AF406545

This is a work of fiction. Similarities to real people, places, or events are entirely coincidental.

FREEDOM

First edition. March 10, 2024.

Copyright © 2024 J.Grayland.

ISBN: 979-8224290857

Written by J.Grayland.

Freedom

J. Grayland

For the most precious people in my life, my family.
And for always eating the last piece of chocolate cake..

Chapter one

S ydney Australia
Casey Tyler

Sitting in the waiting room was on the same level as watching grass grow boring you sit, look at the clock, pick at the imaginary piece of lint on your shirt, listen to the secretary answer calls and tap on the computer keys in front of her looking for a time slot to fit a patient in to see the doctor. It seems ironic that I, as a doctor, am sitting here and waiting to see a doctor huh? Yep, this is what it has come to as a 30-year-old professional woman and surgeon, I am now sitting here on one of those chairs that look nice but feel like you're sitting on a lump of wood. You know the one's that I'm talking about carved legs and a seat covered with soft expensive looking material in a dark green color that ties in with the brown paint on the walls and the framed paintings of flowers, they are everywhere tulips, roses, daisies lots and lots of paintings of flowers I am thinking this shrink loves her flowers Oh yes you heard me right a shrink I am here to see Dr. Susan Colton Ph.D. in psychology and it says it right there in big bold letters on the door right in front of me.

"Tick...tick...tick"

I lean my head against the back of the chair and close my eyes, just for a moment, coming off a twelve-hour shift from the hospital I am exhausted. It's quiet and I am mesmerized by the sound of the clock and darkness lulls me into a light doze, then a spark, a white flash, I'm cold and shivering and I try to open my eyes but they hurt, and when I do open them it is still dark, something is covering them, I try to move my arms but they feel so heavy and they are tied behind me, my wrists burn and chafe as I move them, my whole body aches, I am naked and sitting on a cold surface, it's rough and grates against the skin of my bottom, I try to move but I have no energy, I am drained and I smell, dirt, sweat, blood, and fear, I can smell my own fear I hear the creak of a door and I know he is in the room and I shake with revulsion. "Casey" I feel a soft touch against my arm and I jolt back to reality, looking up into Susan's concerned brown eyes. "Hey there" sitting up straight I rub my eyes and look around trying to re-group my thoughts, I know this place, it's safe. Susan speaks again "They must be working you hard." "Sorry I just got off a long shift." "That's ok honey come on in," she says as she motions me to follow her into her office.

"Take a seat," she gestures with a hand to one of the chairs.

"Thanks," I say, sitting. She sits in the chair opposite me and I look up into her warm friendly face, the face I have been looking into since I was 18 years old Susan is in her mid-sixties with a slim build, her hair cut into a sharp grey colored bob, dressed in loose black pants and a cream shirt. Her eyes radiate towards mine with so much warmth, it always puts me at ease and I instantly feel comfortable.

"You should have moved your appointment honey and got some sleep first," she says with a smile.

"I would have but I need that psych evaluation form signed."

"Ah, yes," she opens the folder in her hands then looks at me concerned. "Well there's no problem with the form, it's already signed, but I do think we need to have a chat about it."

"Somehow I knew you were going to say that." I smile at her.

"Well, I do have some concerns."

"And I knew you were going to say that as well," I say, giving her an amplified sound of exasperation.

"Casey," she says, her tone now reminding me of a mother warning a child not to touch the hot cookies. "It's a three-month contract" she states.

"I know."

"You won't be able to leave," she states again.

"I know."

"And it's what 70% male orientated there?"

"Not sure, " I shrug,

"I'm worried about you being confined," she says and I can hear the concern in her voice so I try to reassure her.

"Susan it's a huge military base. I'm sure it's bigger than one room." She looks down at the open folder balanced in her lap then looks back up to me.

"I understand, but my main concern is that you've come such a long way and I just didn't want you to come in contact with any trigger objects that might just stop your journey forward." I lean closer to her.

"Look, it wouldn't matter where I was anything could be a trigger and you know that so I will tell you what I told Flynn, you both have to let me go a little ok? I love you both to bits but this is something I really need to do."

Susan sits back into her chair and asks "Can you tell me why?"

"I can but..." pausing to take a deep breath I continue "Look sometimes bad things happen in life and you have a choice I could have pulled inside myself and disappeared into my fears and pain, and believe me I came close to doing just that...but I chose to fight, I chose to live, to pick myself up pull myself together and not let that one dark moment in my life define me...define who I am and I chose not to carry that baggage with me for the rest of my life, and I feel taking this job for International Medical Assist will be a new beginning for me I've done my research Susan and I like what I see,"

"And what do you see?" she asks.

"Freedom...I saw a kind of freedom to help; use my skills to help where it's needed; where it's wanted"

"And you don't feel that in your current job?"

"Yes and No. The patients need me to fix them, so to speak, but if it's not me then it will be some other surgeon who is available. I feel with IMA they....they want me. They know that I have chosen to work with them in trying to give these soldiers the best chance of survival and I want that, I want to feel like I am being used for my surgical skills not just because I can fill that shift, or I'm the only one available I want to feel like I am doing something more....and I think this job will give me that sense of achievement, of being constructive in my life"

She's quiet and I wish I knew what she was thinking. *Is she thinking I've lost my marbles? Why would someone who has a stable secure job in one of the largest hospitals in Sydney want to give it all up to go live out in the middle of a hot desert in a tent, surrounded by a bunch of soldiers, in a war zone...yep I guess that would be me."*

"I'm good Susan, honestly" I implore. "This will be a great adventure, give me some balance".

"I know, I just worry about you like you're my own child, but you're right, if you feel like something is missing from your life and this could help you find it, then it's a good decision." I let out the breath that I didn't even realize I was holding, with relief. "Just make sure you keep in touch and, if you have any problems, call me anytime day or night," she said. We both stand and she hands me the signed papers, then she pulls me into a warm embrace. "You take care," she says into my ear.

"I will, and thanks, Susan, for everything".

I drove back to the apartment with a mix of emotions, excitement, fear, panic.... This is it, it's all go from here. All I needed was the green light from Susan and I just got it. IMA had informed me that once I was cleared it would only be a matter of days before I would be leaving the country. Now all I had to do was face Flynn.

Flynn Greyson had been my best friend since we were 10 years old, we were neighbors, went through junior and high school together, he was like the brother I never had. He was my protector, my confidant, my friend and we shared everything so when I had been accepted to a Medical school in Central Sydney, he had applied to law school in the same area so we could share an apartment. We also shared an array of other friends whose number one question was constantly the same "When are you two going to hook up romantically?" But it just wasn't like that between us, We had a lot of love for each other, just not in that way. Oh, he was exceptionally good looking with sandy colored hair that just sat on his collar always messed up and messy. I don't think he even knew what a comb was, let alone how to use one. He just got out of bed in the mornings and gave it a quick rub with his hands, He wasn't overly tall, about 5'11, and he was in great shape. He had a very athletic build from all the sport he had played while we were growing up, and he had a wicked sense of humor. We were very close and we always felt like we were biologically related. I was made an orphan after a car accident took the lives of both my parents when I was 18 years of age. Now that was another file full of pain that I had filed away inside my brain box and decided not to deal with. That was something I had become an expert in. With the death off my parents I had reasoned with myself that we hadn't been all that close as a family anyway I was what is called an "unwanted" distraction that neither of my parents ever wanted, but they ended up with me because of a broken condom I was told this by my mother many times. They both worked long hours and spent the rest of their time socializing with their huge circle of friends. I became what was known as a "Latchkey kid" that's a child that basically brings them self up and the only link they have to the family home is the key to get in the back door, I fed myself, got myself to school, and I entertained myself with my neighbor, Flynn, who became more family to me than my own family.

Now me, I was different. I always felt out of proportion to the other girls. My body was fairly slim and I came in at just under 5'5 with what the boys used to call more than a handful, of boobs that is. I had straight blonde shoulder length hair and the standard blue eyes, I was just...average and, unlike Flynn, I did not have an athletic bone in my body. In fact, the most exercise that I ever got was while I was at work walking around the endless miles of hallways seeing patients. I had promised myself that I would take up going for a run in the mornings. I would start off slow, and when I say slow, I mean snail- pace slow. I needed something other than my music to channel my stress into.

Yes, I loved my music, and it had brought me many hours of comfort and solace in my time of need. The music I listened to depended on my mood. If I was in a crappy "That time of the month" mood, it was always something heavy and loud. When my brain took me to that place I hated to go, I would tune into something soft and reflective and this took me to many different places, away from my reality. It was my escape and it had been my savior in many dark times.

I pulled into the car park at Juliana's Pasta on South Street. This is Flynn's favorite eating place so I had arranged to meet him here, in a public place to give him my news. We had talked about the job at IMA a few weeks ago and he was not too impressed with it then- now he was going to be well and truly pissed.

Chapter two

C *asey*
    Walking into that little familiar cozy restaurant with its dimmed lights, crisp white table clothes and the flickering flames of the candles burning away on each table, I breathe in the wonderful smell of garlic and tomatoes floating through the air and I feel a little more relaxed. Flynn is sitting at our usual table in the corner when he sees me and waves. I walk over and slide into the chair opposite him. He's still dressed in his work uniform which consists of an impeccable grey suit with a crisp white shirt and matching grey tie.

"Hey babes, I ordered us a bottle of Cabernet" he gestured to the glass half filled with a rich red wine in front of me.

"Great, just what I needed, did you have court today?" I nodded towards his suit.

"Yesss" he hissed out "Back again in the morning, unfortunately."

"Hard case?" I enquire.

"Just draining, I need a holiday badly. So how did it go at the shrink?" Looking at him, I actually feel myself cringe as I say " Good.... I'm good to go."

"You're kidding me right?" He sits up straight in his chair slapping his palms on top of the table.

"Nope, I leave Monday," I say nonchalantly, taking a sip from my glass.

"That soon? Holy shit Casey that's in 3 days," he says as he flops back into his chair.

"Yes I know," I say and watch him grab his own glass and take a huge gulp from it. He slowly shakes his head from side to side. And I wait and wait for it....and here it comes.

"I can't believe you're fucking doing it." Now his outburst forces me to push back into my own chair as I swallow and say.

"We have talked about it, Flynn."

"Yes I know but...fuck" he pushes his hand through his hair. "Why?" his gentle eyes look up into mine, searching. "I mean with everything that happened, why would you want to knowingly put yourself into another situation like that ?"

"This is not like, that it's completely different."

"How is it different? You're going into a war zone where you'll have violence, isolation, stress, Tell me, what makes it so different?"

I took a sip of my wine, what could I say? He was right in some ways but this was different, this was work. I was different and I wasn't putting myself in a position where I was going to be by myself, there would be plenty of people around.

"I need it" I finally said.

"But why Babes ?" he says, his voice now quieter.

"I'm not sure, there's just something missing in here," I said placing my hand over my heart.

"And what, you think you're going to find it somewhere out in the middle of a dessert on the other side of the world instead of here ?"

"Maybe."

"Maybe." he almost yells but lowers his voice when a couple at a table nearby looks over at us. "What the fuck is that supposed to mean Casey? Maybe?"

"Well, I don't know until I get there do I?" I hiss back at him.

"I just don't get why you have to go to the other side of the world to find some peace. So what is it? Are you unhappy with your job?

Your life? Or is it just what HE took from you?" Looking up at him with narrowed eyes I warn him.

"Don't go there, Flynn. This has nothing to do with him. It has to do with me, just me alone. I'm not going into this with my eyes closed, I know what I am doing."

"Do you? Then please explain it to me, because I have no bloody idea what is going through that complicated brain of yours." Placing my wine glass on the table, I turn and look out of the window it's starting to rain and for just a second I am lost in the display of the dancing raindrops that start to cover the footpath outside, until I turn back to look at Flynn, his face etched with concern as he waits for me to speak.

"I feel like there's something missing. I don't know what it is or where it is, I just know something is missing, and I keep looking for it, and this is the closest I have come to feeling like its close. I don't know, maybe it's got to do with the feeling of doing something productive and helpful. I just don't know Flynn.... all I know is for a long time now I have this empty feeling inside of me and I keep trying to fill it with work but the emptiness is just getting deeper. You're my best friend and I love you so much but I also need you with me on this....please Flynn." Reaching across the table, I place my hand on top of his and I watch as he takes another sip from his wine glass, swallows, places the glass down on the table then slides his warm hand over the top of mine, the look in his eyes turning from frustration to something softer, then in almost a whisper he says.

"I won't be able to protect you," and I feel a slight prick of tears as I look into his eyes that are now full of pain.

"Oh Flynn, I know you're always there to protect me".

Shaking his head he looks out of the window and sighs "Not this time babes, you'll be too far away and that... that's going to kill me."

"We might be physically apart but emotionally I will have you right here." I point to my heart first "and here" then touch my fingers to my temple. Watching me he shakes his head with a defeated look.

"Please, babes at least tell me you only signed the contract for three months?" Smiling at him now, I know he's caved a little, I reassure him.

"Yes, with an option of renewal once the first three months is done, so if it turns out that it's not what I'm looking for, then all I will have lost is three months out of my life and most likely gained a lot more experience in the process". I say smiling at him.

Tilting his head to one side, his top lip curling into a smile, he says "You always could wrap me around your little finger...Geez, what am I going to do without you?"

"Hopefully get some private time and be able to bring a date home and not have to explain to her that I really am just your roommate and not your wife. " I smile at him then sigh "Flynn I need you to tell me that you're okay with this, you're my family and..." my words trail off and he reluctantly gives me what I want.

"You know I'll support you in anything babes. I will always be here for you, just be careful and I want as much contact as possible either by phone or emails okay?" "I will," I say, crossing my heart with a promise.

Chapter three

Casey

I filled the almost 16 hours of flight time from Sydney to Ashgabat by reading through the information booklet and papers given to me by IMA. They gave the basic information ; geographic area; customs and local weather. There wasn't much about the military base there but I did know it was near a small village called Tayba and that it was a relatively safe zone, mostly used as a base where casualties from the other active areas of Afghanistan could be taken to, stabilized, then sent on to a larger hospital. They also provided healthcare for the local villages in the area.

My contact at IMA, Sarah, had also let me know that there would be a security team at the airport waiting on my arrival who would be escorting me to the army base, which was a relief because I sure as hell wasn't going to take a chance driving myself around this unfamiliar area. Back home I could get lost driving around the car park at the local shopping mall, never mind navigating in a strange country.

I had made sure I had worn comfortable clothing for traveling which included a pair of light-colored cargo pants with lots of deep pockets these came in handy for keeping my papers, phone, and my all-important iPod, with its sixteen gigs of fully loaded music in one the pockets for quick easy access. On top, I wore a dark tank top covered by a white loose long- sleeved thin shirt and a good comfortable pair of hiking boots. I had also tucked a scarf into my backpack to cover my head on arrival. I had pulled my long hair into a ponytail then tightly braided it to hopefully keep it tidy and out of the way. I knew the average temperature at this time of the year was around 30 degrees centigrade.This is where it had come in handy already living in a hot dry country because I was hoping that I wouldn't have to work too hard to adapt to the climate.... fingers crossed.

When an announcement was made by the captain that we would be landing in approximately forty minutes I slipped the earphones into my ears, scrolled through my copious amounts of playlists, lay my head back against the headrest and let Pink's latest album take me the rest of the way.

When the plane touched down with a bump, I looked out the small window at my side and felt small butterflies tickle in the pit of my stomach. When the plane taxied to a stop and it was announced that passengers could now disembark I undid my belt and pulled my backpack from the overhead luggage compartment and made my way to the exit door along with all the other passengers.

Stepping out onto the stairs that went down to the tarmac I was immediately hit by the scorching heat and had to squint at the sun's brightness. It was so arid and there was a strange combination of smells drifting through the air. It smelt like a mixture of sand, engine fuel, cinnamon, and garbage. Hitching my backpack up onto one shoulder, I made my way down the steel stairs and into the airport. Pulling out my papers and passport I took a spot in the long line through customs.

Finally, after what felt like hours, I made it through to the other side and out through the main doors to what looked like total chaos with frantic looking crowds of people pulling luggage and carrying boxes and bags, flagging down taxis and other vehicles. Taking a look around I could see cars and vans lined up on the road in front of the airport. Some were calling out to get the attention of potential customers needing a ride, and others were holding signs with names on them, so I scanned the people and their faces until I spotted a sign that had "Dr. Tyler" in large bold letters on it so I headed in that direction, dragging my wheeled case behind me.

Navigating my way through the crowded pathway towards where I saw my name I noticed a dirty white SUV with dark tinted windows and the name IMA printed on the door and a large red cross printed on the roof. As I got closer I saw that the whole vehicle was covered with a thick layer of dirt and dust, you could barely tell that it's true color was meant to be white. There were two large men leaning against it. The man holding the card with my name on it had what looked like brown short cropped hair; he was tall maybe 6ft? give an inch or two; with well defined muscular arms which appeared to be fully covered in an array of colorful tattoos. He was dressed in a pair of dark green cargo pants and a green t-shirt and heavy boots. He also had on what looked like a heavy black flak vest, but the thing that I noticed the most was a gun in its holster sitting against his right hip. For me this was a little weird to see. Because of Australia's strict gun laws, the only time I ever saw something like that was on a police officer. *"Suck it up Casey, you're not in Kansas anymore"* my inner voice whispered to me. As I got closer to both men I tried to zero in on the other guy, which was difficult because he was leaning against the front of the SUV facing away from me and I could only see the back of him. He appeared to be scanning the crowds of people that were scattered around the SUV but what I did notice is that he was a solid looking guy, and I mean beefy solid, his arms were crossed at his chest and even at this distance I could see the material of his black t-shirt is stretched tight against the muscles of his back, not to mention the size of his biceps that are straining against the short sleeves. Even though he is leaning back, I can tell that he is much taller than his partner. He is also wearing dark cargo pants, a flak vest and a gun in its holster is sitting against his hip and strapped to his leg. It's hard to get a good look at his face from this angle but I can see a strong jawline shadowed by a couple of days of dark stubble, and he has a ball cap pulled over his unruly inky black hair that looks like it's trying to escape its confinement through every tiny gap in the cap. Getting closer now I see that his skin looks tanned from the sun and he is also sporting an assortment of tattoos on his well defined arms. As he turns his head he is wearing a dark pair of aviators that hide his eyes I'm getting closer to them now, and the closer I get to the two burly men the stronger the butterflies churn in my stomach. I pull my own sunglasses down from where they are perched on the top of my head to shade my eyes from the glare of the sun and hopefully also hide the sparks of fear that I am sure they would be able to see in my own eyes. Coming to a stop straight in front of the guy holding the sign, I let go of the handle on my case, causing it to make a loud "clunk" sound that gets his attention as he stares down at me.

"You're here for Dr. Tyler?" I ask him, trying to hide the slight quiver in my voice. "Sure am mam," he drawled in what sounded like a southern American accent.

"Then I guess you're here for me." I smile and hold out my hand to him. After a small pause which includes him looking me up and down like he hasn't seen a woman for a long time, a smile quirks up at the side of his lips and he takes my hand in his own calloused one and with a very firm grip shakes it.

"The name's Jackson Davis mam although most people call me Jax, and this is Nate." he gestures to the man next to him who still hasn't turned around yet but then I notice why he has earbuds in his ears. Jackson slaps him on the arm and he swings around to face us, dropping his cigarette to the floor and stepping on it.

"Nate, this is Dr. Tyler," Jackson tells him whilst still smiling at me.

Nate raises his head in silence, then flips out one of the buds from his right ear. He pushes his glasses up onto the top of his head and his frosty narrowed eyes fix onto mine.

"You're Dr. Tyler?" He questions with a crook of his eyebrow and a low gravely growl. I get the impression he's not too impressed, so I try to lighten the introduction a little.

"Last time I looked at my driver's licence I was," I said.

"You're a woman?" he questions again.

"Yep last time I looked there I was too." I glance down to my crotch area and smile back at him. Jackson let out a slight chuckle and I look from one man's face to the other and ask slowly.

"Is that a problem?" Nate's eyes are steely grey, piercing and icy cold right at this moment.

"It will be if you don't get that shiny blonde hair of yours covered up" he spits out.

"Shit, sorry I wasn't thinking" I said pulling my back pack off my shoulder and rummaging through it until I find the shear black scarf I had brought with me and put it over my hair pulling some around my face to try an cover as much as possible.

"Better?" I asked with a touch of sarcasm in my voice, looking at Nate.

"Much. Come on its a long drive" he says opening the back door of the SUV and gesturing for me to get in. Throwing my back pack onto the seat, I pull myself up onto the dark leather, Nate pulls my seat belt out and thrusts it into my hand. "Buckle up" he says as I look at him he slams the door shut so hard I thought the window was going to shatter with the force. Jackson loads my case into the back, and both men climb into the front seats and pull on their seat belts. I hear a soft click and noticed that all the doors lock at once. Nate starts the engine and slides it into gear and we pull out onto the dusty road.

The streets are crowded and small and it takes some skilled weaving and dodging to navigate the endless crowds of people until finally the SUV cuts a path out onto the open road. I watch as Nate concentrates not only on the road in front of him but also on everything around him in every direction, his eyes seem to dart everywhere and it's not too much of a hardship watching him either, he has such a strong profile, with that strong jaw line and stubble, his thick muscular neck down to his powerful muscled arms and right on down to the large hands that grip tightly onto the steering wheel. I try to look at the various tattoos on his arms but his muscles keep twitching and moving as he drives so I can't see any details of the ink.

"There's a cooler on the floor there" Jackson points down towards my feet. "Help yourself to something cold."

"Thanks." Reaching down I pull the lid back and take out a bottle of cold water, releasing the cap and taking a long drink. The chilled water runs over my tongue and moistens my dry throat "mmm I so needed that" I moan.

"So" Jackson asked "Where's that accent coming from?"

"Australia" I answer before taking another drink.

"Shit, that's on the other side of the goddamn world, what the hell are you doing here?"

"I guess the same as you.... making a living" I say, then look out of the window at the passing miles of sand.

"Well mam I hope you're prepared for the climate out here?" Jackson says.

"Well fortunately the temperature and dry conditions are pretty similar to home so I can only hope" I say, then go back to looking out the window. There is nothing but sand in every direction. I watch as a glassy mirage of heat curls up from the ground, a heat I can see but not feel as the coolness of air humming from the air-conditioning swirls around in the SUV. I lean my head back against the seat and close my eyes, a wave of tiredness and time disorientation suddenly hitting me hard. Feeling the butterflies starting to flutter in my stomach again and turning into something more, a cold fear starts from deep in the pit of my stomach and slowly starts to rise up into my throat *"no, no, no I will not be sick"* I try to swallow back the sour taste of bile in my mouth *"it's ok, it will be ok remember why you're here"* I tell myself then take nice deep slow breaths to calm myself Jackson turns and looks at me with concern in his eyes.

"Are you ok?" he asks reaching his hand over his seat and touching my knee. I nod, then he looks at Nate.

"Pull over" Jackson barks out.

Nate's head turns sharply to look at him "What?" he bite's out in a harsh tone.

"Either pull over or your gonna be cleaning puke out of the back seat for the rest of the day" Jackson tells him.

Nate turns around to look back at me and I am thinking that maybe the color of what I imagine my face to be right now is what makes him shift the SUV into gear and slow to a stop, pulling over to the side of the road with a curse "Oh, you have got to be friggin kidding me," he spits out.

As soon as we come to a stop I open the door and get out, bending and placing my hands on my knees in a half- bent position and, with eyes closed, I slowly breath in and out struggling to center myself. I hear the other doors open and slam shut and I feel Jackson next to me instantly.

"Just take it easy now, nice slow breaths" he soothes.

After a few minutes I could feel myself starting to calm and pull it all back together. The fuzziness in my head was clearing and so was the nausea, thank god. Slowly I pull myself back into a standing position and take the opened bottle of water that Nate thrusts into my hand "Drink" he commands and I take a few cautious sips then look at Jackson.

"I'm ok now thanks. I'm sorry just a bad combination of jet lag and lack of sleep I think."

"It's ok little lady. We understand it's somewhat of a culture shock when you first get out here but it'll grow on you, just like a bad case of foot fungus." Jackson grins at me as I feel his hand rubbing circles on my back. I look up at him and smile in appreciation "Thanks".

Chapter four

Nathanial King

Two weeks earlier...

Standing in front of the large wall of panoramic windows in my office I glance down at the bustling traffic of the city of Portland. Yeah, I know I look like an arrogant rich bastard right now, like I'm watching over my kingdom, arms crossed legs slightly apart in my usual rigid stance, casually dressed in jeans and a white dress shirt, opened at the collar with the sleeves rolled half way up my forearms. I can just hear those exact words coming out of my little brothers mouth if he walked in here right now. Annoying little shit always trying to get me into a suit "It looks professional Nate, it's good for our image." If there is one thing I hate it's a suit, I hate suits they're stiff and uncomfortable and it's very rare that I wear anything close to one, especially to the office, unlike Paxton my little brother...the family lawyer.

I grin to myself and just for a brief moment I'm taken back to when I was about 10 years old, running into this office and finding my father standing in the exact same spot, doing the exact same thing that I'm doing right now, jumping into his big leather chair and him turning to me as he speaks. "Look at that view Nathanial. It feels like we're on top of the world, now I really can say that I'm the King of the Castle." I guess that's what it felt like back then this being the top floor when my father first built the high rise over twenty years ago. We've changed a little in the last few years, added an extra ten floors, the top floor being the Penthouse where I live and we added an events room to the ground floor. King Security was started by my father and since Paxton and I took over its grown exponentially. We've made investments into other companies but our main focus is still on providing security for almost everything from major banks, to clubs and other businesses, and we also provide personal security not just on home ground but internationally as well. The dream that my father started all those years ago has now grown into a trusted, thriving company which I know he would be proud of.

When the intercom buzzes on my desk I reluctantly pull myself away from the view and press the button "Yes." An older female voice breaks the silence through the speaker.

"Mr. King your brother is here to see you" my secretary says.

"Send him in Grace." But before I even finish my words the large oak door to my office opens and Paxton strides through. dressed in a dark colored impeccable looking suit with a file in his hand. Walking up to my desk, he drops the file onto it.

"What the fuck is this?" He points at the file that has now opened and spilled over the large oak wood desk. Moving behind the desk I drop into the leather chair and look down at the paper then back up into the very angry face of my brother.

"Nice to see you too Paxton, please take a seat." I gesture towards the other leather chair opposite me. Paxton ignores the invitation to sit, instead shoving one hand into his pants pocket while pushing the other one through his black slick hair, then he starts to slowly pace in front of my desk. For a minute I can picture him as a cartoon character with animated steam coming out of his ears. Looking back down at my desk I try and hide the grin that vision just gave me. I watch as he paces back and forth in front of me for a few minutes until he finally stops, turns and places both palms on the desk.

"King International Security is one of the largest companies in the country" he says with strength and dignity.

"Yes, I know" I said resting my elbows on the desk.

"Then why the fuck are you taking private contracts?" He grinds out the words like it's painful. I knew when he found out he wouldn't be too happy about my decision. I look down again at the pile of papers that has spilled out in front of me then back up at him.

"It's a favor" I say leaning back into my chair.

"A favor? For who?" he sputters out then backs up to sit down in one of the black leather chairs. Rubbing my hand across the stubble of my chin I look at my little brother, my business partner, my best friend and try to explain.

"Do you remember Steve Peterson the CEO of International Medical Assist?" I ask him, and he nods his head."Well he has some civilian medical staff heading out to the military base in Turkmenistan and he contacted me." Before I can finish Paxton jumps in .

"Then send someone else Nate, there is no need for you to go, and those medical contracts usually last anywhere from three months to a year. King International Security can't do without you for that long."

"No-one ever lasts out the full contract Paxton, it'll be three months at the most"

Paxton looks down at the floor slowly shaking his head then lets out a slow breath.

"Nate you need to stop doing this, it's time to stop."

"Stop what, Paxton? It's just a job."

"That's bull shit and you know it" Paxton hisses out . "Any excuse that gets you back out in the field somewhere and you jump at it. What the fuck are you trying to do Nate? Hope that one day something or someone will take you out? When are you going to stop?"

Leaning back into the comfort of my chair I look at him and I know he's right but I also know that I need this. I need the rush, the insecurity of the unknown, always having to be alert watching your back, being on guard and always having that risk, that edge, that thin small line between life and death. It's what makes me feel alive and reminds me that I am still human, because if I am, then I can feel and I want to feel the pain, I crave it, and I deserve it.

"Nate?" Paxton's voice pulls me back to the now and gets my attention and I turn my head sharply back to him. "Man you need to stop, it's time you moved on and started living. It's been ten years Nate, for fuck sake let it go."

"I've tried and it's not that easy" I sigh with exasperation. "I lost a lot of good men out there."

"Well not hard enough Nate. You were not responsible for any of those men's deaths, you were their Captain and you did your job like everyone else. You need to let it go and start living" he says sitting back down into the chair opposite.

I rub my hand across the back of my neck, breath out and say "Pushy little bastard aren't ya?"

"Well someone has to be, you're such a stubborn hard- headed asshole" he smiles. Leaning forward in my chair I say "This will be the last time, I promise."

"Just call him up and tell him you're not interested," he almost yells.

"I can't, I owe him this one" I said shaking my head slightly.

"What do you mean you owe him?" he grates out between his teeth. "There's something you're not telling me here right?" The question cause my jaw to tighten and twitch.

"Remember last year in Tehran?" I ask him and he nods. "Well the reason we got out of there in one piece is because Peterson pulled some strings to make it happen. He told me then I owed him one..... now he's calling it in".

"Jesus Nate, anyone else but him. He's a shifty, underhanded prick. God knows how the fuck he runs an international medical assist service, for all the illegal shit he's into".

"I know, I know" I say standing and walking around to the front of my desk and leaning against it. "There's also word on the wire that he's surfing pretty close to trouble at the moment and shit is about to hit the fan. Meanwhile the bastard's got innocent people flying in to help our troops."

Paxton looks up. "That's not our problem Nate."

"It is now," I growl, arching an eyebrow at him.

Through narrowed eyes I watch as Paxton sits on the edge of the leather chair with his elbows resting on his knees, his hands scrubbing through his hair, his mind working overtime then he lets out a reluctant deep sigh, "who are you taking with you?"

"Jax."

"Well I guess that's one consolation. If you have to take someone I'm glad it's Jackson." He sighs.

"Yeah, well I figure if I don't officially take him, the asshole will follow me there" Paxton chuckles and stands, but I can see by the look he's giving me he's not impressed.

"Ok let me know what you need and I'll get things moving for you." He relents.

"Thanks" I say giving him a slap on the back.

"You can thank me by coming back in one piece."

"That's a promise." I say giving him an affirmative nod.

Paxton starts towards the door then turns to face me again "Oh and Nate? This will be the last time".

Chapter five

N ate

Driving along the uneven, dusty dirt road towards the base I feel the blood in my veins starting to pump hard. This was not going to be good and I could feel every bone in my body screaming " Big mistake".

"Fucking Peterson never said anything about a woman" "You will be looking after three civvies Nate ,2 surgeons and a nurse, and before you ask the nurse is a male from London" Fuccckk! I should have known better than to trust the bastard, he had slipped it in to the conversation so fast that I didn't even think about the surgeons being female. He knows how bad it is out here for women, especially a blonde western woman, exactly like the one I was looking at in my rear view mirror sitting in the back seat. I knew as soon as I set eyes on her walking towards us outside the airport, blonde hair tied back and glistening in the hot desert sun, like a red flag saying "look at me." I also noticed a few long wisps of her hair had worked its way loose and was now moist with sweat and sticking to the sides of her face and neck, I could see she was of a slim build under the loose comfortable casual cargo pants she wore until I lifted my eyes up to the loose unbuttoned shirt and saw a black tank top stretched over her ample breasts. I had to turn away from her approaching us and let Jax speak first because I knew if I opened my mouth it would not have been pleasant . I could feel a ball of anger starting to cause a knot to form in the pit of my stomach, and then she spoke. It was like nothing I had ever heard before the musical sound of

her accent, the soft tone, and when I turned and looked into her eyes, her perfect fucking big blue eyes that angry knot doubled in size. Anger boiling in my veins, my grip on the steering wheel so hard my knuckles were turning white, I took another glance at her through the rear view mirror. Sitting back against the seat her face slightly turned looking out of the window, she looked incredible, venerable and lost, and those eyes darting around taking in the outside world. Had she known what she was getting herself into? Why would she want to come out here into the middle of a friggin desert for Christ's sake? And how old is she? Like 25, a bored rich chick looking for some excitement? Breathe Nate breathe and remember why you're here- she's just a contract. Do the job and get home" I thought, and steered the SUV towards the base.

Chapter six

C asey
As the military base came into view it was way larger than I had imagined. There were a lot of large green tents around the outside of what looked like a portable hospital base in the center. There were military personal walking around, jeeps everywhere. It reminded me of MASH, a TV series I had watched as a kid, even though I knew this was not a scene from a movie set this was life complete in high definition, 3D reality. After going through the routine paper work and vehicle search at the front armed gates the SUV pulled up in front of the portable building. And once it had come to a stop and they got out I opened my own door, slid down onto the ground and stretched my limbs, then I pulled my back pack out and hooked it over one shoulder. The wide door at the front of the building swung open and a tall slim- grey haired man wearing a uniform came out and down the stairs to where we were standing he thrust out his hand towards me, which I took. "Dr. Tyler? I'm Base Commander Simons. We are so glad to have you here. How was your trip?" he asked as I shook his hand then let it go.

"It was good thank you" I said.

"The other civilian medics arrived yesterday, so if you like we will get you settled in your bunk and then give you a tour".

I smiled and nodded and he motioned for me to follow him. Nate and Jackson had pulled out the rest of the luggage from the back of the SUV and followed as well. Commander Simons walked behind the portable building to another portable block that had what looked like several doors along the front of it. Two small steps took us up onto a thin wooden walkway and I followed the Commander down to the end door where he unlocked it, then placed a key into my hand and said "Always keep it locked even when you're in it ok?".

"Sure" I said looking at Jax questioningly who just shrugged.

The room was better than I had expected. It was small, just enough room for a single bed, a small wooden desk and chair and a small set of drawers with an electric fan sitting on top of it, a window at the back and a small wash basin sitting on a stand in front of it. I dumped my back pack onto the bed and pulled the scarf off my head and pushed my now sweat soaked hair back into its place. Then I reached into the back pack and pulled out a pen and note pad. Commander Simons placed a binder on the desk and tapped the top. "This has all the rules and regulations of the base. It should answer most of your questions but if not, feel free to ask anyone around."

"Thanks I will look through it later. Now it would be great if I could have a look around and get myself orientated a little before it gets dark," I said heading for the door to where Nate and Jax leaned against the building. I looked at them both and thrust my hand out towards Nate. "Thanks for driving me in guys. I think I'll be good now." Jax looked at Nate, then looked back to me with eyebrows, raised and Nate just stared at my out stretched hand.

"Umm... We aint going anywhere sweetheart" Jax drawled.

"Oh, sorry I thought you just had to drive me here" I said dropping my hand and pushing them both into my pockets.

"Nope we're here to stay" Jax continued.

"For how long?" I asked.

"For the length of the contract mam".

"For the whole contract?" I asked shocked.

"Yes mam" Jax said.

"Um isn't that a bit of overkill ? I don't think I will be needing two bodyguards during my stay." I gestured to all the armed military personal walking around.

Nate stood up straight and leaned down bringing his mouth close to my ear and spoke in a low deep tone. "It's ok baby, don't flatter yourself, we're not just here for you we're contracted for two others as well."

Reeling back from him and giving him a look of annoyance, I leaned back towards him ."Tell you what stud, when I get to know my way around this place better I think you might just need to pay me a visit."

"Really? And why is that?" he asked. Those succulent lips of his curving into a wicked grin.

"So I can get you on the operating table and pull that big stick out of your arse". As I walked around him, following the commander, I could hear Jax as he broke into a loud burst of laughter.

"Ha ha ha, I like that woman a lot" he mused.

The base hospital was better equipped than I imagined. It had one area that was used for general medical issues such as minor injuries and illness; another area that was set up as a ward with about five beds but could accommodate more at a squeeze: then there was a small but fully functioning theatre. Outside the hospital I was taken over to another large building that was the canteen. There was also a communal shower and toilet area, officers accommodation, and a tent set up as a communication area for the soldiers that gave them access to the internet and telephones. I also learned that there were cards that could be purchased and loaded with credit to be used in there. I was told that surgeons are practically on call 24/7 and I was given a small beeper and a list of code numbers that they used to determine the urgency of the call. I would also be scheduled to assist the military doctors and nurses with the health of the military personnel on the base doing vaccinations and routine health checks.

Other than that, what time I had left was my own, although I was not allowed to leave the base unescorted, so that meant if I needed to go off base at any time, I had to be escorted by the two beefy bodyguards that had been kindly supplied by IMA .

Just the thought of being under their constant watch gave me an uncomfortable feeling. I mean I could actually see myself getting along with Jax, he seemed pretty down to earth and friendly. As for the other one, Nate, well he just looked like a barrel of laughs....not. He had a huge chip on his shoulder and I am guessing that he is either really bored with his job or just a chauvinistic pig.

We ended up seated in the Commander's office with an older grey haired man who reminded me of one of my old college teachers, Mr. Dickson, although we never called him that- he was always known as Dicko or Dickhead to us. He was a funny, short, stumpy man in his mid 50's but still dressed like he was in the 1970's with his flared tan slacks matching light brown dress shirt and tan tie. He sported a rather severe comb over hair style and every time he would walk under the ceiling fans in the classroom it used to flap around like a limp flag in a breeze. I'm pretty sure that old Dicko played a huge part in global warming because I am convinced he must have gone through a full can of hairspray every day just to try to keep that sucker pinned down. The thought brings a momentary smile onto my face until I remember where I am and concentrate on the sound of Commander Simons voice.

"Dr Tyler these are the other two civilian medics joining you from IMA. This is Dr. Andrew Lancer," He gestured towards Dicko's long lost brother, reaching out my hand to shake his and, yes just as I expected his hand was sticky and sweaty.

"Nice to meet you Dr. Tyler" he said.

"You too Dr. Lancer" I said slipping my hand discreetly behind my back and into the back pocket of my cargo pants where I proceeded to try and wipe the sticky sweat off into my pocket.

"Dr Lancer is an orthopedic surgeon from the UK" Commander Simons continued, "And this is Mike Dawson your Registered Nurse - he's also from the UK." Turning toward the other man in the room I was faced with Mike. He was around the same height as me, with short cropped blonde hair and wire rimmed glasses. He looked pretty young but who knows these days. Mike thrust his hand out into mine and vigorously shook it.

"How do you do Dr. Tyler" he said in his crisp British accent and eyes roaming over me.

"Good thank you, err... nice to meet you both" I said pulling my once again sweaty palm into my back pocket for another secret wipe.

"Please everyone take a seat" Commander Simmons gestured with a swipe of his hand to the chairs sitting around a table, in what looked like a meeting room. It had a couple of computers housed on a desk in the corner and a couple of comfy looking arm chairs. There was also a refrigerator and a bench that housed a coffee machine, toaster and jars of what looked like small cookies. There was an American flag pinned up on one side of the wall and a cork board with lots of photo's of children, babies and what looked like family members of, I am guessing, some of the medical staff here on base. I found it amazing that such a small space felt so comfortable and homely just by all the little special personal touches that everyone had contributed. Commander Simmons saw me taking in the room.

"As you can see this is where staff come to try to relax" he said following my gaze.

"Yes with a little piece of home" I said nodding to the photos. He smiled at me then slid a folder across the table to each of us.

"I know it may seem that you are being inundated with paper work to read, but these folders contain most of the information you will need. Please take time to read it and study it, it contains our protocols and procedures that we have put into place here to try and help everything run as smoothly as possible. It also contains the rules and regulations. Now I know that you're not military personnel and you are exempt from a lot of them, but for your own safety I advise that you try and stick to them as much as possible."

"Not a problem" I said nodding.

"Now Dr. Tyler, as for you I implore you to stick with your security team and do not exit the compound without them or an MP. We have a couple of troublesome rogue groups in the area and please excuse me for being blunt but they would kill to get a hold someone like you."

I gasp at his words then slowly say. "Okay so..."

"So please stay in the compound with your security and unless you're inside, keep your head covered at all times. If they even spot a white woman with blonde hair I'm not sure just how far they would go to get to you."

"Get to me?" I questioned now perplexed.

"Yes, you would make them quite a tidy sum of money on the black market."

"Oh! I see" I say, a little taken back by his words, and I see puzzlement in his eyes.

"I am amazed that IMA didn't explain this all to you before." He said narrowing his eyes at me.

"Err...no they didn't mention anything about my gender, skin or hair coloring being problematic."

The Commander slowly shakes his head, "it should have been a priority...but we are extremely glad to have you here. Your surgical reputation is outstanding from what I have read in your file so, like I said, just stick to the compound and your security team and all should be well."

"Thank you Sir, I appreciate the heads up." I said still slightly stunned by the new information I had just learned.

"Now I will give you all time to settle into your rooms, get some chow at the mess hall and I will see you back here at 0700 hours tomorrow".

Chapter seven

Nate

Eight days, that's how long we have been here and that's how long I've been watching her....closely, not just as a job but really watching her. I don't know what it is that is drawing me to her, but it was strong right from the minute I looked into that rear view mirror and into that innocent face... that innocent beautiful face. With its soft delicate skin, perfectly shaped mouth and the most unusual colored pair of blue eyes I have ever seen. No not blue, more Azure, that color that you get in the sky at dusk as the sun is meeting the moon and the two colors are just touching, fucking amazing. I watch her from the minute she gets up at the break of day and goes for a run around the compound, black leggings that mold to her slim legs and usually a t-shirt that hugs to every curve of her chest. I watch as that shirt becomes moist with sweat the more she runs, ear buds in her ears and an IPod strapped to her bicep, her long silky blonde hair always pulled into a pony tail that swings as she moves. I watch her as she walks into the medical building, always dressed in loose fitting scrubs, and I imagine what's under them. I watch her before she goes to bed. She always comes out of her room and looks out into the night sky before she retires for the night. Her face shows innocence but her eyes show something different.....pain, sadness, and I need to know what it is. She has taken to this place like a duck to water, fitting in with everything and everyone around her. Jax chats and jokes with her but I try to say as little as possible to her. When we speak I need to keep that little bit of aloofness with her and honestly, I'm afraid if I do I will become lost in her completely and that's something I don't do. I don't get involved or attached to women. I just fuck em that's all, no connection, no promises, just sex. I can't give them anything more and I don't want to. So I will keep my distance, finish the job and forget her."

Taking the bottle of water that Jax hands to me I take off the lid and bring it to my mouth chugging it back until it's empty, then tossing it into the rubbish bin, and my gaze catches sight of Casey. She's in what looks like a deep conversation with the British male nurse Mike. But the conversation they're having seems to be animated and strained, and she looks trapped. Jax follows my gaze "What's up bud?" he asked.

"Not sure, she just looks... uncomfortable."

"Well maybe it's cos that little British fucker hangs around her like a bad smell." With eyebrows furrowed I turned to look at Jax "He's harassing her?" I say in a low growl.

"I wouldn't say harassing but I'd say he's interested in getting into her honey pot," Jax throws out with a grin. "Can't say I blame him too much. That little honey pot has been drawing quite a lot of attention around here, but him?" Jackson nods towards Mike. "I'm keeping a close eye on that one. I don't trust that little fucker" he drawls. We both stand and watch their conversation and I watch as the expressions on her face change, her eyes narrow causing a small crease to form on her forehead at something pretty boy has just said to her. Then he places a hand on her arm, and I feel myself walking in their direction cursing under my breath. "Motherfucker".

Watching her stiffen at his touch on her arm, she takes a step back from him, forcing his hand to drop down against his side and, I hear her voice waiver as she says to him "Well Mike I'm going to go get some sleep. I am exhausted." Turning to walk away from him she walks straight into my chest with a thump, and through narrowed eyes I look down into hers then glance over at Mike.

"You Ok?" I ask her.

"Yeah... I'm fine" she nods. Pushing a loose strand of hair behind one ear.

"Goodnight Casey, I'll see you in the morning" I hear the British douche bag say before he quickly retreats backwards making his exit back to his room. She steps sideways to try and get around me but I step in front of her.

"Does he bother you?" I ask her and she shrugs one shoulder "A little, but he seems pretty harmless I also have to work with him."

"Work being the prime word here, that doesn't give him the right to bother you" I tell her. She looks over to where blondie disappeared into his room then looks back at me "Like I said he's harmless, he's got a big ego but I think that's all he's got" she smiles.

"The harmless ones are the ones that you always need to watch closely" I say looking down at her smiling face.

"Good job I have you to do the watching then isn't it," her smile now turning into something playful and wicked.

Leaning down with my mouth close to her ear, I breath in a low rough tone "Don't worry Doc, I can assure you I am watching everything you do," I hear a quick sharp intake of air from those luscious lips of hers, before she steps back from me and looks up through those huge blue eyes framed by long silky lashes and stammers.

"Thank you, I appreciate what you do." My eyes search hers, trying to take in everything in this brief moment, then I look down to where she's nervously rubbing her hands together.

"Do I scare you Doc?" I ask motioning to her hands with a slight nod of my head.

"Err.... no it's just strange."

"Strange?" I ask.

"Yes, this is the first time you have said more than two words to me" and there it is the slight lift at the corners of those gorgeous plump lips, her body now showing a submissive innocence but that mouth, that mouth shows naughtiness and trouble. I arch a brow in response "That's because I don't get paid to talk to you, I get paid to protect you" my voice now deep and husky and I see her shudder in response, our eyes connected for a brief moment until she breaks it.

"Well again Thank you I won't keep you from your job." As she turns to walk away I place my hand on her lower arm and she turns quickly to look at me. "Just remember, if the blonde douche bag harasses you, let me know because Doc? YOU are my job, and I always do my job thoroughly." I watch as her cheeks flush red before she pulls away and walks back to her room.

I walk back to the tent we have set up across from the medical staffs quarters. Jax is sitting in a deck chair with his feet up on a wooden crate, mug of coffee in one hand and a Yankees cap pulled down low over his eyes. "So?" he drawls out.

"So nothing" I shrug.

"So you mean to tell me that while you were over there" he pointed out with his coffee mug, "that you just looked at her and through ESP she knew what you were saying? Geez Nate you're in the wrong business with that kind of power" he laughs.

"Fuck off Jax." I said pulling a cigarette from its crumpled packet in the front pocket of my jeans, I slide it between my lips, light it and inhale deeply then blow out a long stream of white smoke into the night air.

"She's scared of something Jax."

"Yeah, the blonde Brit." He states without even looking at me.

"No." I say, shaking my head. "There's something more." Jax scoots closer to the edge of his chair, leaning his elbows on his knees "Like?."

"Not sure, I haven't figured it out yet. But I will"

"Hey bud, where she is concerned I don't mind doing some investigating" he says wiggling his eyebrows.

"Don't even think about it" I spit out and Jackson raises both his hands in surrender.

"Okay, okay chill, I didn't realize you wanted to tap her, hell I know when to step back ,she's all yours boss."

"It has nothing to do with getting in her pants you asshole."

"So let me get this straight" Jackson muses poking a finger into the air, "you don't want in her pants but you don't want me in there either?"

Dropping the cigarette onto the dirt floor and squashing the butt out I look up at him through narrowed eyes. "Like you said, I'm the boss".

I walk over to the tent, pull the flap back on the door and drop down onto the canvas cot folding my arms behind my head. Jackson follows behind me and sits down on the cot opposite .

"What the fuck is going on?" He levels his stare at me .

"Leave it alone Jax."

"Hell no, I aint never seen you like this over a piece of ass."

Sitting up quickly and facing him, I growl. "She isn't a piece of ass."

"OK, ok she's not JUST a piece of ass, but something is going on. You've been watching her a lot more than the other two."

"Maybe that's because she is a beautiful fair haired woman in a country that would just love a fresh piece of meat like that to put on the black market. Do you know how much she would go for?" I spit out, anger and frustration buzzing through my body making my fists clench. Seeing my anger Jax lowers his tone and sighs.

"I know I've thought about the exact same thing and the one thing I can't work out is why did IMA send her? I mean. they have always sent male civilians out here because this part is known for the sex slave market....so why?"

I shake my head perplexed by the same thought. " I have no idea, that's why I sent an email to Paxton I want to see if he can find out anything more about IMA and the contract they have with the military for this base."

"Good, Paxton will dig like a dog looking for a lost bone I know how much he hates Peterson" Jax chuckles.

"There's just something not right, I can feel it" I said rubbing my hand across the back of my neck." "Well I trust your spider senses bud and I damn well know if we're both feeling uneasy, then something is definitely wrong."

"Let's just hope we're both wrong and watch her like a hawk." "Well I can think of a lot worse things to be doing" Jax smiles. "Just keep your mind out of the gutter and your eye on the target ok?"

"Yes boss" he says giving a mock salute.

Chapter eight

C*asey*

Walking back to my room I close the door and slide the bolt across to lock it, then lean my back against it letting out a sigh of relief. Not only had I once again escaped the claws of Mike but Nate as well. Geez what was it with these men and their stereotypical Alpha male personalities. It's bad enough having to work with Mike in the close quarters of the medical rooms, with his accidental touches and brushes against some part of my anatomy, and that sick thought makes me shiver in disgust, and then when I finally get a reprieve from Mike's unwanted attentions Nate's there watching my every move and quite frankly I was starting to feel like a bloody gold fish in a bowl, it was getting maddening and claustrophobic, just the thought of being in a small enclosed space with Mike and his ego made me feel ill in the pit of my stomach and it wasn't as though I hadn't tried to put him off. Not only had I told a little white lie about having a long term boyfriend back in Sydney but today I had actually told him to his face to back off because not now, and not ever, would I be interested in anything with him, and all I got from him was a sickly sweet over exaggerated smile.

Pulling off my work scrubs and pulling on a pair of grey sweat pants and a t-shirt, I sat down on my bed cross legged, grabbed the IPod off the small table next to it and pushed the ear buds into both ears, scrolling through the list and pressing "play" and the soothing sounds of Enigma floods into my brain. Leaning back onto the bed and closing my eyes, I let it take me into a deep slumber.

When the alarm on my phone bleeps loudly to wake me up at 6am, I groan and hit the snooze button that's set for an extra 5 minutes. I actually feel like I have a hangover- my head feels foggy and aches but this ache isn't caused by alcohol, it's a familiar ache that I get when my brain works over time. I had taken this contract to try and help myself heal but it seemed like it was doing the opposite. Between the over abundance of male testosterone and the constant watchful eyes of everyone, it was starting to feel uncomfortably suffocating.

Sighing and pulling myself out of bed, I splash some cold water onto my face from the small wash basin, and resign myself with the thought of taking a long shower later after my shift.

Pulling on a pair of calf length dark shorts and a navy scrub shirt, I pull a brush through my hair and gather it into a messy bun on top of my head, fixing it with a hair clip, then I pick up the international calling card because today I need to call Flynn. I had managed to send him an email letting him know that I had arrived but today I really needed to hear his voice. It was the one constant thing in my life that always made me feel better. Clipping the two-way radio and my pager onto my pants and tossing a stethoscope around my neck I lock my door, and head over to the mess tent for some much needed coffee.

Walking into the medical tent I am shocked to see the thunderous face of Nate as he leans across the table in the Commander's office "You are kidding me right?" he growls into Commander Simons face.

"I'm afraid not Mr. King. That is part of the contract with IMA. Dr. Tyler has been assigned to work in the local village medical clinic for the day, it is part of her rotation, all the medical staff do it."

"Yes but she is a civilian MD, not military, so send one of your own, they're trained for it." He grates out.

"Calm down King, she's not going in on her own, there'll be other medical staff and a team of MP's." Commander Simons states authoritatively. Nate starts to pace back and forth in the small cramped room, rubbing a hand over his face, suddenly he stops and looks up to me .

"So, how do you feel about this?" he asks. Folding his arms across his chest. I shrug at his question as I sit down.

"He's right, it was part of my contract....I'll be fine." Nate bends down in front me and rests both hands on the arms of the chair.

"Look at me" he demands in a low voice, taking a deep breath in. I slowly lift my face until I am staring straight into those steel gray eyes of his. He looks almost combustible, a muscle ticks in his jaw and he looks like he is using all his strength to contain himself until I finally say "I'm ok with it." His head drops for a split second as he lets out a frustrated sigh then he pushes himself into a standing position "Fine, let's do it." He throws out over his shoulder as he yanks the door open and leaves.

Jax and Nate got into the SUV with Mike and myself and we were accompanied by two other vehicles, a jeep with two MP's and behind that a small military truck that carried supplies for the local village. I found out that a local nurse ran a medical center from the back room of her home. She took care of all the locals as much as she could and once a month the base took her out supplies and some medical assistance to help her out. It was a great idea but the look on Nate's face told me that he was not happy at all. Jax in his usual cheerful way was doing all the talking while Nate concentrated on the road. I'm amazed he could manage to stay on the road with his eyes constantly checking the rear view mirror and zeroing in on Mike. Jax hit Nate on the top of his arm "Chill bud, it will be fine, you worry too much."

"That's my job…bud." Nate said slowly emphasizing his sarcasm.

Jax turned in his seat to look at me. "So Doc how are you doing?."

"I'm fine, thanks."

"You know I love your accent right?" he said with a huge grin spreading across his face.

"Yes I do Jax, you have told me several times before" I said shaking my head at him, "But that's ok because I like yours too." Jax's smile falters and he now looks quite serious.

"Hmm, accent? Me? Noooo, we don't have accents but you guys do" he looks back and forth between Mike and I and I burst out in laughter.

"You're kidding me right?" I ask him "You honestly don't think you have an accent?"

"No mam not at all." He beams back at me.

"Ok if you insist" I smile at him.

"No, now you've started you need to do some explaining little lady, what is weird abouts the way I talks?" he drawls out in an over the top Southern accent. I am still laughing and when I look at Mike he's chuckling away to himself as well.

"Ok first weird American word that comes into my head is Fanny pack? What on earth is a fanny pack?" I ask him. Now Jax looks at me with a really confused look on his face.

"It's, ya know, one of those little bag things that you clip around your waist." Trying to contain my laughter I look at Mike again and Jax asks "What's so funny?."

"Taking in a deep breath I say "Ok, in Australia a fanny is a woman's vagina, so when you say fanny pack I get a vision of a little back pack stuck on a vagina." We laugh again and Jax is still looking confused, then says "Ok, sooo, what do you call your ass then?."

"A bum, a bottom or an arse" Jax points a finger at me and starts to laugh with us. "Ah, now see I like the cute little way you say that word arse" he says emphasizing the letter R.

Nate turns his head and looks over at Jax, "Trust you to have your mind in the gutter."

"What?" he shrugs " I can't help it if the woman has a sexy voice now can I?"

"Jax" Nate warns.

"Oh come on now Nate how much more tantalizing can she get, she's smart, beautiful, talks sexy and comes from one of the most wicked places in the world I mean hell, almost every deadly spider and reptile lives there, shit I bet she's even got a kangaroo for a pet" Jax says looking straight at me. I shake my head at him "No Jax, not a Kangaroo, but I do have a 10 foot crocodile in the back yard." Jax's eyes grow as wide as saucers.

"Really?"

Nate slaps him on the shoulder."No you fucktard she's being sarcastic." Jax rolls his eyes at me then turns back around in his seat and goes back to staring out the window.

The village was small maybe a dozen dwellings I couldn't really call them houses, they were a patchwork of different types of wood and metal, clumped together to form a structure. We pulled up outside one of these structures and Nate jumped out of the SUV turning around to look at me "Stay here until it's been cleared, Ok?" I give him a nod in response.

A small woman came out of the house to greet Nate. She looked tiny standing in front of him I couldn't see much of her face because she had most of it covered by a white scarf she was covered from head to toe in a long sleeved off- white colored dress, the bottom of it gathering dirt as it grazed along the dusty floor. While they talked the MPs walked around the area and checked out buildings and any concealed areas. When they seemed satisfied the area was clear, they nodded to Nate and then they started to unload the supplies from the truck. Nate turned and nodded to Jax "Ok Doc it looks like all is good to get out." Jax said. As soon as I opened the door of the SUV the heat rushed in like an oven. I am so glad I wore a cool thin shirt and cargo shorts today. The only annoying thing was the scarf I had to keep wrapped around my face, it combined with my sweat, had a bad habit of sticking to my skin and making it itchy.

"Doc, this is Salina. She's the village midwife" Nate said, introducing me to the small framed woman standing in front of me. I extended my hand to her and she took it very softly with both hands.

"I am very grateful for your help doctor." She spoke softly, her English surprisingly good. "Please call me Casey."

"Please, we must get you inside quickly, I fear even the dry bushes out here have eyes and ears on us." She steered me into the small building and down a corridor to a back room. There were several people sitting on the floor and leaning against the stained walls of the room more women than men one woman looked to be about seven months pregnant, another woman held a very tiny baby wrapped tightly in a bright orange wrap, so all you could see were a tiny set of closed eyes with long black eyelashes that swept across beautiful olive skin. I walked further into the back of the room to where a tattered old mattress lay in the corner with two small children huddled together. Salina stood beside me and said "These two are very sick, very hot bodies for 3 days now," I dropped my bag on the floor and pulled out my stethoscope and placed my hand on one of the Children's forehead, then gently against his back. He felt hot and his skin was drenched in perspiration. When I pulled up his shirt to listen to his chest I noticed the rash instantly I did the same to the other little boy and he had the same rash. After giving them both a thorough examination, I looked up at Salina. "Are these two brothers?."

"Yes" she answered .

"Looks like they both have measles. I'll give them both a shot of penicillin and I will leave you something to help get the fever down and if you can give them a bath with some oatmeal in the water it will help soothe the rash. I'm guessing they're not vaccinated?"

"No, none of the children here are." She looked at me with concerned eyes.

"Then it may spread to others, I will leave you some medication to help treat any others that may get it."

After I had given the two small boys their injections, I moved around the room attending others. I stitched up two finger lacerations, checked over the tiny baby who was small for her age but appeared to be very healthy considering, gave a dose of laxative to an old gentleman who was complaining of stomach pain and on examination I found he was very constipated, and cleaned and dressed some wounds that were obviously infected. We were there for a good couple of hours before Nate came in. "We need to go."

"What?" I looked up at him from where I was kneeling down on the floor about to dress the wound on an elderly woman's foot.

"Grab your shit we need to go now." he barked at me .

"Hold on I'm almost done" I sighed slightly frustrated at his tone. He grabbed my arm and pulled me to stand.

"Now." He commanded harshly and started pulling me towards the door. Shaking him off I managed to free my arm from his grip.

"What are you doing?" I asked him, now exasperated at his aggressiveness.

"Look I don't have time for details here, we have company coming and I'm getting you out of here."

"What the hell ?" Is all I managed to squeak before he grabbed my arm again and pulled me towards the door and outside, moving me towards the military supply truck, then placing his hands on my hips he lifted me up into the back of it. "I need you to get in the corner down the back and under those bags ok? And I need you to be quiet."

"But... What the.."

"Don't piss me off Doc, I mean it not a peep out of you Okay?" He bent his head down so he was now at my level looking straight into my eyes. "Okay?" He repeated, nodding I moved down the back of the truck and buried myself in the corner under the burlap bags. I felt the bounce of the truck as Nate jumped off the back, then the door slammed shut, a lock clicked, and I was plunged into the darkness.

All I could hear was shouting and the sound of doors slamming, then I heard what sounded like another vehicle skidding on the dirt to a stop. There were more voices, different, heavily accented, I could only make out some words. I heard one say woman and blonde hair, then I heard Nate say, "No, no woman you see blonde man, not woman." The raised voices seemed to go on forever, I lay there under the heavy bags, my eyes stung from the sweat pouring down my face making liquid trails run down my back and chest. The voices seemed to calm now, I heard doors slamming and the sound of an engine start and the truck started to move.

The loud sound of gears grinding as it bumped and swayed over the dirt road we had travelled here. The burlap bags rubbed against my skin- they were itchy and burned, I needed to uncover my face and get some air, my throat was so dry that it felt like it was starting to close up and although I was soaked in my own sweat a cold sensation was starting to gather in my stomach and move up into my chest, a familiar coldness that I knew all too well I had to keep it together. I tried to slow my breathing but it had an agenda all of its own, it became rapid and panicked and I felt myself slowly sinking, it was dark.....and I was starting to lose it and drift back to that place where I have struggled to control for years I tried again to regulate my breathing and slow it down. *I will not let you win, you have no power over me, and you never will."* I silently chant to myself and take slow breaths in and out. I had to get this feeling of fear and panic under control I listened and concentrated on the bumps and shakes of the truck as it moves and I close my eyes and imagine that I am on a beach watching the roll of the waves coming into shore then sweeping back out again. I start to smell the salt of the ocean in the air and feel a breeze against my face, and I let myself keep sinking and sinking slowly back into the warm sand of the beach until I reach a place where the calmness of my thoughts starts to make me feel safe, and there I stay.

Chapter nine

Nate

"Nate" I heard Jax call out. When I turned around and looked in the direction that he was looking a dirty white van was heading along the dirt road towards us at full speed. Running into the house I grabbed Casey and, ignoring her questions and resistance, I pulled her outside and got her into the back of the supply truck pushing her towards the back of the truck and under a pile of some empty feed sacks. There was no time to explain, I just hoped that she trusted me. As I closed the doors behind me I got a brief glimpse of her haunted face as she buried it under the bags and I saw fear in those blue eyes of hers. Shaking away the image and jumping down to the ground, I shut both doors and bolted them, leaning against the corner of the truck just as the white van skidded to a halt in front of me.

The door of the van slid open and several casually dressed men jumped out. They would have looked like a group of tourists if it wasn't for the AK47 rifles they were carrying. One of the men started shouting as he came right into my face and shoved the rifle against my chest. In broken English he yelled "Where is the white woman?" With eyes locked onto his I calmly spoke "There is no woman here." "You lie" he spat back at me . "No, No woman here, only what you see" I said spreading out my arms motioning to the others around me. "You dog, you lie, where is the white woman with white hair?" His words came out slow between gritted teeth, I inhaled deeply to calm myself and keep hold of my anger, because having this guy yelling and spitting into my face was starting to piss me off so much I thought the muscle that was twitching against my jaw bone was going to snap like a rubber band any minute. "There is no white woman here, we have white man with white hair" I said pointing over to where Mike sat in the SUV. "Maybe you saw him." There was a long pause as we both looked at each other- neither one backing down. The other men took off in different directions and scouted around the house and inside. After what felt like hours of standing face to face with this asshole invading my space the others came back to stand behind him and one whispered something into his ear and then he finally broke his gaze and pointed a finger into my face. "It may not be today but we will have her, she was promised." I took a step back putting my hands up in front of my chest. "Look, we don't want any trouble, we are only here to give medical help and deliver supplies." He narrowed his eyes at me then spat on the floor near my feet turned, then motioned to the other men to get back into the van. Letting out a relieved breath, I watched as the van took off leaving behind a cloud of dust.

"Ok let's move it out" One of the MP's shouted as he jumped into the truck and motioned for the driver to go. Jax and I jumped into the SUV with Mike in the back seat and followed the truck back along the dirt road. Hitting the steering wheel with the palms of my hands I shook my head "What's going on Nate? How the hell did they know we were here? And what the fuck did that mean, she was promised?" Jax asked. I changed gear and looked at him "I don't know, but I intend on finding out. I'll get onto Paxton as soon as were back on base and see what he can get out of Peterson. What I do know" I said, "is that she is not safe, and we need to get her out ASAP." Jax said nothing just nodded in agreement.

After the initial search at the base gates by MP's, once we were back inside, I jumped out of the SUV and motioned with my hands for the truck to pull up behind the shower block and quickly jumped up onto the back of the truck and unlatched the bolt, swinging the heavy doors open with a loud bang. In two strides I was in the back pulling at the sacks. "Doc," I called out to her, but there was nothing. Pulling back the last feed sack, I saw her laying curled up into a tight ball, her hands covering her face. "Shit" Crouching down next to her I let my fingers stroke her dusty sweat soaked hair away from her face and gently moved away her hands. Her eyes were closed and she lay completely still. Softly I stroked the back of my knuckle down her cheek. "Doc," I said, speaking more softly now. Her eyes flew open and she sat up quickly pulling her knees up to her chest "It's ok, we're back at the base." She looked terrified. I spoke soothingly and stroked a hand up and down her arm, gently I took both her arms and pulled her into a standing position. Pushing her hair away from her face and placing a finger under her chin, I lifted her face to look at me and with my eyes searching hers I reassured her "Hey you're ok." I watched as her eyes flitted around the inside of the truck looking disorientated until they finally focused on mine and she nodded. "Come on let's get you out of here and cool you down." Guiding her to the edge of the truck then jumping down I lifted my hands up and gripped her waist, lifting her down to stand on shaky legs on the ground in front of me Jax pushed an opened bottle of water into my hand and I lifted it to her dry lips. "Take a drink" I urged. Slowly she put her mouth to the opening of the bottle and drank until it was empty. Leading her back to her room, I sat her down on the edge of the bed "Are you ok?." Crouching down in front of her so I could see her face she nodded. "You need to drink some more water then take a shower, you need to cool your body down, ok?" She just nodded. "Just rehydrate, relax and we'll talk after." Placing two more bottles of water on her desk I turned to leave when she said "Nate?" I turned to look at her "Thanks," Giving her a quick nod I left and went straight to the glove box of the SUV, pulling out the satellite phone I punched in Paxton's number and waited for it to connect.

After several rings Paxton answered "Nate, How is it going?."

"Not good Paxton I'm going to need you to do some digging for me."

"Digging? What kind?" Paxton questioned.

"There's something deeper going on here and I can't put my finger on it but after what happened today…"

"What happened? Is everything alright?" He fired out.

"Grab a pen and paper I need you to write this stuff down." I proceeded to tell him everything that had happened including everything that was said. There was a pause on the line then Paxton spoke.

"Ok, got it all I'll see what I can find out." He said.

"Oh, and Paxton, I need you to get me what you can on a Doctor Casey Tyler, I'll email through what I know but whatever you can get, including any phone records from before she left Sydney Australia including any calls or emails while she's been here."

"Yep, got it, I'll get onto it and get back to you as soon as I have anything."

"Thanks Paxton."

"Just be careful Nate" he said in a serious tone.

"I always am little brother". Just as I ended the call to Paxton, Jax walked over to where I was leaning against the SUV still holding the phone in my hand.

"What are you thinking boss?" he asks, pushing the phone back into the glove box I scrub at the back of my neck in thought and let out a deep breath.

"Not sure yet, Paxton is going to see what he can dig up. What about you? You've talked to her more than me, what do you know?"

"Shit, man not that much."

"Ok, so what do you talk about?" I ask.

Jax leaned against the SUV and ran his fingers across his chin in thought before he said. "Not much, music, what down under is like, shit like that, nothing overly important, just general conversation."

"What about when she uses the base phone at the contact center? Any idea who she's calling?" Jax's eyes dart back and forth as he scans his memory.

"She never said anything to me, but when I was near her the other day she was talking to someone and I think she said the name Flynn."

"Flynn ? a guy?" I let out sharply, my body instantly stiffening.

"Well yeah, I guess so it doesn't really sound like a chick's name to me."

"What, a boyfriend?" I asked him and he lets out a weary sigh.

"Not sure. She's never mentioned anyone and she's working here so I presumed she was single, dang it, don't tell me I've been hitting on a taken woman man." Jax said wearily.

Looking straight at him I asked angrily "What?" he flinched at my tone, then gave me a playful man- slap on the back.

"Just kidding boss, just having some fun at your expense" he chuckled.

"Do I fucking look amused?" I say tightly.

"Not too much. Why don't you just go talk to her yourself ?" Just as Jax spoke the words we both turned at the slam of a door and watched as Casey, dressed in cargo shorts and a green scrub shirt, take off towards the medical building "Here's your chance" Jax nodded towards her.

"Maybe later. I wanna do some research for myself in the computer lounge."

"Then I guess I'll be staying right here and keeping my eye on the little lady" Jax smiled then winked at me........ the asshole.

Chapter ten

Casey
Looking down at the seconds hand on my watch I counted the steady pulse of the young soldier who I had performed an appendectomy on last night. All his vitals were stable and the wound looked clean. The wound getting infected had been a worry. As hard as they try with infection control out here, there was still a much higher chance of any wounds getting infected compared to any other modern facilities. Grabbing the soldiers file and a hot cup of coffee, I sat down to do some documentation, taking a sip of the coffee, it's bitter taste running into my mouth. I swallowed begrudgingly and tipped it out into the sink. "Yuck" There is no way I am ever going to get used to drinking that crap unless I find some milk and sugar to go into it, then it may improve. Finishing off the notes and leaning back in the chair I pulled out my IPod, pushing the tiny buds into both ears. I slid through the music playlist until I hit the song "Glitter in the air" by Pink. Closing my eyes and relaxing deep into the chair I let her soothing voice sweep into my ears and take me into a relaxing music coma. This was somewhere I often visited to distribute the stress from my overloaded brain. Flynn was the one who called it my "music coma" but it worked, and that's why I had made sure that I had filled up the IPod with as much music as would fit onto it and after today I really needed it.

Looking back on the day's events made me grimace. I must have looked like a total idiot, like some pathetic weakling, the way I had reacted to being hidden in the back of that truck. But the confinement just sparked something I hadn't had to deal with for so long and my body just froze with the familiarity of having to be hidden like that.

Just breathe and let it go, I tell myself, you made the decision years ago that what happened in the past, stayed in the past and there was no way I was going to let it have any effect on me now. *"It's gone, let it go"* I whispered to myself- well I thought it was to myself -until I felt a light tap on my arm. With a jump I open my eyes and look into the dark hooded eyes of Nate. Flipping out one of my ear buds he asked "What's going on Doc?".

Bowing my head I shake it slightly "nothing" I whisper. He sits down on the coffee table in front of me, leaning his elbows on his jeans- clad knees and looking at me as I flip the other ear bud out and turn off the IPod. Raising my head to look at his dark eyes searching mine, his strong jaw with its little muscle twitch and dark stubble, and his tousled black hair, he is quite a spectacular specimen. He breaks into my carnal thoughts with the low rumble of his voice.

"We need to talk."

"OK, what's up?" I ask.

"Today was pretty intense" he started slowly "Are you ok?"

"Yes, I'm fine" I swallow hard.

"You see, now that right there" he said pointing to my throat "That tells me that you're not."

Feeling a little nervous I ran my tongue across my bottom lip and gave it a slight bite. "No I'm good, it was, like you said- intense".

Nate looks up at the ceiling and lets out a long exhale. "Intense is an understatement Doc. You see I think there's more going on here than meets the eye" he continues. Looking at him I try to figure out where he's going with that statement.

"What do you mean ?" I ask. And he seems to take a thoughtful moment before he continues, in fact he actually looks pretty angry but with whom? Himself? Me? "Are you going to continue or do you want me to guess what you're talking about?" I ask with a slight bite to my tone, and that was enough to make his head whip up so fast I thought he might actually hurt himself.

"What happened out there today was not just some bored guys out looking for trouble, they had an agenda, they were there for a specific reason, they were there looking for something in particular and I'm pretty sure they were looking for you."

"What? Why would they be looking for me?" I ask him perplexed.

"I don't know I was hoping maybe you could tell me the answer to that." For a moment I just stared at him, before standing and pushing my IPod into the pocket of my pants "Why the hell do you think I would know?" I asked him. Shrugging his shoulders he continues. "I guess that's the big question here" He was standing in front of me now, his huge solid body towered above me, his hands pushed into his jeans pockets.

"Look I have no idea what's going on here and I have no idea what's going on in that pea- sized brain of yours. Have you ever thought that you're just too suspicious of people?" he peered at me through a narrowed pair off infuriated eyes and said "I am always suspicious of everyone Doc."

"Then maybe you have a problem" I said and picked up my paper work heading for the door.

"Hey" he called out after me "I haven't finished talking here."

The look I threw at him right at that moment could have sliced through steel. "Fuck you" I hissed through gritted teeth as I opened the door to the outside "What a fucking arsehole." I cursed just loud enough for him to hear.

"I've been called much worse than that sweetheart" I heard him say behind me.

"I just bet you have" I threw back the words at him and started walking back to my room but I could hear his heavy boot steps behind me so I just picked up my pace until I felt his strong large hand grab onto my wrist and spin me around to face him. "I said we're not finished talking" He said slowly.

Pulling my wrist from his grasp I said "What the hell is your problem? For the first couple of weeks that we arrived here you couldn't even be bothered to look at me, never mind speak to me, you just sent your little minion Jax in to do all the talking but now, all of a sudden, you think I have some big conspiracy thing going on that you don't know about? Oh! fuck yeah I forgot you're an American so everything is a big conspiracy." He came in close to me, breathing hard, the little muscle in the side of his jaw twitching faster.

"You have a very dirty mouth for such a pretty lady" he said with a smirk.

"Oh! this is nothing mate compared to what I am capable of." Now we were both breathing hard, staring at each other until the lock of our eyes was broken by the sound of Jax's drawl as he slipped his way in between us.

"Hey, now what on earth is going on here?" I look at Jax then point at Nate.

"Your friend here is a dick head, that's what's wrong," I said, planting my hands firmly on my hips.

"Come on now Doc, cool it down, let's just bring the heat down a little and talk about it."

"That's what I was trying to do but she is impossible." Nate gritted out not taking his eyes away from mine.

"I will talk to you when you learn to speak to me like I am a person and not an inconvenience" I say, then I walked away and up to my room slamming the door behind me, leaving Nate rubbing the back of his neck and pacing back and forth with fury. I peek out of the window and watch as Jax speaks while Nate looks at him, furious. Listening closely, I strain to hear what they're talking about. "What the hell did you say to her Nate?" Jax says. Nate points over towards my door. "That woman is so...so...infuriating, I just wanted to ask her some questions and she exploded like a cherry bomb."

"Well you're not actually Mr. Charming are you?" Jax retaliates.

"I don't want to be Mr. fucking Charming I want to get to the bottom of this shit and get the fuck out of here and back to my air-conditioned office" Nate yells loudly turning his head towards my room, hoping I would hear him.

"Jesus Nate what the hell is wrong with you?" Nate looks at Jax, his anger radiating through his eyes "Nothing, forget it" he spits out and walks back over to their tent shaking his head.

In my room I start to do my own pacing which is hard considering how small it is in here. I could not believe how this man could make me explode so fast, what the hell was going on. I'm always so calm and collected but he just seems to know how to push my buttons. I mean, he went from a silent arsehole attitude to an over protective alpha male, to accusing me of being a liar and hiding something from him. He was like a rollercoaster- admittedly an extremely handsome- one but still I didn't have to answer to him, or his damn rollercoaster personality.

Over the next couple of days I tried to keep my distance from Nate and things were fairly calm Nate had gone back to not even looking at me and keeping to himself while Jax and I were always talking. He was great and hilariously funny, the complete opposite to Nate. He reminded me a lot of Flynn, and we seemed to have this comfortable, easy banter between us. He told me that he and Nate had been friends for quite a number of years before he came to work for him. Apparently they both met when they were in the military. He also dropped a few lines into our conversations about how Nate lives a very private life back home, and tried to excuse his hard personality and his unsociability on his experiences while on tour with the military.

"Once you get to know him he's a great guy, he's the only man I would ever trust with my life" Jax said, and I could see the loyalty and adoration in his eyes as he spoke. He and Nate had a very close brotherly relationship, one that it appears had been built over a lot of tough years.

Chapter eleven

Casey

On Saturday it was low key celebrations all over the base due to it being American Independence Day back in the States. In the mess hall they had set up a huge barbecue area and supplied steaks, burgers and hot dogs all through the day that included a wonderful selection of desserts, and I had put away more than my fair share of chocolate brownies, but they tasted heavenly. Later on that night they had built a fire pit that now roared with flames and sat around drinking beer and toasting marshmallows, people kept drifting in and out as they came off duty and went on duty and everyone seemed to look like they were in a food coma from all the food they had grazed on throughout the day.

I was walking back towards my room after finishing up some paperwork when I heard Jax call out "Hey Doc, come on over here and have a beer with us." Looking over at him I gave him a smile but shook my head declining his invitation. "Thanks, but I'm really tired." Jumping up from where he was sitting he jogged over to me and placing his hand on the small of my back as he ushered me towards one of the logs placed around the fire pit. "Now come on girl, there's a time for work and a time to relax. And right now it's time to relax and have a beer."

"Ok, cowboy" I relented and sat down on one of the logs and where a cold bottle of beer was placed into my hand. "Thanks" I said looking up at Jax as he sat down next to me and clinked his bottle against mine, then took a huge pull of beer from his bottle. "Happy Independence Day" I said as I put the bottle to my lips and drank down some of the ice cold amber liquid and let out a low moan "Mmmm." "I see you like American beer ?" Jax asks and I nod giving him a smile.

"It's good and it's been a long time since I've had a cold beer" "Really? I thought you Aussies lived off the stuff." Laughing I shake my head at him "You Americans do have a lot of misconceptions about us." "Then maybe you need to educate me darling" he chuckles leaning closer to me. Ignoring his playful innuendo I ask "So where's your boss tonight? Not celebrating?"

"Not sure, he'll be somewhere around".

Jax and I relax into a comfortable conversation comparing different holidays and celebrations in each other's countries and before I realized it he had handed me another bottle of beer and as I lifted the bottle to take another drink I noticed Nate. He was standing over near their tent, a beer in one hand talking to a pretty dark haired woman and he was actually smiling at the her. "I see he's found a friend" I said pointing over to where Nate and his female friend stood with the neck of my bottle. Jax looked over to where I was pointing and let out what sounded like a grunt. "Dang, must be her lucky night cos he's smiling." At his words I felt my stomach drop into the bottom of my feet, and I actually felt queasy as I watched him absorbed in conversation with this other woman. What the hell was wrong with me? It had to be the beer that was making me feel this way after all it had been a long time since I had drank one. Shaking my head I tried to clear it but the more I watched them the sicker I felt, it was like a mixture of nausea and anger, anger? Why would I be angry seeing him with a woman? It didn't make any sense, I couldn't stand him, he was an egotistical arse. No it had to be the beer, there was no other explanation to it. As though he felt me staring at him Nate turned and looked straight at me, my face flushed instantly with the thought of him catching me staring at them, and then he smiled, the bastard smiled a huge confident and flirty smile at me. Quickly looking away and back at Jax, I stood "Thanks for the beer Jax. I'm going to go to bed I'm really tired." "Oh, Ok darlin, I'll see you in the morning".

"Night" I said as I dropped the empty beer bottle into a garbage bin and walked back to my room, and with every step I took I could feel those steely grey eyes burning a hole into my back.

I really needed to talk to Flynn right now. Checking the time and working out the difference I grabbed my calling card and headed over to the base phone and dialed his number. He picked up on the third ring. "Hello? Flynn?"

"Casey?"

"Hey mate how are you?" I asked feeling instantly at ease hearing his voice.

"I'm good, how are you?" he asked.

"I'm...ok" I answered with as much confidence as I could muster.

"Just ok?" he asked with concern.

"No, I'm good, really I just wanted to hear your voice." Feeling a little more at ease I slipped into a comfortable conversation with Flynn, catching up on what's been happening back home and by the end of the half hour call he had me laughing and feeling completely relaxed, as usual. Sighing, I say "I had better go Flynn I need to be up pretty early."

"Ok, babe , you know I miss you." "I miss you too, so much." The last words came out in a whisper. "Not long now though hey?" Flynn says.

"Nope and I'm sure we'll have fun making up for all the lost time." I smile at the thought.

"We will babe, just be careful and look after yourself." He said sternly.

"I always do....love you." "Love you too babe." And with that I hung up the phone, stared at it for a lingering moment and smiled to myself. Turning around I walked straight into the solid hard chest of Nate. Looking up at him I mumbled an apology and attempted to walk around him but he moved in the same direction blocking my way, so I tried to move around the other side but once again he moved to block me again. Looking at him with frustration I ask "What?"

"Who's Flynn?"He bites out.

"What?" I ask slightly confused by his tone.

"You heard me the first time Doc and I hate repeating myself, I only ask once." He said crossing his arms across his chest. Annoyed at the now smug look he has on his face, I shake my head, "Piss off Nate, first you shouldn't be listening into other peoples conversations; second it's none of your business; and third, I don't have to answer to you," I say prodding a finger into that rock hard chest of his emphasizing my points until he catches my wrist in his hand.

"Who the fuck is Flynn?" he asks again this time more slowly, his deep voice now a rumble. Pulling my hand out of his grasp I start to walk away but he moves in front of me so that my back is now pressed up against the wall that the phone is connected to. Placing his hands flat against the wall one on either side of my head he leans in close, his face almost touching mine, and shakes his head "You are a very trying woman Doc and you are wearing my patience very thin."

"Then maybe you need to go back to your little friend." I nod in the direction of where he was standing earlier talking to the dark haired woman, I watch as both his eyebrows arch and a faint smile curves at the corner of his lips as he moves his mouth closer to the side of my face, his breath is warm and smells of coffee as he whispers against my skin "Are you jealous Doc?"

Anger spread through my body as I pushed at his muscled chest with both hands moving him only slightly backwards."Don't flatter yourself Nate, you're nothing special" I spit out.

"Are you sure about that?" he asks sliding an index finger against the side of my jaw. Pulling away and ducking down under his arm, I manage to escape his trap making my way quickly towards my room but I could hear him coming up fast behind me. "Ok, Look, I'm sorry." He says making me stop and spin around to meet him face to face and I can see the sincerity of his apology in his grey eyes. Looking at him I extend my hands outwards as I ask "What do you want from me Nate?" I almost plead and I watch as he rubs his hand over the back of his neck.

"I want you to talk to me." He says.

"Why? Why am I so interesting to you? I'm just a job remember? Now all of a sudden you want to talk, no...no...sorry, interrogate is more the word, because for some reason you think I have something to hide from you." Shoving his hands deep into his pockets and lowering his head I hear him let out a long breath before he speaks.

"Ok, I get that I'm not the easiest person to talk to but in these circumstances, to me, time is too precious to waste and I think that there's something more going on here than you just being here for your medical skills Doc, and I'm just trying to piece things together." Looking into his eyes I see uncertainty and a true concern in them, so much so that I pull in my claws and calm my voice.

"Look I applied for the job through a colleague at work. I was accepted by IMA and shipped out here and that's as much as I can tell you."

"Did you know the work colleague personally?" he asks.

"Well no it was kind of a friend of a friend type situation, but it all seemed above board. I researched IMA to make sure they are a legitimate company" I told him.

"Oh they're legit alright" he interrupts, then continues, "But it's what's hidden underneath that has me more concerned."

"Well, like I said, you know as much as me, and I'm sorry that I don't have anything more to give you Nate but there is no conspiracy going on and I'm not hiding anything from you. So if we're done here I'm going to get some sleep." He gives me a nod but before I walk away he asks "One more thing?"

"Sure." I sigh.

"Who is Flynn?" Giving him a sheepish look I just smile and say "Well Mr. King I do remember you telling me that you never ask a question twice sooo, I'll pretend I never heard that." As I turned and walked back to my room I heard him let out a string of curses under his breath.

Chapter twelve

Nate

Looking up to the sound of my name I see Jax waving the satellite phone in the air above his head. "It's Paxton" he shouts making me jog over to him and take the phone. "Paxton?"

"Hey big brother how are you?" Paxton asks.

"I'll be better if you have something for me." I tell him.

"Well I've been doing some digging around and as we already guessed IMA is pretty much a front for illegal activity."

"What kind of illegal activity?"

"You're not going to like it Nate." He pauses as I close my eyes and say.

"Go on?"

"It seems like our old friend Peterson has been moving a lot of black market stuff under the radar."

"What kind of stuff?" I ask gritting my teeth waiting for his response.

"Cars, electronics, weapons, it appears he's been supplying the head of an underground militant group there with a lot of luxuries and getting paid handsomely for it."

"Do we have a name?"

"He's known as the Red Dagger AKA Asferat Halmid, he runs a militant posse there and apparently is quite wealthy and wields a considerable amount of political power as well."

"Ok that's standard out here but what's this got to do with Miss. Tyler?" This time there was a much longer pause before Paxton spoke again .

"He also likes collecting things like...... women."

"What the fuck Paxton?" I exploded into the phone.

"Apparently he has quite a harem of women for himself so I'm thinking if Peterson has been supplying him with what he wants, maybe he put his order in for a blonde intelligent western woman." Now pacing back and forth in front of the tent, I rub a hand down my face in frustration and revulsion at Paxton's words. "Do you think someone would go to all that trouble just to fill his harem?" Paxton asked.

"I think if someone has more money than brain cells they would, but why would Peterson call in his owed favor for me to get her here?" I said .

"Now that I do not know. He would have to know that you wouldn't let her out of your sight Nate, but then he also knew that if he needed to make sure something was delivered in one piece that he has the right man for the job."

"Fuck, if that shifty little prick thought he could pull me into his diabolical illegal business dealings he's got another thing coming," I spit out angrily.

"So what's the plan brother?" Paxton's voice broke into my thoughts.

"Well I think for one I need to get Casey out of here and back home."

"What Australia?" He asks.

"No, Portland."

"Here?" Paxton asked "Why here? Nate, don't you think it would be better to send her back to her own country, surely they wouldn't go after her there." He says now sounding slightly exasperated.

"And you know that for sure Paxton? You can guarantee that can you?"

"Well no, but..."

"That's right and neither can I."

Once I had disconnected the call to Paxton I found Jackson sitting in front of the open fire. Taking a seat down next to him, I filled him in on the latest information Paxton had given me and watched as the anger spread across his face. "That mother fucking son of a bitch" Jax raged.

"Exactly" I agreed, feeling just as frustrated as he did right now.

"So what are we going to do?" He asks me.

"I'm planning on taking her back to Portland until I can work out what Peterson's plan is. At least there I have my own resources at hand."

"Pftt... good luck with that one man, there is no way you will ever convince that woman to go to Portland with you" he chuckled.

"I know" I said rubbing my fingers over the stubble on my chin "She's like a wild cornered cat, but..." my words trailed off in thought for a moment taking some pleasure in the thought of her wildness. Until Jax cleared his throat.

"I think you need to keep your mind on the job" Jax said and I looked at him through narrowed eyes.

"Don't you think that's what I'm doing?" I growl at him and he lifts his head up towards the sky like he's searching for the right words "Jax?".

"I don't know man; there's something....different with you, I've never seen you act like this before. I mean what is it about this woman? I've seen you watching her like an eagle watching its prey, and I have never seen you do that to any woman before, and now you wanna take her back to your home for protection, why don't we just get her back to her own country?"

Scrubbing a hand across the back of my neck I look at him and ask "Honestly? I don't know Jax there's just something about her I'm not sure what it is but fuck, it's there I can feel it. What I do know is that I have a bad feeling about this whole situation, I keep going over what Paxton told me and it just seems to be a lot of planning and preparation to go through for them to just give up once she's gone from here, and you know me, if anything did happen to her..." I said blowing out a breath.

"I know, I get it you don't have to explain to me, but you do have to explain it to her and I'm telling ya now there is no way she will agree." Jax says shaking his head.

"Well I guess I'll have to be gentle and convince her then" I said with a smirk.

"Ha, you? Gentle? Now that I can't wait to see".

The following morning I gave Paxton a call giving him the go-ahead to get the wheels in motion to bring Casey back to Portland on the quickest flight possible and this is when it came in handy to still have contacts in the service that were always willing to help me out if need be and this was one of those times, and fingers crossed I wanted to be out of here by Friday. That would give me three days to keep Casey on the base and hopefully safe. Jax was going to stay behind and finish out the contract securing the other civilians on base, although we both new Casey was the target here not the others, but whatever logic told us we never reneged on a job and we had never cut out on a contract. That's why the company had such a high reputation because we had high standards, when King Security International took on a contract, that contract was honored, whatever the circumstances were. After I made the call to Paxton I went to have a chat with Commander Simons who I am guessing was not going to be too happy about the plan I had set in motion, but I'm pretty sure he wouldn't want to have an international kidnapping scandal happening on his base either. I wasn't expecting too much opposition from him, but the Doc, now that's a whole other kettle of fish, so now all I had to do was face the kettle and try and hook myself a fish and reel her in.

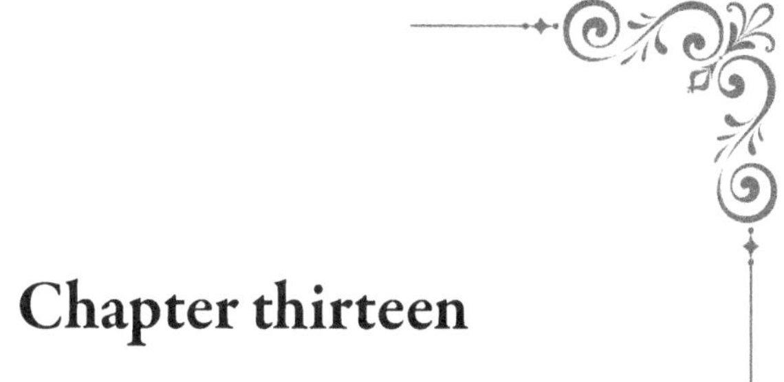

Chapter thirteen

C asey
Waking early, I started off the day with a quick run around the base. It was something I had only taken up while being here, I thought it might help me to de-stress and give me something to channel my frustrations into; the stupid thing is all the frustration I was feeling was caused by the person who was supposed to be making me feel safe, Nate... Such an infuriating person and so egotistical, his personality was like a rollercoaster so up and down I didn't know if I was Arthur or Martha . Every time we had to speak to each other he seemed to show a whole new part of himself, he was actually more wishy washy than the drum on a washing machine and it was driving me nuts.

Feeling sweaty when I got back to my room, I grabbed a towel, toiletries and some clean scrubs and headed down for a shower. A few people had come down with the flu bug and Commander Simons had decided that some flu shots should be given out and I was that lucky person picked for today. Needless to say this day was going to be long and hot as usual.

By 2pm that afternoon I was reminded by the deep grumble coming from my stomach that it needed some fuel, so I headed down to the mess hall to see what culinary delights they had on offer today. Grabbing a bottle of water and one of the biggest well- stuffed chicken salad sandwiches that I had even seen I took it back to the small area that sat behind my room. Just after I first arrived here I managed to drag a chair out here and at this time of the day the wall from the building that housed my room gave it perfect shade from the blazing sun. Flopping down into my pilfered chair, I pulled my sunglasses down from the top of my head, then pulled my IPod from the pocket of my scrub pants sliding my finger over the screen to the music icon and pressing play on an Enigma album. With my ear buds in, I relaxed back into the chair and devoured the chicken sandwich like a starving animal, washing it down with the water. Leaning my head back against the chair I closed my eyes and felt my body relax as the warmth in the air spread through my body. I was just starting to drift off into a nap when, for some reason, I felt a presence near me. Opening one eye with a squint I saw Nate looking down at me. "You know if you fall asleep there you'll get burnt."

Letting out a sigh I said "What do you want Nate?"

"Just to talk." Sitting up, I pulled the ear plugs out of my ears and pressed the pause button on the IPod.

"You like to talk a lot don't you?" I said.

Nate lifted his hand and scratched at his head. "Not really, well not usually, but I don't normally have so much resistance from someone I'm trying to protect" he said with a slight grin.

I put my hand over my heart "Aww, you make me feel so special now" I said, with a bite of sarcasm.

His boots crunched on the gravel as he crouched down in front of me. Looking into my eyes he paused for a moment then said "Maybe that's because you are." That statement caused me to look away from his gaze just for a second before I stood up and collected my rubbish .

"Spare me the bullshit and honey Nate and get to the point" I said wearily.

When he stood up he towered over me with his huge frame and as I looked up into his icy stare I saw that little muscle twitching at the side of his jaw, which I had now learned meant he was losing his patience. "Why are you so damn aggressive woman? Every time I want to talk to you, Bang! You get defensive. What the hell have I done to offend you? Is it my driving? My face? Do I smell?" he said lifting up one of those wonderful defined muscular arms and taking a sniff under his arm pit.

Letting out a deep breath of exasperation I placed my hands firmly on my hips. "Hmm, where should I start? Number one," I said lifting my hand up displaying one finger to him, "Decision to leave family and friends and go the other side of the world ? A big one." Raising another finger I continued. " Number two, choosing to leave my well established job to come here? Stressful." Holding up another finger I said "But the condescending look on your face when you came to pick me up at the airport?....Priceless" I said putting firm emphasis on my last word before I continued. "I came out here to help, I didn't ask for a personal body guard and I am sorry that you got stuck with that job, but that doesn't mean I have to put up with your hot and cold personality fluctuations. One minute you're looking at me with daggers in your eyes and the next minute you're trying to have a friendly conversation with me, and to be honest it is doing my head in." He stared at me until his lips curved into a smile, which only managed to make the situation worse. I looked down at my feet and shook my head exasperated. "See, now you think it's all funny." He took a step closer to me and pushed his hands into the pockets of his jeans.

"Sorry, you look really angry and hostile but all I can hear is you talking in that weird accent and saying things that are just going straight over my head." Looking at the grin on his face made me cave and admit defeat, his smile made my own lips curve into a matching one.

He took a step closer "Is that a smile I see Doc?"

"You are so frustrating," I said in almost a whisper, then he took another step closer until he was now standing right in front of me.

"So can this frustrating man share a coffee with this crazy Aussie?" he asked, bending down a little so he was looking into my eyes, until I gave him a nod.

He guided me over towards the mess tent, the palm of his hand gently touching the base of my back, and then he grabbed two cups of hot coffee from the machine and gestured towards a table outside. "Okay, first things first, what does quote "doing my head in" mean exactly?" he asked, taking a sip of the hot brew.

"It means that you are driving me crazy" I said with a chuckle.

"Ahh, I see, well I know what that feels like" he said with a knowing tilt of his head then he extended his hand out towards me and said "Let's start again? Hello, I'm Nate King and I am here for your protection for the duration of your contract." With a smile, I placed my hand into his large, strong hand and gave it a gentle shake.

"Hello Mr. King nice to meet you. I am Dr. Casey Tyler." When I looked down at my small hand in his it felt warm yet rough and magnetic, tiny prickles of what felt like static electricity lightly tingled along my palm and up my fingers, making me quickly pull my hand from his. I heard him breath in a hiss of air and looking up I see his eyes searching my own, until I picked up my coffee and took another sip, looking down into the cup and breaking that awkward feeling.

"So" Nate started "I guess I owe you an apology in regards to our first meeting? I...Err... guess I was a little pissed at the time, but not at you," he held up his hands in a defensive manor, "Just at the situation."

"Situation?" I queried and he rubbed a hand down his face and started to look... uncomfortable.

"Look you're an intelligent woman Casey and I don't want to beat around the bush with you."

"Then please, don't" I tell him.

Nate's eyes seemed to flitter around everywhere like he was searching for the right words until he said "I know I've said this before but I think there is something more going on here than you think, so many things are wrong; out of place; I had my brother Paxton look into IMA and although it is a legit company it's the CEO I have my doubts about."

"What do you mean?" I asked slightly confused.

"The CEO of IMA is a man called Robert Peterson and he has a very questionable past. I haven't had much to do with him so I'm going on the information my brother Paxton has found so far."

"So, if you haven't had much to do with him, how did you come to work for him?" I watched Nate's body instantly stiffened at my words and the look he gave me was one of disdain. Then he slowly said "I do not work for anyone Casey. A while back he got my crew out of a bad situation with some transportation and he asked me to come here and return the favor, and yes before you go there, he was checked out and cleared until he took over as CEO for IMA, and that's why I need to know as much as you know about what happened at your end. Like how did you get the contract? Who hooked you up with IMA?" Thinking back and trying to remember every detail I absently run my tongue over my bottom lip. Looking up at Nate he closed his eyes for just a second and said "Please don't do that" gesturing to my mouth with his eyes.

Ignoring his comment, I told him of how a co- worker had taken a contract with IMA and how they talked about what a fantastic experience it was, and how it had sparked my interest, so he passed on the information to me and I had contacted IMA and left my details. "Then what happened?" Nate asked.

"They called me in for an interview and I had to go through an evaluation process and paper work, you know credentials, resume psych evaluation and that was it" I finished and took another drink from my coffee.

He looked frustrated as he ran a hand over his face in thought "Ok, so what about mutual friends with this co-worker?" He seemed to put emphasis on the word co-worker almost like he hated the sound of the word.

"Maybe on social media, I do have a lot of co-workers on my Facebook page." I shrugged nonchalantly but the look of disgust on his face made me sit back on my chair.

"If there is one thing I hate the most it's social media" he said through clenched teeth. "It is the easiest way for someone to find out all your personal information."

"That's why it's called social media so your friends and family can keep up to date with what's happening in your life." I said.

"Exactly" he pointed at me "It's not your family and friends that's the problem. it's every other mother fucking stalker slash psychopath that also knows what you're doing and where you are." Now he had me running my own hands down my face in exasperation.

"You're right, but this situation is not something that comes up in my life all the time. This is an unusual predicament, I mean shit this is nuts, it's like something out of a book or a bad dream." The fast thoughts that started to run through my head also made me start to fidget in my chair and I felt the slow coldness of anxiety starting to form in my lower stomach, that was quickly manifesting into something bigger, I felt a light sheen of sweat starting to flush over my face, and I became aware of the rapid beats of my heart thumping in my chest. I saw Nate pull his chair closer to mine, then he placed his hands on my shoulders and turned me to face him. "Casey? look at me" I heard him say, but I couldn't, my breathing was getting faster, the thoughts running through my mind were rapid and sharp and my breathing was trying to keep up the pace .Closing my eyes I tried to slow my breaths down. I needed to get control now or my thoughts would take me back where I had no intension of letting them. My eyes flew open with the barking command of Nate's deep voice "Look at me" instantly my eyes locked onto his, "That's right now slow that breathing down and keep looking at me, don't think of anything else just me, here, and now okay?" I nodded and put all my concentration on his face, mapping every line, every tiny scar and every mark, and as my breathing slowed, my mind started to clear and it started to process and organize itself into a clearer thinking pattern and I could feel myself climbing back up from that familiar dark, deep hole I had been in many times before.

"I'm okay" I shrugged at the grip of his hands on my shoulders.

"You know that's twice now that I have seen you start to have a panic attack and you don't seem to be the kind of woman who rattles easily, so where were your thoughts going just then?" he asked with concern.

"Nowhere, I err... had a couple of anxiety attacks when I was younger, but I haven't had one for years.....until I came here." The words came out in almost a whisper and Nate sat back in his chair.

"Yeah well, I guess I can understand that, after all this isn't the kind of place you would come to have a good time, it would cause even the toughest of people some anxiety it can be stressful and daunting." His voice was a lot lower now but the way he spoke made me feel like he was talking to a teenager that had gotten herself into something bigger than she expected.

"I didn't come here for a good time," I said through narrowed eyes, "I came because I thought I might be able to do something right for once in my life, you know? Give back to others. I'm not some stupid bimbo that thought I would be coming to a holiday resort out in the desert to get a good tan."

"I didn't say that" Nate said defensively.

"No but it's what you were thinking. See this is why we cannot talk on a normal level to each other Nate, in one breath you're concerned and respectful and within a split second you turn into an arrogant, condescending, egotistical dick." When I stood up he placed his hand on my forearm and forced me to sit back down. Smiling, he said, "I can assure you I will take that onboard Ms. Tyler but before you take off on me again please for once can we finish this conversation? Damn it woman," he sounded exasperated but I really didn't care. I just sat and waited for him to speak because the less I had to talk to him the better. Crossing my arms across my chest defiantly I said, "Fine. Talk" He shook his head, took a deep breath and said "I know you're going to be pissed at me for this next question but it needs to be asked, I need to know if you have any personal relationships going on at the moment, you know a boyfriend or any close relationships with a co-worker?"

"Nope." I answer quick and sharp.

"No current boyfriend, no one been paying you more attention than what's normal? At work? Back home?" He continued.

"Nope."

"So there's nothing else you have to tell me?" he asked, eyebrow raised.

"Like?"

"Well I've seen you using the base phone to make personal calls, so what about any family?"

Shaking my head, arms still crossed and with pursed lips I said "Nope" and now he looked pissed. Abruptly he stood, rubbing both his hands at the back of his neck, "Goddamit, Casey give me something here" he pleaded. I looked up into his face and directly into his piercing eyes.

"Like what? I have nothing to give you I have no family, no boyfriend, no lover, I can't give you something that's not there. I'm sorry Nate." Getting up and turning, letting him know I had nothing more to say I walked back to the med building, leaving him standing there.

Chapter fourteen

N ate

Sitting back down on the chair I watched as Casey walked away. My stomach dropped down into my balls, the way she looked up at me with those multifaceted colored big eyes of hers and told me she had no-one, made a lump form in my throat that I found so fucking hard to swallow. This woman, so intelligent, so stubborn and tough, yet so sad.. and distant... so fragile.

"Fuck" I swore to myself. What the hell was I doing? What the hell was she doing to me? I didn't even know anything about her, she was so secretive and hidden, so why was I so drawn to her like a fly getting pulled into a web? Holy shit, when she placed her small hand in mine when we first sat down, there was a spark I felt it, and I saw it in her face she had too. So what the hell was that? Jesus! I needed to remember that she was a client and just a client and I needed to keep that straight in my head. I don't do this; I do not let anyone in...Ever...it's just business.

By the afternoon my temper was starting to fray. I had been mulling over our conversation the whole time. Never in my life had a woman had me this mad, so I went over to the med tent to try once again to talk to her about us leaving for Portland on Friday. I wanted to give her plenty of time to process it because I knew I was going to have another fight on my hands, but when I got to the tent I was told that she was in surgery, so I ended up grabbing some food from the mess tent and going back to my own tent to eat and wait for her to return after her shift was done. The last time I looked at my watch it was almost eleven pm and I must have dozed off because the next thing that I remember was hearing her voice quietly talking to someone. Sitting up, I strained to hear more. Who was she talking to? Lifting the flap of the side window slightly, I could see her standing at her door, and leaning with one arm against the other side of the door was that fucking muscle headed Brit, Mike. Watching them talk, I could see her attempting to close the door, but Mike moved his arm down to now rest against it, stopping her from moving it at all. The smile on her face dropped and turned into a scowl as she brushed his arm off the door and attempted to close it again. This time Mike moved closer into her room and she placed both her hands on his chest and I saw her mouth say that little word " NO," and that was enough to have me out of the tent and jumping up onto the small balcony and wrapping my hand around the back of that smug little fucks neck, pulling him away from the door. I turned him towards his own room and shoved him so hard he stumbled into it "I'm not sure what language you speak but usually in any language when a woman says " NO" it mean back off."

Mike straightened himself up and puffed out his chest like a bull frog, his hands fisting. "What is wrong with you ?" he asked in his little snooty accent.

"Nothing now." I growled. He took a step towards me and I took a bigger one towards him, *"Go on you little fuck take your best shot and I will be scraping you off my boot like a dog turd in about 10 seconds."* I was so wishing for him to take that first swing, so I could put my fist right in the middle of that smug face of his. After a minute of the weak stare down he had aimed at me, he turned his head, gave a little huff sound and went into his room.

When I turned towards Casey she was standing just inside her room with her mouth slightly open and her eyes wide. "What...what did you just do?" she stammered. Looking at her I put my hands up in surrender. "Oh, I'm sorry was I interrupting something here? Because it looked to me like you were trying to push him out the door, or did I see wrong? Were you actually trying to pull him in?" I asked with a sarcastic sting.

"No...I" she stammered out again.

"You what? Did you invite him back here?"

"NO" she almost yelled out "We just finished in surgery and he wanted to come in, what are you doing here anyway? Were you spying on me?" she said, and her voice actually sounded angry now. I looked down at the floor and shook my head "You have got to be kidding me right? That jumped up snooty little ass hat just tried to push his way into your room and if I hadn't been here he would have been nailing you to that bed right now, and all you can ask is was I spying on you? How about a thank you Nate for saving my pretty ass." She sat down on her bed and pinched the bridge of her nose between two fingers.

"I'm sorry, thank you Nate, now why were you spying on me?"

"I wasn't spying, I was waiting for you to come back to your room because we need to talk, well more like I talk and you listen." Her head shot up fast and her eyes pinned me like a note to a cork board.

"Is that right?"

I pinned her back with my own stare "That's right Ms. Tyler, no more kid gloves I've tried to talk to you calmly but it seems to be getting me nowhere so now I'm just going to get to the bottom line. You have three days to pack your stuff. This place is not safe for you and I am taking you back to Portland with me until I can figure out what the hell is going on. The plane leaves at 1900hrs Friday so be ready." She stood up and placed her hands on her hips in a defiant manner.

"What the...?" She sputtered out.

"You heard me the first time" I told her.

"I am not going anywhere. For one I still have a contract to fulfill and two, when I leave here I will be going home to Australia and not with you."

"Well I just cancelled your contract and you will be leaving with me, on Friday."

"No I'm not." She said shaking her head.

"Yes you are." I said nodding mine.

"What are you going to do force me?" She snorted.

"If that's what I have to do then, yes"

"Then I will contact the embassy and call my lawyer. You cannot force me to go anywhere with you Nate." I moved up closer to her, my voice low and close to her ear as I say "try me." Then leaving her with her mouth hanging open with, for once, nothing to say, I left and went back to the tent and fell back onto my cot.

"She aint gonna go that easy Nate," Jax said smugly from where he was laying on his own cot .

"She doesn't have a choice in it Jax" I said my jaw starting to ache from all the tension in it .

"I don't think you're gonna be able to steam roll this one, she's smart, you're gonna have to come up with something to out- smart her" Jax said tapping a finger to his temple.

"I don't care if I have to pick her up and carry her on that damn plane myself, it will be happening." I sat up on the edge of the cot and leaned my elbows on my thighs." She already threatened to get the embassy and a lawyer involved" I said pulling a cigarette out of its crumpled packet, I stuck it in my mouth and lit it, drawing the smoke back hard into my body. I was hoping the nicotine fix would calm me down enough to think clearly Jax sat up to face me.

"Why don't you tell her the planes going back to Australia? Have a word with the pilot and get him to keep his mouth shut; it will be dark when you leave; just don't tell her where you're going and once you get there, well at least you're half way to solving the problem at least you will have her in the States."

"And then what Jax? Keep her tied up to the desk in my office?"

"Hell, I don't know Nate, you will just have to think of something once you get there, although the tying her to the desk sounds pretty hot." He smirked.

Tossing the cigarette out the tent doorway onto the gravel outside, I lay back on the cot and pushed my hands behind my head and went to sleep hatching a plan to get that stubborn ass woman back to where I could protect her the best, on my own territory.

At the first peek of the morning sun I was woken by the sound of a slamming door. She was going for her morning run. Standing and stretching out my tight muscles, I longed for the day I got back to some home comforts, one being my huge bed. I was past sleeping rough on a tiny stiff cot now I had gotten a taste of the luxuries of home and damn I was missing it. Grabbing a towel and some soap, I headed to the showers, while Jax kept a close watch on Casey I really wanted to avoid her today as much as possible I saw the feral look in her eyes last night and I just knew that today, if we came in contact, she would be gunning for blood...mine!

Never in my whole life had I met such an argumentative person as her. She was spirited, he had to give her that, but damn she was going to be the death of him at this rate. Hopefully once she had cut his balls off with a blunt, rusty razor for bullshitting her into going back to Portland, he would have to work on trying to break down the walls she had erected around herself and see what lay beyond. Yeah, he knew he was asking for trouble, but she tweaked something inside him that he had never felt before and that had him intrigued, curious and challenging. And he never backed away from a challenge.

After my shower I headed back to the tent to where Jax was and asked "So? What type of mood is she in today?"

"Oh, she's pissed, well at you that is" he laughed.

"Ha! What's new?" I said tossing my towel over the end of the cot.

"She was going to call her lawyer friend until we had a chat." Jax handed me a steaming mug of coffee.

"And?" I asked eyebrow lifted.

"I told her we had a talk and even though it was hard to convince you, you'd decided to escort her back to Sydney." He smiled.

"And she bought it?" Now that surprised me!

"Hey, come on, your ole buddy here always knows how to charm a lady" Jax motioned to himself with his thumb.

"You're an ass you know that? But thanks man, I wasn't game enough to tackle her again this morning." I said with relief.

"Ha Ha Ha, don't tell me you're scared of that pretty little lady now?"

"Are you fucking kidding me? I would rather do another tour in Afghanistan than spend a single day with her."

"Ah! That's just the sexual tension between you two." Jax gave me a wink that made me spit out a mouthful of coffee.

"What? Sexual tension? fuck no, never."

"Hm hum you say that now, but once you get that little spit fire between the sheets of your bed, everything's gonna change." He said knowingly.

"Not going to happen man, not in a million years."

"Then why are you taking her back to Portland?" Jax asked.

"You know me, I can't let it go until I know the job is over and there is too much going on with this one that I don't think it's going to be over until I finish it myself.... So until I know for sure that she's safe, I want her where I can protect her properly and the only way to do that is to have her right next to me."

"Well at least you can be sure of one thing." Jax said.

"What's that?"

"It definitely won't be boring".

Chapter fifteen

C asey

Dialing the number, I waited for Flynn to answer I was guessing he was asleep because of the time difference, so I was prepared to be patient, but on the fourth ring he answered. "Casey?" he asked, his sleepy voice full of concern. "Flynn? It's okay, don't get worried I'm ok." I said quickly trying to alleviate his fear.

"Jesus, Casey, what's wrong?" The sound of his concerned voice made me miss him more than ever.

"Did I wake you?" I asked.

"As if I give a shit about that, what's going on? you sound... upset."

"I just needed to talk to you, there's a bit of a problem here and I wanted to get your advice.' I said unsure of how much to tell him.

"Okay" he said slowly. So with carefully chosen words I took a deep breath and tried to explain as much as I could of what had been happening here and about Nate's thoughts and conclusion. "What the fuck Casey? that sounds crazy I'll have you booked on the next flight back here pronto, you need to come home."

"That's what I'm planning to do Nate wanted to take me back to the States with him until he found out exactly what was going on, but after I kicked up a bit of a stink, he's agreed to escort me back to Sydney." I hear Flynn breath out in relief.

"Well at least he sounds like a smart guy and he's looking after you. You'll be fine once you get back here and then I can look into this legally, it just sounds so nuts." "I know, tell me about it, so much for coming here to do some good for mankind" I said with a hesitant chuckle.

"Are you okay?" Flynn asked, this time in a more comforting tone.

"I am now I've talked to you, I just needed your input." I sighed.

"Well babe, you've got it, always, let's just get you home then we'll figure out the rest I'll feel a lot better when you're here."

"Me too... Thanks Flynn I'll let you get back to your beauty sleep and I will email you my itinerary for the flight as soon as I get it from Nate."

"Great....Just be careful ok? Love you babe." "Love you too Flynn night." Hanging up the phone, I pushed the calling card back into the pocket of my jeans and turned around to see Nate leaning against a guard rail I paused for a moment, then continued to walk past him. I was trying to ignore his presence until he said in a low gravelly voice, "You lied."

Turning to face him I asked "What do you mean, I lied?"

Straightening himself out to his full height and shoving his hands into his front pockets he said "You said you weren't involved with anyone."

"I'm not," I defended .

"So... who were you professing your love to just then?" he gestured towards the phone with his eyes.

"Well not that it's any of your business but it was my lawyer." Nate's eyebrow crooked as he stared at me .

"Really? Your Lawyer? Not sure what world you come from baby but I don't think there are many people who could honestly say that they loved their lawyers." Frustrated and tired, I really didn't want to argue with him, it was so exhausting. "Maybe that's because most people's lawyers are not their brother's." I said annoyed at him.

The look on his face seemed to relax and soften. "Your brother?"

"Yes, my brother, satisfied?" And with that I swiftly turned around and, as I walked away, I heard him say "Baby with you? I don't think I will ever be satisfied."

Going back to my room, I paced. In two days I would be back home, and then what? Besides all the problems surrounding my presence here, I have enjoyed everything; the workload, the people, my team; it's been a wonderful experience and I was actually starting to feel myself getting stronger, getting away from the demons that are still stuck in that small corner of my brain gripping like a vice, holding on and waiting to rear their ugly heads when I least expect it. The decision I had made to come here was a good one in spite of all the problems it had caused. It had given me a small glimpse of the control I did have over my actions, my feelings and my future. I felt like that empty pie dish that I was carrying around inside my chest called a heart, actually might have gotten its first slice of pie back into it. I lay on my bed and looked up at the ceiling.

As I lay thinking my mind wandered onto thoughts of Nate. What was it with him that rubbed me the wrong way all the time, I mean he was arrogant and frustrating and I bet he was always used to getting his own way in all aspects of his life. He had that commanding presence about him and I am pretty sure he had no problem with the ladies; he was perfectly built, too much in fact, his body was so... hard, so well defined and sculptured, so... too good to be true, too perfect. Blowing out a deep breath, I plugged in my music and hopefully I would drift into a music coma because laying here thinking about Nate's perfect body and those wicked piercing, eyes that reminded me of dark storm clouds, a contrast to the strong angles of his jaw covered in a dark shadow of stubble that matched his unruly inky black hair. Eventually the music soothed my thoughts and lulled me into a sleep with thoughts of Nathanial King entwining into them.

The next day involved me going through my notes and paper work and making sure everything was up to date on the patients I had been taking care of while I had been there, and swapping contact information with some members of the team that had been great to work with and wanted to keep in contact. I had been told that Jax was staying behind to look after the other civilians until the contract that King International Security had was fulfilled. It would be sad saying goodbye to Jax, he was good to talk to while having an early morning coffee, and he had been a great buffer between mine and Nate's explosive personality clash. Always there to calm things down and smooth things out, he would make a great negotiator. Funny how he and Nate were such good friends and yet so different from each other personality- wise. Anyway, maybe that's why the friendship worked, they balanced each other out.

Damn, I was thinking way too much into those two, they would both be just a distant memory in a couple of days and so would this whole experience. Sighing deep at the thought, I started the job of packing, which was pretty easy considering I only had one suit-case and I wanted to leave myself enough time to have a last walk around the base and a final round of goodbyes.

Chapter sixteen

Nate

Seeing her small suitcase sitting outside her door, I walked over, lifted it and put into the back of the SUV. They were due to fly out at 1900hrs and they needed a good hour to get to the airport Jax was driving them out there so he could bring the SUV back to the base I was a little apprehensive about leaving Jax here, but it was the only option that they had and Jax was fine about it. He just told Nate that he owed him a nice bonus is his paycheck and a cold beer when he got back to the States. Besides Jax didn't anticipate anything major happening once Casey had left after all as Jax had pointed out, "Remove the cause and you remove the problem".

I watched as Casey walked over to the SUV and dumped her back pack into the back seat, then pulled herself up into it and clicked her seat belt in place. Jax slid into the driver's seat and, after closing Casey's door, I climbed into the passenger seat next to him Jax turned around to look at Casey. "Now, darlin' you sit back and relax and let the expert here show you what a smooth journey should feel like." "Let's hope your driving is as smooth as your talking then" Casey told him with a smile. By the time we reached Ashgabat Airport the sun was just disappearing into the horizon and taking some of the heat with it Jax pulled up out the front and I grabbed the bags while Casey covered her head with a scarf. Turning to Jax, I held out my hand to him and he gave me a firm hand shake, then pulled me in for a short man hug with a slap to my back. "Watch yourself ok?, no heroics" I said, giving him a stern look and pointing a finger at him.

"Who me? Never" he said with a grin.

"I'll call you in a couple of days, Ok?" I told him. Jax nodded, then turned to look at Casey. He pulled her into a strong embrace "I'm gonna miss our chats little lady, you take care okay?" "You too," she said as she leaned into him for a hug that lasted a bit too long for my liking. When they pulled apart, I found myself staring at both of them just for a split second, but it was enough for Casey's eyes to lock onto mine. Giving my head a shake, I grabbed the bags and took her by the elbow, leading her into the airport lounge area then taking a turn in the opposite direction and down a long hallway that led away from the main boarding area. "Umm.. Boarding is back there" she pointed behind us.

"We're not going commercial" I told her.

"We're not?" she asked as she followed me.

"Nope". We walked down to the end of the hallway until we came to a stop in front of a door, where I pulled a swipe card from my pocket and swiped it through the terminal until the door clicked open and I held it and motioned for her to go in ahead of me. It wasn't a very big room, there was a desk, a few chairs scattered around and a wall of windows and a glass door that opened up out onto the tarmac. To the right she could see some of the commercial airplanes lined up and some taxiing down the runway I dropped the bags onto the floor, then looked at my watch . "We're a little early, take a seat" I said, and she sat down.

"So what airline are we using?"

"Military cargo plane had to make a drop of supplies here." I said giving her a sideward look.

"We're flying in a military cargo plane?" Casey asked through narrowed eyes. "But isn't that miss- use of government property?"

"Not if you know the right people, and it was the only flight travelling in your direction this week."

"So an American military cargo plane just happens to be flying to Sydney this week? How convenient" she said with a sting of sarcasm.

"Hey, never look a gift horse in the mouth, we were lucky" I said, turning away from her stare in the hope that her suspicious, inquisitive mind would be sedated until they were in the air. Luckily, before she could ask anything else, there was a loud rumble from outside. Looking out the large windows you could see the lights on the tip of a wing then the full body of the plane as it taxied to the front of where they stood. The noise from the aircraft lessoned as it powered down and a door fell down into a set of stairs. Someone came down the stairs and towards us, the glass door pushed open and in walked Steve dressed in a military issued green Nomex flight suit and immediately pushed his hand out towards mine. "Nate, it's been a long time" he said.

"Yes, too long buddy, and I appreciate the favor."

"For you? Anytime" He grinned. I turned towards Casey and introduced them. "Steve, this is Doctor Casey Tyler, our passenger Doc? this is an old buddy of mine Captain Steve Davids." Casey took his offered hand and shook it.

"It's nice to meet you Steve" she offered taking a quick glance in my direction. "The pleasure is mutual mam," Steve said with a perfect white smile beaming as his eyes gave Casey an appreciative glance. He stood a few inches shorter than me with short buzzed brown hair and what you would call boyish looks. "So," Steve said slapping his hands together "Let's get moving, we have a long flight ahead." "What about refueling?" I asked him.

"No problem. We'll be stopping in Morocco, refuel then back in flight."

"Sounds good" I nod. Grabbing our bags we headed out onto the tarmac towards the huge grey twin engine bird and up the short stairway onto the plane. Looking around the empty space, Casey's eyes wandered over the metal tracks that ran down the middle of the floor where pallets of cargo would sit and be moved. "Just over the back there's some seats for you to sit, it's not first class, and we don't have any cabin crew to serve you cocktails, but it's functional," Steve said, pointing to an area at the back of the plane where a row of four green airline chairs with seatbelts were anchored to the fuselage of the plane. Stepping carefully over tracks and ropes that lay around, we made our way over to the seats stashing our bags behind the seats. I motioned for Casey to take a seat "Let me know if you need anything, it's a long flight but I brought some snacks and water," "Thanks," she said adjusting her belt and clipping it into place as I took the seat next to her and did the same.

The twin engines fired up to a roar and within a few minutes the plane was taxiing to a smooth lift off. As soon as we leveled out it was announced by Steve that they were free to undo their seatbelts and relax Casey reached around and fumbled in her back pack and pulled out her IPod and plugged it into her ears. "You use that a lot," I said gesturing towards the IPod with a nod.

"Yeah, it's been a good friend to me" she smiled wistfully.

"Friend?" I questioned with curiosity and she gave me a nod."Ok Doc, now you have me curious to know how an IPod becomes such a good friend?"

"This little piece of modern ingenuity has done a lot, it's helped me study, to relax and recharge, it's dependable, it's brought me a great deal of comfort and it never wants anything in return."

"You know you can get a lot of those qualities from human friends as well" I said.

"You can, but the only thing this wants from me is a recharge" she said giving the IPod a little shake .

"You know not everyone you meet wants something in return for your friendship Doc."

"I'm afraid I haven't met too many people like that in my life." She said with a small amount of sadness.

"That's too bad, because a friendship is like a good wine, it gets better with age" she gave me a little smile. "Now that sounded like something out of a birthday card." Smiling back and rubbing my chin I said "It did, didn't it?."

I watched as Casey slowly drifted off to sleep with her music plugged into her ears, her blonde hair tied up into a pony tail, a few wisps had fallen free and snaked down the side of her face close to her ear, then continued to follow the delicate column of her neck. She wore not a scrap of make-up on her face but she didn't need anything, her skin was so smooth and clear, it looked like porcelain. With her eyes now closed her long eyelashes fanned out against the top of her cheeks, her lips slightly parted as she inhaled air in and out. Following the movement down until I could see the swell of her breasts peeking just above the top of her shirt, I watched them slowly move up and down with each breath, she was so beautiful and it took everything I had to not run a finger down the side of her face and rub those delicate wisps of hair through my fingers.

Standing up, I moved further down the side of the plane and stretched my arms behind my neck, moving my head from side to side and stretching out the taut muscle there. I really needed to move away from her for a few minutes and try to center myself because I was feeling like such a prick right now. I had lied to her big time and when she woke I was going to have to come clean and tell her that she wouldn't be going to her home but to mine. I knew she was going to fight me, but the decision I had made was the right one because I couldn't, wouldn't let anything happen to her and if that meant she was going to fight me on it, then so be it.

Sitting back down next to her as she slumbered I found that my mind became flooded with a wave of irrational thoughts like why the hell was I so drawn to protect this woman? Was it obligation?

Was it a case of honoring a contract? Or was it that she had ignited something in me? The thought of anyone else being in control of her protection made my back teeth grind against each other *"What the fuck? Why would that bother me? She's made it clear she can't stand the sight of me and she doesn't need me, so why am I sticking my neck out here?. Because she caused something to spark in my chest and I want more, and not only am I talking to myself right now but I'm answering my own questions as well. Great, I'm losing my mind."* Leaning my head against the back of the seat in utter frustration with my thoughts, I looked over to where Casey was starting to stir from her sleep I watched as the pink tip of her moist tongue slid out and along her bottom lip and her eyes slowly fluttered open.

Breaking my gaze from her mouth, I reached into my bag and handed her a bottle of water . "Thanks" she said taking it and drinking down half the bottle.

"You hungry?" I asked.

"No, thanks, I'm fine." She wound the ear plug cord around her IPod and pushed it back into her backpack, then leaned back into her seat. "Did you get some sleep?" she asked, but I shook my head.

"No, I'm afraid I have been procrastinating"

"Oh....do you have something on your mind?" she asked with concern.

"Yeah unfortunately"

She looked over at me and tilted her head to one side "Do you want to talk?"

"I don't know about that Doc, me and you, well we don't seem to have much luck talking" I said my mouth curving into a grin .

"I know," she said quietly, rubbing her fingers against her temples. Leaning back into my seat I found myself absently rubbing my palms along my jeans- clad thighs. "Look if it's personal, that's fine."

"No, no" I cut her off "It's not so much that's its personal, it kind of has a lot to do with you I'm just trying to find the best way to explain it all to you."

"Okay.." she said slowly and I felt her stiffen in her chair as I turned to face her more and took a deep breath.

"Remember I told you that Paxton, my brother has been doing some digging?" she nodded and I continued. "Well he's found some disturbing things."

"Like?"

"Well the CEO of IMA, Peterson, he's pretty dirty. He's been doing some... shopping for the head of one of the rebel groups back in Ashgabat ."

"What kind of shopping?" She asks.

"Anything he wants apparently, drugs, weapons....women" I say and look straight into her eyes.

"What the hell?" she gasps.

"Look, I think Peterson had an order for a fair skinned woman and somehow you showed up on your work colleagues social media page and bingo, just like online shopping. That's why when we were helping the villagers that day, they were looking for something specific."

Her eyes grew wide with a realization. "Me?"

I looked down at the floor and nodded "Yeah."

"That sounds.....ridiculous, I'm sorry Nate but I am no-one important, there is nothing special about me.... this is just crazy." She sputters.

"You might not think you have anything to offer but to him you're an expensive, beautiful intelligent toy, that he can play with."

"A toy?" she almost yells.

"Yes, a toy. The first challenge is to obtain you. He will use your skills as a doctor for his rebels, then he will share you around, use you until he finds a new toy to replace you, then he will discard you, or sell you onto someone else." I say harshly, I need her to know how dangerous this situation is.

Her eyes start to dart around in earnest like she's trying to make sense of what I'm saying. "But why me? I'm sure there were plenty of other women on his social media page."

I shrug at her question, "Who knows, he seems determined though so anything is possible, maybe he saw something in you that he thought was a weakness that would work to his advantage."

"Shit, shit, shit" she curses and returns to rubbing her temples. After a slight pause she looks back at me. "But now I've left he has no reason to pursue me won't he just move on to an easier target?" she says hopefully.

"Oh he will pursue you, now it's just become more of a challenge, a game, and one that he will have no intensions of losing."

"Ok, then when I get home I will go to the embassy."

"This is not something they will want to get involved in, not with everything that's going on in the east, it would be a political nightmare." I tell her.

"Then what the hell am I going to do?" she throws up her hands and I could hear the desperation starting to form in her voice.

"This is it King, it's now or never." "That's why I wanted to take you back to the States where I'm on my own territory and have access to my own connections and resources, and I would have a better chance to find Peterson."

There's a pause, her voice now almost a whisper, as she asks "Why are you telling me this now and not before?"

I take in a deep breath and go for it. "Because we're not going to Sydney, I'm taking you to Portland Oregon." I blow out in one sentence. Her eyes zero in right onto mine and in them I see a mixture of emotions; anger, shock, betrayal and fear. "You son of a bitch, you lied to me" she seethed .

"Well you didn't give me much choice." I said in exasperation, shrugging my shoulders "you're so stubborn and defensive it was either this or let you go home and...." I couldn't even put into words what might happen if I let that happen. "Okay, okay I agree I could have listened to you better, but why? Were not actually best friends or anything, I mean once I get home the contract is finished, you're not responsible for anything that happens once the contract is over." she says and I quickly stand, anger spearing through my chest.

"Nothing is over until you are safe" I yell, but when I look into her face she's gone pale and pulled her body inwards protectively. Holy shit had my outburst caused her to cower? Taking a calming breath, I sit back down next to her "I'm sorry" I said in a gentler tone.

"No, I'm sorry, for not listening to you and being more grateful for help with this friggin unbelievable, ludicrous situation that I'm in" she waved her hands in the air in exasperation "But I will be going home Nate, this is not your problem anymore and believe me I can fight my own battles....I'm used to it."

Closing my eyes for a second trying to calm my temper down once again with this stubborn ass woman, I put an end to this "It's not open for debate Doc, we are going to Portland and this discussion is over." I look at her with determination and am surprised to see that the only argument she gives me is the sight of her pouty lips and her arms crossing over her chest as she thrust herself back into her seat in defiance.

I spent the next few hours lightly dozing, and every time I open my eyes they went straight to looking at her. She must have been exhausted because she slept almost the whole time. I watched as daylight slowly lit up the cabin and I felt the plane starting to slowly make its decent. Leaning over to where Casey sits, I gently clipped her belt in, but the noise woke her and I watched as she looked at me through weary sleep- filled eyes, taking a few seconds to focus on what had woken her before she pulled herself into a straighter sitting position. "What's going on?" she asks rubbing her eyes with the back of her hands.

"We'll be landing soon," I tell her and she nods and reaches for her back pack and pulls a comb from one of the side pockets. I watch mesmerized as she loosens her hair from its pony tail and pulls the comb through it. As she does, it transformed from slightly messy bed hair into long, straight lengths of pure gold, shimmering through her fingers; the sun light in the cabin just catching it right and I have to look away before I reach out and run my own fingers through it, just to see if it's as soft as it looks. When I turn to look at her again she's pulled it back into its original pony tail and dropped the comb back into her back pack and my brief moment of pure serenity was gone.

With a bump, the plane was on the ground and taxiing until it came to a stop. Steve came down from the cockpit "You guys good?" he said giving his hands a quick slap together I stood and shook his hand. "Yep, very smooth flight, thanks Steve, I owe you one."

"Ahh, for you? Anytime." Steve released the door and it dropped down into stairs to a blast of hot sun in our faces. I pulled my sunglasses down off the top of my head and Casey lifted up her hand to shield her eyes. Turning again to Steve I said "Give me a call next time you're in town and we'll get together for a beer." "Sounds like a plan." He says turning to Casey, "And it was a pleasure to meet you mam" he said with a slight dip to his head "The pleasure is mutual, and thank you" she smiled back at him.

I grabbed the bags and motioned for her to follow me into a side area of the airport where passports were checked and we were ushered through customs. Once outside the Portland International I slid open the screen on my phone and pushed a few numbers. "Hey Paxton, we're at the airport."

"That's great, give me about 10 minutes" he says.

"That's fine just send Nick down" I told him.

"Right on it" he said and I ended the call and looked at Casey "Paxton is sending a driver to pick us up shouldn't be too long."

"A driver?" I didn't answer her, I just pushed my phone back into my pocket and looked the other way, then pulled out a cigarette, lit it and inhaled deeply. "You know that's bad for you right?" she said motioning to the cigarette now hanging out of my mouth.

"Yes Doc, I'm well aware of the evils of smoking." I smiled and before she had time to continue and before I even had time to finish my cigarette, a familiar sleek black Lincoln Navigator pulled up at the curb. "This is us." I grabbed the bags and the boot of the car flipped open and Nick got out "Mr. King."

"Hey Nick" I nodded him a greeting as he took the bags from me and proceeded to place them in the back. Opening the back door I motioned for Casey to get in, but she didn't even attempt to move. Letting out a sigh, I said , "Now what?" She turned her head to look over at the main entrance of PDX.

"I was just thinking how much easier it would be for you if I went in, got a ticket and went home." I looked at her through narrowed eyes, she was chewing at her bottom lip.

"Not happening Doc, in you get." She still didn't attempt any movement and I saw a small glint of fury in those beautiful blue eyes of hers. "Casey" I growled a warning, then motioned to the back seat of the Lincoln. Moving closer into her, I leaned down placing my mouth at her ear. keeping my voice low, "If you don't get in the mother fucking car right now I will throw you over my shoulder, carry you back into customs and tell them you're an illegal here, and it can take quite a long time to sort that kind of thing out and believe me, I don't think you want to be in the holding cell of the local prison for a few months, do you?"

"You wouldn't?" she said shocked at my determination.

"Try me." I answered. She let out a hissing sound, then slid into the back seat, while I got into the front.

Taking the highway, we crossed the Willamette River into the heart of the city, and within minutes we had pulled up out the front of the twenty storey glass building that was King International Security. Nick took care of the bags and I lead Casey by her elbow into the lobby and straight for the elevator. Once inside the elevator I swiped my access card over the screen and the doors close.

Chapter seventeen

C asey

The doors of the elevator opened up to a white marbled floor and what looked like frosted glass panels from floor to ceiling Nate swiped his card once again over a panel at the side of the glass door and, with a click it opened, and he motioned for me to enter. Beyond the door was a magnificent sight, the white marble floor ran all the way to two steps down into a huge sunken living area and over to where floor to ceiling glass took over a whole wall. Stepping down into the living area, where two long black leather couches sat opposite each other, a large black and white oriental looking rug sat on the floor in between them. On the wall to my right was a huge flat screen T.V that took up almost the whole wall and on my left hand side there was a long black marble kitchen island and beyond that a whole wall of cupboards, everything fitting together neatly, the stove, sink and a huge double fridge. Roving my eyes around the huge open apartment, I noticed that behind me was a modern black staircase leading upwards.

Scatted around the walls were various pieces of art, some paintings that looked somewhat abstract and some black and white photos. The whole area was breath taking and neat, no clutter, everything in its place. I looked at Nate as he placed our bags down on the floor. "This is.... beautiful, the rent must be a real bank breaker," I said in awe as I kept looking around the enormous space in front of me. The corner of his mouth twitched and turned up into a tiny smile and he shook his head "I wouldn't know about that, I own it."

"You....own....this?" I said, spreading my hands out in front of me.

"I do. Come on I'll show you to your room." He picked up my bags and I followed him up the stairs and down a long hallway that had several doors. I followed him until he reached a door at the bottom and opened it, then moved back for me to enter. The bedroom had the same large floor to ceiling windows, it was a whole wall of clear glass. A huge bed sat almost in the middle of the room I walked over to it and ran my hand over the soft covering, plump black and red colored pillows leaned against an ornate carved wooden bed head. It looked so inviting after all the travelling we had done over the last twenty four hours Nate dropped my bags on the floor at the end of the bed and pointed to another door. "In there is a bathroom and closet area." He looked down at his watch and asked "Are you hungry?" "No...thank you, just tired"

"Okay, well take a shower and get some sleep, and... make yourself at home." He turned to walk out of the door.

"Nate," I called and he turned to look at me "Thank you." He gave me a quick nod of his head and just walked away closing the door behind him.

The hot water from the shower streamed over every tight muscle in my body and it felt so good to have a decent shower with constant high pressure and steaming hot water. After washing my hair and body until I felt clean, I reluctantly got out, dried myself and slipped into a clean t-shirt then slid in between those soft, clean sheets, inhaling the aroma of freshly washed linen I closed my eyes and drifted off easily.

Opening my eyes I glanced over at my phone and looked at the time it was 2.15 pm holy-crap I had been asleep almost the whole day. Getting up I pulled on a black pair of yoga pants, went into the bathroom and splashed some water on my face to try and clear my sleepy hangover eyes then pulled my hair up into a messy bun. When I opened the bedroom door I could hear two different male voices, they sounded muffled and somewhere downstairs. Walking down the stairs, I headed to the kitchen and quietly opened some cupboard doors looking for a glass. It felt really weird and uncomfortable going through someone else's cupboards but my mouth was so dry I needed some water. To the left hand side of the kitchen there was another door slightly open and just as I had found the glass that I had been looking for, Nate walked out dressed in a pair of very snug fitting jeans and a white button down shirt, his sleeves folded mid way up his arms. "Hey" I said filling the glass up in the sink.

"How did you sleep?" he asked.

"Like the dead" I smiled, taking a drink from the glass.

"There's some coffee in the pot and help yourself to something to eat, the refrigerator is pretty well stocked."

"Thanks, I'm not a big coffee drinker." I took the glass of water over to the large windows that dominated the living area and looked out. The sky was so clear and blue and there was a fantastic view of the city below Nate didn't have to speak but I could feel his eyes watching me closely. "What a great view," I said turning to sit on the couch.

"Yes, It is, especially at night time." He said glancing towards the view. Putting the glass down on the small table next to the couch I looked up at him, his eyes were focused entirely on me. "You okay?" he asked. I nodded and that intense focus that we had on each other was broken by a male voice. "Nate, we will have to make a move on this ASAP" turning I watched as a clean- cut, brown- haired man looking very much like Nate, only a few inches shorter and dressed in a stylish grey suit walked from the room next to the kitchen looking at some papers in his hand. He came to an abrupt stop and lifted his head and saw me sitting on the couch. "Oh, Hi, I'm Paxton, Nate's brother." He came over and held out his hand to me. Standing, I took it and looked into his friendly smiling face.

"It's nice to meet you Paxton...I'm sorry for all the trouble I seem to have brought to your doorstep" I said apologetically.

"Oh, hell no, you haven't done anything you need to apologize for here, Peterson is an ass. Not only has he put you in danger but he screwed us over as well I'm glad you're here and hopefully it won't take too long for us to get you back home."

"Thanks I appreciate it." I said.

Paxton looked back at Nate."Okay well I'd better get moving and I'll meet you back down in the office later."

"Sure, thanks." Nate said to Paxton as he got into the elevator and the doors closed behind him. Nate went to the refrigerator and pulled out a plate and some containers I walked up to the kitchen island and sat on one of the stools and then watched as he pulled a platter out of one of the cupboards and filled it with pieces of fruit, cheese, olives, and crackers, lifting a lid on another plate that was full of sandwiches, "I hope you like turkey" he said motioning to the food spread out in front of us. "It all looks great, you really didn't have to go to so much trouble." "Believe me it's no trouble, I just picked up the phone and it came up from catering on the second floor, help yourself." Going back to the refrigerator, he pulled out a jug of orange juice and filled two glasses.

I think I was more hungry than I first thought because I am pretty sure I could hear the thud of the food hitting the bottom of my empty stomach and I had to keep reminding myself to chew before I swallowed. Nate ate and looked at his phone, thumb flipping through screens and tapping away at the keys and then the phone beeping back in rapid responses. I watched him, no I ogled at him, he was such a wonderfully built specimen of a man, the corded muscles in his arms flexed as he played with his phone and I found myself mesmerized by that ever present twitch at the side of his jaw that kept flicking under the dusting of dark bristles along his jaw line, and his unruly messy black hair where a stray lock had dropped down onto his forehead.

My thoughts turned to the spacious area that was his home and he had a driver for Christ's sake! What the hell kind of security business did he and Paxton own? Breaking my thoughts, Nate looked up from his phone. "When you're done eating, you need to get dressed."

"Oh, ok... where are we going?" I asked, slipping off the stool, grabbing the dirty plates and heading for the sink.

"Just leave those, we need to meet Paxton in my office so we can go through some things then I've arranged for Charlie to take you out to do some shopping." My head jerked up to look at him.

"Umm...Charlie? Shopping? I..... Don't do shopping," I said slowly, "but thank you for the offer."

A smirk danced over his lips. "All women shop," he said with a smug look on his face.

"Maybe in your world, but not in mine, and who the hell is Charlie?" I said placing my hands on my hips.

"My PA, and you will need to shop, you only have the clothes that you took with you, good for the dessert Doc, but not for here." He said matter-of-factly shaking his head.

I pondered for a moment what he just said and I suppose this time he might actually be right I didn't really have much with me to wear at all. "You're right, I do need to pick up some things, but I don't need an escort to shop just point me to the nearest Discount shopping mall." He gave me a weird look before he asked "Discount mall?"

"Yes, you know like K-mart, Target..... You do have those here don't you?" looking down at his phone again and shaking his head he said "I have no idea Doc, Charlie will take you shopping, and Nick will drive you and be your escort."

"You mean like a body guard?" I said under my breath.

"Whatever you want to call it, but while you're here, where you go he goes……. understand?" he glared at me sternly.

"Yes sir" I said giving him a mock salute, then before he could say anything else, I made a hasty retreat up the stairs to change.

Dressing in a pair of black skinny jeans and a loose white shirt, I slipped into my hiking boots and grabbed my purse I brushed my hair out and pulled it into a pony tail and went back downstairs to were Nate was waiting. He handed me what looked like a small credit card. "You'll need this to get back up here when you're finished, just swipe it over the small box in the elevator and it will bring you straight up to the penthouse."

"Ok" I said taking the card and shoving it into my purse while following him into the elevator, the next time the doors opened we faced a set of large glass doors with "King Inc" etched into the glass Nate opened up the door and motioned for me to enter. Walking forward we passed an empty desk, then another large set of dark wooden doors that he pushed open into a huge office with more floor to ceiling glass windows that took up the whole back wall. A large wooden desk sat in front of them. On the desk were three computer screens and a keyboard. On one side of the room was a small compact wall unit that looked like a bar, with bottles and glasses of different sizes and a coffee machine. Tucked into the side was a small refrigerator and sitting on the other side of the room was a black leather couch with a couple of matching chairs. Nate walked over to the desk and pulled a note pad and pen from one of the drawers and handed it to me. "I need you to write down all your social network addresses and passwords, and also any email addresses that you use." I gave him a wary look as I took the pen and pad from him.

"Don't worry, we can change all the passwords afterwards, but we need to go through everything." Sighing, I wrote down the information that he wanted and handed him back the note pad, then sat down on the couch. Nate moved back behind his desk and pushed a button on the desk phone "Charlie, can you come in here please" he said and a female voice quickly answered. "Yes Mr. King." With a knock on the door, it opened and in walked an elegant looking woman. She looked to be around mid twenties, slim build with long waves of auburn colored hair that fell over her silky cream blouse; her black pencil skirt sat just above her knees; the skin on her long legs looked flawless under the fake tan she wore I only saw the back of her when she walked into the office and up to stand in front of Nate's desk. "Charlie, this is Casey" When she turned around to where Nate was looking at me sitting on the couch, the smile on her face faulted just for a split second, then it was instantly back in place as she came over and held out her hand for me to shake. Standing up I took it and looked at Nate.

"This is Charlie?" I asked him with a raise of my eyebrows, but before Nate could answer, Charlie did it for him "Yes, it's really Charlotte but Nate likes to call me Charlie, it's his little pet name," she purred. I choked back a small laugh that I managed to cover with my hand but that didn't stop her eyes turning into little green slits as she gave me the ultimate death stare which was eventually interrupted by Nate handing her some cash. "I need you to take Casey shopping. She didn't bring much with her, so take her down to Pioneer Place we have an account there so just charge anything she needs."

"Hey, hold it there" I said, placing myself to stand right in front of Nate. "I have my own money and I will buy my own clothes thank you." His eyes locked onto mine and that little tick at the side of his jaw started it's little dance of agitation. "The cash is for tipping, something I am sure you're not used to."

"I have credit cards and I believe that you do have those little things called ATM's right?".

"Yes, and a large currency exchange rate to go with them when you use a card from overseas." He said with a slight quirk of his lips.

"I'm sure I can handle that, but thank you for the offer." He let out a curse under his breath and I turned to Charlie. "Come on Charlie, let's go shopping, apparently every woman just loves to shop," I sang sweetly to her while giving Nate a smile.

On the way out of Nate's office she grabbed her purse and we went down into the lobby we walked out into the heat of the day to where Nick was leaning against the black Lincoln, parked out the front of the building. He was a pretty solid looking guy, maybe in his late thirties, dressed in black dress pants and a black button down shirt, but the dark sunglasses and his shiny bald head made him look badass.

As soon as we reached him he opened the back door and Charlie got in and slid up the seat giving me room to sit next to her. When Nick slid into the front seat she said "Pioneer Place please Nick," then she looked me. "It's got some great top end retailers there."

"Sounds expensive," I answered.

"If you call Macy's, Tiffany and Saks Fifth Avenue expensive, then yes it is." She said sounding snotty.

Letting out a sigh I said "I just want a cheap shopping mall, nothing fancy and over- priced." And from the look she gave me you would think I had just slapped her across the face .

"I guess it depends on one's taste and up-bringing," she retorted. Smiling to myself, I just turned and looked out of the window. "So where are you staying?" Charlie asked.

"Up in the Penthouse."

"The Penthouse," she sputtered out. "With Nate?"

"Yep. With Nate." I didn't even have to look at her to feel the angry heat radiating from her, then she slowly said.

"You know Nate and I are very close."

"That's nice," I shrugged and she continued, "I mean I do a lot for him as his PA, and we have been out on quite a few dates as well."

Turning now to look at her, I ask "So you and Nate are..dating."

"Well kind of. We're trying to keep it on the low because he is my boss after all."

"I see, funny he never said anything to me about you." I said giving her a knowing smile. She stuttered now, trying to think of something to cement her claim, "Like I said, he doesn't want it getting out yet."

"Uh, huh." I smiled to myself.

"You have a very strange accent, is it British?" She asked, changing the subject.

"No," I laughed at the friggin bimbo, "Australian."

"Oh, so you like have koala bears in the backyard and snakes everywhere?" "Yeah, and I ride my pet kangaroo to work every day as well." I sighed and she actually paused at what I had said, like she was thinking about it, then she let out a small air-headed giggle "That's a joke right?" I just shook my head from side to side, thinking wow, how the hell was this girl working as a PA?

After spending what felt like an eternity in and out of small expensive clothing stores, I finally found a small inexpensive store that had everything I needed without sending me broke. Within a few minutes of entering the store, Charlie snubbed her nose and loudly let me know that she would be waiting for me in the car. Looking around, I picked up some shirts, pants and a couple of summer dresses and some comfortable strappy flat shoes. I also managed to buy some new underwear, something that was greatly needed. I paid for my purchases and came out to walk into the cosmetic store next door. There I grabbed some shampoo, deodorant, body-wash and a few cosmetic items. I have never been big on plastering my face with layers of make-up but I still like to use a little touch here and there. Swiping a bottle of perfume that sat on the counter. I paid, picked up my bags and went back to the car.

Once we were back at King International Charlie got off the elevator on the fourth floor I said a quick thanks, then continued up to the top floor. On entering the living area I noticed an Iphone sitting on the kitchen counter with a note under it. Picking up the note it read "Casey, please use this phone, I have installed my number in it, feel free to call home, don't wait up for me, I will be late, make yourself at home Nate." I was torn between being happy that I would be able to call Flynn now and a little disappointed that Nate was going to be late. Now why the hell is that bothering me? I mean the poor guy has also been away from his home and family and.....the comfort of Charlie's company? And with that thought a shiver ran through my body. Stunned at the way I was feeling, I gave myself a shake and went up to my room to put my purchases away.

For dinner that night I just grabbed the cheese and fruit platter that was still in the refrigerator from earlier in the day, sunk into the soft leather couch and dialed Flynn's number. He answered quickly, shouting into the line "Casey? Where the fuck are you?"

"Hey, it's ok, I'm ok Flynn." I reassured him.

"What the fuck is going on? I was on my to pick you up from the airport when I got your text."

"I know, there was a change of plans at the last minute. I'm so sorry Flynn. I didn't mean to give you a scare." I said as I nibbled on some cheese.

"Ok, just give me a minute to breath here, then talk." He breathed deeply into the phone. I spent the next twenty minutes explaining to my best friend about everything that Nate had told me and why he had brought me to Portland. "So really the fucker has kidnapped you" Flynn said .

"Kind off, I guess." I chuckled, "He's a good guy Flynn."

"That he might be, but do you trust him?" he said seriously. Now that right there was a question and a half, and it was something I had to think hard about.

"Flynn? you know I can't...." my voice faltered and Flynn picked up where I had left my sentence. "I know, I know. It's hard for you to trust babes."

"I trust him to protect me," I said.

"That's all I'm asking Casey." he sighs into the line.

"Nate and his brother are doing some digging Flynn, and that worries me." There's a slight pause, I know that Flynn knows exactly what I'm worried about, "Don't be, nothing will be found."

"But what if..." Flynn cuts off my sentence sharply. "No! Casey, there's no if's or buts about it, they would have to be pretty damn good to find anything about Max I buried it myself, I promise you." I let out a sigh. "I hope so."

"Let's just concentrate on what's happening now, ok? I'm looking into Steve Belson, the one who hooked you up with IMA in the first place, I've got an address on him so I want to pay him a visit and see what he knows." Flynn says.

"Please Flynn, just be careful." "Always Casey, always." After I hung up from our phone conversation I took a quick shower, changed into my black yoga pants and a black t-shirt, grabbed the T.V remote, got comfortable on the couch again and did some channel surfing until I found an old musical, "Singing In The Rain" to watch until my eyes grew tired and slowly closed.

Chapter eighteen

Nate

Paxton had been doing quite a bit of research on this Steve Belson, the so called work friend that had put the first link between Peterson and Casey, but there was nothing too damaging. He was a general practitioner, forty years old, single with a crystal clear record. Paxton had already called him and was satisfied that he hadn't known anything other than he had a great experience with IMA and thought that it was something Casey would also enjoy. Paxton said he seemed pretty sincere, and there didn't seem to be any holes in his story. The other interesting bit of information that he found out was about her "so called brother" Flynn Cooper, who turned out to be some shit- hot lawyer with no biological ties to Casey at all. So why had she lied to me about him? What was she hiding? There was something, I could felt it in my gut, but for now we were back to square one for tonight. Tomorrow, it was Petersons turn.

We'd had a late night tonight, catching up on work and looking into that Belson guy, so we had gotten some Chinese takeout and eaten in the office along with a couple of beers. By the time the elevator doors opened up into the Penthouse it was way past 1am, I noticed that the big screen T.V was on and the credits from a movie were rolling up the screen. Walking further into the room to find the remote to turn it off, I notice her, laying curled up on the couch, clutching the remote in both hands against her chest. Stepping closer to her, I see that her eyes are closed and her pink lips are slightly parted as she breathes in deeply from sleep. Moving my eyes down her body she has the remote pressed into the middle of her ample breasts that are gently moving up and down as she breathes. I hold my own breath as I try to ease the remote out from between her fingers without waking her, but as I slip it free, my fingers brush against one of her breasts; she stirs moving her head to one side; a blonde lock of hair falls over her face, and I move it away tucking it behind her ear. Inhaling, I sit back onto the coffee table and watch her sleep.... Again. I'm starting to think this is becoming a habit, but she is so exquisite to look at, she looks so pure, so innocent, and I have this strange need to protect her, whatever the cost is.

Eventually pulling myself away from watching her sleep, I go to my bar and pour myself a large scotch and take it into my office I need to get a head start on tracking down Peterson as he appears to be the eye of this tornado, and that's where I intend to start first. I've found in the past forgetting the symptoms and curing the cause has always worked in my favor.

Leaning back into the comfort of my chair I swirl the amber liquid around in the tumbler before taking a drink, when I hear a soft noise that sounds like a whimper. Placing the glass down on my desk, I tune into where its coming from, silence.... then a small cry that starts to ascend louder, and in such a pained tone it makes my stomach churn. Jumping up, I move quickly from the office and into the living room to where I see what was just a few minutes ago a beautiful woman in a peaceful slumber, was now a woman writhing around on the couch like a tortured soul in pain; legs moving, arms flailing in the air; with her head rapidly shaking from side to side. Walking over to her, I place both my hands on her arms and softly speak to her. "Casey, wake up."

"Nooo, please" she cried out.

"What the fuck?" I shake her again, this time a little harder, until her eyes open and she pulls herself into a sitting position pulling her legs up and wrapping her arms around them.

"What? Shit..I'm sorry" she breathed out.

"Are you ok?." I ask smoothing a hand over her arm.

"Yeah, just a bad dream or something, I don't know." With her rapid breathing starting to slow she looked around the room and then to me, with such a mix of emotions in her eyes. I got up and grabbed a bottle of water from the refrigerator and brought it back to her.

"Here, drink," I said putting the bottle into her hands. Within a few minutes she had calmed herself and took a drink of the water. I sat next to her on the couch "Better?"

"Yes, thanks." she breathed out.

"Do you want to tell me about it?" I ask, cautiously but she shakes her head. "Like I said, just a bad dream."

"That looked a lot more than just a bad dream Doc?" I said tilting my head slightly to look at her.

She looked down at her hands. "I'm sorry, I was watching T.V and I must have fallen asleep."

"Don't worry, I want you to make yourself at home. It's just late, I thought you would be in bed by now, is your room comfortable?"

"Yes, it's great I just.... hate being cooped up in a room that's all. If you don't mind, I would prefer to leave my bedroom door open?" she said with some apprehension.

"Sure, whatever makes you feel comfortable I didn't mean to leave you here alone on your first night but I wanted to get started on our little problem." "Oh, I thought you were out on a date or something."

I shook my head and chuckled "Nooo, what made you think I would be out on a date when I have a house guest here."

"More of a house invader I think but hey, don't let my being here stop you, I'm the one who has unexpectedly stepped into your life, besides I'm sure Charlie missed you a lot, I figured you two had some catching up to do."

With a raised eyebrow, I asked "What has Charlie got to do with anything?." She looked from where she was rubbing her hands together in her lap up to me.

"Well she made it pretty clear to me today that you and her are....close?" she said uncomfortably.

Throwing back my head and letting out a loud laugh, I said "No, I can assure you Charlie is my PA and that's all I mean, she's very beautiful, but a little too plastic for my tastes I like my women more... realistic. Just don't tell her I said that or she'll probably spike my coffee with chili powder or something." I was still trying to contain my laughter but looking at her she actually looked relieved and seemed to relax a little.

"So did you find anything out?" she asked.

"Paxton managed to talk to Steve Belson but he couldn't give us anything to go on, I did find some information on Flynn Cooper though." I eyed her.

Her eyes went from looking at her hands straight up to mine, the look on her face changing instantly. "Flynn has nothing to do with it." She said fiercely.

Holding up my hands in a defensive move, I placated, "I know, I also know that he's not your brother." She stood up, hands on her hips, fury seeping out of every part of her body.

"Not in the biological sense, no." she said lifting her chin.

"Then why did you lie to me?" She moved closer to me and jabbed her finger into my chest as she spoke. "He may not be my brother by blood but he is in every other sense. We have been best friends since we were kids, and we have shared everything together, he's my rock- my anchor."

"And your lover?" I asked.

"Oh my god, really?" she said and started to pace back and forth in front of me, and I am sure I could see steam coming out of her ears.

"I asked you to be truthful about him and any other relationships that might be of some significance, and I find that not only is he not your brother, but you live together as well. So it seems pretty appropriate for me to ask if you are lovers?" "No! it's not appropriate, just because I've been friends with a male for many years and we share rent does not mean we sleep in the same bed, I mean it might in your world, but not in mine."

"Look, I brought you here to help you, so give me a fucking break and be truthful with me" I said, raising my voice in frustration. She threw her hands up in the air and started to walk towards the stairs. "Well that I can remedy." She says without even turning.

"What the hell are you talking about?" I spit back at her and once again this conversation we're having is just as frustrating as she's making me.

"I'll be leaving first thing in the morning. This just will not work."

"Like hell you will" I growled out and grasped her wrist stopping her from going up the stairs.

"I am not your prisoner Mr. King and obviously your lack of trust in anything I say is only going to cause you a huge headache. Now please let go of me." She said trying to pull her arm free.

"No" When she tried to push me away from her with her free hand I grasped that wrist as well.

"Let go," she yelled, and she started to fight me, pushing and pulling, trying to free herself from my grasp. Moving her close to the wall I pulled both her arms up above her head and held them against the wall pressing my body against hers, pinning her against it in hope of containing her thrashing limbs from taking out my nut sack. But she continued to wriggled and fight me. "Stop" I growled out but her movements become more frenzied and her breathing was starting to accelerate rapidly as she moved against me. "Casey, stop" I say again, only this time calmer and softer, and over the next thirty seconds or so her movements slow until she stops fighting me and we're both breathing hard. Bending down a little so I can look into her face, I see she has her eyes tightly closed. "Look at me," I say softly, and slowly her eyes open and what I see in those beautiful blue eyes hits me hard. It's not anger but a torturous pure fear that sends a chill through my entire body. My eyes are searching hers for some kind of clue as to what the hell is going on in her mind right now, and what the hell is she so scared of. Then my gaze moves to her mouth, her lips look moist, pink and wet and I take the chance to do what I've been wanting to do for the last few weeks. I dip my head down and take her mouth with my own running the tip of my tongue across her bottom lip, waiting for her to open and accept my invasion. Pressing my body harder into hers I feel her start to soften, then very slowly her mouth opens slightly and she accepts what I am offering, and she starts to kiss me back, our tongues meet and tangle, her lips are warm and soft and I nibble at her bottom lip, pulling it into my mouth. Her taste makes me hungry for more and I delve deeper into her warmth, our lips moving together as I feel my body starting to heat, I know this is where I need to pull back. As I do I lean my forehead against hers and we are now both breathing hard as I ask her "Why won't you let me in Doc?."

"Because I can't" I hear her say in a low whisper. "Nate please, let me go." Reluctantly I release her wrists from my hold, her arms drop down in front of her and she rubs at her wrists."Damn it, did I hurt you?" I asked looking down at her wrists. "...No," then she ducks under my arm where I had her encased against the wall, and walks quickly towards the stairs. "Casey?" I call out to her and she stops but doesn't turn to face me and just says "I'm going to bed, I'm tired."

"FUCK." I yell into the now empty room, running my hands through my hair with frustration "What the fuck are you doing to me?" I yell up the stairs after her. "Driving me fucking nuts" I answered myself, falling into a chair, my stomach in a tangle of knots and my mind soon to join it I must be losing it big time my brain has never been this scrambled over a woman for fucks sake. Never in my entire life has a female made me have multiple emotions all in one hit, it's like I've walked into a bar and told the bar tender to hit me with everything he's got, and he gives me a huge glass filled with anger, frustration, possession, fear, lust and chemistry, and then watches me drink it all in one hit before telling me that the cocktail is called Casey Fucking Tyler. Grabbing my half empty bottle of beer, I put it to my mouth and drain it in one gulp, slamming the empty bottle back onto the table with a "Thunk".

I needed to get this shit worked out and get her back home. There's only so much control I have, and with her I am losing it fast. This feeling it's new and uncomfortable. I have always had control of everything in my life, in business, in public, in private and in bed. Maybe it's just the chase with her, I mean that's something new for me, having to work hard to get a woman into bed. No it wasn't just lust with her, it was definitely so much more than a dance between my sheets. I want to consume her I want to get into her mind and sooth every bit of that pain and fear that I see behind those beautiful eyes of hers. I need her to trust me. I need her to need me. I need her to want me.

I wake to streams of sunlight flickering across into my eyes. Rubbing a hand over my face I look at my watch. It's just after 7am and I have slept on the couch. Feeling the scruff of my unshaven face, I stand and stretch out my aching muscles, the couch may look comfy but not if your 6ft 3. I Make my way up the stairs and to my bedroom, I desperately need a shower. As I get to my door I look over to where the door to the guest room is wide open and I can see

Casey laying across the bed in just a black t-shirt. She's laying on her stomach clutching onto a pillow, her shirt slightly raised to reveal her ass covered only by a sheer pair of black panties I was tempted to stand there and watch her for a while, but knew that was a really bad idea. Moving quietly and quickly, I walk through my bedroom and into the bathroom.

Showered and shaved, in clean clothes I felt almost human again I headed down the stairs grabbed my keys and to the elevator. I didn't even stop for coffee. I just wanted out of there before she woke up I needed to keep a clear head and get back into the office.

Charlie was sitting at her desk as I walked through the doors. As soon as she saw me she jumped up and came around the front of her desk and before she could say anything I said "Coffee, black." "Yes Mr. King" she nodded and took off towards the kitchen. I pushed open the heavy doors to my office and as I sat down at my desk she strolled in with a mug and placed it in front of me, "Is there anything else I can do for you?" she said in a sexy drawl so sweet it made me look at her with a raised eyebrow and her cheeks flushed red. "No, Thank you" I said curtly. I watched her turn and walk out, and realized that when Casey had said that Charlie had a thing for me, damn if she was right, why had I not noticed it before? I just saw her as an employee, nothing more and that's the way I planned to keep it.

Sipping on the hot coffee which gave my brain just the kick it needed, I flipped on the lap top and started to do some work. I needed to catch up on some contracts that Paxton had emailed me. One was for a chain of banks that wanted to upgrade their security supplier and another was for a new night club that was opening downtown, and it was quite a complicated intricate contract. Looks like I had left my little brother with a huge job while I was away ,and looking over this contract he had done a damn fine job.

My phone buzzed and Charlie announced that Paxton was on his way up to see me. Stretching my arms up and behind my head, I looked at the time. I had been working on this night club contract for over four hours, no wonder my muscles were feeling stiff. A knock at the door and Paxton strolled in holding a folder which he dropped down on my desk in front of me. "Hey," he said flopping down into a chair "How is the club contract doing?"

"It looks good, just working out a few kinks, otherwise it will be good to go by the end of the day." I said.

"I've been doing some research." He nods towards the folder he just brought in.

"And?"

"I tracked Peterson down, he won't be back in the country for another week I also found something interesting about your house guest."

"Okay, you have my attention." I said leaning back into my chair. Standing and pushing his hands deep into his pockets, Paxton looked slightly uncomfortable

"She has a history gap."

"What do you mean a history gap?" I asked narrowing my eyes at him.

"Casey Tyler has a gap from the age of 14 to 17 years old. Now I'm not sure why yet, but I'm working on it." Standing, I picked up the folder and thumbed through it. There was personal information, place and date of birth, address, education and job history and a newspaper article on the death of her parents when she was 18 years old. Dropping the file back onto my desk, I let out a low curse. "Shit man, both parents at 18?" I cringed.

"I know, shitty hey? but it's weird Nate, I got everything from her birth until now but nothing for the missing three years, it's a complete blank." Looking at Paxton with an arched brow, I could see that we were both thinking the same thing.

"That's because it has been blanked out, it's been erased, covered up, but why?" I tap my chin with my finger.

"Exactly," Paxton points at me "but your little brother here has connections in the right places, it won't take me long and I am sure we will know soon enough."

"Thanks Paxton I know this is taking up a lot of your time but I do appreciate it."

"No problem, I mean she is our client right?" I looked down at the file. Then back at Paxton "meaning?" I say more sharply than I intended to. Paxton holds up both hands defensively. "Nothing man, nothing at all, I just thought with that moony look you just had on your face she might be....something more."

"Moony look, what the fuck does that mean?"

"You know, like she might be testing your libido," he said grinning. I shook my head and this time let out a choked laugh . "More like testing my patience."

"So...." Paxton asks with a questioning look on his face, sitting on the edge of my desk.

I crossed my arms across my chest and sighed in defeat, smartass little shit knew me too well. "Yes, maybe... I don't know Paxton. There seems to be a lot going on with her."

"Have you talked to her?" he asks.

"I've tried to, but she's got this god damn cast iron wall that comes into place as soon as I ask her anything."

"Maybe that's the problem I mean look, she's been dragged from a strange country to another strange country with a strange guy in his house, under some unseen threat, that's got to freak you out man." I nodded, he was right.

"So what do you suggest?" I ask him.

"Well you could try something normal like, bringing her over for dinner. I'm pretty sure Lynda would love to meet her, and she might relax more at the beach I have heard the Aussies love their beaches. Come stay over for the weekend."

"I'm glad you feel safe enough making plans without talking to your wife first." I laughed.

"Lynda will love it." He swats his hand in the air.

"Yeah, okay that sounds good thanks Paxton".

Chapter nineteen

Casey

I lay on the bed for what seemed like hours trying to process what had just happened. Once again I had freaked out on Nate, which was really starting to piss me off, because I'd had this shit under control for years. Well I thought I did, I mean I had managed to build a huge wall around myself for protection but for some reason when Nate entered my space that seemed to all go out the window and it was confusing as hell. He made me feel something that was new to me, stirred emotions that I didn't think I would ever be capable of, emotions that I had been alienated from for so many years now, and it was seriously messing with my head. Squeezing my eyes closed, I see Nate's face close to mine, his breath whispers warm across my face, his hard body pinning me to the hard wall, his strong hands gripping onto my wrists, the strength and heat of his body so close....and then the picture changes and the face so close to mine is no longer Nate's but one of pure evil and that feeling of warm breath has changed to a hot alcohol- ridden smell, and that warm hard body pinning me to the wall is now claustrophobic, dominating and painful. I can feel the adrenalin starting to course through my body, quickly I open my eyes, take a deep breath and will the image away as quickly as it came.

My thoughts were turning into a huge jumbled mess. Had I spent so long protecting myself and ostracizing myself from feelings, that I didn't recognize any show of emotions from others anymore? Or did he just want a quick easy lay? I'm pretty sure he wouldn't ever be short of willing bed partners, so why did he kiss me with such passion that my legs almost gave way and sent tingles shooting through every inch of my body? Logically I know in my head that he needs to ask me questions if he is going to put an end to all this madness that is happening, but every time he asks me anything it feels so intimate and personal and I just don't know how to do personal with anyone but Flynn. He is the only one who knows everything, my past, my present, my anxieties, my fears....my insecurities. Nate had taken his job further than was ever expected of him he had brought me to his own home, to protect me, so somehow I needed to find a way to let my barriers down, just a little and try to trust again. I need to get " me" back right now " Fuck you Max" I whisper into the dark room. "Fuck you".

By the time I woke in the morning the Penthouse was empty. I'm guessing that Nate had gone into his office I had a quick shower and pulled on a pair of shorts and tank top and made myself some breakfast. After washing the dishes and tidying up the very tidy Penthouse, I logged onto the computer and typed out an email to Flynn writing down what was happening here and how I was feeling and, as usual asking for his advice. I thought it was much better to put it all in an email and he would read it when he had time I hated using him as my crutch and imposing on his life, but if I said that to him he would probably skin me alive. He was my "go to" guy, he also gave great advice, he would definitely make someone a great husband one day. Now that sounded weird my BFF Flynn a husband.!

Going back into the kitchen I took a look in the cupboards and a scan of the refrigerator and made plans to cook dinner for Nate, kind of like a piece offering for my erratic behavior last night. He probably thinks I'm a lunatic or something I needed to try harder to communicate with the poor guy, so I would start with his stomach.

I was just adding the creamy chicken garlic sauce to the pasta when I heard the elevator come to a stop and the doors slide open. Nate walked in, placing his phone and keys on the coffee table, then came to stand at the kitchen island where I was placing the hot pasta into two bowls. Placing both hands on the marble top, he looked at me with a raised brow. "You cooked?"

"Don't sound too shocked, I can cook" I said smiling at him.

"Smells great." He said after inhaling the aroma coming from the pasta. I pushed a full bowl towards him and handed him a fork.

"Thanks, I'm starving," he pulled out a stool, sat and shoved a forkful of pasta into his mouth then looked at me. "Mmm.. this is really good."

"Thank you" I smiled, perching myself on a stool next to him and digging into my own bowl. Giving him a quick glance now and then, I noticed that he was wearing a pair of jeans that clung to every taut muscle in his thighs and a dark button down dress shirt with the sleeves folded half way up his forearms, and every time he moved his arm a tiny glimpse of ink would peek out. There was no doubt about it, he was an incredible looking man. After the last bit of pasta went into his mouth he took his and my bowls to the sink and pulled a bottle of wine from the rack and two glasses. I watched as he poured us a drink, then handed me a glass. "You know you're a guest right? I don't expect you to cook for me" he said with a slight grin.

"I know, it was more of an apology meal."

"Apology? What for?"

"Last night" I said softly.

"Hey" he started, but I stopped him by holding up a hand, "No really, I haven't been the best house guest so far and I know you're only trying to help. I just..." I shake my head looking for the words to explain, but nothing comes out, he motions for us to sit on the couch.

Placing his glass on the coffee table and leaning back into the leather he said "Look I understand the situation is difficult, and I admit I'm not the easiest person to get along with. I'm used to taking charge and bull dozing ahead, I don't do delicate and I don't tip- toe around a problem, but you...you have me perplexed."

"Oh, really? why is that?"

With a slight shake of his head he continues. "Well, to start with, I don't think I have ever come across someone like you. On the outside you're opinionated, strong, independent and very closed, but on the inside I see something...more"

"Okay" I say slowly "And what do you see Mr. King?"

He sits forward leaning his arms on his thighs and pauses for a moment then his eyes connect with mine. "On the inside, I see someone who is in a lot of pain, someone who is used to hiding and protecting herself so well that she now can't find herself anymore. She's lost and the question here is does she want to be found?"

Looking down into my glass of wine, I take a sip then look back at him. "We all have baggage, Nate."

"Then maybe you need someone to help you carry that baggage?" he says. Searching his eyes, I see so much compassion in them and I try so hard to put strength into my words, but all that comes out is weakness as almost in a whisper, I say "Some things are just meant to stay lost." Looking from my glass back to him, his eyes now show confusion as they search mine for a moment, then he changes the course of the conversation completely.

Leaning back again he asks "Tell me about you, I mean from as far back as you want to go." Placing my glass on the coffee table, I pulled my legs up, tucking them under me, and try to think where to start.

"Hmm....well I was born to parents who didn't plan on having any kids in their life. They were both lawyers and happy with just each other, then I guess nature stepped in and my mother found herself pregnant. Abortion wasn't an option for them because off their religious beliefs and so I was born. They fed and clothed me and put a roof over my head but that was it. As long as I stayed out of their way and didn't interfere in their lives they were happy. When new neighbors moved in next door to us they were so different to my own family. They had two kids, a girl a few years younger than me, Sophie, and a boy my age."

"Flynn?" Nate asks .

"Yes, we became inseparable. He became my protector, my confidante, my brother in all ways, and anything other than that was just unthinkable between us. He shared his happy family with me, he gave me normal I guess." I said wistfully.

"He sounds like a good person," Nate said .

"He is." Taking a deep breath I continued. "Then, when I was around eighteen, my parents went out to dinner one night and when they were returning their car skidded of the road into a ditch.... they were both killed instantly."

"Jesus Doc." He says in a low whisper.

Shaking my head at his shocked tone, I said "it's ok, they went together so at least at the end they would have been happy. So after the house was sold and their debts paid, I had enough to put myself through medical school and I lived at Flynn's family home until my residency was done. I got a job at the local hospital in surgical and Flynn went on to study law and we became house mates."

"And IMA comes in...." he drags out the words slowly.

Thinking for a moment while subconsciously chewing on my bottom lip, which seems to draw Nate's eyes directly to my mouth, I continued. "You mean Steve? I don't even know him that well, just someone at work but we have a social network page that everyone at work is a member of, it's kind of like an information page for the staff - you know, to swap ideas and information, swap stories and stuff like that. Then this one day in the cafeteria at work he started talking about IMA. How it had been a great experience and how much he thought I might get something out of it. He also gave me a card for IMA and a few days later I gave them a call. From there the process was pretty quick," I said with a shrug off my shoulders .

"So why IMA?" he asked curiously.

"Honestly? A change, a challenge, the experience."

He chuckled , "Well you definitely got an experience alright."

"Well that's not really the kind of experience I was looking for."

"So what were you looking for Doc?" he asked with a tilt of his chin.

Draining the last inch of wine in my glass, then staring into its emptiness, I said, "I'm not exactly sure.... something though." Standing and picking up both glasses I took them into the kitchen and slipped them into the dishwasher, turning to see Nate now watching my every move as I go back to sit next to him. "So, I showed you mine, now it's your turn."

He gave me a puzzled look, "Excuse me?"

"Well I've given you my brief life history so what about you?"

Shaking his head, his eyes still on mine he says "I don't remember saying anything about sharing life stories Doc."

"Come on, fair's fair" I said, and he lets out a deep sigh.

"There's not much to tell I was born and raised in Portland, My dad was a city cop that ended up starting his own security business. He started small and over the years built it up to provide security on a larger scale for most of the major banks and many other assorted businesses, until he branched out into international security which provides personal security for people who need it."

"Like a bodyguard?" I ask.

"Something like that mostly dignitaries, politicians and the occasional celebrity."

"You sound very busy."

"We do well and It pays to have a good solid reputation." He says with pride.

"So have you and your brother always been in the family business?"

"Not always, Paxton had always worked with my father... until he suffered a heart attack 6 years ago." He says rubbing his hand over his chin.

"Oh Nate, I'm so sorry." He gave me a nod of his head but the glimpse of pain that shot through his eyes told me how much he missed his father. "And you're Mother?" I continued cautiously.

I watched as he rubbed the palms of his hands over his jeans-clad thighs uncomfortably then said "Mom retired to Hawaii a few years after Pop passed but she never recovered from losing him... one night she just went to bed and never woke up." I put my hand over my mouth with a gasp. "The autopsy said that her heart just stopped in her sleep, but we know she really died of a broken heart."

"Wow Nate, I'm speechless." I say as he leans back into the couch.

"So you see Doc, we do have something in common after all." All I could do was nod, and he continued, "So Paxton had been running the family business on his own for some time but as it was growing big fast, I left the military and joined him."

"So, you were in the army?" I asked.

"Marines, for a good fifteen years, joined up at 20."

"Then I'm guessing that would make you 35?"

"36." he corrects.

"Wow that's a lot of time in the service."

Turning away from me, I heard him say "Yeah, too damn long."

"And...I'm guessing by that answer you're carrying some baggage of your own then." I said softly.

He turned back to look at me a resigned look in his eyes. "Don't know anyone who came back from a tour who doesn't have a shit load of baggage weighing them down, unfortunately it's part of the parcel." I could see by the expression on his face that this was not a subject he wanted to continue to discuss, so I let it go, and that left a very uncomfortable pause in the air between us. Looking at his profile, I watched as the muscle in his jaw started to twitch.

I placed my hand on his thigh. "Hey, I'm sorry."

He ran a hand through his hair and stood up. "I have some work to do in my office, but thanks for dinner" he said, and walked in the direction of his office, leaving me sitting there realizing that I had just seen a piece of Nate that I don't think he showed anyone too often.

After cleaning up the kitchen, I went up and took a shower before slipping into bed and flipping my IPod to the soothing tones of Enigma that quickly lulled me into a deep sleep where for the first time in a while, the only image that entered my mind was that of Nathanial King's handsome face.

Waking in the morning I glided my hand over the sheet searching for my Ipod that always becomes lost somewhere amongst the bedding. Finding it, I brought it to my sleepy eyes and looked at the time, it was just after 9am, so I knew it was safe to go down to the kitchen and grab a cup of coffee in just my tank top and panties. Nate was always gone way before eight, so I knew once again I would be on my own for the day, but as I got closer to the kitchen I could hear movement. Stopping half way down the stairs, I glanced down and saw a half naked Nate filling up the coffee machine. He looked like he had just gotten out of the shower, his black hair was messy and wet and beads of water still ran down his muscled back, all the way down until they disappeared into the towel wrapped around his tapered waist. My eyes wandered over the planes of his muscular back, his skin looked tanned and the huge tattoo that spanned over his back was breath taking it looked like a man in a kneeling position, with his head cradled in both of his hands, with a pair of majestic wings made from intricate feathers opened behind him. It was a spectacular piece of work that must have taken hours in the chair.

The naked parts of skin that I could see were flawless, apart from the ink on his shoulder that looked like a collection of skulls. When he turned to get some water from the sink my eyes got a peek of the rest of him, the muscles of his shoulders and arms and chest all defined perfectly like he had been sculptured from a piece of marble. He had some more ink down the side of his chest which looked like more words, these ones lined up in a row. Another tattoo took up most of his other shoulder and the top of one arm. It looked like some kind of bold tribal pattern. He had various other small tattoos on his forearms but I couldn't see from this distance what they were. Drifting down the front of his body, I could see the muscles of his abdomen twitching with every movement. A thin line of dark hair slowly trailed down and disappeared under the towel. He was definitely not hard on the eyes. With the thought of where that trail of dark hair on his abdomen lead to, I felt my heart rate beat a little faster than usual, *"Go back to your room, he hasn't seen you yet, you pervert"* I told myself, but before I could turn, he looked up to where I was standing. "Morning, want some coffee?"

"Err... sure" I murmured as I slowly walked down the stairs and onto a stool at the kitchen island. Pouring out two mugs of the steaming brew he slid one towards me, as well as a carton of milk. "Thanks," I said adding the milk to the mug of coffee and taking a sip. After a few minutes of silence between us, he went to the refrigerator and pulled out a carton of eggs and some butter then a bowl and whisk from one of the cupboards. Cracking the eggs into the bowl, he started to beat them. "Breakfast?" he gestured towards the bowl "Sure." "Just scrambled eggs though. I'm no chef in the kitchen." He grinned at me.

"Do you want me to do that while you get ready for work?" I nodded to where he was whisking the eggs.

"Nope, no work today, it's Saturday and I have plans."

"Oh."

"For us" he motioned with his hand from him to me.

"We do?"

"Yes, we're taking a trip down to Paxton's."

"Your brother's home?" I asked surprised at his change of mood from last night. "Yep, he and his wife Lynda have a place right on the beach and he invited us down there, so you will need to pack an overnight bag." He poured the beaten eggs into a pan and started to stir them, then turned to look at me, "and I'm guessing you don't have anything to swim in but I am sure Lynda will have a spare suit that you can use."

"I...I don't mind staying here while you go visit your family," I stammered out. "Not going to happen Doc, besides he invited us both, you'll enjoy it and I am sure Lynda will enjoy some female company as well."

He served the eggs onto two plates, added a piece of toast and pushed it in front of me with a fork. "Eat, we have a two hour drive in front of us."

"Two hours?" I asked.

"Yep, they're down at Rockaway Beach." None the wiser to the destination he was talking about, I just scooped some eggs into my mouth and gave him a small smile.

Within the hour I was dressed in shorts and a light long sleeved shirt and sitting in his SUV. We had been driving for about an hour and I was busy taking in the different scenery until he broke the silence. "You're very quiet."

"Sorry, I guess I prefer to concentrate on the view more than having a heart attack watching you driving on the wrong side of the road." I smiled at him and he chuckled . "Yeah, I guess it would seem weird to you."

"Weird is an understatement." I said shaking my head.

"You know you should do that more often." he said softly.

"What?"

"Smile."

I felt a slight flush of heat across my cheeks. "I'm trying," I said thoughtfully.

"Do you like the beach?" he asked glancing quickly from the road to me.

"I love it; I was in the little nippers growing up." He gave me a puzzled look.

"What the hell are little nippers?"

"It's surf lifeguard training for kids, It teaches children water safety and confidence, and educates them I guess, on how to read the unpredictability of the ocean."

"And what about you?" Nate asks.

"I used to live close to the beach so I did it until I was maybe eleven or so."

"Then you will love where were going, the beach there is phenomenal." I smiled again at him, then leaned my head back against the head rest and went back to watching the scenery outside.

When we pulled off the main road onto a series of winding roads, I could smell the salty ocean on the breeze that was now drifting through the window. We turned into what looked like a drive way that wound its way along until a beautiful two storey white house came into view, and behind it sat a back drop of the wide expanse of the ocean. It looked like something out of a photo journal. I let out a small gasp. " Wow! This is beyond words," I said looking at Nate .

"I told you it was." He said smiling and pulling up in front of the house, turned off the engine and got out. Coming around, he opened my door and I slid out onto the gravel path, then he reached into the back seat and pulled out our bags. With his hand gently touching my lower back, he guided me towards the front door where, as soon as we put a foot on the bottom step, it opened wide and there stood Paxton dressed casually in jeans and a t-shirt. "Hey," he said ushering us inside and closing the door. "How was the drive?" he asked looking at me.

"Great, your home is beautiful Paxton."

"Well thank you, come on in and make yourself at home, Lynda's just in the kitchen getting us some lunch." Once again I felt Nate's hand, warm on my lower back, as he guided me down a long hallway into a huge kitchen where at the bench cutting up lettuce was a petite slim woman with dark blonde hair cut into a pixie style. When she looked up, her green eyes sparkled, and she broke into a huge warm smile. "Hi guys," she said, leaving the knife she was using on the bench and wiping her hands on a towel.

When she came from behind the kitchen bench she was wearing a light yellow summer dress that flowed over her bulging belly. She came over and gave Nate a hug. "How's that baby cooking?" he said patting her belly.

"Oh, it's still got a bit longer to spend in the oven yet" she said rubbing her belly. Turning towards me Nate said. "Lynda this is Casey," I held out my hand and she took it in a warm embrace placing her other hand on top. "It's so lovely to meet you Casey."

"You too, and thank you for inviting me to your home," I said smiling at her.

"Oh, my what a beautiful accent Paxton told me your from Australia?"

"Yes, Sydney."

"How exciting. I hope you're not going to mind me talking your ear off and asking lots of questions?"

"Not at all." I smiled at her enthusiasm.

Paxton stood at the fridge. "Wanna beer?" he asked Nate and at his nod he grabbed a couple of bottles out. "Casey?" He held up a bottle towards me, but before I could decline, Nate said "Better not Paxton, the Doc is a bit of a lightweight where alcohol is concerned." I just looked at him and shook my head with a smile, then said to

Paxton, "No thank you, as your brother has so nicely pointed out I'm not much of a drinker." The two brothers opened their beers and walked out onto the back porch, looking at Lynda I asked.

"Do you need any help with lunch?" I asked Lynda.

"Nooo, I'm almost done, you go follow the guys and have a look around and please make you self right at home," smiling at her I went out to where Nate and Paxton sat in two easy chairs enjoying their beers. There was a long wooden deck that ran the full length of the house, with chairs scattered along it and right in front of where I stood was the best sight I have seen for months, four wooden stairs led down onto the huge expanse of white sand, and out towards the crystal blue ocean. The swell wasn't big, but the white foamy waves crashing into the shore made me feel like I was home.

Chapter twenty

Nate

Watching Casey completely at ease while we shared lunch with my family had me mesmerized; from her infectious laugh and wide smile, to her easy flowing conversation. As we sat out on the back porch enjoying the beautiful ocean view, she looked more relaxed than she had done in days. Looks like my little brother was on the right road when he suggested this weekend. I will have to make sure to thank him later.

Lynda bombarded Casey with questions about Australia all through the meal and Casey looked like she was enjoying talking about her home country, between nibbling on her lunch and occasionally taking time to gaze out into the ocean. When we finished eating she insisted on helping Lynda with the dishes and I could still hear them talking away in the kitchen while us men were politely told to sit and relax. Taking a pull of my beer, I nodded to the kitchen, "Looks like they're getting along well."

"Yeah, I know, see I told you this was a good idea." Paxton grinned.

"I know, I know, smart ass." I said and Paxton snorted.

"Told you I was the brains in the family."

"Yep, you're a legend in your own mind." I smiled back at him.

After several minutes pause, Paxton spoke again "Nate?"

"Hmm" I hummed swallowing the rest of my beer.

"If I ask you something, will you keep your cool?" Giving him a curious look, I gave him a nod to continue. "She's more to you than a job isn't she?" Leaning forward in my chair, I ran my hand down my face.

"Honestly? I'm torn, there's definitely some kind of chemistry there."

"Well she is living in your Penthouse, and she's certainly a beautiful smart woman."

"You know what I'm like with women Paxton, I'm lucky if I have the same woman in my bed twice, it's always been just sex, but with her..." I shake my head, not knowing what the hell I'm feeling.

"Remember Nate, you do like to protect, it's in your nature." Paxton shrugged.

"I know but this is beyond just protecting her I can't seem to get her out of my head and the thoughts are so consuming."

"So do you think she has any idea about how you're feeling?" Paxton asked. Shaking my head, with a grunt, I said, "Not exactly, she's not an easy person to talk to, although saying that we did manage to have a conversation last night without it getting out of hand."

"What do you mean?" he asks, brows furrowed.

"I don't know, sometimes we can talk and she seems like she's opening up and relaxing, joking around then Boom! all of a sudden it's like the shutters come down on the conversation and she closes off."

"There must be some reason behind it though Nate I mean we don't know much about her but what we do know doesn't look great."

"She has nightmares as well, bad ones." I tell him.

"Shit Nate."

"I know, someone or something hurt her Paxton, and I want to know who and why?" I say absently peeling the label off my beer.

"Well hopefully we'll get some more insight this week and as soon as Peterson steps one foot back in the U.S we'll know."

"Good, I want a piece of that prick first." I growled.

"Don't worry you will, served on a platter" he grinned.

Coming out of Paxton's home office later that afternoon after finalizing the club contract, Lynda was relaxing on the couch with her feet up. "How you doing?" I ask her.

"I'm good, I just get tired quickly." She sighed.

"Well you are carrying a whole new person in there," I nodded towards her belly.

"Tell me about it."

"Where's Casey?" I said looking around.

"Oh she changed and went down to the beach. She is so fascinating to talk to Nate"

"Yes, she is, and I'm sure the topic for the day was babies?." I quirked an eyebrow at Lynda.

"Some, but not much I got the feeling it was an uncomfortable subject for her to talk about."

"What makes you think that?" I said curiously.

"I don't know, just a feeling I guess."

"Well I'll let you get some rest and I'll go check on Casey." As I turned to leave, Lynda spoke "Nate? I like her she's a good person" I gave her a smile before making my way to the porch and down the stairs onto the sand. Pulling out my sunglasses and slipping them on to block out the glare from the afternoon sun, I scan the beach and see her standing at the water's edge, looking down at her feet, as the water runs over them. I lower myself into one of the sun lounges that sits just at the bottom of the deck and put my arms behind my head, which brings my head up enough so that I can see her without her knowing. She stands looking out into the horizon. Her hair moves in the gentle ocean breeze, her white peasant shirt hanging low on one side where one shoulder peaks out. She's wearing a short pair of denim shorts that show off a pair of long, lean, tanned legs. She is exquisite to watch as she slowly walks down the beach a little then stops again, concentrating on making circles in the wet sand with her toes. She looks so deep in thought and I want into those thoughts, I want to know everything about her.

I see her fiddling with the front of her shorts and she bends slightly and slips them down her legs and tosses them behind her on the sand. She's wearing a one piece black swimsuit that moulds to her perfect ass. Grabbing the bottom of her shirt she lifts it up over her head and it joins her shorts on the sand behind her. Casey adjusts the thin straps of the top of the suit. Its low cut at the front, showing the top of those perfect breasts, and cut even lower in the back. And then I see it. Pulling my glasses up to the top of my head, I sit up quickly and squint my eyes to clear my vision. Getting up I start to walk closer to her. I need to see what I think I am seeing. As I get closer to her it comes into clearer view. On the left side of her back, starting down near her hip, is a huge tattoo. It's a tree done in black ink, an old weathered looking tree with branches that reach out towards her left shoulder and the leaves at the tips are blowing away on the wind; then the leaves slowly turn into black birds that end up on her right shoulder. As she turns to walk into the surf, I can also see some script written along her ribs. "Holy shit Doc, you certainly are an enigma, who would have known it," I say to myself as I watch her dive into a wave and come up on the other side, wiping her now wet hair away from her face. With long graceful strokes, she starts to swim through the water with ease. I stand and watch her for a while, until she looks at me and smiles.

Going back up into the house, I grab a towel, then walk back to meet her as she walks through the waves and back onto the shore. She stands in front of me and I wrap the towel around her shoulders and briskly rub her back as she shivers from the now cool air. "Thanks."

"How's the water?"

"Exhilarating" she breathes picking up her clothes from the sand. I want to ask her about the ink on her back but at this moment she looks so relaxed and sedate that I don't want to push her. We walk back up to the house and sit on the steps while she dries herself off and slips her shirt back on. "Thank you for bringing me here Nate, the beach, your family, it's been...wonderful."

"I'm glad," I smile as I slide the back of my fingers across her cheek. "I like to see you smile," I say in a low voice, as I move a lock of wet hair away from her eyes and tuck it behind her ear, letting the pad of my index finger stroke from the lobe down her neck. I see her eyes close and her head tilt to one side as my finger stops at the pulse at her throat and I am hypnotized by the thumping beat under my touch. Slowly I move my hand up and cup one side of her face and she leans into my palm, her own hand moves on top of mine, it's so soft and warm, then her eyes flutter open and look straight into mine. "Nate, we can't," she whispers.

"You know there's something between us, you just have to let me in."

"It's not that simple....you're a good man Nate and I'm not... good." She shakes her head and gently removes my hand from her face. "This," she motions between me and her with a hand, "Can't work...ever, I can't give you what you want Nate. I'm....broken. unfixable."

"Nothing is unfixable, you just have to want to fix it baby." I say.

"Oh, I've tried, for years Nate... but I don't want to hurt you." She looks down at her hands now twisting in her lap. I tilt her chin up so she has to give me back those eyes. There is so much pain behind them, it makes my chest ache.

"You won't hurt me and I promise I will not hurt you; just..don't shut me out okay?" Her eyes search mine as she chews on her bottom lip, and then she gives me a nod. I lean in and give her a soft kiss on the tip of her nose, then stand up pulling her with me. "Now let's get you inside and dry".

That night I lay in my bed knowing that she is laying in a bed just on the other side of the wall next to me. Images invade my mind of her walking along the beach, her beautiful blonde hair moving in the breeze and that moment when she looks up and notices that I'm watching her. My heart shifts into over- drive and starts pounding out of my chest as I take in her beautiful smile. *"Holy fuck, what am I doing? Why the hell am I pursuing this woman? She has me so tangled up she's invading my sleep now. I keep trying to keep the relationship straight in my head, trying to win her trust, to protect her but its bull- shit. That will never be enough, she's got under my skin and I want to touch her, taste her, I want to be inside of her."* "Fuck," I let out a low curse into the night and try to adjust the painful ache between my legs enough so I can get some sleep.

Coming down to the kitchen the next morning I grab myself a cup of coffee and join Paxton in his office. "Morning," I said, flopping into the leather couch in the corner of the room. "Hey," Paxton continued looking through some papers in his hand. "Where are the women?" I asked him.

"They went for a walk along the beach before you leave." He said briefly looking up.

"They've gotten along really well this weekend."

"Yeah, Lynda has loved the company and it looks like Casey enjoyed it too." He said with a smile.

"Yeah, she did relax a lot more being here."

"So, did you manage to talk to her about... you know her history?"

Shaking my head I said, "Nothing much different than what we already know."

"Well I did get a call from my contact early this morning. He's following a lead and thinks he should have something soon."

"Great, because I don't think Casey is going to give us any more than what she already has, whatever she's hiding I think she's been doing it for so long she's become an expert."

"Do you have any ideas?" Paxton asks.

"Some, but I'm hoping I'm fucking wrong Paxton." I said shaking my head.

"That bad, huh?"

"With her body language, nightmares, the defensiveness and Paxton, she has a big ass tattoo on her back and it spells out pain and lots of it."

"Fuck Nate." Paxton's eyes narrow at my words.

"I know, let's not go there until we have more information ok?"

"Sure thing" he nodded .

The drive back to the city was a quiet one. Casey didn't say much at all, just concentrated on looking out the window until she fell into a light sleep, her head pressed against the head rest, her lips slightly parted. I could hear her softly breathing, and while I drove I couldn't help but keep taking glances at her perfect sleeping form and thought to myself that I will be bringing her to the beach more often if it makes her this relaxed and peaceful.

Its late by the time we get back and as soon as we hit the Penthouse Casey, walks up to her room and I hear the shower turn on. Grabbing myself a glass from the bar, I fill it with two fingers of scotch and take it into my office to check my emails and messages when my phone pings with a text. Looking at the screen, it's from Paxton. Sliding my thumb across the screen to open it, I read, *A little bird just informed me that Peterson will be back in his office tomorrow around 10am.* I type back to him, *"He's mine."* My phone pings again with *"be careful bro." "Always."* Throwing back the remains of scotch, I take the stairs two at a time up to my room. Looking over I see the guest room door slightly open and Casey in bed.

I'm up early and leave before Casey even wakes. I need to pick up some paperwork from my office, then I plan on heading over to Petersons. I want this fucker before he disappears again. I sit in my SUV, sipping on my coffee, while I watch the front of his building, scanning who goes in and who comes out for what turned out to be a good couple of hours. Then I see him exiting a cab, short balding little bastard in his Navy Armani, and now at least I have some idea of how he can afford such an expensive suit. I wait until he enters the building, then I follow. Checking the board, I see his name and floor number and take the elevator up. The doors open out into an office, with modern furnishings. One wall to the right has IMA in huge red letters on a white background with a desk in front of it, and a older looking petite woman sitting behind it. I look at her, then turn my head and look at the double wooden doors to the left hand side, that I presume is Petersons office. I look back at the secretary . "Can I help you sir?" she asks.

"Nathanial King here to see Mr. Peterson."

"Do you have an appointment?" she asks looking down at the diary in front of her. "No, but I am sure he will be expecting to see me," I say as I start walking towards the doors to his office I hear her moving around the desk. I'm presuming she is going to try and intercept me entering his office.

"Please sir, Mr. Peterson is very busy. You really must have an appointment." Ignoring her, I push open the doors and there he sits behind a huge glass desk, his jacket off, and he has a phone pressed against his ear. His head shoots up to look at the intrusion into his office and he quickly lets the person on the other end of his phone conversation know that he will call them back.

"I'm sorry Mr. Peterson I tried to stop him..." the secretary flustered.

"It's okay Sarah" he gestures at the woman to leave his office and I take a seat in the chair opposite his desk. "Mr. King it's good to see you. What is so urgent that it has you barging into my office today ?" I look at him, and lift an eyebrow at his question.

"Really? You want to play it like that?"

"I'm sorry obviously you have me at a disadvantage here, so please enlighten me." He spreads out his palms in front of him. I feel my teeth start to grind and my jaw tighten as I look at the greedy little pathetic vermin in front of me. Reigning in my fury I manage to growl out two words "Casey Tyler." He purses his lips as he looks up to the ceiling like he's searching his tiny brain, trying to put a face to the name.

"Ahh, yes, the doctor from down under. I seem to recall she left her position without informing IMA. Very unreliable, and she broke her contract," he said with a shake of his head. Not being able to sit still any longer, I stood and placed both hands on the desk in front of him.

"I believe you broke any contract when you employed her under false pretences." I grate out between tight lips.

"I have no idea what you're talking about Mr. King."

"Listen I'm done playing this game with you, I know what you've been doing and what I want you to do is get in contact with your buyer and tell him that the deal is off."

Petersons façade dropped for just a moment, then he continued, "like I said, I have no idea what you're talking about. I was informed that the stress of her position had turned out to be a little more than she had anticipated and you had taken her back to her own country, as she had requested.....after all I do know that you always do your job to the highest of standards Mr. King, that's why I asked you for the favor in the first place. Although, I didn't expect you to be there personally yourself." Looking at him through narrowed eyes I ask "What are you talking about Peterson?" I watch him look at the pen he was rolling between his fingers.

"Put it this way Mr. King, I did not expect the head of a big company such as yours would have had the time to take on a 3 month contract overseas, and when you turned up there instead of one of your employees, it... caused a tiny hiccup." His mouth turned up into a smirk and I had to take a deep breath to gain some control because the realization of the words he had just spewed out and that look on his face right now, I wanted to rip this fucker's head off and shove it up his ass. Through gritted teeth, I said "I was your hiccup?"

"Something like that. You see this time it involved a military base, much harder to get access to, hence the set up at the clinic in the village, it was supposed to go smoothly but..."

"I got her out," I finished for him. "So it back fired on you."

"It did, but a good business man always has a backup plan." He says leaning back into his chair.

"And that is?"

"It's as simple as she was found; paid for and delivered; it's not my fault that she didn't get to her owner because of some over-protective security guard. I have done my part now, it's on your head." When he pointed his pudgy little finger towards me I could no longer hold back the fury that now pumped through my body. I wanted to kill this bastard right here, right now. Rounding the desk, I grabbed him by the throat, slamming the back of his head into his chair. As my fingers squeezed and tightened into his skin, his hands started to pull and claw at my hands, trying to break my hold. I pinned my eyes on his as I watched his eyes grow wide and glassy with fear. As he struggled to breathe, his face started to change into a nice shade of crimson, as his lungs started to suffer from oxygen starvation, his lips move as he tries to beg and bargain for me to stop. I can feel his fight getting weaker and his body getting heavier. He's starting to lose his fight. Just as he is a second away from unconsciousness, I relieve a small amount of pressure on my hold, just enough to give him a tiny promise of air, just enough to keep him coherent, enough to hear what I need to say. Leaning down close to his face, my voice reverberating in a deep low growl, I say, "I don't know who has been feathering your nest, and honestly I don't care, but this ends now. She was never for sale. I don't care what or how you do it, but this is all on you, pay them off, bargain or beg, I don't give a fuck do you hear me?" He managed to nod, then I continued. "I have a paper trail on everything you have been up to and if you don't fix the mess you have caused, I will fuck you up, and if you or anyone comes near Casey Tyler, I will take them down as well. Do I make myself clear?" He nods again in understanding. Letting go of his throat, I straighten, keeping my narrowed eyes on his without breaking contact, and I watch as he rubs the reddened skin around his throat and gulps in air like a fish out of water. The earlier smug look on his face is now replaced by one of fear. Turning and walking out of his office and into the elevator, I suddenly regret restraining myself from snapping his fucking neck.

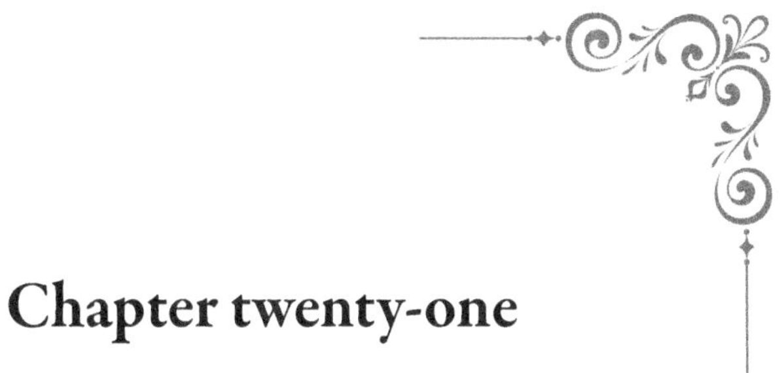

Chapter twenty-one

Casey

When I came down stairs this morning Nate was nowhere in sight, he must have left really early. I didn't hear a thing last night as soon as my head hit the pillow I was out to it, completely exhausted thanks to a weekend of sea air and swimming. It was probably the best deep sleep I'd had in ages, and thankfully, one free of any dreams. Looking around the kitchen, I grab a glass and fill it with juice from the fridge then take it up to the master bathroom and run the water on the huge bath. Sitting on the shelf above the tub is an arrangement of bottles full of bath oil. Trickling some across the top of the water, I place my glass on the side, undress and slide into the steaming hot water, and lean my head back. It feels wonderful, and I feel my body relax and my mind drift into thoughts of the weekend at the beach, and Nate, and my inner turmoil about him. Whenever he's close to me my body seems to go into over –drive, I physically feel my heart rate rise. Yes, I am aware that there is a spark there, but isn't that just a physical attraction, a sexual urge? But then his actions, his words, his gentleness with me, is that part of the whole ploy to get me into bed as well?

All these questions going around in my head don't change the fact that no matter how much I am attracted to him, I just don't think I am capable of giving him all of me. He has that possessiveness and dominance about him and I see that in his eyes, he's used to getting what he wants, so am I a challenge? A body to be conquered?

Fuck, this is driving me nuts, maybe I am just thinking too deep into it, but that's what I do, think 24 hours a day 7 days a week. It's something I've never been able to turn off, thanks to...... Standing up fast from the water and grabbing a towel, I wrap it tightly around myself, and with just that tiny glimpse of a memory I feel the need to protect and hide myself. That's what that fucker did, not only did he steal my past but he's still stealing my future and why the hell am I letting him? "Son of a bitch" I cursed out into the steam filled room.

Drying quickly, I pull on a pair of yoga pants and a tank top and head back down to the kitchen. Pulling open the bottom drawer, I see the packet of cigarettes and lighter that I have seen Nate pull out when he goes out onto the upstairs balcony to get his nicotine fix, now and then, and although I have not placed a cigarette in my mouth for years, right at this moment I have a bad craving for one. Out on the small balcony I light it and draw back the smooth smoke into my lungs. Oh my god that is so friggin good, is my first thought, until I take another draw and my head starts to spin and I feel nausea rising into my chest, making me toss the rest into the small plant pot filled with sand in the corner of the balcony. I sit down on the tiled floor, putting my head down between my knees until the dizzy spell is gone. "Holy shit, now I know why I quit, yuck".

I was still sitting in that position when I heard a buzzing noise coming from inside. Intrigued to know where it was coming from, I looked around until I saw a green light flashing on a intercom on the wall. Picking up the receiver I say, "Hello?"

"Hello madam, this is the front desk in the lobby. There is a gentleman here to see Mr. King. He said his name is Jackson Steele." What the hell? Jax is here? "Sure, send him up." I said excitedly then replaced the handset back onto its cradle and went over to the elevator. I really hope this is Jax coming up here and not some crazy psychopath or, even worse, one of Nate's girl friends. Now the sound of that word on my tongue really did make me feel sick in the stomach.

When the elevator doors open, out saunters Jax with his cowboy swagger. "Hey, Aussie how the hell are you?" He moves in and grabs me into a friendly bear hug, then pulls back, his eyes moving from the top of my head and down the length of my body. "Damn woman you're looking great."

"Thanks, you're not looking too bad yourself, but what are you doing here?" I asked him.

"I called Nate and he told me to meet him here." He answered simply.

"No I mean, I thought you were going to be staying at the base for a while?"

"Yeah, well things got a little sticky, so the other civvies got pulled and sent back to good old England".

Looking at him through narrowed eyes, I asked, "What do you mean sticky?"

He ran a hand down his face and let out a sigh. "Let me talk to Nate first ok? Then we'll chat." Seeing the disappointed look on my face he added, "Hey it's nothing for you to worry your pretty little head over ok?" Grudgingly I nodded and he clapped his hands together. "Now woman, where can I get me a beer round here?"

I didn't realize how much I missed chatting with Jax his sense of humor is so quick and naughty, he just has a knack of making me laugh... a lot. He's a great guy. He reminds me so much of Flynn, very brotherly and protective, it's a good feeling.

We are deep in conversation. Jax is telling me about the ranch that he owns in a place called Superior Montana. I watch as his face lights up with pure pleasure as he talks about the horses that he breeds, and how much he loves the open air of the country. I am so busy listening to him talk that I don't even hear the sound of the elevator doors opening until I look up and see Nate standing near the bottom of the stairs staring at us both with fury in his eyes. Jax stands and pushes his hands into the pockets of his jeans his stance reminding me of a naughty child waiting to be chastised. "Hey buddy, hope you don't mind, I took one of your beers?" Nate moves towards the bar and drops his keys and cell on the top of it, then pours himself what looks like scotch into a glass tumbler. Knocking it back in one gulp, he says, "Not at all buddy. You know my home is your home." Those words just come out of his mouth, but his face and rigid stance is saying something totally different.

Nate leads Jax into his home office and closes the door. "Well excuse me," I softly say to myself as I feel my phone vibrate in my pocket I pull it out to see Lynda's name on the screen. "Hello?"

"Hi Casey." Her voice is so bright and friendly.

"Lynda, is everything ok?" I ask with some concern.

"Yes, fine, I just wanted to know if you were planning on going shopping for an outfit for the opening of The Bazaar."

"The what?"

"The Bazaar, It's the night club that Kings just took on the contract for."

"Oh, no sorry I had no idea."

"Oh well, maybe Nate hasn't gotten around to telling you yet but Saturday is the big opening and it is going to be huge." She enthused into the phone.

"I don't know Lynda, he hasn't said anything, but I'm sure he's probably already got a date lined up."

"Nooo, I am pretty sure it's just slipped his mind." I hear the uncertainty in her voice and the last thing I want is for her to feel bad. "Hey it's ok, it's fine, night- clubs are not one of my favorite places, so it's all good, but I will be glad to help you shop for an outfit if you like?"

"Really?" she says excitedly.

"Sure."

"Great, how about tomorrow around 11am, then we can grab some lunch as well."

"Sounds perfect, see you then."

"It's a date then" she giggles, then hangs up. I walk into the kitchen and discreetly try to listen in on what's going on behind the closed door of Nate's office but all I can hear is the low deep hum of their voices. So I walk over to the huge windows and pace back and forth in front of them. I want to know what's going on in there, are they discussing me? Why is Jackson back so soon? And why the hell did Nate look so angry when he came in? Eventually, after what felt like hours but realistically was more like minutes, they came out and both looked at me, then Jax turned to Nate and said "Ok buddy, I will see you Saturday night, then I am heading off back to the ranch for a few weeks."

"Sounds like a good plan, you deserve it." Nate says slapping a hand on Jax's shoulder. Jax lifts his chin at me and says "Ok girl I will be seeing you later."

"Bye Jax" I smiled at him and Nate walks him to the elevator and when Jackson is gone he turns back towards the bar, grabs a beer, flips the cap off and leans against the bar. "So..." I said breaking the silence in the room "Is everything ok?" Looking up at me he takes a pull from the bottle and I watch as his throat bobs as he swallows.

"Everything is just great" he says with sarcasm dripping from his mouth.

"What about with Jax, I thought he wouldn't be back for weeks, did something happen?"

"Just you" he snorts.

"What's that supposed to mean?."

Putting his bottle down on the coffee table and sitting on the sofa, he blows out a sigh. "The contract is done. After what happened with you, the other civilians wanted out and went back to the U.K.

Jax only had to stay and tie up some loose ends." He shrugs his shoulders as if to say, "and you know the rest."

Looking down at my phone still in my hand, I decide to change the subject. "Your sister- in-law called me, she wants me to go shopping with her for a new outfit for Saturday I told her it would be Ok, if it's alright with you?" Looking at me now through narrowed eyes he says "So... now you're asking me for my opinion?"

"Err yes I was under the impression I had to while I was here, under the circumstances."

"Mm-hum" he murmurs.

"Is there something wrong Nate?" I ask.

Sitting forward on the couch he leans his arms on his thighs. "Now why would there be something wrong?"

"Because you sound like you're really pissed about something." I said putting my hands on my hips.

"Hmmm and why do you think I would be pissed? Let me see," he thinks and taps a finger against his chin, "Maybe it has something to do with the fact that I have busted my ass trying to get you to relax with me, we've even spent time at the beach around my family, yet with all that I've still only managed to get you to open up to me a tiny fraction of what I saw when I came in here and saw you and Jax together; talking, laughing and you totally relaxed; so what is it? What magic button does he hold? Or is it that you just want to fuck him."

"What? nooo, of course I don't."

Standing, he runs a hand down his face, then spreads out both hands. "Then why can't you give me what you gave him?"

"I don't know." I shrug.

"You don't know?" his voice now rising to match the anger on his face. "Well, I guess it's not just me you don't want to fuck at least," he spits out with such venom. I stand to face him my own anger coming to the surface to match his, "You arrogant bastard. What, did I bruise your ego because I haven't jumped into bed with you as quick as some of your other women? It's not all about sex Nate. Maybe you need to stop thinking with your dick and give your brain a chance."

He shakes his head and a smirk pulls at the edge of his lips."My ego huh? I guess you might have a point there, but don't worry Doc, I get the message loud and clear," With that he starts to walk away towards his office, then turns around "Oh and the answer to your question. I will have Nick drive you and Lynda tomorrow and you need something to wear because you will be attending the opening as a guest, purely from a security point of view of course, so don't worry it's not a date or anything that might taint your virtue." Going into his office he closes the door with a loud thud, and all I can do is fall back onto the couch completely stunned and bewildered by his angry words.

I didn't see Nate for the rest of the night. I went up to my room and closed the door and busied myself catching up with unanswered emails and surfing the web. In the morning he was gone and when a text came through from Lynda telling me she was waiting in the lobby, I went down to meet her and Nick was waiting out by the car. Now I'm not much of a shopper, I just like to get in, get what I want, then get out, and it didn't take me long to realize that shopping with Lynda was an experience all of its own. Endless stores and clothes, for hours, and just when I thought I couldn't take one more dressing room, she found the perfect dress that fit over her pregnant belly that she loved. The knee length silk red dress with short sleeves, fitted her to perfection. It molded to every one of her curves with enough room for comfort, and once it was paid for we found a cafe and ordered some lunch.

"Now we just have to find you something," Lynda says around a bite of a huge sandwich.

I shake my head. "I think I'll be staying in my room."

"What? No way, hasn't Nate said anything yet? Typical man they never realize that a woman needs plenty of notice for these things." She says with a scowl.

"No, he told me about Saturday night, I'm just choosing not to go."

"What? Nope, not happening girl, you are coming, I need you there to keep me company." Her expression changed and she gave me a sideways look. "Hold on, what do you mean he told you?"

"Just that, he told me I was going because he needed to keep an eye on his security problem."

"What an ass" she says, slowly shaking her head in disgust, then her face suddenly brightens and she gives me a very wicked smile. "Then all the better to go. We will find you a knock out dress and show him just how much of a security problem you really are," she says making little quotation marks in the air with her fingers emphasizing the word "problem". I was just about to cut off her bright idea when I remembered Nate's lousy behavior today. Why should I miss out because he has a problem with me being friends with Jax? "You're right?" I tell Lynda.

"I am?"

"Yes, Saturday night I will be busting out of the Penthouse prison and having some fun, so eat up, I need to find something to wear."

"Now you're talking my language girl," Lynda laughed.

The day was long and tiring and so much fun I haven't done a girls day out for years, in fact I don't think I have ever done a girly day shopping for clothes... ever. Going up to my room I hang my dress in the closet and place the rest of my bags on the bed. Lynda dragged me into a lingerie shop called Lapurla and I purchased an expensive strapless body suit in black lace, with some thigh high black stockings. I needed something to keep all my curvy bits together under the body hugging black strappy dress that she also talked me into buying. "Oh Casey it will go great with your skin tone and blonde hair." Add to that a silver pair of 4 inch heels and a small matching purse, she pretty much fitted me out for the night, and now looking at the dress hanging up I'm glad I had Lynda there to make the decisions for me, she did a great job.

Around eight o'clock that night there was a knock at my bedroom door. Opening it up Nate stood there, looking striking with his black ruffled hair and unshaven jaw, wearing a black t-shirt that molded to every crease and line on his chest and clung around those huge biceps, together with a pair of low slung jeans and bare feet. I think I can feel my mouth watering. "I brought some pizza, it's in the kitchen," he motioned behind him with his thumb.

"Oh thanks, it's ok, I'm not really hungry." I went to close the door but he stopped it by placing a hand against it.

"Hey you need to eat."

"I'm good, really, I think I'll just crash early, I'm pretty done in after all the shopping with Lynda today."

Nodding his head he said, "You didn't leave your door open last night?"

"No, I didn't want to get in your way." I said and he raised an eyebrow at my comment.

"Please just leave it open, I know it makes you feel safe, and I promise not to bother you". And with that he went back down the stairs to the kitchen.

That night I left my door slightly ajar.

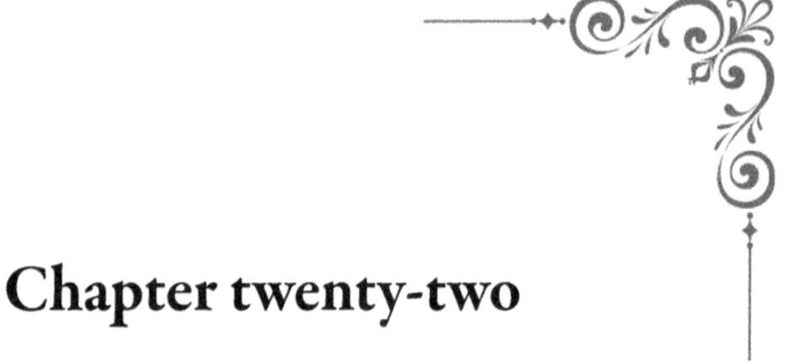

Chapter twenty-two

Nate

The week went from bad to worse. First there was the meeting with Peterson. That smug bastard made me feel like I was going to combust in his office. Then the scene walking in on Casey sitting on the couch, huddled next to Jax. I saw the look on her face, she was laughing and happy with him, and that made my anger level go up another notch. I hated the fact that he had made her look that way and not me. Then later she wondered why I was pissed at her. Is she fucking kidding me? Holy shit, I thought we were starting to break through that barrier. Yes I know she keeps fighting me and she's clearly told me that there is no chance of anything happening between us, but that came from her mouth, and her body is telling me something different, or is it? Fuck I have definitely let my guard down with this woman. To make her feel comfortable, I have compromised my own personality and toned down my penchant for being an asshole, and Jax walks in and accomplishes in what five, ten minutes? what I haven't been able to in weeks, and damn, she's right, it is a blow to my ego. Hell, she might as well have just kicked me right in the balls because seeing them together, so comfortable with each other, that's exactly what it felt like. So no more pussy- footing around I now get the message, loud and clear, if she wants me to back off then that's what's going to happen, Just get this shit cleared up with Peterson, then bye bye Ms Tyler.

I didn't see much of her for the rest of the week. I managed to avoid talking to her at all apart from letting her know that I brought pizza back one night and that she could keep her door open. I knew it made her feel safe and I know I'm a prick, but I do want her to feel safe in my home. On Saturday afternoon I let her know that Paxton and Lynda would be picking her up around seven because I had to be at the club early and I would see her there. Just for a split second I thought I saw a look of disappointment on her face when she knew I wouldn't be accompanying them, but it was just as quickly gone.

Nick dropped me off out the front of what looked like a huge red and white circus tent. There were colored lights and loud music, and entertainers dressed like evil looking clowns. There were scantily dressed women in tight fitting corsets and feathers, it looked like a circus gone bad, but I guess that's why it was called "The Bazaar," because it was meant to be a bazaar place to be in, It was a mixture of a B&D club, burlesque and a circus, all rolled into one, and by the looks of the queue to get into this place, I could see this was going to be a long evening, ending in a huge headache.

The lines of people waiting outside to get in was crazy. I walked into the huge doorway where one of my security guys let me into a dark corridor with flashing lights on the floor, that made a path to yet another ornate gold door. Pushing it open, I was blasted by a pounding beat. The building was circular in shape, which kept with the circus theme inside. Around the outside was a bar that ran around the whole room. Booths and tables with chairs followed the same pattern, then a few stairs down, took you to a huge arena and a dance floor.

At different areas throughout the club there were mini stages which each held some type of activity on them. One had a huge gold bird cage on it and inside sitting on a bird swing, swinging, was a blonde woman wearing only a gold swimsuit. On another, a scantily dressed male and female were embraced in each other's arms moving provocatively against each other to the music. On another mini stage further towards the back, was a blonde woman dressed from head to toe in tight black leather. From her pointy thigh high boots, all the way up to a pair of huge breasts spilling out of a leather bra decorated with silver studs, she was sitting on what looked like a red throne, where she kept changing into different sexual poses. The waiters and waitresses were all in various dress from full leather suits to burlesque- type corsets with different length skirts. There were also different performers walking around juggling everything from glow in the dark crystal balls, to daggers and glass pins, and one guy exhibiting his fire breathing talent. This place surely did mirror it's name.

Walking up to the bar, I signal the barman for a water and perched myself on a stool at the end near the back wall where I have a perfect view of almost the whole room, to sit and supervise and, fingers crossed, hope that everything runs smoothly tonight.

Watching the crowd starting to expand in the arena dance floor, I watched as a tall solidly built Alonzo Reed the club owner starts making his way through the crowd towards me. "Mr. King, I'm glad you're here, it looks like it's going to be a great opening night."

"Yes, it seems so," I nod at the crowd of people still spilling in the door.

"I see you didn't bring a date?" he asks.

"No but I have some family members joining me soon."

"Good, well enjoy the night and we'll meet tomorrow and revise whether we need to make any changes to the security." I give him a smile and a nod and when he walks back into the crowd I go back to scanning the room and over towards the door. Looking down at my watch, I see it's just past 7pm. Moving my eyes back to the door, I notice Paxton entering holding Lynda's hand. As they make their way through the crowd following Lynda is Jax, who is holding the hand of a leggy blonde, her head bent, she appears to be concentrating on where she's walking. They're moving through the crowd like a snake, making their way up to the bar towards me, and when the blonde finally looks up, I am sure the floor just crumbled beneath my feet. This stunning woman heading in my direction, her blonde hair in soft waves falling around her shoulders, her body encased in a snug fitting black dress that is clinging to her every curve, my eyes follow down a pair of beautiful long legs that finish up in a pair of the sexiest high heels I have ever seen on a woman, is no other than the Doc, and she's holding tightly onto Jax's hand.

Standing to greet them, I motion for them to move to a booth that has been reserved in one of the corners and they all slide in. "Wow!" Paxton exclaims, "This place is freaky."

"You can say that again," I agree, trying not to stare at Casey sitting next to Jax. A waitress dressed in a black leather mini skirt and matching bra comes over to take everyone's drink orders. Paxton and Lynda opt for water, Jax orders a beer and Casey orders a beer as well. Giving her a questioning look, I ask "I thought you didn't drink Doc?"

"I don't normally but tonight I intend to enjoy myself," she answers sheepishly. "That's my girl, you need to loosen up a little," Jax tells her and I look at him with an eyebrow cocked in annoyance. *"That's right Jax, see my face right now, it's saying don't push your luck buddy"* and he gives me a grin *"Yeah you know exactly what I'm thinking."* "You going to sit with us?" he asks looking at me.

"No I'll stay at the bar. I have a good view from there."

"Suit yourself" he says with a smile and I turn and walk back to my bar stool and continue to scan the crowd, watching and analyizing the crowd of people everywhere and thinking, do we have enough security to handle the crowd? Are there any dark zones? Why the fuck is she sitting so close to Jax? *"Reel it in man you're losing it."* I find that every few minutes I am glancing back at the booth where I notice their table filling with empty glasses. I watch as

Paxton and Lynda get up and move to the dance floor when the fast paced music changes into a slow track, leaving Jax and Casey in the booth, sitting way too close, laughing and throwing back shots, and I feel blood starting to pump through my veins, my anger palpable. My sight of them is interrupted by a female figure standing in front of me in a snug fitting silky blue dress. Looking up my eyes rove over her ample breasts spilling from the top half of the dress and up to a pretty face with red lips, bright green eyes and long red hair cascading down her back."Hi," she says, "buy a girl a drink?" Taking another look at the booth, I signal for the barman. "A drink for the lady."

"Stacey," she introduced herself holding out her hand to me, and I take it "Nate".

Over the next hour or so I learn that Stacey is single and she works as a secretary at a local law firm, and I can tell by her body language and how she has now moved from sitting on a bar stool next to me to standing in between my thighs, that she is looking for a warm body to share a bed with tonight. I glance over the top of her head and right into a pair of wide blue eyes staring back at me. *That's right baby you keep watching cos two can play at that game."* I watch her face as I slip an arm around Stacey's waist pulling her closer into my body, those blue eyes widen more for a moment, then soften as she moves closer into Jax's side and I see his arm move around her back and my jaw starts to twitch. My back teeth grind against each other in anger. Casey grins at my reaction and before I know it, my head has tilted down and my mouth is on Stacey's lips. She moves her mouth against mine but there's nothing, I feel nothing, it feels cold and detached and......all wrong. Pulling away from her and wiping my mouth across the back of my hand, I look up to the booth, and Jax and Casey are walking towards the dance floor. The music changes and I recognize the slow pulsating beat of Groove Armada's "Edge Hill" and I watch as Jax pulls Casey against his body and they start moving to the music, their bodies molding together, swaying, grinding, his hands moving up and down her back, and I suddenly have this urge to break my best friend's legs. Breaking Stacey's hold, I excuse myself and move towards them, pushing through the crowd until I tap Jackson on the shoulder. "I think this dance belongs to me," I growl at him. He says nothing, just gives me a lift of his chin and moves back and I pull her into my body, my hands sliding down to her lower back. She attempts to move away but I pull her firmly back against me. Leaning down close to her ear I say "If you're going to grind that body on anyone tonight it will be mine no-one else, do you understand?" Her eyes widen in shock at my words but she gives me a slight nod of her head. Our bodies slowly move to the hypnotic slow beat of the music, her body is pressed hard against mine, and I stroke my hands up and down the smooth material against the skin of her back. Her hands are pressed against my chest and her head is nestled under my chin, and every time I breathe I smell the combination of vanilla and spices in her hair. Her hands slip down and into my jacket and slide around my waist, a move that brings us even closer together. We stay like this until the song finishes and turns into a more heavy frantic beat that breaks our embrace. She drops her hands and tries to move away from me and stumbles until I grab hold of her tightly around her waist. "I think you may have had a little too much to drink Doc." I guide her back over to the bar area. "Get your purse," I tell her.

"Why?" she asks giving me a weary look.

"Because I am taking you home."

"Somehow I don't think we'll get any flights to Sydney at this time of night, do you?" she chuckles.

"My home." I tell her firmly and she pulls her arm from my grasp.

"And what if I'm not ready to go yet?" she says now with her chin lifted defiantly. "Oh you're ready." I reach out to grab her arm again but she takes a half step, half stumble, backwards then pulls herself upright. Smoothing down her dress and tucking her purse under her arm. she brushes a stray lock of hair away from her face, and those beautiful eyes of hers are now narrowed and angry. "Look. I'm pretty sure I am old enough to decide when I need to go home. ok? Besides I'm not into threesomes." She sneered.

"What?"

"It's ok Nate, you take the red head home for some bump and grind, I'm sure I can find something to occupy me, I'll just grab a cab back later."

"Bump and grind?" I laughed, but stop when I see the look of scorn on her face.

"Well I can assure you that you will not be looking for something or someone to occupy your time because I have no intensions of doing anything with the red head." I say more seriously now.

"Didn't look like that before when you had your tongue down her throat." she bites out.

I looked down at the floor and push my hands into my pockets. "That was a mistake."

"What? Sorry I don't think I heard you then, it's pretty loud in here," she said putting a hand to her ear to emphasize her point.

Walking closer to her I said. "That was a mistake, I wasn't thinking straight."

"You looked like you knew what you were doing to me." She said quirking a brow.

"Well I didn't, ok?"

"So why Nate?" she asks her face set into an angry yet slightly hurt look.

Blowing out a large breath of air in defeat, I say, "Because... I was watching you and Jax and it pissed me off okay?"

Looking at me, she shook her head, "You're an idiot" she said then turned and walked back over to the booth where Paxton and Lynda sat. I followed her and stood while she said goodnight to them both then headed for the door.

"Everything ok?" Paxton asked, brow raised.

I rubbed a hand down my face. "Yeah, I'm just going to take her back to the Penthouse. She drank way above her limit. Are you two ok?" Paxton nodded. "Yep, you go man, we'll be leaving soon anyway. It all seems to be running smoothly and Lynda's getting tired."

"Ok, drive home safe and we'll talk tomorrow." I leaned down and gave Lynda a kiss on the cheek then headed out to try and catch Casey before I lost her in the crowd outside.

Chapter twenty-three

C asey

Grabbing my purse off the table of the booth, while saying a quick goodnight to everyone, made me look rude, I know but all I wanted to do was get out of this place and as far away from Nate as possible. The uncomfortable feeling of anger that was building in the middle of my chest felt like a large air bubble was about to pop and that combined with my rather large alcohol consumption tonight, made my brain and my mouth very unpredictable. Pushing through the doors I moved to lean against the outside wall and try to contain my rapid breathing before hailing a taxi from the other side of the road. As the taxi pulled at the curb, I reached to open the door, when I felt a hand grab my arm and I am turned to face Nate's solid chest. "I'm parked down here." He said tucking me against the side of his body and walking towards his black SUV, he pulled out the keys and with a click the doors are unlocked and he pulls open the passenger side door. "Get in," he growled. Crossing my arms across my chest as an act of defiance, I hear him take in a deep breath before he says, "Get in the fucking car now or I will pick you up and throw you in."

"You wouldn't dare," I challenged.

"Try me." he said tilting his head.

Looking up at his face, his lips pressing so tightly together it makes the muscle at his jaw throb, with his eyes now narrowed their grey color looked more like steel. With an exasperated breath I slide into the passenger seat, slamming the door. He moved quickly around to the driver's side, got in and started the engine shifting the SUV into gear and pulling out into the traffic. Turning to look out of the side window, I watch as the lights melt into each other as we drive towards the Penthouse at a swift speed.

After what seemed like an endless silence he spoke."Look, I have no idea what's happening between us but I do know that it's driving me to the doors of insanity." Looking over at him I can see his hold tightening on the steering wheel, his eyes shift to glance at me briefly before looking back at the road. "What, you have nothing to say now?" he bites out sarcastically.

"There's nothing to say." I tell him.

"Oh fuck, yeah baby, there is plenty to say so don't clam up on me now." His words come out so sharply that I actually feel them sting and prickle at my skin.

"Look, just drop me off and go back to your red head, I'm sorry I ruined your plans for the night."

Pulling to a stop at the traffic lights he swung his head to look at me. "Is that what this is all about? Jealousy? Why, I feel so flattered Doc," he smiles placing a hand over his heart.

"Keep dreaming Nate" I say, then splaying his hands out in front of him he says with an unabashed smirk on his lips, "What can I say, a man cannot live on bread alone sweetheart and you have made it quite clear that you don't want any part of me." Looking down at my hands now twisting together in my lap I feel the heat rising into my cheeks. I glance up quickly to his face, then back down at my now knotted fingers, and I almost whisper the words to him.

"I didn't say I don't want you …. I said I can't." I hear his sharp intake of breath and I look up into the burning heat of his stare just for a brief second before his concentration turns back to the road, then into the underground parking area under the Penthouse. Stopping briefly to punch in his security code, he drives down and pulls the SUV into his reserved parking space. Jumping out as soon as he turns the engine off and heading towards the lifts, I hear the click of the lock on the SUV and within seconds he is behind me. When the doors open he almost pushes me inside and against the back wall, his body hard and warm against mine. Leaning his head down so he is eye to eye with me, he speaks one word "Explain?" Looking away from his face, I try to squirm my body away from his imprisonment but he doesn't budge. With both of us breathing heavily from the struggle, we just stay in that position staring at each other until the ding and the sound of the elevator doors opening breaks the contact and he takes a step back giving me room to slip from under him and into the foyer of the Penthouse. As I start to move towards the stairs he almost shouts "NO! Do not run away from me Casey." Turning, I look at him, "Look I'm tired and my head is fuzzy from the alcohol, just leave it, okay?" I say, as I continue up the stairs and into my room. Tossing my purse on the bed side table and slipping off these painful heels, I flop down onto the bed.

Closing my eyes against the dizzying effects of too much alcohol that seems to be kicking in hard right now. I put my arm over my eyes and curse myself for saying what I said to him. It was stupid. True but still stupid. Yes I do feel something for him and the chemistry between us is palpable, but I am lost, I have no idea how to have a relationship with anyone never mind being intimate with anyone, so how the hell do I do this with him? I just can't.

While I am contemplating getting up and undressed and into bed, I hear him coming up the stairs and walking down the hall. Moving my arm, I glance at my doorway and he is standing, arms folded, leaning against the opening. He's taken off his jacket and his button- down silk shirt sleeves are now rolled half way up his forearms, letting little pieces of his ink peek out. Clearing his throat, he says, "Do you think that maybe we should talk? You know like real humans, no arguments or tension or judgments, just two people getting to know each other." Letting out a deep sigh, I move myself up the bed and tuck a pillow under my head, leaning against the bed head. I nod for him to sit on the bed. Unfolding his arms, he also pulls a pillow up against the bed head and mimics my position. His arm brushes against mine and I quickly move it away. He's next to me, in my bed and he's close, so close I can feel the heat emanating from his body. Sensing my apprehension at his closeness, he moves to widen the gap between us, which makes me feel like I can breathe a little more easily, and I am glad when he breaks the somewhat awkward silence in the room by speaking. "So... what you said in the car, can you elaborate more on that statement?" My brain is struggling with how to tell him my thoughts, my feelings, without delving too far back into my past and I'm not sure where to start and when I don't answer him he speaks again. "Okay, let's start with something easier. Do you feel the chemistry between us?"

"Yes" I answer, my voice barely a whisper. But I am determined to answer his questions.

"Are you afraid of something?" he asks.

"Yes."

"Of me?"

"Yes...no, not of you, I don't know what of exactly, the intimacy I guess."

"As in.... sexual intimacy?" he asks, his voice now dropping a little and I hear the concern in it.

"Yes."

"Okay, so have you had any long term sexual relationships?"

"No"

"Never?" his voice rising with what now sounds like shock.

"No, never."

"No boyfriends, no lovers in the past?" he says slowly.

"No." Rolling onto my side so I can see his face, watching as he rubs his finger tips back and forth over his lips I say. "And before you ask, no I'm not a virgin, I have had sex before, it was just not... normal, and something I would rather forget..." My words trail off and I watch his face change, harden, and the little nerve in his jaw starts to twitch again until he says in a low, controlled voice "Did someone hurt you?"

Not sure how to answer that question, I just go with "I would just like to leave it at that okay?" he closes his eyes for a brief moment then gives me a nod, then he turns on his side, so we are face to face. He is breathing harder now and he slowly lifts his hand up to my face and strokes his thumb over my cheek.

"How long ?" he asks. I turn my face away from him and his voice gets lower as he asks again "How long?"

"About twelve years," I breathed out.

"Shit!" he curses under his breath and with his thumb still gently caressing along my jaw line. He tilts my face up to look at him. "You know I would never hurt you, don't you?" Closing my eyes and leaning my face into the touch of his hand, I nod, "but you need to talk to me, you need to tell me what you want, and what you need from me okay? Let me know what's happening in that stubborn, argumentative head of yours." He grins when I smile. "There's no hurry baby, we can take all the time you need. I want you to feel comfortable with me okay?" Nodding again, I feel his hand slide down my arm to my waist and move me closer to him, his other arm slipping behind my head so I am now tucked against his body and wrapped in his arms. laying my arm across his stomach, I breathe him in, he's warm and inviting, he smells of clean linen and spice, and it feels so calming, peaceful and... safe. My eye lids feel so heavy and I can feel them starting to close. I am drifting into serenity, and into the darkness of sleep.

Darkness, my body shivers when a cool breeze brushes over my naked body. I hear footsteps, then a click of the lock and a door open . Pulling my legs up close to my body I hug them against me and sink into the corner and close my eyes as tight as I can, My head is telling me that if I squeeze my eyes closed hard enough I can disappear into the wall. It's silent, but I know he's there, I can hear him breathing and I can smell his pungent body odor more than I can smell my own. Then I feel a sting against my leg as I am hit with something that feels thin like a cane, maybe, and I flinch away from it. "Wake up slut" thwack!, another sting and I let out a small moan. When a small overhead light is turned on, I try to shield my now open eyes from the harsh glare, and the bindings on my wrists burn with my sudden jerky movement."I see you managed to remove the cover from your eyes again, when I told you not to." he snarls."Stand up," he barks at me and I struggle to do as he says, pulling myself up on thin wobbly legs where he slams my body against the wall with his arm pressed across my throat."You are a useless slut and you know that you will have to be punished now don't you?" he says as he presses harder against my throat. I can feel my breathing getting shallower from the lack of oxygen. His face is close to mine, his putrid breath turns my stomach. "But you like being punished don't you?" I nod in agreement. I know what I need to do, agree and don't fight, if I struggle his punishment is much more painful.

I wake with a gasp and a jolt of my body, my eyes opening quickly. I try to focus on where I am then I feel a large hand spread against my stomach, a cold wave of fear spreads through my body until I feel warm breath against the side of my neck and a deep, soothing voice. "Shhh! Baby I'm here, it's okay you're safe." He pulls me closer into him and gently kisses my temple and I am quickly orientated to where I am and start to relax back into his hard body behind me. We are both still wearing the same clothes that we wore out to the club last night so, I am guessing that we fell asleep on my bed while we were talking. I feel his warm rhythmic breathing against the back of my neck, and it brings me back exactly to where I am. I sigh and it feels....good, and strange, it's a feeling I'm not used to, never had before. I've always been guarded and cautious, always looked at everyone as a potential threat, and yet here I lay with this typical alpha male with his strong and dominant personality who could really hurt me, and yet I feel so safe. I have no butterflies doing somersaults in my stomach, or nausea, or any signs of panic; no feelings of restraint or control; just an overwhelming feeling of peacefulness that feels wonderful and inexplicable. I am resolved and determined to try my hardest to let this man into my life, which will be difficult without telling him everything. I just need more time before I open up that vault. I need...I need...fuck, I have no idea what I need right now but this is a start.

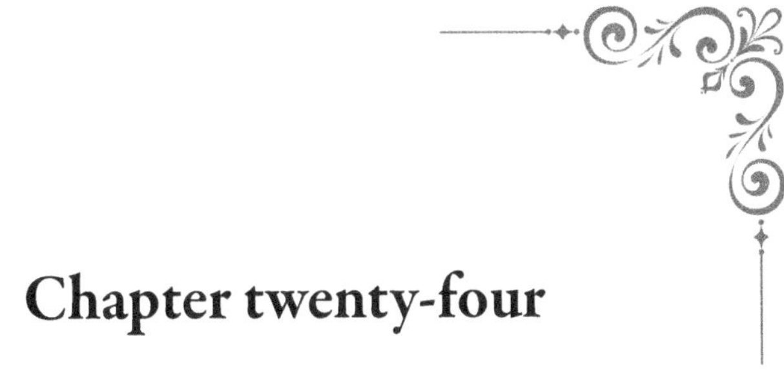

Chapter twenty-four

N ate

Waking early, before the sun had even risen was a habit I'd acquired from being in the military for so many years and normally it didn't bother me but this morning I wanted to stay exactly where I was. It had taken me so long just to get this far with her that I didn't want to let her go and she felt so damn good tightly pressed against me. After she woke suddenly earlier, with what I presumed was a bad dream, she had turned around and she now had her head against my chest and I had an arm around her back. Looking down at her now peacefully sleeping, I am in awe, taking in every inch of her beauty from her long eye lashes that are fanned out against her creamy soft skin to her moist luscious lips that are slightly parted, her elegant neck and her soft blonde hair that tumbles across my arm and onto the pillow. I watch as her eye brows pull together and I gently stroke a finger across them whispering "Shhh" until they relax.

I need to know all of her. She has stirred emotions in me that I have never felt before, and I want to give her..... everything. Besides my country and my family, I have never wanted to fight so hard for anything before, especially a woman's attentions. I have never even entertained the idea of being in any kind of relationship, it's just not me, but she...brings me to my knees. Sure I admit to start off with it was all about getting her in my bed and the allure of her body. That dammed sexy accent and the stubbornness and spirit of the woman just drove me out of my mind. Damn, I'm turning into a goddamn pussy thinking about relationships and shit, what is she doing to me?.

I don't want to wake her but the temptation of that creamy skin is too much and I gently slide my fingers down her arm to where her hand is resting against my abdomen. Gently tracing her fingers right down to those perfect nails, she breathes out a low moan and moves her head against my chest. Looking down at her, I watch as those beautiful eyes open and sleepily look up at me. I lift my hand up and my fingers stroke a lock of hair away from her face, letting my thumb gently brush over the lobe of her ear, then I stroke down under her chin, tilting it upwards slightly. Her sparkling blue eyes stare straight into mine, and in that swirl of blue and sapphire I can see the trepidation she has, and I want to take it all away, every ounce of fear she has. I intend to absorb all her pain, I want her to trust me. As I lean down to take her mouth with mine, her eyes close and she tilts her head up more. That first touch is slow and soft, until I feel the warm tip of her tongue touch my bottom lip and her opening up to the invasion of my tongue caressing hers. We are both lost in this intimacy. Moving down and pulling her into my body, I need her closer. With one hand at the nape of her neck and the other holding onto her hip, I dive deeper into the kiss and when she moans into my mouth heat runs down to my groin and it throbs with passion. I feel her hand slip around my torso and slide up my back and that ignites more heat through my body. Moving my hand from her hip and sliding it down to the hem of her dress I move the material up until I feel the lacey top of her stockings. "Sweet Jesus." I breathe into her mouth, letting my fingers caress the top of the stockings then following the clip of the garter belt up to the junction of her thighs I feel the soft silkiness of her panties and they are so moist against my finger tips. She moans again at my touch and my body is starting to slowly combust inside, she feels so good, and I start to pull her dress further up her body. I want this mother fucking thing off now. I need to feel skin against skin, but as I get the dress, up to her waist she breaks the kiss and grabs the dress halting its ascent. Looking at her confused. "What's wrong baby?."

She looks away for a moment then down at her dress "I... have....scars" she says in a low whisper. I lean my head down so we are now eye to eye and try and rein in the instant anger I feel at the thought of her being hurt by something or someone. In a low calm voice I say "Show me." After a few moments hesitation she pulls the dress up and over her head and lays back down on the bed turning her head to face away from me. Turning on the bed side lamp, my eyes drift back to her almost naked body and I see first some tiny white scars across the top of her breasts. When I touch them with my finger tips she inhales a sharp breath but still keeps her head turned away from me. Slowly I let my fingers run down to her ribs where there are several short scars in a perfect line and as I move to her stomach there are more marks, some straight like they were made with a sharp razor, and some jagged, and then there are a few that are perfect circles and look like old burns, like they were made from a lit cigarette being pressed into the skin. Gently I touch every mark and that burning heat that was once in my groin has moved up into my chest and has turned from lust to pure anger. This is not from some kind of accident, these marks where deliberately made, and that thought is now causing a throbbing pain deep in my chest. My voice still calm, I tell her "look at me." Slowly her head turns and the eyes that were full of passion a few minutes ago are now brimming with tears. "Who....who did this?" I ask motioning to the marks across her beautiful body. Sitting up, her head bowed, she reaches down to grab the sheet and pulls it up in an attempt to cover herself, until I stop her. "No! don't." Lifting her face to look at me, a tear runs down her cheek and I collect it with a brush of my thumb. "You don't ever have to hide from me. You may see scars but I see perfection. You. Are. Stunning and you. Are. Mine".

Her moist eyes looking at me tear something inside, and I pull her into my arms again, our mouths crashing against each other with a passion, every nip and bite igniting us both, and I feel her fingers slide down the front of my shirt and open the buttons. Then I feel her hands working it down and over my shoulders, her hands moving over my arms first then down my chest. I lean back against the bed head and lift her to straddle me. I need her to have complete control of what's happening. I want her to have all the power to do whatever she wants, and fuck that thought makes me even harder. Our mouths still hungry and joined together, I feel her slowly grinding against me, then suddenly she breaks the connection and moves back slightly. Before I can question her, she reaches behind her back and unclips her bra. I let my hands slide up the soft skin of her arms and move the silky material from her shoulders until it drops and she is bare in front of me. Her breasts are perfect, creamy mounds of plump softness. I pull her closer so I can pull one of them into my mouth. Her hands run through my hair, alternating between pulling and smoothing, as I draw a soft pink nipple into my mouth and suck hard. She pushes harder against my mouth and the moan she lets out sounds so fucking good. She moves one of her hands down my shoulder, across my ribs, down my stomach until she reaches the bulge pressing against the front of my jeans and she stops and looks at me, her eyes wide, her mouth slightly parted and panting and I see a flash of concern cross her face. "What is it" I almost pant.

"You know some of my sexual history Nate.... I've only ever experienced pain and it's been a very long time." She says hesitantly.

"It's ok baby, we don't have to do anything you don't feel comfortable with. Shit, it's my fault, I shouldn't have let it go this far this soon." I run a hand through my hair but before I can say anything else, she presses a finger against my lips, stopping me .

"No, it's not that, it's just... I've never felt like this before. I've never wanted more before, but I'm a little scared of..."

"Of what baby?" I ask running my fingers over her cheek.

"Of not knowing what to do, to feel.... of this," she said stroking her hand across the rock hard erection in my pants.

I let out a low chuckle. "You're scared of my dick?".

"It's not funny Nate, look at the size of it?"

"Come here baby." I pull her back into my chest. "Listen, first I guarantee it will fit and second, you do what you feel, this isn't a case of pass or fail honey just trust me, and trust yourself okay?" She nods, then strokes a hand through my hair. "Now give me your mouth, I need to taste it some more. I haven't had my fill yet." Grinning she presses her mouth against mine and in an instant that passion and heat from before is quickly re-ignited and her heat engulfs me. Slipping my hand down to the front of her panties, I run a finger over the silk that is now soaking wet, moving my hand to the small strap of silk at the side of her panties I roll it around my fingers and with a quick tug it snaps and the panties are gone. Now I feel her wetness against my fingers as I gently run them through her folds, she is so slick and hot and I can't stand it anymore, I have to be inside her. Without breaking our kiss, I gently flip her onto her back and I feel her undo my belt, then my zipper, and then her warm hand slips into my boxers and her fingers wrap around my hardened length ."Fuck," I exhale, "give me a minute babe you're killing me here." Getting up from the bed I shed my jeans and boxers. then cross the hall into my own room and grab a condom from my bedside table. Returning to where she lays naked sprawled across the bed, her body flushed with desire and wanting. Ripping open the condom packet I slip it over my length. Kneeling onto the bed I nudged open her legs with my knee and cover her body with mine. Reaching down I slowly guide my hard shaft into her warm waiting body, pushing in inch by inch, looking down at her languid face, her eyes open wider and stare into mine, and I can see the apprehension and fear starting to gather in them. Stopping my intrusion into her body, I lean my head down close to her ear and whisper, "It's ok baby just relax and open for me." I feel her legs open wider and her sex relax around me and I continue to slowly bury myself deep inside her, until I am fully sheathed in her warmth, and with great restrain I still my movements. She is so god damn tight, I need to give her time to adjust to my size. I take little nibbles against her throat and up to her jaw, licking and softly biting. Moaning at my open mouth kisses over her neck and shoulder, she starts to move under me, her hands running over my back. "You ok baby?" I pant into her neck. "Yes," she hisses out, "more" and with her plea I give her what she wants and I start to move in and out of her hot, wet, tight body, slow at first but the more she moans the deeper and harder I drive into her. Feeling her legs wrap around my waist makes her hips tilt up more taking me in deeper than I ever thought possible, and I am lost in her.

Chapter twenty-five

C asey
With my legs instinctively wrapping around his waist, he moves deep inside me pushing me into a world of euphoric ecstasy. His ridged stomach pressing against mine, his hard chest rubbing against my breasts, my nipples tingling with his every move as his skin caresses mine. With one elbow pressed into the bed, his hand holding the back of my head while our mouths assault each other's, then his hand moves down gripping my hip, pulling me into him with every grind of his hips, rolling and grinding. Little sparkles of electricity dance up and down my spine, making my sex throb and pulsate and Nate breaks our kiss. "Look at me" he demands. Looking into his grey eyes I see a hunger and all that I manage to breathe is "Nate."

"Just keep your eyes on mine and feel baby, feel me and let go." With his lips close to mine, my body arches into him and those once little sparkles of electricity now increase with every one of his hard, long thrusts, pushing me up higher until I reach the height I was seeking and with another last thrust I am pushed over the top, writhing and moaning in pure rapture. His mouth is on mine, breathing in every one of my gasps and moans until his head pulls back and I see the thick corded muscles of his neck bulging as he reaches his own plateau of pleasure and growls out an explosive, " Fuck."

Holding his weight on his elbows above me, but still inside of me, we both continue to pulse and throb around each other, then looking down at me he lightly touches the tip of his index finger at the top of my forehead and slowly slides it down between my eyebrows, over my nose and lips and down to my chin then lightly kisses my lips. "That was…"

"Wonderful," I finished for him. Eventually sliding himself from my body he walks into the bathroom to dispose of the condom then comes back and slides back into bed. Engulfing me back into his arms and pulling the sheet up to cover us then he kisses the top of my head. "Sleep baby." And with my head pressed against his warm chest, I drift off.

When I wake again it's just becoming daylight outside, and we had become disentangled from each other. Nate lay on his back, one arm laying across his stomach, his chest slowly rising and falling, and I watch for a few moments just taking in this man lying next to me, who had just given me so much more than he would ever be able to understand. Quietly sliding from the bed I scoop up my panties and Nate's shirt and pull them on as I quietly creep out of the bedroom and down the stairs to the kitchen, where I get myself a glass of juice and take it out onto the balcony, grabbing my IPod off the kitchen island on the way. Sinking down into a lounge chair, I pull my legs up onto it and plug in my ear buds, scrolling through the music list until I find my favorite Pink album and press play. Leaning my head back against the chair and closing my eyes, I relax into my thoughts of what just happened. I have never let anyone get as close as Nate did tonight, and I am amazed at how it feels. I feel…different, unbound, released and so intoxicated by this feeling, it's sublime the way he makes me feel and I trust him, holy shit! I trusted him enough to let him in to my fucked up body and my fucked up mind, no, no, not fully into my mind…yet, I gave him snippets of my past, I mean I had to give him something to explain my scars, my apprehension, my anxiety. Fuck, I sound like a real nut job. Why the hell would he want to be involved with someone like me? There were so many things he still didn't know about me, somehow I had to tell him everything so there's were no secrets between us. I needed to speak to Flynn.

With my mind made up to give myself a fighting chance with Nate, I felt even lighter. I always told myself that the past needed to stay in the past, where it belonged. I needed to break free from its bindings and I'd always thought that I was trying but after how Nate made me feel inside. I'd just been doing the opposite, I'd been making those bindings tighter every year since it happened, until they had a strangle hold on me and now it was like a light bulb moment and holy shit! I'm the one who keeps them there, Jesus! Twelve years of fucking therapy and it takes one night of hot sex to wake me the fuck up and smell the coffee? I'm the one who controls my life, my mind, my body me...just me alone.

With music soothing my brain and my eyes closed, feeling the warmth of the early morning sun on my face, it's heat is interrupted by a shadow blocking it. Opening my eyes and pulling out the ear buds, I look up to see what is causing the shadow. And I see a sleepy looking sexy man, his black hair mussed, a dark shadow of stubble across his jaw line, his broad shoulders and bare hard sculptured chest moving down to the tight muscles of his abs that lead right down to that sexy V that disappears into a black pair of loose sleep pants that are sitting low on his hips and that's right where my gaze has stopped, until I hear the low grumble of his delicious voice. "Everything okay?"

Jerking my gaze from his crotch to his face, I see worry in his eyes. "Everything is great." I beam at him.

"I woke up and you were gone and I thought...." He trails off.

"No, honestly Nate everything is just perfect, I just needed some thinking time." His fingers lightly pulled on the cord of my ear buds.

"This helps?" he asks curiously.

"Yes, it helps me to stop over thinking" I say smiling at him.

"And are you?"

"What? Over thinking? Always, but not now."

"Good, so there's no reason for you not to get that sexy ass back into bed so I can explore some more of that body then," he says grabbing both my hands and pulling me to my feet.

We ended up spending most of the day in bed discovering each other for what felt like the first time. We touched and tasted and shared our bodies and took little naps in-between and the only words that were spoken were whispers of endearment, filled with passion until, while laying with my cheek pressed against his chest, I heard the distinct sound of his stomach growling. He glanced down at his watch. "Wanna get dressed and I'll take you out for some food?"

"Hmm a date huh?" I looked up at him with a smile.

"Yes a date," he said, leaning down and kissing the corner of my mouth.

"So we've kind of done this the wrong way around haven't we? I think you're supposed to take me on a date first, feed me, then get me into bed." I smile at him and he shrugs "What can I say; I never do anything the easy way baby."

After dressing in a pair of jeans and a t-shirt I pulled my hair up into a pony tail and went down stairs to where Nate was waiting at the bottom, dressed casually in jeans and a snug fitting black T-shirt, with his hands pushed into his pockets. I walked up to him and brushed a hand through his messy hair trying to tame it a little ."You look like you just got out of bed" I laugh.

"Not sure where you've been all day woman but I'm pretty sure I just did," Taking my hand he lead me to the elevator and pushed the call button. Once inside we travelled down to the lobby and placing his arm around my shoulders he guided me to the front doors and out onto the pavement. "So what do you feel like?" he asks. "Hmm something typically American, surprise me". We walked down into an array of lights and wonderful smells coming from all the different restaurants that spilled out onto the side walk until we stood outside a small place with "Stella's" printed in red over the front window. Nate pulled me inside and we were instantly greeted by a short older-looking woman wiping her hands on her apron, her face breaking out into a huge warm smile as she came towards us. "Nathanial, my boy where have you been?" she said as she walked into his open arms and he wrapped her into a hug.

"I've been busy working Stella. How's business?"

Pulling back, she looked at him with concern. "Business is good, but you look so skinny, take a seat and I'll get you some of my ribs."

"Now that's just what I'm looking for. Stella, this is Casey, and she's from Australia and I have promised her some good, tasty American food." Looking at me, her smile seemed to grow even bigger, "Then you've come to the right place, you both take a seat and I'll feed you up good and proper".

Leaning back I licked the last bit of barbeque sauce from my fingers. "Holy crap, I think I am about to pop," I said running a hand over my full stomach.

"I take it you liked it then?" Nate asks.

"Like is not the right word, that was phenomenal, I have never had ribs that taste so good and they were so bloody big." Looking at the smile of satisfaction on his own face, I could see that he was happy with his choice of restaurant he had brought me to. As we walked back to the Penthouse I spied a vendor's cart at the side of the road. "Nate, I need one of those," I said, pointing to the large pretzels hanging from a rack on the cart. Dragging him over, he purchased one and handed it to me, and I bit into it. "Oh wow, I have always wanted to try one of these," I said, around moaning and chewing the warm, soft, buttery dough Nate. just stared at me with an amazed look and shook his head "What?"I asked with a mouthful of pretzel.

"If I'd have known how happy and relaxed you are with a mouth full of dough, I would have brought you a whole cart load to yourself." I bumped him with my elbow and we continued walking back to the apartment, where we spent the evening spooning on the couch watching a movie and trying to recuperate from our night of feasting. When the movie finished Nate turned off the T.V and dropped the remote on the table. Stroking his fingers through my hair he said "Can I ask you something?"

"hmm hmm" is all I could manage through the food coma I had sunk into.

"The guy in your past, the one that hurt you." He said slowly making me stiffen instantly in his arms. "Relax" he whispered into my ear.

"What about him?"

"Did he pay for what he did...to you I mean"

Pausing for a moment to think I answer."Yeah, he paid legally and illegally,"

"Illegally?" he questions.

"Yeah, Flynn got to him first and gave him a dose of his own justice." Nate's voice sounded slightly strained when he said "I like the sound of this Flynn, he sounds like a great friend." "He is," I sighed.

"And...the scars? Did he...." He trails off and I knew where he was going with his question so I stopped him.

"No! That was just from an accident when I was younger." He nodded, but I saw the flash of interest in those curious eyes and I hoped that my answers would satisfy that inquiring mind of his for a while longer.

That night in bed I was encased in Nate's strong arms. There was no making love this time, just sleeping. The last thing I remember before my eyes closed was Nate whispering against my temple "Get some sleep baby, I think you've had enough sexual discovery for one day, besides I don't want to give you too much of a good thing, I might scare you away".

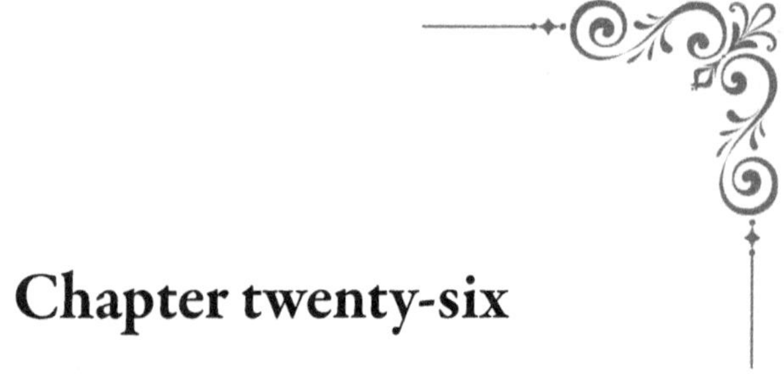

Chapter twenty-six

N ate

Turning my head, I looked at this beautiful woman that lay beside me, her hands clasped together and tucked under her cheek, her blonde hair spread out over the pillow, her eyes with those luscious long eyelashes closed and those succulent lips slightly open breathing in slumber. The wonderful curves of her body covered only by a sheet, she looked so serene and untroubled by anything, it was hard to believe that this was the same woman from the other night. Once she opened up to me and embraced the chemistry that had built up between us she let me see the real her. Now, I just had to keep her this way.

Quietly slipping from the bed, I went into the bathroom and took a shower. With a towel wrapped around my waist, I pulled out a shaver and shaving cream. I desperately needed a shave before I went into the office this morning. Spraying some foam into my hand, I looked up into the mirror and saw the reflection of pure beauty staring back at me. She was standing behind me dressed only in a thin black tank and a black pair of panties. "Morning."

"Hey," she said, tracing a finger over the tattooed wings on my back. "Can I?" she pointed at the shaving foam.

"You want to shave me?" I asked and she answered me with a simple raise of a brow. "Have you ever shaved a man before?" I asked and she scooped the foam from my hand. "No, but trust me, I'm a surgeon" she winked.

Making some space next to the hand basin, I lifted her up and sat her in front of me moving her legs apart so I could step closer into her. With soft tender strokes she coated my face in foam, then picked up the razor and moved it over my stubble. My eyes never left hers as I watched her concentrate on every stroke she took with the razor. When she finished, she wet a wash cloth and wiped any excess foam away from my face. I looked over her shoulder into the mirror, "You did a good job Doc, there's only one problem."

"What's that?" she asks, and I move in closer to her and rubbed my erection against the crotch of her thin panties then lean in closer to her ear. "You have made me incredibly hard." I kissed the side of her neck and down to her collar bone.

"Sorry," she whispered.

"No, I'm just sorry that my dick will have to behave itself until later, I have to get into the office and although I would love to take you here fast and hard, I have a feeling you're pretty sore from yesterday." She pouted her lips and dropped her head in defeat, letting out a long sigh. Placing a finger under her chin and tilting her face up to mine, I gave her a quick kiss. "You'll thank me for it later ok?" smiling, she nodded.

"Do you want me to make you something for breakfast?" she asked.

"No, that's ok, I have an early meeting so I'll grab something later, remember if you want to go anywhere today Nick's number is next to the phone in my office, just give him a call and wait for him ok?"

"I will," she nods, giving her a knowing stern look she holds out both hands in defeat, "I promise".

Pulling on a pair of jeans and a navy button down, shirt I roll my cuffs up my forearms and pull on my boots. When I get down stairs Casey is pouring herself a glass of juice. Grabbing my keys and phone, I went to her and took her face in my palms "I'm sorry you're cooped up in here, but hopefully it won't be for too much longer."

"Its fine. After back to back shifts for years, I'm enjoying the rest." Brushing my lips across hers once more, I got into the elevator and down to my office. I had only just unlocked my door, sat down and flipped on my computer, when Paxton came in.

"Paxton".

"Morning Nate." He greeted. "I brought you the revised contracts for the club," he said handing me a folder and I take a quick glance down at my watch.

"Thanks, I've just got enough time to check my mail then I'll head over there." "Sounds good." Looking up at where Paxton was still standing in front of my desk, his hands pushed into his pant pockets, he had a weird grin on his face.

"Is there anything else?" I asked him.

"You tell me" he shrugged his grin growing wider and I lean back into my chair.

"What the fuck is wrong with you?"

"Nothing, I just thought you might have something you wanted to talk to me about"

"Like...."

"Oh come on, the other night? At the club? What? you don't think anyone with half a brain saw what was going on between you and Casey?"

"Nothing was going on." I matched his grin with my own.

"And I'm calling bullshit." He said, shaking his head.

"I'm not getting into the details of my private life with you little brother, although I will tell you that I did managed to break down some of that wall she hides behind."

"Damn Nate, you got her in the sack?" I gave him a warning look.

"Ok, ok chill, I get it." Paxton held his hands up defensively, then asked "Did you manage to get any more information about her history, I mean anything new?" I blew out a breath and leaned back into my chair.

"She had a bad experience with a guy, I'm not sure if he was a boyfriend or just someone she new, but he messed her up Paxton. Reading between the lines, he forced sex on her and I'm not sure what else, but she has scars. Now she told me they were from some kind of accident when she was younger." Running my hands through my hair, I tried to dampen the anger that was starting to build again at just the thought of someone causing her pain.

"Shit! Nate, that's a terrible thing to have to carry around with you, no wonder she's guarded, she's protecting herself." Paxton said with concern.

"Yeah I know and it seems she's been doing it for at least the last twelve years."

"What the fuck? Nate Twelve years, holy shit, and now she has to deal with this situation with Peterson?"

"Yeah, well let's hope the warning I gave him is enough."

"Well if it's not, then he has a death wish. I've built quite a file on all the dirty shit he's been involved in including his current side business, so if push comes to shove, we'll just bring him down the legal way." He says with such conviction I know he's got what we need.

"Thanks Paxton, I always know you have a back- up plan."

"We need one, specially with that slimy bastard." He spits out.

"I know."

I spent the first half of the morning in the office going through my emails and reading through some of the contracts that Paxton had drawn up. This is where it pays to have a brother who went through law school. Pulling everything together for the meeting with the Bank of West this afternoon was my priority today. King Security had secured a contract for supplying all the security for every branch and sub-branches across the country, so I was going over everything with a fine tooth comb, making sure everything was in order.

Looking at my watch and seeing it was getting close to 1pm, I buzzed Paxton's office. "Hey Nate, everything good?" he answers.

"Yeah it all looks great. Listen you want to go get some lunch before this meeting?" I ask.

"Sure thing. I'll meet you down in the garage in about 10 minutes."

"Great I'm starving," I said, as my stomach let out a groan. We ended up at Fires Restaurant and grabbed a couple of pizzas and spent some time talking once again about Casey. "Sooo, it this thing serious between you and Casey?" Paxton asked, before he took a large bite of the cheesy goodness.

"You are not going to give up with the questions are you?" I ask quirking a brow at him.

"Nope." He asks before taking another bite of pizza.

I sighed in defeat then nodded, "Yeah I think it could be."

Paxton's eyes grew wide and he started to cough on the pizza he was chewing.

"You. Serious. About a woman? Holy crap, I guess there's a first for everything after all." He grins.

"Shut the fuck up." I threw a balled up napkin that bounced off the side of his head.

"Hey, no violence now."

"Then mind your own business."

"Are you kidding me? For years I have watched you bed women and that's it, no second date, no relationships, no promises, not even a friggin phone call, and now after all those years, my big brother has serious feelings for a woman? Geez Nate, are you sure the world hasn't just started turning the other way, because I feel like I've been knocked on my ass," he chuckled.

"Ok, ok just contain yourself around Casey with your excitement. I don't want to spook her with your over-zealous excitement".

The meeting with the Bank of West board members took way too long for me, through most of it all I could think about was getting back to the Penthouse and seeing Casey. I was relieved that Paxton took on most of the questions regarding the contract because, for the first time in my life, my mind was somewhere else instead of business. After all the contracts and paperwork were signed and the deal was sealed, I was eager to leave, but it was suggested that we head down to the bar for a celebratory drink and I knew when Paxton gave me that "It's part of the job" look, that my plans for getting back to Casey would be detained.

One drink turned into two for me. Paxton kept the same drink in his hand the whole time we were there, which was a good idea because he had quite a drive to get home. Eventually I made our excuses to leave and after dropping Paxton off at his car, I drove back to the Penthouse. Walking out of the elevator, I dropped my phone and keys on the table looking around for Casey. Not seeing her down on this level, I was just about to head upstairs when I heard talking, looking around it sounded like it was coming from the balcony. As I got closer to the sliding glass door, I saw her she had her back to me and she held her phone up to her ear. Stopping, I waited and watched, as she pushed a hand through her hair and squeezed the back of her neck as she started pacing. She looked like she was getting agitated with whoever she was talking to as her voice grew louder. I moved closer, "Look, you know I appreciate everything that you do for me Flynn, but things have changed and honestly I don't want to do this anymore." She sat down in a chair and bowed her head. "Yes, I understand...ok..I will...bye." Pressing the button to end the call, she stood up and as she started to come inside she saw me standing watching her.

"Hey" she smiled at me.

"Who was that?" I asked nodding towards the phone in her hand. There was a slight pause, a sigh, then she said "Flynn."

"Everything ok?"

She pursed her lips. "He's pissed at me, he wants me to come home." As she spoke those words, I felt a jolt run up my spine.

"Did you tell him that's not going to happen?" I asked my voice tinged with anger.

"I told him I would talk it over with you."

"And you just did and I gave you an answer." My body started to feel tense at the thought of her leaving and I needed to keep a cool head about this. I walked over to the fridge and pulled out a beer, flipping the cap I took a draw on the icy cold liquid, then placed the bottle on the kitchen counter. She came over and pulled herself onto a stool and rested her elbows on the island, her hands propped under her chin, and those icy blue eyes zeroed in on mine.

Silence, she said nothing, just watched as I took another long pull at my beer, our eyes never leaving each other's, and I could see her mind working like the cogs inside a clock, ticking over and waiting for the right time to strike and knowing her it was coming...right...now. "So, like I told Flynn, I would discuss it with you." I felt my lips twitch at her smoothness.

"And I gave you my answer, it's not happening" I said, pronouncing the words slowly. I could see the tension starting to build in her, then she holds out her arms and starts to inspect them. Pulling up her shirt revealing her stomach, she looks down at it, then she turns her back to me with her shirt still pulled up in her hands. "Could you just take a look at my back for me?" Now she has me baffled at her actions.

"What?"

"Well I can't see a tag or a label that has property of Nathanial King hanging off me anywhere, so I am guessing it's my decision if I go home or not, right?" With her hands firmly planted on her hips and her chin slightly tilted upwards, I make my way around the kitchen bench until I am standing in front of her. I place my hands on both sides of her face, and bring my mouth down close to hers.

"Baby, the minute you opened your legs and took me inside of you last night, you became mine." I breathed against her lips. "And I don't care what Flynn thinks you are not going anywhere."

"Really?" She whispers.

"Really," is all I said as my mouth slid against her lips. I felt her tension slowly start to ease as she wrapped her arms around my waist and opened up to me, as my tongue slid in between her lips. She tasted of fresh mint and the kiss that started off slow and languid, changed, as she softly bit my bottom lip and moaned into my mouth. Slipping my hands down her back and grabbing her ass I squeezed, and pulled her harder against me, placing light kisses down the side of her neck. As I licked and sucked around to the base of her throat, she tilted her head back, giving me better access. Moving my hands slowly up to the hem of her shirt, I pulled it up over her head, dropping it to the floor and ran my hands over the soft satin of the white lace bra she was wearing. Letting my thumbs move in small circles around her nipples that puckered into hard nubs under my touch. I felt her fingers move up the front of my shirt and work on the buttons, opening it, then sliding it off my shoulders, dropping it onto the floor. Then those soft, nimble fingers of hers were moving over my chest and down over my abdominal muscles until she came to the top of my jeans, where she slid her fingers along the top of them. Working down to the button, she opened it and slowly slid down the zipper. I was so fucking hard, it felt like an instant relief from the pressure of the tight denim that was containing me. Breathing hard against her neck, she slid a hand into my jeans and wrapped it around my length. "Jesus," is all I could say before I took her mouth with a growl of passion and, as our tongues tangled, I worked her shorts and panties down her legs until they pooled at her feet. Lifting her up, I sat her on the back of the couch. "Wrap your legs around me" I commanded, and as she did, I slid my length into her trying to hold myself back as much as humanly possible and not take her too hard . Once I was fully seeded in her from root to tip, I was lost. She let out a gasp at my invasion, but soon tightened her legs around my waist and threw her head back as I thrust in and out of her moist, tight, heat, pushing deeper and deeper into her body. I couldn't get enough of her. The air filled with moans and heated breath, it was fast and uncontrolled and so damn good. When I felt her tighten around me and she moaned my name, I plunged in deeper, claiming my own release, throbbing and filling her warm body with my own hot liquid.

We stayed connected while we steadied our breathing with soft kisses and she unlocked her legs from around my waist, as I let her feet touch the floor I slid out of her. That's when it hit me. "Fuck." The curse came out with such force that Casey jumped ."What?"

"No fucking condom." Running a hand through my hair and down my face, I shook my head and she placed a hand on my chest.

"It's ok, I'm on birth control and I can assure you I am healthy."

Closing my eyes I felt some relief and pulled her into my arms. " I am too, it's just I have never lost control before...ever. Did I hurt you?"

"No."

I kissed the top of her head. "I'm so sorry." Moving away from me she collected her shorts from the floor and pulled them on.

"Don't worry about it, I was just as carried away as you were."

"I know, but it was a stupid mistake to make." I said pulling on my jeans.

This time when she looked at me, I saw something flash in her eyes. Was she angry at what I had said? "I didn't mean that the sex was a mistake, that was incredible, I meant an un-planned pregnancy would be a mistake."

She started to walk towards the stairs, then turned to look back at me. "You're right, it would be, but don't stress about it because if for some reason my birth control fails you have nothing to worry about Nate, because an un-planned pregnancy is hard to accomplish when you can't have children." With that she turned and walked up the stairs.

I pulled my jeans back on and grabbed a beer from the fridge and a cigarette from the small wooden box on the bar, then went out onto the balcony. Sitting down, I took a drink of the cold liquid, then lit up the smoke, inhaling deeply. I felt the nicotine rush into my veins I know how much Casey hated the smell of cigarette smoke, and logically she was right, it was time for me to get rid of the habit, so I had managed to cut it down to the bare minimum, but right now I needed it. The look on her face as she went up the stairs tonight made me feel like a bastard. Her beautiful blue eyes that minutes ago were filled with passion and desire, had changed to being empty of emotion. Damn, she was like a kaleidoscope, turn her one way and you have beautiful sparkly colors, move another way and you get a mixed up mess, and she can't have kids? What the hell? My mind started whirring through more questions now, why? What had happened? Was it from her accident or her attack? Would it affect us? Do I want children? I've never even thought about any of this shit before because I never saw anything permanent happening in my future with any woman, and now I'm sitting out here bursting a blood vessel over my future. For Christ's sake.

I sat out on the balcony for about an hour contemplating my next move. Going inside, I found my phone and pulled up Charlie's number and pressed the button. "Mr. King?" she answered after the third ring.

"Yeah, Charlie, listen we got the contract for the Bank of West today, so I want to organize something for everyone who put in all the hard work."

"Wow! That's great, so you want me to book the Club room on the ground floor and get some catering in?" she asks.

"Yeah, just organize the usual stuff you know, finger foods, desserts and an open bar down there as well."

"Not a problem, when for?"

"Make it Friday around 7pm and send out memos to the staff."

"I'll get on to it first thing in the morning Mr. King." Charlie enthused.

"Thank you." Pressing the button, I disconnected the call then started for the stairs. Her room door was open and she lay on the bed facing the door. When I saw that she wasn't asleep yet, I stood in the door way. "So am I banished to my own bed tonight?" She didn't answer, she just pulled back the blanket as an invitation. Slipping my jeans off, I slipped in next to her. "I'm sorry if I said something that upset you."

"It's ok, it's not important."

"Rolling over to face her and pulling her into my arms, I tucked her head under my chin and kissed the top of it. "You're wrong, everything about you is important to me, and when you're ready I want to know everything about you."

"Don't ask for things you don't need Nate." She said her voice almost a whisper.

"Believe me, I need it, and eventually you will give me everything."

"Ok caveman, but the only thing you'll be getting now is me sleeping," she yawned. "I can live with that baby..For the moment".

Chapter twenty-seven

C asey

When I woke the next morning, Nate had already left. He did leave me a note on the kitchen island letting me know that Paxton was bringing Lynda into the office for lunch today, and to come down around noon, which put a smile on my face. In the short time that I had known Lynda, we had started to become close. We talked quite often on the phone through the day. We were very similar to each other, and talked about everything and anything, from favorite movies and music to her missing not being able to do much painting at the moment because of how the baby was zapping all her energy, which was understandable at this stage in her pregnancy. She was well into her third trimester, so I was always reassuring her that she needed all the rest she could get right now, and that she will always be an artist and it wouldn't be too long before she would get back into her painting.

It actually felt weird talking about getting back to work. Lynda was getting frustrated with not being able to paint, yet here I was not even thinking about my own professional career that was on hold at the moment. To be honest, I didn't miss it at all, maybe it was because I had buried myself in it for so long it had burnt me out. Shit, I just reminded myself, I needed to contact the hospital and let them know what was happening and where I was. Making my way into Nate's home office and turning on the computer, I sent them a quick email, then checked my own before taking a shower and changing into a pair of black jeans and a white silk shirt and slipping on a pair of white sandals. Grabbing my purse and shoving my phone into it, I headed for the elevator and down to Nate's office.

Lynda was sitting in one of the leather lounge chairs that sat outside his office and as soon as she spotted me coming out of the elevator, she attempted to get up. Quickly moving to her side. I bent down to give her a hug. "It's ok, you stay seated."

"Thanks," she puffed out."It's so good to see you. I was starting to go stir crazy at home so Paxton organized lunch."

"Now how can living on that beautiful beach cause anyone to go stir crazy?" I asked, smiling at her, and she swatted my arm."You know what I mean." Just as I sat down on the chair next to her, Nate's office door opened and out walked the immaculately dressed Charlie.

Leaning closer into Lynda, I whispered "Here comes Charlotte the Harlot."Lynda let out a snort of laughter that caused Charlie to give us a stern look as she walked around her desk and sat down. "Paxton should be down soon Mrs. King," she said smiling sweetly at Lynda, while throwing the look of death my way. "Wow, she doesn't like you does she?" Lynda nudged my arm. "Really? I wouldn't have noticed." I said wickedly.

Paxton came down from his office first and bent down, kissing Lynda, and putting both his hands gently on her stomach. "How you feeling honey?" he asked in a smooth and tender voice, "I'm good." Then he turned to me. "Hey Casey."

"Hi Paxton," I said giving him a smile Paxton stood looking over at Charlie. "Give my brother a buzz and tell him to get out here, we have too beautiful ladies to take to lunch." She gave him a slight nod and picked up the desk phone and relayed Paxton's message into the mouth piece. Within a few minutes Nate came out, pushing his phone into the back pocket of his jeans.

"Hey" he greeted, giving Lynda a peck on the cheek, then turning to me he leaned down and brushed his lips softly over mine then his hand came up and brushed a loose strand of hair away from my face. "Ok, let's go get some food," he said jingling his car keys in his hand Paxton took Lynda's hand and helped her up from the chair, and proceeded to the lift. Nate slid an arm around my waist and as we started to move I took a quick glance at Charlie. She looked at where Nate had placed his arm, then back at me with a scowl I gave her a huge smile in victory as I placed my arm around Nate's waist and ran my hand up and down his back.

We ended up going to this great little Chinese restaurant and ordered quite a few dishes that were placed on a large lazy Susan serving platter in the middle of the table so we all could just take what we wanted. The food was heavenly and everyone was so full by the time we were served with coffee. Nate told me about the celebration party he and Paxton had organized on Friday evening to thank all the office staff for their hard work on the contract they had just won.

That night in bed after we had made love and he was completely naked, I made it my mission to explore his wonderful tattoos. On his back was a man crouching with his hands covering his face and he had a large pair of wings that kind of drooped around his body. Under his feet was a scroll that had the letters USMC. Running my hands over his back as I straddle his naked butt, "When did you get this one?" I asked him. He had his arms folded underneath his head and his face turned to the side. "That one about 15 years, got it as soon as I enlisted." Leaning back I ran a hand along the back of his calf muscle where a skeleton wrapped in an American flag, holding a rifle and wearing a helmet was, and before I asked he said, "That one and the ones on my side, about 6 months after the first." Moving my fingers up to the words that ran down the side of his chest, they read "Death is only one breath away," Sliding onto the bed, I urged him to turn over so I could look at his other tattoos . On one shoulder he had a collection of skulls in different sizes that ran down and over his huge bicep, that also included the words "Semper fi, never forget the fallen." On the other shoulder he had a tribal pattern that covered his shoulder and a small part of his chest on that side. It's intricate swirls and pattern moved down his arm, covering it in a sleeve. With my fingers tracing along it, I looked at him with arched eyebrows. "That's been a work in progress I started it about 10 years ago and kept adding to it."

"And this?" I touched the tattoo on his right forearm. It was of an old fashioned hour glass and etched in the sand running through it were the words "Mom & Dad." "This one is beautiful, I can see you and Paxton loved both your parents very much.

"Yeah, we did" he said wistfully.

I curl into his side and he wraps an arm around me, running his fingers up and down my back. "Your turn," he said, tapping a finger on my own back tattoo."I got that about 10 years ago. I guess I was in a dark place at the time, and the old dark tree kind of emulated how I was feeling."

"And how was that?" he asked.

"I don't know..... empty, alone...abandoned. I added the dead leaves turning into black birds flying away later on." Lifting my hand and turning it over he ran his thumb over the tattooed word on my wrist that said, "Breathe" "And this?" he said placing a kiss on the space where his thumb was stroking.

"Same thing I guess with the anxiety I was suffering from it was like my reminder."

"Well," he breathed out, "I can't ask you about any more because I have been over every inch of that body and I know that you don't have any."

"Nope, that's it, what you see is what you get".

The next few days passed quicker than I expected and before I knew it I was getting ready for the celebration party that was being held downstairs. I had piled my hair in a knot at the back of my head and left a few wisps of hair to dangle free. I had chosen a white loose-fitting summer dress, as I was told to dress for comfort not style. I had just applied some cherry lip gloss to my lips when I heard Nate shout up the stairs. "Casey, Paxton and Lynda are here."

"Coming," I answered, and slipped my feet into a flat pair of sandals and headed down the stairs. Looking at Lynda in a pretty light blue summer dress, and the guys in jeans and t-shirts, I felt relieved that I hadn't over dressed. As soon as I hit the bottom stair Lynda's smile made me feel instantly relaxed I think I had been doing some over- thinking about this party. I've never been big on socializing, I've always been a loner out of habit I guess, but since Nate broke into my life I am seeing another side to it that includes, family and friendship.

Once we were in the elevator, Paxton pushed the button for the ground floor Nate stood next to me and I felt his hand snake around my waist and pull me closer into his side. Leaning down close to my ear he whispered, "You look beautiful." Looking up, I smiled. "Thanks, so do you."

The corner of his mouth turned up a little, "Not sure I've ever had a woman say that to me before."

"I bet you haven't," I rolled my eyes at him. The elevator opened and we all walked down to the club room, pushing through the huge wooden doors into an equally huge ball room, it had tables and chairs set around the perimeter of a dance floor. Along one of the side walls was a long table full of what looked like finger foods and desserts, and at the back wall was a fully functioning bar. Nate told me last night that the club room was usually rented out for weddings and parties. The ceiling of the room had what looked like black and white lengths of silk stretched from one side of the room to the other in an alternating pattern, with large crystal chandeliers hanging under the silk. The walls were white and the floor looked like shiny black marble. It was a stunning room Nate ushered me over to a table and pulled out a chair for me to sit, then sat in the chair next to me, placing his arm around the back of my chair. Paxton seated Lynda, then headed over to the bar, returning a few minutes later with two beers for himself and Nate, a glass of water for Lynda and a glass of white sparkling wine for me.

As we sat, chatted and munched on an assortment of tasty finger food, I glanced around the room taking in King's employees. They all looked happy and relaxed. Every so often someone would stop at our table and talk to Nate and Paxton. It was good to see such content looking staff who obviously had a lot of respect for their boss's and vice versa. The music that had been playing in the background suddenly stopped and a older looking man with a bald head, wearing jeans and a polo shirt started walking towards our table holding a microphone then speaking into it. "Ok, can I have everyone's attention please." The bustle of noise and talking grew silent and he continued looking between Nate and Paxton as he spoke. "I just want to say on behalf of your employees, we thank you for appreciating us." Paxton and Nate both laughed and in unison said "You're welcome."

"So if everyone will raise their glasses in the air and let's toast two of the most honorable men in the business." The bald man said holding up his glass and voices sounded out all through the room in appreciation, then the microphone was passed to Nate. Taking it he stood and cleared his throat.

"Thank you everyone for all your hard work. Without it we wouldn't have scored the contract for one of the biggest banks in the country." Nate paused momentarily and the room was filled with clapping and whooping sounds from the crowd. "So, enjoy the food and the open bar, but not too much because we'll expect you back at work early Monday morning." The crowd let out a groan and then the background music grew louder as the lights dimmed slightly and people started to gather on the dance floor.

Nate leaned in toward me. "I'm just going to go and talk with some of the employees will you be ok?" he asked "Sure. You go mingle I'm fine." He brought my hand up to his mouth and planted a kiss on my palm, causing my cheeks to warm slightly. He tilted his chin up to Paxton motioning for him to join him, Paxton gave Lynda a kiss on the cheek and left with Nate then Lynda turned to me.

"They're like a pair of bookends."

"I know but It's good to see they get along so well." I said.

"They certainly do, I guess it came from only having each other for a while."

"Yes, Nate told me about his parents, did you ever get to meet them?" I asked her.

"No, they had passed away before I met Paxton, but from what I know they were very close knit, I wish I would have met them they both sounded like wonderful, loving parents." I nodded at her response then asked."So how did you and Paxton meet?"

A warm smile spread over her face at my question. "He came into a gallery exhibition where I was one of the featured artists. He was interested in buying one of my paintings, we started talking, followed by dinner and that's all it took."

"Must have been love at first sight then huh?" I said.

"Something like that." She smiled.

"That's wonderful, you make a beautiful couple."

"So do you and Nate," she said lifting a brow.

"I'm not sure we're a couple exactly." I said hesitantly.

"Really? Are you blind?, he is awestruck by you Casey. I have never seen him so...so comfortable and at ease with a woman like he is with you, not that I've met many of his lady friends, but occasionally we would meet up for dinner with him and he would bring a date, but that would be it, we would never see them again."

"So no long term relationships then?" I asked curiously.

"Never. He spent so many years in the Marines, I don't think he liked to get too close to people, you know? He lost a lot of good buddies over the years from what little Paxton has told me, so he was always very guarded, but with you he's...different."

"Yeah, but you're forgetting I'm living in his Penthouse at the moment, so he doesn't have much choice but to see me."

She placed a hand on my arm. "Believe me it's different. Remember I'm here on the outside looking in and I can see plenty. Now, if you'll excuse me for a moment, this baby needs a trip to the powder room." She smiled and rubbed her protruding belly, stood and headed to the back hall next to the bar. Bringing my glass up to my mouth to take a sip of my wine, I looked up and saw someone walking towards me that I didn't particularly want to see tonight, Charlie, slithering towards me like a snake in her skin- tight little black dress and spiked heels, right down to the way her tongue slipped out of her mouth and over her bottom lip, I'm pretty sure I could hear the hiss from here.

Helping herself to a chair at the table next to me, she sat elegantly crossing her legs. I took another sip of my wine and placed the glass on the table. "And what do I owe the pleasure of your company, Charlie?" I asked, giving her a sideways glance. She looked around the room, then brought her head back to face me.

"Nothing, I just thought I'd be sociable." She said sweetly.

"Really," I sighed. "That's very considerate of you but I'm sure there are plenty of other's here who would love your company, I'm just not one of them."

"Now don't be like that I just figured we both have something in common."

"And what would that be?"

"Nate," she said, nodding in the direction to where Nate was talking to a couple of people next to the bar.

"That would be Mr. King to you, wouldn't it?" I said with a bite, and the sweet smile she had been displaying the whole time she had been sitting here faltered a little.

"Let's just say it's Mr. King in the office, but Nate in all the other places." She said grinning.

"Huh huh" I sighed out, now bored with her innuendo's. She moves a little closer to me and lowers her voice.

"Come on now, don't tell me you think you're the only one he's fucking."

NOW, she had my whole attention. "Funny, I didn't see anyone else in bed with us last night...or this morning, come to think of it" I chuckled, and she snapped out her hand and gripped my arm. Looking down at where her long pink nails were just starting to make indentations in my skin, then looking up at the somewhat psychotic look on her face, I calmly say, "You have about 2 seconds to get your hand off me before I break every bone in it." Instantly pulling her hand away she snarled. "You are one of many. You're disposable, you're a temporary toy for him to play with until he gets bored with you."

"And what makes you think he'll get bored?" I said.

She paused for a moment then stared straight into my eyes, when she said, "You see, what I'm sure you haven't figured out yet, is that Nathanial King is a dominant in the bedroom. He has very particular sexual needs, he likes to fuck hard and rough and he doesn't care who he hurts in the process, and I know all about your sexual hang-ups, about your broken past and how he pursued you until he got you into bed. Even you're smart enough to realize you were a challenge to him and he loves the pursuit."

I am temporarily stunned by her words, but I quickly recover, because there is no way I am going to let her see that she has shocked me. Looking at her, I press my hand against my mouth and fake a yawn. "You're boring me Charlie, and aren't you late for your night time shift, you know the one where you stand on the street corner and swing your purse to attract the customers?" The anger that spread over her face made me think for a moment that I might have to duck from her girly slap, but we were interrupted by Lynda coming back to the table. As she sat down, Charlie stood up and quickly walked away. Lynda looks at me questioningly, "She's a bitch," I shrug, and we both laugh.

A few minutes later Paxton circled back around to the table and sat next to Lynda, placing an arm around the back of her chair, leaning in and kissing the corner of her mouth. "How you doing honey?" he said to her with such love and concern it made me smile.

"I'm getting tired and uncomfortable," she sighed.

"Ok, then it's time for me to take you home," he said kissing her again.

"You're not driving home this late are you?" I asked Paxton.

"Sure, it's all good, we're used to the long commute."

"Why don't you just spend the night up at the Penthouse in the other guest room? I'm sure Nate would agree." I said.

Paxton looked at Lynda. "I am pretty tired but it's up to you babe, and Nate." She said placing a hand on his thigh.

"Casey's right, Nate would insist I'm sorry honey I didn't realize we would be here this long. I should have thought it out better." Paxton said.

Lynda cupped the side of his face. "It's fine babe."

"Ok, I'll just let Nate know and I'll take you up." Paxton stood.

"It's ok babe, I can get in an elevator by myself and put myself to bed. You stay and enjoy some chill time with your brother." Seeing the look of hesitation on Paxton's face, I jumped in, "I'll take her up and get her settled Paxton. I'm pretty tired myself." Paxton looked back at Lynda .

"Are you sure?" he asked her again.

"Yeah babe, go, I'll be fine." Kissing her cheek, he said, "Ok, but I'll be up soon."

"Just let Nate know where I've gone, ok." I said to Paxton standing.

"Sure thing and thanks Casey." He smiled.

"Not a problem".

After settling Lynda in the guest room I took a shower and slid in between the cool soft sheets of the bed but when I closed my eyes all that was going through my head was what Charlie had said. *"I know about your sexual hang-ups and your broken past."* How would she know anything personal about me? And how the hell does she know so much about Nate's sex life? He told me that he had never slept with Charlie but she sure seemed to know a lot about him, something just doesn't add up, and the more I mull it around in my brain the angrier it's making me. Logically I know that she is a manipulative bitch who wants Nate. I'm pretty sure there is no level low enough that she wouldn't go to, to have him, but still how would she know anything about my sexual past unless she had heard it from someone. *"You can't give him what he wants, he likes to fuck hard and rough."* Did he? Every time we had made love he was always gentle and patient, was he doing that for me? Was I denying him something? My stomach rolled with anxiety and I could hear my heart starting to beat loud in my chest, working its way up into the thumping in my head. Taking some deep calming breaths in through my nose and out through my mouth, I eventually relax enough to fall asleep.

Chapter twenty-eight

Nate

Looking over at the table where Casey and Lynda had been sitting, it was now empty and Paxton was heading towards me. "Where are the girls," I asked.

"Lynda was tired and I think Casey had had enough so they went upstairs. Sorry bro, it looks like you have house guests for the night."

Waving away his apology with concern, I asked, "Is Lynda ok?"

"Yeah it doesn't take much to exhaust her these days." Paxton slapped me on the back. "All's good, this should be winding down soon, drink your beer and relax." Giving Paxton a nod, I tilted the neck of the bottle to my mouth and drained it of what was left of the amber liquid.

Paxton was right and not too long after people started to slowly drizzle out of the club room. We headed up to the Penthouse. It was quiet with only the light from the stand lamp that stood in the foyer lighting the stairs. After saying goodnight to Paxton as he entered the guest room, I quietly opened the door to Casey's room. For the past week I hadn't slept in my own bed at all and truthfully, I didn't miss it. I was getting used to Casey's hot little body snuggled up to me all night and I had the added benefit of morning sex- not to mention sex through the night. Moving to the side of the bed, I could make out the outline of her curves under the sheet. She was facing away from me and her blonde hair spilled out over the pillow behind her and, through the silence of the room, I could hear her breathing, heavy

206

and deep. Not wanting to disturb her, I slipped off my jeans and shirt and pulling back the sheet and slowly slid into bed behind her. As I placed my arm around her waist she flinched slightly but relaxed back into me, and the warmth of her body instantly made my own body relax and before I knew it, I had drifted off.

Waking up, I had to squint against the glare of the light that was coming in around the edge of the blind on the window. Of all the places on my body it could zero in on, it managed to find my left eye. Groaning, I rolled over onto my side and run a hand over the now empty space next to me. "So much for my morning sex, sorry boy looks like you'll have to wait," I said, looking down at the erection that was now tenting the sheet. Sitting up on the edge of the bed I pulled last night's jeans on and went into my own room, took a quick shower and changed into a clean pair of sweats and a t-shirt and headed down the stairs I came to a stop half way down at the sight of Casey, dressed in a loose fitting white shirt and a pair of shorts, standing at my stove stirring what looked like scrambled eggs in a pan. Lynda and Paxton both sat on stools at the kitchen island that separated them from Casey. Lowering myself to sit on the stair, I leaned my elbows on my knees and watched her move around the kitchen efficiently and freely. How can someone look so elegant and sensual cooking breakfast? She looked so carefree and comfortable right now, and I wanted to just sit here and watch her for the rest of the day. That's when it hit me right in the gut like a sucker punch, I wanted to watch her cook in my kitchen every day, every month of every year from now on. I couldn't let her go. Just the thought of her not being here gave me an ache right in the middle of my chest and damn if I was letting her go...not now...not ever...she is mine.

Making my way down the rest of the stairs, I slid onto a stool just in time to have a plate full of fluffy scrambled eggs, bacon and toast pushed in front of me, followed by a mug of steaming coffee. "Thank you," I said looking at Casey but she avoided my eye contact as she served Lynda and Paxton, then herself. "So," Paxton said, "What are your plans for the day Bro?"

"I'm taking Casey out for the day." I said looking over at her.

"You are?" she asked with interest.

"Yes but it's a secret," I said, placing a finger to my lips.

"Hmmm sounds intriguing," Lynda said looking at Casey.

"It does" she agreed but still didn't make any eye contact with me. and that was starting to bother me.

After breakfast was done, Lynda and Paxton headed out for the drive home, and I helped Casey stack the dishes in the dishwasher. "So," she started, "What do I need to wear on this secret outing you have planned?"

"Just something comfortable."I grinned.

She nodded, then said "I'll just go take a shower then," wiping her hands on a towel, but before she walked away from me I grabbed her hand and pulled her against me. "What's wrong?" With those beautiful blue eyes looking up at me I searched them for an answer.

"Nothing's wrong," she said, and looked down at my chest trying to avoid my eyes.

"Hey" I placed a finger under her chin and tilted her face up and her eyes back to mine.

"I'm just tired, I guess" she said quietly.

"Talk to me." There was a pause and then she shook her head.

"There's nothing wrong really, I just got caught up thinking about an email I was reading last night, from the hospital where I work."

"And?" I pressed.

"They were just enquiring about a time line for returning to my position."

"And you told them?" I asked, Silence again. "Doc, you have to give me something, I feel like this is a one sided conversation here, " I said, motioning between us with my hand.

Shrugging she said, "and I told them that it wasn't possible for me to give them an exact answer." She said nonchalantly.

"Ok, and I'm guessing by the little lines creasing your forehead, they weren't too happy with that?"

"Let's just say they expected me to be back scrubbing in for surgery first thing Monday morning."

"What the hell? That's two days away." Releasing her from my arms and taking a step back from her, I rubbed a hand at the back of my neck in frustration.

"It's ok Nate, I told them that was impossible." Feeling slightly relieved, I had to ask her, even though I had an idea of her answer.

"So did they give you more time?"

"Nope, so I told them they could shove their job where the sun don't shine." She said. Jerking my head up and looking at her, she was smiling.

"Shit, Casey, I'm really sorry."

"Don't be, it's not your fault I can always find another job." She shrugged one shoulder.

"Damn it, and you look so heartbroken as well."I grinned at her. Still smiling, she patted her hand against my chest as she walked past and up the stairs to take a shower.

When she came back down dressed in shorts and a blue tank and her hair pulled into a ponytail, I picked up the knapsack I had packed, grabbed her hand and led her down to the garage. Pulling out onto the street she said "So where are we going?"

"I thought we would go to Washington Park and have a picnic." Looking at me with a surprised look I asked her "What?"

"Nathanial King does picnics?"

"No, not usually, but I'm feeling guilty about you spending so much time being inside, so I thought you might enjoy being out in the sun."

"That sounds nice, thank you."

"Your welcome".

We spent hours strolling around looking at the flowers that were out in full bloom at the moment, then to the holocaust memorial. We walked along the pathways under the enormous trees there until we found a great place to sit. Pulling a blanket from my pack and placing it down on the grass, I motioned for her to sit and I joined her. Reaching back into the pack, I brought out two bottles of water, a box of crackers, and a container filled with an array of cheeses and another filled with strawberries.

"Wow, domesticated too." She laughed.

"Ha! I picked these pre-made up at the deli yesterday." Casey pulled the lids off the containers, took a cracker and a piece of cheese, and slid it into her mouth. Just watching the way her mouth opened and her lips engulfed the morsel of food with a moan, I instantly thought of something much better I'd like to see slip between those luscious lips of hers.

By the time we got in that night it was late, so we grabbed a pizza on the way and sat eating it while watching a movie. The movie was inconsequential but watching her devour the pizza was not. All that lip smacking and sucking up the cheesy strings of mozzarella was making me hard. When she had popped the last bit in her mouth, I grabbed her hand and pulled her into my lap and moved her around to straddle me, my hands grasping her ass. She smoothed a finger over my forehead moving a piece hair away from my eye. "Thank you for today, it was really nice," she said, then placed a kiss where her finger had just been.

"You're welcome." Moving my hands over the curve of her ass, I felt her thighs tighten as she wiggled and pressed into the bulge of my jeans.

"Hmm I didn't realize eating pizza was that exciting." She looked at me, her brow lifting and her mouth turning into a mischievous grin. Placing my palms on her face and pulling that sassy mouth down to mine, I growled, "Come here, I've wanted to taste this mouth all day".

When her lips connected with mine, warmth ran through every vein in my body. Deepening the kiss, she sucked my tongue into her mouth and moved, rubbing against me, that caused the bulge behind my zipper to swell more. Moving my hands up, I unbuttoned her shirt and pushed it off her shoulders and cupped her lace covered breasts in my hands. Her nipples grew hard as I ran my thumbs over them, pulling down the cups of her bra, exposing that beautiful lush skin of hers, I took a nipple into my mouth and sucked greedily at it. She dropped her head back and arched into my mouth. With one hand on the small of her back I ran the other up the middle of her breasts, up the soft skin of her throat until my fingers ran along her bottom lip. She moaned, then took one of my fingers into that hot mouth and sucked. "Holy fuck Doc, I need to be inside you, now" I snarled. Both her hands moved down to the front of my jeans, where she unbuckled the belt, the button popped, the zipper opened and as I sprang free from the confinement of my pants her hand wrapped around my length and she slowly caressed it, then she ran her hand deeper down and cupped my balls with a moan. "You are so hard," she whispered into my ear, then sucked on the lobe of it.

"And if I don't get inside you now I'm going to come in that pretty little hand of yours baby." Moving to stand, she slipped her shorts and panties down her legs and stepped out of them. Breathing harder she asked "Condom?".

"I've got a clean bill of health honey and you're on birth control, it's your decision." She looked up at the ceiling, then back to me, a pause, then she moved back onto my lap her legs straddling me. Reaching down between her legs and running my fingers through her hot wet folds, I groaned, holding my shaft and rubbing the swollen head at her entrance. "Lower yourself down baby, take as much as you can." Slowly she began to lower her hips, taking me inside of her inch by inch. Watching her face, she closed her eyes and lowered her forehead against mine. We were both breathing hard now. With my hands on her hips I guided her until her heat was almost at the base of my shaft, god she was exquisite, her warm breath on my lips, the flush of pink in her cheeks, the tightness of her sex engulfing me and the brush of her hard nipples against my chest as she slowly started to move. Moving my mouth to hers, I gently bit into her lip which caused our mouths to once again fuse together in a symphony of hot, wet, kisses that quickly caused me to thrust my hips up harder into her. She moaned and panted into my mouth and I could feel she was close. A shrill ran up my spine when I felt her legs start to tremble with the movement of her hips as she ground down harder onto me, and when her head fell back and that blonde hair grazed along my thighs, I lost myself inside of her, hot liquid filling her as her sex pulsated around me. Pulling her hard against my chest, her head burrowed into my neck, until our heavy breathing and shuddering slowed and calmed.

Being woken early by the buzz of my phone on a Sunday morning while having Casey's warm naked body wrapped around mine, was not what I wanted right now. I tried to ignore it but the fucking thing was so persistent. Reaching over to the side table, I blindly slid it to answer and pressed it against my ear "Hello."

"Mr. King, I'm sorry to call at this time but there's been a break in at The Bazaar night club and the technicians are having a problem turning the alarms off." Charlie's voice sounded as annoyed as I was feeling.

"Did they try the master key?" I said rubbing my hand over my face in an attempt to wake myself up.

"Yes, but nothings working and it's been going now for over an hour."

"Ok, I'm on my way." I sighed and disconnected the call.

"Who was it?" Casey's groggy voice asked.

"An alarm at the night club won't turn off. I have to go down there, just go back to sleep, I'll be back before you know it." Leaning down, I placed a kiss on her forehead and slipped out of bed and into my own room to get dressed.

Chapter twenty-nine

C asey

Rolling over in bed, I reached out and slid my hand across the space to where Nate slept. It was still empty he must still be working on the alarm. Stretching and yawning, my thigh muscles ached and I smiled remembering the reason why they were aching. Looking over at my phone the time read 9.36am, so I pulled myself out of bed and into the bathroom, taking a quick shower and dressing, then heading downstairs. I thought I might find Nate asleep on the couch or in his office, but he was nowhere in the Penthouse, so I resigned myself to grabbing a bowl of cereal and headed for the couch, picking up the remote to turn on the TV and watch the morning news. Before my ass hit the leather, the intercom on the wall beeped. Placing the bowl on the coffee table, I walked over and picked up the handset. "Hello."

"Good morning this is the front desk. Mr. Kings secretary is downstairs, she has some papers to bring up for him." Damn, really? This chick never gives up, but what can I do? It's not my place. Sighing, I said, "Ok. Send her up."I hung up the receiver and went back to my cereal and flicked through the hundreds of channels until I found something that resembled world news.

The elevator pinged and I looked at the opening doors. She wore jeans and a green silk blouse, her hair pulled up in a tidy chignon, her make-up flawless. Fuck what does she do, sleep with that crap on her face, it's so thick, if she smiled too wide I am sure her face would crack. Turning my eyes back to the TV, I continued spooning cereal into my mouth, hoping if I ignored her she would do what she had to do and leave. It was too early in the morning for a fight. She walked past me carrying what looked like some white folders in her arms, and went through to Nate's office. A few minutes later she came back out and stood right in front of the TV. "I've placed the files that Nate wanted on his desk, He forgot to take them when he left this morning. Oh, and he forgot this too." she said, placing what looked like his phone on the coffee table. I looked down at the phone and then back up to her. "It must have been a busy night if he left his phone somewhere."

"Oh he was busy alright, but not just with the alarm." She said smugly. Jerking my head up to look at her so fast I almost gave myself whiplash, I peered at her through narrowed eyes."What's that supposed to mean?" She smiled and picked up her purse and headed back towards the elevator .

"Let's just say, the alarm was fixed within a few minutes of him arriving but he didn't want to disturb you, so he came back to my place for coffee and we found something.... fun to do for the next few hours." Jumping up from where I was and almost running over to the elevator, I swear I was going to crack that pretty little face of hers, but before I could get to her she was in the elevator and as the doors were closing I heard her smug laugh as it descended. I banged against the metal doors and yelled, "In your dreams you Bitch".

Infuriated, I paced back and forth in front of the elevator doors contemplating whether to go after her and punch her perfect pearly white teeth down her throat, or make a wish with her skinny legs. Anger bubbled inside of me at just the thought of Nate touching any part of her body. My brain started to work over time, thinking over what she had said. If the alarm was fixed that quickly, why hadn't he come back here? And why did she have his phone? And if he had spent the night with her, where the hell was he now? Was he feeling guilty and couldn't face me? Or was she just such a spiteful bitch she would try anything? My head started to throb from all the fury that was running through my body, and walking in circles around the apartment wasn't doing anything to calm it down. Grabbing my IPod, I headed to the back room where Nate had it set up as a gym area. Pushing the ear buds in and selecting the fast paced music of the heavy metal group "System of a Down," I cranked up the volume and jumped onto the treadmill selecting a run speed. With the thumping music silencing my thoughts, I ran until my sweat covered body couldn't take any more, my mind felt clearer and my body felt sated.

And that's where Nate found me. Laying on the seat of the bench press, my clothes soaked with sweat, panting and trembling from the hard work out and the fury that I had inside me. "Casey?," he said, with concern coming over to the bench press. I sat up and held up both of my hands.

"Don't" I said giving him a warning look. Standing, I walked out of the gym and down the hall into the bedroom with him following.

"What the hell is going on?" he asked. Pulling off my wet clothes, I walked into the bathroom and locked the door, ignoring him completely. I just didn't know where to go with this right now. All I knew is I needed a shower. As soon as the cold water hit my skin, it stung but I needed to cool down. Running my face under the spray, it felt so good right then, I washed my hair and body and got out wrapping a towel around myself. I unlocked the bathroom door and went into the bedroom Nate sat on the edge of the bed his elbows resting on his knees. As I started to dry myself off I could feel his eyes watching my every move. Without saying anything, I pulled on a pair of shorts and a t-shirt, then brushed my hair out. His eyes never leaving my movements. Once I had my hair up in a messy bun, my eyes met his, they were full of confusion with a hint of anger. Taking a deep breath in and releasing it, I sat next to him on the bed, feeling exhausted and shattered by my now depleted anger.

Finally he spoke. "Are you done now?" I just shrugged my shoulders. "What the hell just happened ?" His voice was deep, low and calm I closed my eyes and slowly shook my head. " No, you did this yesterday morning and you gave me some bullshit excuse about your job and I let it go, but not this time, this time you talk." Closing my eyes I searched for the words to try and start this conversation without looking like some possessive, jealous idiot, and I came up blank. Waving a hand nonchalantly, I headed for the bedroom door and mumbled "forget it," as I headed down the stairs. He followed.

"Not going to happen Casey" his voice now sounding slightly angry as he followed behind me. At the bottom of the stairs he grabbed me at the elbow, spinning me around to face him. "Don't run from me, just talk to me."

"I said forget it, it's nothing important."

"Well it certainly was important enough to get you this pissed off, holy shit you looked like you were going to implode up there," he said gesturing up towards the gym with a tilt of his chin.

"I'm sorry I was angry and I couldn't deal with it in the normal way like going for a run outside, so I did the next best thing."

"Yeah, I get that, but you're still not explaining to me what the hell happened to piss you off in the first place?"

"More like who."

Narrowing his eyes, he said, "Someone's been here?" I nodded "Who?"

Chewing on my bottom lip, I said, "Charlie."

"Charlie was here?" he asked sounding slightly surprised.

"Yes this morning" Looking at him now he actually looked relieved.

"Fuck Casey, you scared the shit out of me, what did she want?"

"She brought some files and your phone. She said you left it at her place this morning." He dropped his grip from my elbow and took a step back, folding his arms across the wide expanse of his chest. A smile started to appear on his lips and he looked smug.

"Ok I get it now. Look, once I got the alarm turned off and reset, I didn't want to come back that early and wake you, so I went back to Charlie's place for a coffee, and I left my phone there, and you're thinking something happened between me and her right?" That arrogant look that he had on his face right now made my anger start to resurface.

"You egotistical prick. See this is why I wasn't going to say anything, I knew that's exactly what you would think, puffing your chest out like a caveman on ego overload. I don't have to think anything about Charlie because she's made it clear to me on several occasions that you and her are fucking and I'm just the flavor of the month." That wiped the smile off his face.

"What?"

"This morning she made it quite clear that you had spent the rest of the night in her bed."

"What the hell? I went there for coffee and that's all, nothing happened" he said in a low growl I walked over to the couch and sat down leaving him running a hand through his hair. "Why the hell would she say that?"

"Have you been so oblivious to her behavior that you haven't noticed how she feels about you."

"Obviously" he said with a blank look on his face. "She actually said that?" "Oh she's said a lot more than that," I said, and noticed that now he was rubbing at the back of his neck with fury.

"Go on" he encouraged.

"She knew things...about me, personal things that she said you had talked to her about."I said hesitantly.

"Fuck me," he spat out. "This is just getting better by the minute." He sat down on the couch opposite me. "I have never spoken to her about you, my private life is just that- private." I could see a myriad of emotions in his eyes- anger, confusion but the one that caught my attention the most was honesty.

Closing my eyes I sighed,"I know Nate, I know nothing's going on between you and her. I could see the game she was playing from a mile away. She has a crush on her boss and when another woman comes into the picture she feels threatened and she'll try anything and everything to get me out of the picture." Those deep steely eyes of his looked slightly relieved.

"Yeah well it's not going to happen first thing tomorrow it stops"

"What are you going to do?"

"Fire her ass" he half yelled.

"Can't you just move her somewhere else?" I asked.

"You're kidding me right?"

"I know, but she's young and immature. Being in love with someone can make people do weird things."

"I'm not going to keep her employed just because she's immature Casey, actions have consequences, and I won't have someone like that working for me. Not now, not ever" I didn't say anything to that, after all it wasn't up to me. It didn't stop me from feeling bad about it though. After a few minutes silence between us, his eyes narrowed at me and he said "There's more isn't there?"

"What do you mean?"

"If you didn't believe what Charlie had told you then why were you so pissed ?" Looking down at the floor, I shrugged. "No, don't do that I want an answer, not silence, you're not shutting down on me again. She said something to you that's gone deeper in that over -thinking brain of yours, and you need to tell me...now." I could hear the anger starting to come back into his voice, and he was right, we had come so far the last few weeks and when Charlie had told me about his sexual preferences in the bedroom, it had been like a punch to the stomach.

Standing up I started to pace back and forth in front of him. "Casey," he growled out my name and it made me jump. Blowing out a slow breath, I said, "She said that you like sex.... Rough, and because of my sexual inadequacies that you'd get bored with me" I cringed at my own words.

"What the fuck?" he cursed, and stood up from where he sat and headed towards the elevator grabbing his phone and keys from the kitchen island on his way. I quickly followed him. "Nate, where are you going?" Spinning to look at me I saw the sparks of fury in his face, that little muscle at his jaw line ticked and jerked. "I'm going to see Charlie, this is bullshit" he spat out as he gripped the back of his neck in frustration.

"What now?"

"Yes, now. Besides the fact that she disrespected and upset you, I want to know where she keeps getting all this shit from. Is she listening in on private calls, on meetings, on private conversations between me and Paxton?" He continued towards the elevator.

"Nate, wait" I said getting closer to him.

"What?"

"Is it true?"

"What the hell Casey?"

Stumbling through my words now, I tried to get them out. "I mean, if you think that she may have listened in on private conversations, then she must have heard you and Paxton discussing your sex life." I looked down at the marble patterned floor of the entry.

"Really, do you think I discuss my sex life with my brother in the office all day?" "I didn't mean that, I'm just saying...I don't know what I'm saying any more." Looking up into his face I asked the question that had been bugging me since the staff party.

"Is our love making satisfying for you, or are you...holding back?" His eyes searched mine. I could see he was trying to find the words to placate me, and that pause that he took before he answered, was the answer to my question. I started to back away from him and he stepped forward reaching out a hand to touch me, but I moved.

"Casey"

"It's fine Nate, I understand."

"No you're jumping to conclusions." He growled.

"No, I knew from the moment I met you, you were strong and commanding. Until we got back here, then you changed your whole personality. Was that for me?"

"Nooo"

"Because I don't want that Nate, I don't want to change you, I couldn't live with that. My life has already been fucked up beyond belief and I will not be responsible for dragging you into it."

"You have it all wrong, yeah I toned my over bearing, arrogant personality down a notch or two. but that was because I realized that someone in your past must have hurt you and I didn't want you to be afraid of me, but don't ever doubt that what happens between us in the bedroom is false baby."

"I don't doubt it, but I don't want to stop you from being you Nate, because if I do, eventually you will get bored and dissatisfied, and after what I've experienced with you over the last weeks, I don't want to go back to what I was. Nate, you have given me freedom and I like it too much to give it back." Before I knew what was happening Nate had backed me up against the wall and caged me in with a hand on either side of my head.

"Baby," the words were almost a soft whisper but I shook my head. "Listen to me when I tell you, I would never do anything to hurt you, please don't destroy what we have." Looking up into his eyes they were swimming with emotions, this tough man that stood in front of me at that moment looked so vulnerable and open. I swallowed down the lump that had formed in my throat. "I won't, I just need some alone time, ok?". His brows furrowed and I continued, "things have been moving pretty fast and I just need to ground myself ok?" Slowly he nodded and backed away from me."Ok" Relief flooded through me as I said, "Thank you".

Chapter thirty

Nate

The next morning I sat in my office going through the blow out Casey had the previous day. I'd come in early this morning, before anyone else. I found it too hard to sleep in my own bed without her next to me, but given all that had happened and the need to fiercely protect her from everything, and anything I also know that underneath her tough exterior she's fragile and so, respecting her request for some alone time, I had gone to my own bedroom last night, leaving my door open so she knew I was still there.

Flipping on the computer I went through my agenda for the day, then went through my emails. I'd texted Paxton earlier letting him know to come to my office as soon as he got here so when he waltzed through the door not long after, I told him to sit down and went through the whole story of Charlie's antics. When I finished, he looked just as pissed as I was feeling, and he agreed with me that there was no room for someone like her in King Security.

When my phone buzzed just after 9am, I let Charlie know that she needed to come to my office before she did anything else. Knocking before she entered, she slowed when she saw Paxton sitting in one of the chairs in front of my desk. "Is there something I can do for you Mr. King?" she asked.

"Yes you can take a seat." I gestured to the other chair and she slowly lowered herself into it.

Nervously she looked at Paxton, then at me. When I shook my head she asked, "Is there something wrong?"

"I guess you could say that," I said raising a brow. "When you dropped my phone and files off yesterday at my home you had an altercation with Ms. Tyler."

"No, not at all," she said innocently.

"Sooo-you're saying nothing happened?" I asked.

"Nothing of significance."

Blowing out a breath of air in annoyance, I said, "Look Charlie, I'll cut to the chase here because frankly I'm done with the whole thing. You and I have never had a relationship, correct?"

"No Mr. King."

"Well at least we have that straight. So why have you been telling Ms Tyler that we are in a relationship."

Her eyes grew wide like saucers as her jaw dropped open, "I-I-I haven't Mr. King."

"So what? Are you telling me she's making it all up?"

"I...I don't know" she stuttered.

Charlie started to fidget in the chair. She looked uncomfortable, good, that's just what I was aiming for. "The thing that I want to know is, where did you get all the information from, you know about my sexual preferences in bed, did you hack into my emails or listen in on calls and private conversations, because if you did then we will be looking at pressing charges for invasion of privacy and breaking your non disclosure contract." Looking over at Paxton, he nodded in confirmation. "Oh, absolutely," he agreed .

"What? No," she almost shrieked out, I knew that would get her attention, her hands twisted in her lap and there were tiny beads of moisture gathering along her top lip. Swiping an imaginary hair away from her face, she sat up straight and squared her shoulders. "Ok, I didn't break any non disclosure rules or invade your privacy. I was bringing some files into your office one day and happened to hear you both having a conversation about Ms. Tyler and I didn't want to interrupt so I didn't come in."

"But you stood around the door long enough to get what you wanted, right?"

"Nooo-it wasn't like that, you don't understand."

"Then enlighten me Charlie," I said, coming around to the front of the desk and leaning back against it, folding my arms across my chest.

Looking up at me she cleared her throat. "I just wanted to make her think there wasn't a future between you and her." Taking one stride away from the desk to stand in front of her, I thought about what Casey had said about this woman and her crush, and even though right now she was pissing me off, hurting a woman, even her feelings, was not who I was. I may be an arrogant prick but, never to a woman.

"And why would you want to do that?" I asked her.

Lowering her gaze to her hands that sat in her lap, her shoulders visibly shrank back. " I don't know, I just thought that maybe, one day, you and I...." immediately I cut off her words.

"No, there never was and never will be anything between us Charlie." When she brought her face back up to look at me, I saw the tears well in her eyes.

"But you're always so nice to me, you give me time off when I need it, you always smile at me and ask me how I am. I thought it was just a matter of time before you asked me out."

"Just because I treat you like a human being and not like my slave, does not mean that I want to date you Charlie."

"But you might have one day...if she hadn't come into the picture" she sniffled.

"She has a name. Ms. Tyler is already under a lot of stress due to the situation, she's in a strange country with strange people and what you did was disgusting behavior that has ultimately thrown a spanner in any progress that we've made so far, not to mention you have disrespected your employer with lies and we don't work like that. We rely on honesty and integrity from our employee's and trust, and I'm sorry but we don't trust you any longer."

She stands quickly, "Please Mr. King I can't lose my job." She pleads.

"You should have thought about that before Charlie."

"So... you're firing me?" she asks, eyes wide. I pause for a moment and just look at her and all I see is fake tears. This isn't some innocent woman with a crush, this is a opportunist, a phony, everything about her is fake, she will change herself to get what she wants. Why the hell didn't I see this before? She wants a man that can provide her with security, and I don't think this revelation will put an end to her plans. This time when I look at her, I feel nothing when I say "Pack your stuff up, I want you out of this building within the hour, you're fired."

"What?" she gasped looking at Paxton for confirmation.

"You heard him," he said, and she instantly stiffened her body in response, lifted her chin and left.

Paxton looked at me. "Phew what a bitch."

"Yeah, well I'm not too proud of letting her go, she was good at her job, but I can't trust her and I won't have her upsetting Casey." Walking over to the bar in the office I poured him a mug off hot coffee and refilled my own, and handed it to him.

"So how is Casey?" he asked.

"She's...mad"

"I bet she is," he scoffed.

"But she trusts me and we did hash the whole thing out but her shutters started to come down again and she needed some time to herself. She handles things differently to any other woman I've known."

"It sounds like it. If that was Lynda, she would have my balls on a plate right now. They must build women tougher down under."

"She sure is a tough cookie, well on the outside anyway, but on the inside...now that's a totally different story." Paxton stood. "Give her time bro."

"I intend to Paxton don't you worry".

Later that morning I had another meeting to attend with the Bank of West board, some papers needed to be signed before we could start implementing their security take over. The meeting was supposed to be short but it ended up including lunch with drinks. I didn't get back into my own office until well after 4pm and I still hadn't answered any of the multitude of emails that were clogging up my in- box. I needed to sift through them and flag the ones of interest, and forward them on to Paxton for viability. Picking up my phone, I checked it for any messages from Casey, but there was nothing. It seems I had already gotten used to receiving at least several text messages from her during the day, but not today.

Paxton came back into my office as I was trawling through emails, with a folder in his hands. He dropped it onto my desk. "That's everything for the Bank of West, everything is signed, sealed and delivered, so you can start strategizing security plans." He said looking relieved.

"Great, I'll take it home and look it at it later."

"Just remember you have 30 days from today to have everything in place for the take- over." Before I could answer him my phone buzzed. Looking at the screen, Nick's name came up. Tapping the button, I brought it up to my ear ."Yes Nick"

"Err, we have a problem Mr. King" his tone made feel uneasy.

"What kind of problem?"

"It's Ms. Tyler... I lost her."

Standing up, I yelled into the phone ."What do you mean you lost her."

"I don't know, I took her to buy some groceries, she went in the store but never came out. I've been through the whole place Mr. King and she is no- where." Rubbing my hand down my face I could feel the anger starting to fill my veins and before it got to my mouth, I asked "Tell me Nick, why the fuck was she in the store by herself while you're outside, when I specifically told you to be her god damn shadow?" My last few words came out in a harsh angry yell.

"I'm sorry Mr. King, but she always tells me to wait outside."

"She isn't paying your salary Nick, I am, and you were supposed to stick to her like glue...FUCK! Just text me the address where you are and stay there. I'm on my way." Disconnecting the call, I shoved the phone into my pocket and looked up to a worried looking Paxton.

"What?" he demanded.

"Casey's missing, I have to go." Grabbing my car keys.

"I'm coming," he said following me to the door.

"No, stay here and pull some of the guys in to assist. I'll text you where I am when I get there I have a tracker on her phone, so go down to the surveillance room and see if you can find it" I said, jotting down the number of the phone and handing it to him then heading for the door.

"Done, just go find her Nate," Paxton said. I gave him a quick nod and headed down to the garage.

Once Nick had sent me the address, I was there within a few minutes. We scanned the area again and went back through the grocery store, talking to the manager. He showed me to the two exit doors at the back of the store and Nick and I went over the area looking for something, anything. At the back of the store was an alley coming in from the main road. I'm guessing this is where the delivery trucks come in to drop off stock. Walking up the alley, scanning, I scanned every crack and fracture in the road and there at the end of the alley laying near the side of the wall was a small black hair tie. Picking it up, it had a single strand of blonde hair entwined in it. Quickly turning back towards Nick, I said "She came up this way." Jogging back to the store, the manager I had spoken with was standing next to a short older woman wearing the Safeway uniform. The manager gestured towards her. "This is Louise, she works out the back here, she said she saw a man taking a woman out the back." Calming my breathing, I asked Louise, "Did you see what they looked like?"

"Yes sir, the woman was a slim, blonde woman."

"And the man that she was with?" I asked her hastily.

"He was a big white guy with a bald head." She said holding up her hand to indicate that he was about 6 foot in height.

"Do you remember what he was wearing Louise?"

"Yes sir, he just had a black t-shirt and black pants. I saw them coming through the back here," she pointed to the door that lead from the front of the store into the back area. "I said to him, hey you can't come through this way, but he told me to shut my mouth. I was going to give him an ear full but the woman, she gave me a look that said don't mess with this guy, so I figured I'd just let them go about their business."

"Did the woman say anything?"

"She looked too scared to say anything, he had her pulled into him close like he was forcing her to walk the same way."

"That's great Louise, did you see which way they went?"

"No sir, I only saw them leave through this door and down the alley."

"That's great, thank you for your help".

Heading back towards the car, my phone buzzed. Answering it I said, "Paxton, tell me you have something?"

"Ok, well the tracker shows her leaving the back of the Safeway, down the alley and left on to 14th Avenue then down to Johnston Street, where the signal was lost."

"What?"

"I know, I've notified the local police and I pulled in some of our own guys. They're down there now going over everything. Oh! And Jackson's heading your way. He's bringing a detailed map of the area." Closing my eyes and taking in a deep breath, I had to keep a lid on the rage that was coursing through every inch of my body, I needed to channel it into finding Casey, instead of thinking about what I was going to do with the mother fucker who was behind this. Paxton's voice broke into my thoughts.

"Nate?"

"Yeah I'm still here." I answered.

"We'll find her, Ok?"

"Just keep me posted. I want to know as soon as anyone knows anything and I want to know when the tracker on her phone comes back on."

"Absolutely, now go do what you're good at and find her".

Minutes turned into hours. We went over every inch of ground, following the different paths that we thought she may have been taken, figuring she was on foot then changing tactics for if she was taken by vehicle. The local cops had road blocks checking cars and trucks, but nothing, it was like looking for a needle in a hay stack, with the small amount of information we had. I hung on to hope that Casey still had her phone and she would turn it on again, if she could... "Fuck" I cursed, sitting down on a bench. I took out my phone and pressed her number for the hundredth time tonight, only to get her message bank service. Putting my head into my hands and rubbing my face. "Where the hell are you?" I asked into the darkness of the night.

"That's exactly what I want to know too," a gruff voice answered. Looking up, I see Jax amble up and sit next to me on the bench.

"How the fuck did this happen?" his voice was low and tinged with irritation.

"Someone grabbed her at the grocery store" I said.

"She was supposed to have someone with her 24/7 Nate."

"She had Nick with her."

"And he didn't see it coming?" he almost spat the words out.

"No, he said she made him wait outside." I said.

"What the fuck? And he listened to her? What the fuck is wrong with him?"

Nodding in agreement, I said through gritted teeth."That's what I want to know." Jax stood up shoving his hands into the front of his jeans.

"You know if something happens to her this whole thing was for nothing, right?" he said, arms out stretched. Standing up to face him, my rage now coming to the surface again, I got in his face.

"You don't think I know that you asshole? Nick fucked up but I'll deal with him later, right now Casey is more important."

"If anything happens to her..." I cut him off in mid-sentence.

"Don't even think about any other alternative but finding her" I said through gritted teeth. Jax blew out a breath and my phone buzzed in my pocket. Pulling it out I saw Paxton's name on the screen, shoving it against my ear and answering "Paxton, tell me you have something."

"Phone came back on about 3 minutes ago, tracker is showing it's at Oaks Amusement Park."

"Got it, we're on our way".

Chapter thirty-one

C asey

Why I had convinced Nick to wait outside the store while I ran in and grabbed a few things was beyond me. How could I have been so stupid? *Because this whole situation is beyond believable, that's why, this stuff only happens in the movies not in real life. That's it, I must have fallen asleep while watching a movie, but that doesn't explain the wetness soaking through my jeans right now or the stinging of the graze on my cheek, or the burning sensation in my lungs either.*

Images flicked back and forth through my mind, making a story board. Nick looking pissed as I left him leaning against the SUV, grabbing a basket instead of a cart at the entrance, placing some bananas and apples in the basket, reaching up onto a shelf for a jar of honey, turning and running into a brick wall of a man, his arm wrapping around my waist, his fingers pinching hard into my skin. Something hard pressed into my ribs, then he leaned down and in a low voice said "I have a gun, put the basket on the floor and come with me, make a scene and I will shoot anyone in here who gets in my way, you got that?" I tried to speak but the words were stuck in my throat somewhere so I just nodded and placed the basket down onto the floor. "Give me your phone.

"What?" I stammered out.

"Your phone, now" he growled. Reaching into the pocket of my jeans and pulling out my phone, I slapped it into his hand. He

232

flicked off the power switch on the side and shoved it into his own pocket, walking briskly towards the back of the store and through an opening that read STAFF ONLY across the top of it. Confronted by an older woman, I tried to warn her with a look that this was not someone to be starting an argument with. Once we hit the alley I dragged my feet on account of this guy being so big, he had a lot of weight behind him and he was using it to force me to walk forward at a fast pace.

When we got to the end of the alley he stopped, breathing hard and looking around, he let out a curse, the gun that he was pressing into my side moved and he shoved it behind his back and into his pants, then he pulled out a phone and pressed a number. "Where the fuck are you? Well hurry up." He grumbled into the phone. This was my chance, he had to put the gun away because he couldn't hold it and me and use the phone to find out why his ride wasn't were it was supposed to be. Pulling all my strength together, I struggled to break his hold from my wrist. His grip was like steel. He pushed me against the wall, my cheek scrapping against the brick, but I struggled and turned to face him. Bringing up my knee I thrust it forward with every bit of energy I had, and I swear I heard his balls make a cracking sound as my knee made contact. Letting go of my wrist, he bent over clutching his junk, moaning. I gave him one big shove and he toppled over onto the floor. Reaching down and shoving my hand into his pocket, I grabbed my phone and I ran. I had no idea where I was going, I only knew I had to get as far away as possible from him before he got up.

Staying out in the main streets, I ran up one street to another taking turns and side streets, my mind was coursing with fear and my body with adrenalin. I had no idea what I was doing, the only thing going through my mind was to get somewhere safe. The sun was starting to go down, it would be dark soon. Running into a small park, I saw what looked like amusement rides. Looking around I couldn't see anyone and everything was in darkness, slipping through the gate I jogged over towards a small white building, pushing through the door and collapsing onto the concrete floor I pulled myself into a corner. The floor was wet and cold and there was a stench of urine in the air that made me heave as I tried to gulp air into my burning lungs. I felt like I had been hit by a freight train full of emotions and it had just smashed into my body, exhaustion, terror and trepidation flooded through me and it's so dark in here, so fucking dark. Wiping the damp hair off my face, I rubbed my eyes trying to clean the sweat out of them so I could focus. After a few moments my eyes adjusted to the darkness and I took in where I was, with two doors and a sink in the corner, I had come into a public bathroom.

Standing up I turned the water on in the sink and scooped some into my hands bringing it up to my mouth and greedily drinking, then I splashed some onto my face. The sting of cold water hitting my skin helped me to sober to my situation and clear my fogginess of anxiety. Sliding my hand into my back pocket, I pulled out the phone and turned on the power switch, waiting for it to boot up and give me just a glimmer of the light that I was so desperately craving right now. Flipping to the contacts, I pressed Nate's number, ringing twice he answered "Casey?"

"Nate" I breathed out in relief.

"Are you ok?" his voice was full of concern and haste.

"Yes…I'm in some kind of amusement park, but it's dark" I told him.

"Hold tight baby we're on our way, just stay with me on the phone ok?" I moved into the corner again and crouched down.

"I'm sorry….I was so, so stupid" I sobbed.

"Shhh," he soothed, "It's ok, it's not your fault."

"I should have listened, but this is just so…crazy."

"I know baby, I know." The soothing sound of his voice brought some warmth into my body.

"I see lights Nate" panic riddles my words.

"It's ok that's me and Jax pulling up out the front, just stay where you are and we'll come to you ok?"

"Yes...ok"

Hearing the slamming of car doors and the crunch of boots on the gravel brought me some relief but when the door pushed open and I heard his voice, I felt my fear deflate like a balloon. "Casey." Nate's voice was low and calming as he came over to where I was crouching in the corner. Bending down and placing one strong arm around my waist and hooking the other arm under my knees he scooped me up into his arms and against his body. I wrapped my arms around his neck and burrowed my face into his shoulder. He carried me back to the car with ease and soothing words. Once we were back at the car, I felt the warmth of a blanket being wrapped around me, and I heard Jax say, "Thank fucking Christ." A door opened and Nate bent and slid into the back seat with me still in his arms, adjusting me and the blanket on his knees.

With the cars movement I pressed in harder to Nate's hard chest. I could feel his heart beating against my cheek, his warmth calming as he pressed a kiss to the top of my head. When the car stopped he got out with me still in his arms, his astonishing strength never wavering. Keeping my eyes tightly closed, I felt the ascending of the elevator, then out and up the stairs into the bathroom. Letting my legs slide down to a standing position, holding onto my arms until he was sure I had my balance, he turned the water on in the bathtub and steam started to fill the room. Turning to me and without saying a word, he peeled off my clothes, piece by piece, and while he held my hand he motioned for me to step into the steamy water, sliding into the warmth and comfort that made me shiver. Sitting on the side of the bathtub he picked up a washcloth, dipped it into the water and brought it up to my sore cheek, gently pressing it against the raw skin. "I just want to clean the dirt out of it ok?" Nodding I let him take care of me, watching as he rubbed soap on the washcloth and this time ran it over my arms, pausing and cursing under his breath when he saw the dark finger mark bruises on my wrists and arms. His eyes flickered back and forth from my skin to my eyes, a mixture of emotions so pure and raw that I had to look away.

"I'll go down and make you something to eat, you must be starving?" he said in a low voice, I gave him a nod. "Will you be ok on your own?" Another nod of my head and he stood and left me to wash my hair and let the warmth of the water seep through my skin and slowly bring my body back to life.

After drying myself off, I looked in the mirror at the deep red scrape on my cheek, and winced. Wrapping myself in a bath robe I headed for the stairs to the low sound of voices. Nate, Paxton and Jax were deep in conversation and as I hit the bottom stair they all stopped and turned to look at me. Nate walked over, took my hand, and led me to sit on the couch. On the table in front of me was a steaming hot mug of coffee and a plate with a sandwich on it. "Eat something baby," Nate soothed. Picking up the sandwich and taking a bite of it, I swear it was the best thing I have ever tasted, and when it hit the pit of my empty stomach, it agreed.

They all stood and watched me first eat the sandwich, then take a mouthful of coffee "Guys please sit down. You're making me feel really uncomfortable here." I said looking up at them. Nate took a seat on the couch next to me, Paxton sat on the couch across from us and Jax just stood with his hands shoved into his pockets. "I think you should go to the hospital and get checked out," Nate said.

"I'm ok apart from what you've already seen" I said gesturing to my cheek.

"He's right, better to be safe than sorry," Jax said.

"I'm fine. I would know if I needed any medical treatment because us doctors kind of know these things," I said, with a slight grin trying to make a joke and lighten the mood in the room, but looking at the serious looks on their faces they were not amused. "Look, I'm sorry I convinced Nick to wait outside. It was stupid and I'm sorry for causing so much trouble and wasting your time."

"Stop" Nate ordered. " Yes, what you did was foolish and reckless, but don't ever think that you're trouble or a waste of time. We were all worried and frantic. I've had almost every person and cop out looking for you and before you think it, not because you're a client, but because we care about you." Looking up and taking in the somber looks on all three of their faces, I let out a sigh.

"I'm sorry, it was my own fault."

"I think we need to share some of the blame as well," Jax said. "I think we thought after Nate's visit to Peterson the threat of anything happening was significantly lower than what it was."

"Looks like he'll be getting another visit very soon," Nate said tipping his chin at Jax.

"But do we know if it had anything to do with him?" I ask, and Jax shakes his head, "Not a hundred percent but I wouldn't put anything past him".

Nate looked at Jax then turned his gaze to me "Are you ready to go through what happened?" I nod and sink back into the couch, then starting at the beginning I go through everything that had happened pausing here and there trying to recall all the details that I could. "Yep I'd say that's Peterson, he's the only asshole that would pull such a second class shoddy stunt" Jax drawled, standing Nate ran his hand over his face, then he turned to Paxton.

"I need you to take Casey to the beach house Ok?"

"Sure thing" Paxton nodded. Nate then turned to me "We need to get you dressed and pack you a bag for a few days ok?"

"Err, no it's not okay" I said jumping up from where I was sitting.

"Doc" Nate started but I cut him off.

"No Nate I'm staying right here" now standing in front of me he ran his hands calmly up and down my arms.

"Babe, don't fight me on this, I need you to go with Paxton just for a few days, I want to be able to sort this out and know that you're safe."

"Look, I would rather stay here and take my chances than drag this shit down to Paxton's beach house and put his pregnant wife in any danger, I will not do that to either of them."

Paxton jolted up from his seat "Casey, he's right the beach house is safe and secluded and it's fitted with one of the best high tech security systems, plus I'll take a couple of our own guys down there."

"Paxton no, Lynda doesn't need this type of stress at this stage of her pregnancy" I argued.

"Casey she will be more stressed by you being here I promise you, I wouldn't take any unnecessary risks with the safety of my wife and baby" sitting back down on the couch I dropped my head into my hands this all felt so wrong and so surreal, what I really wanted to do was get into bed and sleep then wake up to find out this was all a bad dream, but looking up and seeing the look on all three faces of these intelligent, strong men and the potent over powering testosterone in the air, it brought me back to reality, standing I threw my hands up in defeat "Fine, you win" I said heading up the stairs to my room.

Dressing in a pair of jeans, a tank and pulling on an over sized sweat shirt of Nate's that I had borrowed out of his wardrobe one night I slipped into my sneakers and hastily shoved some clothes and toiletries into my back pack, picking up my IPod and phone on the way down stairs "Ok, let's go" I called out. Nate walked across the room until he stood right in front of me "Paxton will take you to the beach house and I'll follow you there in a couple of hours ok?" giving him a slanted look I asked "Why?"

"Jax and I have some business to take care of first" Looking between Nate and Jax I watched as they gave each other a knowing look then looked away from each other. "You're going to see Peterson aren't you?" neither one of them answered me Nate just placed his hands on my shoulders and kissed the top of my head "Go with Paxton I'll be right behind you" looking up at his face those gray eyes of his searched mine and I saw unease, I also saw a restrained fury.

"Nate, please" I pleaded.

"Everything will be fine, I promise" he lightly brushed his lips over mine and the next minute Paxton and I were standing in the elevator heading down to the garage.

Chapter thirty-two

Nate

Pacing back and forth in front of Jax, I was relieved that Casey had actually done what I had asked without too much argument and gone to the beach house with Paxton, I knew she would be protected there and after the events of the day, the ocean brought her so much calmness and comfort and I needed for her to feel safe, my thoughts were interrupted by Jax. "Geez man stand still your making me feel tired here just watching you" stopping and rubbing my hand along the back of my neck I looked at him.

"I think better when I pace."

"There's nothing much to think about, let's just pay the bastard a visit and knock him the fuck out!"

"Ahh, if only it was that easy" I laughed, then I remembered the file that Paxton had left me a few days ago the one with all the information on Peterson that he'd compiled, walking to my office I retrieved it from the bottom draw and opened it up, pulling up my chair I pulled out the many pages and started to read, Jax came in a few minutes later with a couple of tumblers and a bottle of single malt, pouring us both a drink he handed me a glass "What's all this?" he motioned to the papers spread out over the desk.

"This my friend is insurance."

"Insurance?" he asked quirking his brow.

"Yep, this insures that after we knock him the fuck out we have enough here to keep him out."

"Really?" Jax sat and took a sip from his glass, picking up one of the sheets of paper I watched as he started to read.

After about an hour of reading through the file that was full of not only papers but photo's and numerous flash drives, Jax spoke. "Damn Nate that brother of yours is one smart cookie" he said with amazement.

"Don't I know it" I nodded.

"Well let's get this over with, you got his home address?" Jax asked nonchalantly. "Sure do" picking up the file, I pushed the flash drives into the top draw of my desk and exchanged them for a couple of random ones there was no way I was taking the originals with me, grabbing my keys and phone we headed down to the garage. Climbing into the SUV and throwing it into gear we pulled out into the traffic and headed for Petersons home, intent on putting an end to this tonight.

Pulling up outside the gated address Jax jumped out and plugged a decoder box into the electronic gate release, pressing a few buttons the gate opened and he hopped back in the truck "Well that was a piece of shit lock" he laughed and I continued to drive up the gravel path and parked in front of a large Spanish style house "I can see the asshole does well from his ill gotten gains" Jax said.

"Isn't that always the way? " I said with a raised eyebrow, pressing the door bell, after a few minutes the door opened and there he was, Peterson dressed in a pair of casual shorts and a polo shirt his smile dropped the instant he saw us and he backed away when both Jax and I stepped through into the entry.

"Nate, Jax what are you doing here? How did you get my address?" he stuttered nervously.

"I think you know the answer to that question yourself" Jax drawled, moving fast within an instant I had Peterson pinned against the mirror in the hallway pressing my forearm into his throat "What are you doing?" he asked in a choked voice, getting in real close to his face I lower my voice to a low growl.

"I warned you to leave Casey Tyler alone, but you didn't listen did you?" trying to break from my hold his arms flailing around he squeaked "I'm sorry, please I can't breathe."

"What a shame" I toyed.

"Please, let me explain" he pleaded.

"Give him a little air Nate I really want to hear this" Jax said, releasing the pressure just enough for him to clear his throat and get more air into his lungs. "Talk" I barked into his face.

"I had a guy watching her weeks ago but after our chat I tried to call him off but I haven't been able to get a hold of him."

"Bullshit" I spat.

"Honestly, I swear."

"So let me get this straight you hired someone to grab her but didn't have a correct contact number for him?" I almost laughed in the dumb shits face.

Nodding he said "I know right? He must have had a burner phone or changed his number, honestly Nate that's the truth" releasing my arm from his throat Jax handed him the copy of the file that we had brought with us.

"What's this?" Peterson asked nervously as he reluctantly took the file.

"This is a copy of every scam and every deal you ever been a part of for at least the last ten years" I said pulling out the fake flash drives from my pocket and waving them in his face "This is over Peterson, I have enough here to bury you with for a long time" Petersons eyes flittered between the flash drives in my hand then back to my face, "So for the second time and the last time, if I see or even smell you in a ten mile radius of Casey Tyler or King security I will start digging that grave and put you in it myself do-you-hear-me?" punctuating the last four words slowly for him to understand he said.

"Ok, ok I got it" he stuttered out and with the look of terror that had imprinted itself on his face, and the wet spot on the crotch of his shorts, somehow I believed he did.

On the drive over to the beach house I couldn't stop thinking about the look on Casey's face when we found her, crouched in the corner of that stinking filth pit of a public bathroom, dirty, wet and shivering from the cold she looked like a frightened rabbit, the last thing I want her to do is pull down her shutter's again it's taken so long just to get my foot under them and the shit that went down today would be enough for her to close up completely.

Just the thought of her being hurt or frightened makes my stomach churn, from the minute I saw her I had the need to engulf her in my protection and keep her all to myself, she's such a contradiction on one hand she's a spit fire and guarded and on the other hand she's innocent and terrified of the world and everyone in it, she has me mystified, yet enamored and captivated all at the same time.

Pulling up at the front of the beach house just after midnight the house was in darkness so I let myself in with my own key, going inside I notice that the kitchen light is on, walking into the kitchen Paxton is sitting at the table, standing when I enter the room "Where's Casey?" I ask him.

"She's asleep in the guest room"

"Is she ok?"

"Yeah, Lynda fed her a glass of brandy and they talked until the alcohol hit her, she couldn't keep her eyes open" Paxton smiled.

"Good thing she's a light weight with alcohol then, I guess it came in handy" I gave Paxton a knowing grin and sat down at the table.

"So how did it go?" he asked.

"Well considering I wanted to snap his neck in two I think he might have got the message this time loud and clear, he had some excuse that the guy he hired to grab the doc changed his cell number or some shit, and he couldn't get in contact with him to call everything off."

"Do you believe him" Paxton asked rubbing at his chin.

"I think he is such an incompetent ass that it's possible but when I produced your little blackmail file on all his so called business deals, well let's just say he lost quite a bit of color from his face...not to mention control of his bladder" Paxton's mouth twitched at the corner.

"Let's just hope it's enough" he sighed.

"Oh, I think that the dirty file we have on him and the threat of having every bone in his body broken should seal the deal" Paxton let out a low laugh as he got up from the table and gave me a nod.

"Well I'm going to hit the sack, I couldn't even think of sleep until you got here" "Yeah go sleep, I think I might crash in the spare room I don't want to wake Casey up I want her to get a good night's sleep."

"OK, I'll see you in the morning, night Nate."

"Night Paxton".

Quietly walking up the hall to the spare room I opened the door, it held a single bed and some storage boxes in it, closing the door behind me I went to the huge bay window and opened it letting in the fresh ocean breeze that filtered into the room taking a deep breath I stripped down to my boxers and stretched out on the bed.

Opening my eyes it was still dark but something had woken me glancing down at the illumination of the dial on my watch it was only 3.20am, sitting up on the side of the bed and rubbing my hands over my face I heard a noise, getting up and opening the door I lean against the frame and listen, silence, nothing and then a whimpering, moving down the hall towards the direction it seems to be coming from I find myself standing outside the guest room where Casey is, pressing my ear against the door I hear the sound of sheets rustling then another low painful whimper, slowly opening her door I see her tossing and turning and as I get to the side of the bed she starts to mumble words, leaning down closer to her I try to hear what she's saying. the mumbles start to become clearer until I can pick out words here and there "No, please, it hurts, let me out" her face is as pained as her words and I can't watch her like this, gently stroking her hair away from her face I lean in close to her ear "Casey, Casey wake up baby" still stroking the side of her face with my knuckles I watched as her eyes slowly open, those magnificent eyes that show so much fear and confusion until she realizes it's me touching her and then I see them fill with tenderness and trust "Nate" she says sleepily.

"It's ok baby you were having a bad dream."

"Did I wake you I didn't hear you come back?"

"I was sleeping in the spare room when I heard you" pulling herself up into a sitting position she moves her hands over my chest then up to cup my face.

"What happened? Are you ok?" she asks with concern.

"I'm fine I just didn't want to wake you" letting out a breath then scooting over to the other side of the bed she pulls back the sheet in an invitation for me to join her and I gladly slide in next to her pulling her warm body into mine and breathing her in, this is where I want to be every minute of the day, her warm body in my arms, her soft hair against me and that smell of vanilla from her creamy soft skin permeating my senses, here right now I feel like if I hold her close to me we will eventually melt into each other.

Her fingers stroke across my chest, following the lines of muscle definition and she lifts her head up to look at me "I was worried about you" she whispers.

"No need, everything's good" I said gently guiding her head back against my chest I stroke my hand up and down her back basking in the warmth of her skin, her fingers slowly slide over my chest and around my nipples then down to my stomach muscles and around my belly button , the pads of her fingers are so soft followed by the light scrape of her nails, her fingers follow the line of hair that trails down into my boxer shorts then she moves them underneath the waistband and down the length of my growing shaft, fingers slowly moving all the way down and under my balls until she cups them and strokes the skin until it pulls tight, then her fingers move up and down, stroking, caressing closing my eyes I groan with the pleasure of her touch, reaching back up to the top of the boxers she starts to pull them down my legs and I tilt my hips up to accommodate her action, as she pushes them completely off she slides her body down and settles in between my legs resting her warm cheek against my balls, I can feel the warmth of her breath against my inner thigh and I involuntary shudder at the feel of her between my legs, my shaft starts to throb with anticipation, reaching down my hand I stroke her hair " Babe you don't have to..." I start to say but she cuts me off with a "shhh, I want to" she murmurs thickly and she places small kisses and tiny flicks of her tongue along my length starting at the base and working her way up to the tip, looking down I watch as her tongue licks at the head once then her lips wrap around it and she takes my whole thickness deep into her mouth "Fuck" I breath out, the warmth and silkiness of her tongue moves along my throbbing hardness I am so deep in her mouth when a charged sensation travels from my shaft up my spine like little balls of electricity and back down into my balls, her fingers begin to stroke and massage at the muscles in my thighs that are now so taut and solid from her languid caress, she strokes my shaft up and down with her warm mouth and I can feel myself starting to spiral into ecstasy quicker than I'd like to, sitting up and causing her to release me with a slight popping noise I flip her over onto her knees "I need to be inside you right now" I growl kneeling behind her I move her legs apart with my knee and run a hand down her spine to the middle of her shoulder blades and gently push her torso so it lays flat against the bed and with one swift push I slide deeply into her slickness and start to grind into her in hard, long, deep strokes until I feel her starting to tighten around me, reaching between her legs and pressing my thumb against her swollen nub, she moans and spasms against me, feeling the hotness of her orgasm sets my own off and with one more pump into her I lose myself inside off her body so much I swear I see stars.

Chapter thirty-three

C asey

Waking in the morning and trying to move was impossible, with the huge body of a man wrapped around me from behind. His arm braced around my waist. I lifted the arm and slid into a sitting position on the side of the bed, turning my head to look at his beautiful sleeping face shadowed with a three- day growth of dark hair. He looks exhausted, and I am stung by a guilty pang in my chest, because I know I am the cause of it all. I don't want my complicated life to connect with him, he means too much to me now, he has brought so many new emotions and feelings out in me that I find it confusing and disorientating to even comprehend them.

Forcing my aching leg muscles to stand, I pull on a pair of shorts and a t-shirt and quietly head out onto the back porch and down onto the sandy beach. Walking down to where the ocean is rolling in and up onto the sand, I sit with legs crossed, and watch it's gentle calmness as I drift into my thoughts of Nate and ultimately a decision that needs to be made about the relationship we have fallen into. I know I have fallen in love with him I also know that in the long run I'm no good for him, he deserves more, and I'm not sure if I will ever be able to give that to him. I have tossed my own truths around in my mind many times. I even told Flynn that I needed to tell Nate everything, to which he assured me that decision was mine to make, he wasn't happy about it but I know he will always stick by me whatever happens. I just don't know if Nate would be able to accept and live with my shame, my past, that is my burden to bare, not his.

I got up and walked back to the house. When I heard the stirring of movement coming from it, heading up the back stairs I was greeted at the screen door by Lynda holding two mugs in her hands. Opening the door for her, she handed me a mug. "Tea?," she said, before I even asked.

"Great, thanks I'm over you Americans and your constant need for coffee." I laugh, and we sit down on the out- door sofa. "How are you feeling?" I ask her nodding to her belly.

"I'm good, I have been getting some tightening sensations, but please don't say anything to Paxton or he will have me at the hospital before I can blink."

"Just Braxton Hicks? No pain?" I ask concerned.

"No pain, just little practice contractions," Lynda says with a smile, giving her belly a rub. "Paxton tells me that he doesn't think Peterson will be bothering you anymore," she says with a raised eyebrow, and I nod "So.... That means no more threat for you huh? You must be relieved." I nod again ."So... why the long face?" I take a sip of my tea and take a minute of thought before I answer "No threat means I go home."

"Oh Casey, I never even thought about that, I've got so used to you being here with us, with Nate what are you going to do?"

"Honestly? I'm not sure," I sighed.

"But you and Nate...." She trails off.

"That's why I'm not sure. I mean Nate and I don't have any kind of commitment to each other. We were just two people who were thrown into a difficult situation together and it got out of hand."

"That's a load of crap Casey and you know it. Any idiot can see that you two have feelings for each other."

"I know, I just...it's complicated."

"Everything has a solution Casey, sometimes you just have to look harder to find it," she says looking at me with eyes full of sincerity, and we both fall silent for a few minutes. Then she rubs a hand across my arm and stands, "Just talk to Nate before you decide anything, Ok?" Nodding again I watch her go inside.

Over breakfast I could feel Nate's eyes watching me and every time I looked up at him they seemed to be full with concern, and I'm not sure why, unless I was reading him wrong. What I did know is he wanted me alone, so once breakfast was finished he suggested a walk along the beach. Walking down to the shore line, our feet sinking into the wet sand, the cool water exhilarating at this time in the morning. We hadn't walked far before he took hold of my hand and looked down at me. "Can we sit for a while. I think we may need to talk." The serious look on his face made me feel a little jittery inside. "Sure," I answered and we walked up onto where the sand was dry, and sat down next to each other. After a few moments he turned to face me.

"Did I hurt you last night?" he asked, and I noticed a pained look in his eyes.

"What do you mean," I asked perplexed by his question.

"You know when we..." then it clicked what he was talking about.

"No, it was wonderful." I smiled at him and he blew out a relieved breath.

"I didn't mean to be rough with you, but when you put your mouth on me I lost control just a little," he smiled and held up two of his fingers showing me a gap of about a centimeter in between them, making me grin.

"Yes, I did notice that." Lifting my hand up to his mouth, he pressed a kiss against my fingers.

"So you going to tell me what's on your mind?"

"Lots of things."

"Like?" he asked.

"Like is the threat over now? What happens next? What do I do next?." He looks at me, then glances out towards the ocean.

"I think at this stage Peterson is done. We have too much on him for him to be any kind of threat and now he knows it. As for what happen next, well I think I still want to keep you close for a little while longer just to be on the safe side, and what you do next, I guess that will be your decision to make." His voice trails away with the last few words and I struggle a little with what he just said. I think I expected more resistance or at least more of an argument from him, not just him telling me that it's my decision, is it that easy? Had I seen too much in the intimacy we've been sharing. Maybe it was just as simple as sex between two people. It just didn't make sense though and the thought of leaving him and going home started little ripples of anguish to bubble in my stomach. Taking a deep breath and standing, I brushed the sand off my behind and said, "I guess I should start to think about going home then." Starting to walk away from him, tears pricking in my eyes, he grabbed my arm and spun me around to face him. Looking at me I see his eyes searching mine. "Hey, not yet, please."

"It's my decision you just said."

"Fuck," he spits out and runs a hand through his hair in frustration. "I didn't mean it like it sounded."

"I believe it's called a Freudian slip Mr. King, you know where your true thoughts slip out of your mouth without thinking."

"No, you've got it all wrong."

"Yep, I'm seeing that now," I say and try to walk away from him again, only this time he pulls me back into his arms and holds me tight against his chest.

"Stop, you damn stubborn woman, and listen to me." Closing my eyes, I calm my anger which was starting to bubble, and relax into his embrace. Placing both his hands on either side of my face and tilting it up to look at him, he says " Look, truthfully I never even entertained the thought of a long term relationship with any woman. I've never been the settling down type of person and I still don't know if I am. I'm arrogant, possessive and I can be an ass most of the time, but no-one has ever challenged me the way you do... no-one has ever made me feel the way you do when we're together. You drive me bat shit crazy sometimes but you also make me feel so comfortable and relaxed I can't promise you forever Casey, but I need you in my life. You take my breath away, but you also help me to breath baby, so please can we take it one day at a time and see where it leads us?" The sincerity and pleading in his voice relaxes me more. Smiling, I nod my head, then rest it against his chest, hearing the rhythmic beating of his heart. I feel his mouth kiss the top of my head and breathe into my hair. "I don't know what you've done to me baby, but you have certainly knocked me off balance, and I know you will have to go back home eventually, but let's just have now, okay?" I nod my head again and he takes my hand in his and we continue to walk back down towards the beach house.

That night we sat around the dinner table, enjoying bowls of creamy garlic pasta with fresh crusty bread, and a nice bottle of dry Riesling, while Paxton and Nate shared some of their childhood stories with Lynda and I. The way they both laughed recalling some of the sticky situations they had been caught up in as kids, I'm pretty sure their parents had their hands full. It was nice to see how many memories they shared and I was mesmerized as I watched these two handsome, strong men that had so much love and respect for each other. You could feel the strength of their bond emanating around us.

The next morning we headed back to the Penthouse. It was a quiet drive I looked out the window, taking in the beautiful scenery while Nate drove I guess I was a little lost in my thoughts again, thinking over what he had said to me on the beach the day before and still trying to sort out what is going on between us. I mean logically, I know we have feelings for each other, but I also know Nate's playboy history, never committing to anyone in the past just a gaggle of woman and one night stands. The thought of him being with someone else so intimately now just pisses me off, but that's in the past, and I'm an expert on keeping the past buried, so what he did then is just inconsequential.

But deep in the back of my mind I still have that nagging question that keeps gnawing at me, have I changed him somehow? Have I interrupted his solitary single life? Have I chucked a huge spanner in the works of his comfortable existence? In my heart I want to tell him everything, lay myself bare and take that chance, but my head is warning me that my shameful past may be too much for him to handle, and when he sees the real me, will he realize the mistake he's made?.

Chapter thirty-four

Nate

Silence is all I get from her the whole drive back I want her to talk to me, let me in, but I also know that when she's silent she needs it to try and reset herself, but it still pisses me off, and I try to think back to what I said to her in our conversation on the beach. Only the truth, I told her I had feelings for her. I also told her I can't make her any promises either, is that why she's withdrawn back into her bubble of silence? But shit, I have to be truthful, and I honestly don't know where our relationship stands. I care for her I don't want to let her go, and the thought of her being with anyone else but me, fuck I can't even go there. I feel my grip on the steering wheel tighten and my knuckles turn white. No that's not going to happen, but can I ask her to give up her life, her home for me? And what happens if she does and things don't work out between us. Could I do that to her? Damn, why does this have to be so complicated? My head's now starting to scramble with so many questions I need to shelve my thoughts and concentrate on the road and I need to talk to Paxton, use him as my sounding board, just to try and work out what the fuck is wrong with me.

As soon as the elevator opened, Casey started for the stairs, only stopping to look over her shoulder at me and say, "I'm going to take a shower." Then continuing up the stairs. Dumping my keys on the entrance table I head for my home office to check my emails and any messages that might have come in while we were at the beach house. Sitting back in my chair and idly moving the mouse back and forth, my mind wanders back to the frustration with the woman upstairs who I am imagining is standing in the shower with steaming water cascading over her luscious body, while rubbing shower gel over every curve. It's a constant irritation, just trying to get into her mind. It's like having a watch that has broken into a hundred tiny pieces and I am trying to fit them all back together into a tiny space with a magnifying glass. If I place a cog in the right place everything ticks but if I accidently place it in the wrong place, it upsets the whole balance and I need to pull it all apart and start again. Fuck me.

Then it hits me, we've spent a lot of time together but it's been under pretty difficult circumstances, so maybe I need to roll things back a little and take her out on a real date, so we can get to know each other better as a couple and not so much like a job responsibility surrounded by so much drama. Moving the mouse, I bring up the directory and find the phone number for Higgins Restaurant downtown and make an online booking for two for tonight. Then onto the Indian Head casino for some fun on the tables. Pleased and satisfied that I now have a plan in action for a night of relaxation with my beautiful woman, I push up from my chair and head up to where she is just coming out of the bathroom, a thick black towel wrapped around her body. She rubs her long blonde hair with another towel and I follow her as she walks into the bedroom and grabs a comb from the bedside table before sitting on the edge of the bed. "Everything ok?" she asks, watching me as a slide behind her on the bed, my thighs resting on either side of hers. I reach out taking the comb from her hand and gently start to run it through her hair. "Thank you." "No need for thanks, I love your hair, the color, the feel and the smell drives me crazy." She lets out a chuckle as I inhale that wonderful vanilla scent that she always has. "I have a proposition for you."

"Oh, Really ?" she asks turning her head slightly so she is looking at me.

"Yes, I would like to take you out tonight...on a date."

"A date ?"

"Yes, a date."

Shaking her head, she says, "Nate, it's fine, you have done so much for me and really I can assure you that you don't need to wine and dine me to get laid tonight."

"Ha ha ha that's good to know, but really I want to take you out, tonight, on a real date, just you and me." She looks at me and I can tell with that look on her face that my plan was a good decision, as her beautiful full lips turn into a smile before she says, "I would love to".

When she walks down the stairs later that night dressed in a strapless figure hugging black dress that sits just above her knee's and shows off those long tanned legs in a pair of silver four inch heels, and her long blonde hair that's hanging down her back and moves with every step she takes. I want to take her back up stairs to bed and forget going anywhere, but when she reaches the bottom stair with that beautiful smile showing me just how happy she is right now, I think that dirty thought can wait because I want to take my woman out and show her to the world. "You look stunning," I said, moving into her and pressing a kiss against her neck. "Thank you, you don't look too bad either," she said running her hand beneath my jacket and against my white button down shirt. Taking her hand in mine, we head down to the garage. She starts walking towards the SUV but is stopped when I grip her hand a little tighter. "No baby, not that one tonight, we're taking the Audi 8" I say, pointing to the sleek midnight black sports car. Her eyes open wide as she looks from me to the car and then lets me lead her over and open the door for her.

Dinner consisted of a beautiful juicy rib-eye steak, and I watched every bite she took and every moan she made while chewing it. She caught me staring at her. "Something wrong?" she asked with one eye brow cocked.

"I think we need to order dessert. Sitting here watching your mouth devour and enjoy that steak so much is making me uncomfortable," I said, through narrowed eyes.

"Why?" she asks bewildered.

"Because I have something much better for you to enjoy and it's straining against my zipper right now, I think it might be envious of your steak ." She covered her mouth and let out a giggle.

"Now I know why you haven't been able to sit still, but you know I could fix that," she breathed out sensually.

Now she had my full attention, and with a raised brow I asked, "Really, tell me more."

She slowly ran her tongue over her bottom lip which brought my eyes directly to her mouth, then said, "just stop watching me eat" she grinned.

"Damn woman, I thought you were offering to get on your knees under the table."

"Later" she mouthed giving me a naughty wink, and I was wishing we were back at the Penthouse, NOW.

After our meal, we drove over to the Casino and I watched as her eyes grew wide in awe at all the lights and glitz. The excitement that had flashed across her face was fuelling my own. Placing a hand against her lower back, guiding her into the casino and to the nearest roulette table. Dropping several hundred dollar bills down they were quickly exchanged for chips. Looking down at the chips I had just placed in her hand, then looking back up at me, she stammered "I.. don't know what to do."

"Just place them on random numbers where- ever you want" I said motioning to the table.

"But..."

"No buts, no thinking, just do," I said, placing a kiss on the tip of her nose. She turned to the table and hesitantly started to place her chips down. Signaling for a waitress and ordering us both a drink, I stood back and watched her face change as she watched the croupier roll the ball, and then her smile fade as her chips were taken away. She turned to look at me with pouty lips. Smiling and handing her a glass I say, "It's ok, place some more bets."

"But I'm losing your money" she said taking a sip of the vodka martini, then letting out a hiss. "Wow, that's..strong."

"Enjoy, and place your bets."

Turning, she placed down some more chips and on the next spin the croupier was pushing over her winning chips. "Holy shit we won," she said, her face beaming with elation at me. She looked utterly adorable right now, like a kid in a candy shop. The next time she leaned over the table to place a bet, I noticed the guy next to her lean back and take a good look at her ass. Moving in closer behind her and blocking his view, I turned and gave him a primal look of ownership that seem to make him move pretty quickly to the other side of the table trying to avoid even looking our way. I think I may have made him uncomfortable as I locked my gaze on him for the next few minutes.

After a few more drinks and spins of the wheel, Casey was giddy with excitement at her growing pile of chips and I'm guessing feeling the effects of the vodka martini and the two margarita's she'd consumed. Knowing she was a light weight, when she asked for number four, I lead her away to cash in her chips and we headed back to the car. Before she got in she leaned down and pulled off one of her heels, then the other.

"Sorry my feet are killing me I don't think I'm used to wearing these things for so long."

"Not a problem" I laughed and helped her into the passenger seat of the Audi. Pulling her seat belt over to lock it in place. Sliding into the car myself and starting it up, I slipped it into gear and headed towards the Penthouse. "Thank you so much for tonight I don't think I have ever had so much fun," she said, placing her hand on my thigh.

"You're welcome, it was a good night." Taking my eyes briefly off the road to take a quick look at her leaning back in the seat, she looked so relaxed and content.

"What were those last drinks I had?"

"Margarita's"

"Hmmm I think they are my new favorite drink," she cooed.

"Really? I would have never known that." I smiled to myself at the sound of the slightly inebriated tone in her voice. Taking another look at her face, with her eyes now closed, she stayed like that until I pulled into the garage and shut the engine off.

As soon as I opened the passenger door her eyes flew open, and she took the hand that I offered her, getting out on some- what wobbly legs and leaning into me. "Wow that was fast" she said.

"Come on my little gambler, let's get you upstairs and into bed."

"Hmm I like the sound of that," she breathed into my chest.

Letting out a chuckle at her dirty insinuation, I said, "To sleep."

"Noooo," she moaned. Taking her hand I lead her towards the elevator and press the call button. She looks so beautiful, bare feet, holding her heels and purse in one hand and that wonderful smile of hers. The doors open and I direct her in and swipe my card then pull her against me. "We really have to go to bed...to sleep?" she asks.

"Yes, we do." I feel one of her hands move down the middle of my chest towards the front of my jeans and I place my own hand on hers and move it back up.

"Casey," I warn in a low voice.

"Hmm"

"Not tonight baby you've had just a little too much to drink."

"And?"

"And I'm being a gentleman."

"But I don't want you to be a gentleman, I want you to be wild, rough and dirty," she breathes into my neck. That sends a shiver down my spine, right to my groin, and in a more sober voice she says, "Honestly I'm not drunk just a little merry. The drive back cleared my head." Looking into her eyes and seeing the lust in them was driving me insane. The elevator pings at the Penthouse and the doors open. Taking her hand I lead her to stand at the kitchen island and take off my jacket. Leaning down close to her ear, I whisper, "Don't move." Pulling out my phone I scroll through the music list until I find what I'm looking for. Sitting it on the sound system docking station and cranking the volume up, I press play and the slow thumping beat of the Arctic Monkeys song " Do I wanna know?" fills the air. Walking over to where she's standing at the kitchen island, I move her to face it and press my hand at the middle of her back bending her so that the top half of her body is lying flat against the marble island. Running both hands down the back of her dress until I reach the hem, I slowly pull it up over her ass and leave it bunched up around the top of her waist, and suck in a breath. When I see the black lace panties and the thigh high stockings that she's wearing. Running both my hands over her peach of an ass and the lacy material, then down to the top of the stockings. Slipping a finger under the lacy top of the stocking, I run it around against the warm, soft skin of her legs and she squirms a little. "Stand still," I say in a hard, deep tone.

"Sorry it tickles," she breaths out.

"Shhh," I hush. "No movement, no sound" I say sternly to her, and she acknowledges what I have said with a slight nod of her head. Bending down onto my knees behind her and sliding my fingers around the top of her panties, I take my time slowly sliding them down her legs, tapping her ankles one at a time to lift her feet and slip them off completely. Looking up I am face to face with her beautifully perfect ass I lean in and lean my cheek against the warm skin of it and I hear her breath hitch with the connection. "No sound," I say, giving her a quick slap on her ass cheek, making her jump slightly, then stop as I press small open mouthed kisses over the red mark just starting to appear on her skin, and when I give the skin a slight nip with my teeth, she squirms again, earning her another smack to the other cheek. When she stills again I continue to kiss, nip and bite at the red tainted skin, sliding my hand down between her legs and pushing them apart. I run my fingers over her sex, it's so fucking wet that she has just given me the answer that I was seeking, she likes this...a lot.

Sliding a finger through her slickness, I hear the slight change in her breathing. Bending down behind her, I gently open her slick naked folds and run my tongue over her wetness and I feel her moan vibrate through her body. Her juice is so sweet and addictive that I need more of it and just like I am intending on eating a peach, I open my mouth over her sex and gorge on her sensitive flesh, running my tongue back and forth over her swollen nub until I am satiated. Standing up behind her, because frankly I am torturing myself much more than I am her, and if I don't release my dick from my pants I am pretty sure I am going to do myself some damage. Undoing the zipper and releasing my erection letting it slap against her ass. I bend into her so it's sitting against the warm skin of her lower back and slip my hands underneath to where the top of her strapless dress begins and pull it down, along with her bra, then I fill my hands with her breasts, feeling the smoothness of them first then pinching those hard erect nipples between my finger and thumb. She lets out a low moan in her throat. Moving a hand up to where her long hair is spread over the marble bench, I move it away from her neck, clearing a path for my lips, kissing and licking little swirls from her shoulder up her neck, then biting and sucking just below her ear, while rubbing myself against her. Fuck, she feels amazing. When I suck on the lobe of her ear I whisper to her "Tell me what you want?" She moans out "You, inside of me." Breathing heavier into her ear, I say "ask me."

"Please, Nate now" she whimpers.

"Tell me, what you want me to do to you?" I growl and her hips grind back into me and she turns her head slightly to look at me and breathes. "I want you to fuck me.... Hard" and with those words I was done. I scooped up her hair in one hand wrapping it's blonde silkiness around my fist and gently pull it until her head tilts back. At the same time I enter her with one quick, deep thrust that makes her jolt against the kitchen island with a loud moan.

Steadying myself and taking a deep breath just for a moment while I feel her tight inner muscles constrict and adjust, I start to move, slow, deep and hard to start with and it doesn't take long for my rhythm to change into fast, deep and hard. The louder her moans and breathing gets, the harder I fuck into her body to the beat of the music and damn, she's meeting my every thrust. Leaning down I bite into the skin of her neck again, not too hard but just enough to feel her tighten around me. Her breathing now turning into a mixture of pants and moans ." Do you need to come baby ?" I growl into her ear.

"Yes," she answers, between breaths.

"Then come for me baby." With those few words I feel her clamp down onto my shaft and let out a compilation of expletives and moans as her muscles spasm and squeeze around me. The sound of her orgasm and her still writhing against me sends me into a spine-tingling frenzy, and I find my own climax soaring and with one last thrust, I bury myself to the hilt and loose myself inside of her, with my own loud moan and a completely drained, "Sweet, Fucking, Jesus".

We stayed exactly where we were for some time, with me leaning against her back and bracing my hands on the kitchen island from behind her to take most of the weight from my spent body, until our panting breaths and heaving bodies calm and become sated. Gently pulling myself out of her and tucking myself back into my pants, I place my hands on her shoulders and guide her to stand. When I turn her around to face me, her eyes meet mine and I see so much in those beautiful hooded blue eyes; trust, contentment, and a sweet serenity. Pulling her into my chest with one hand and holding the back of her head with my other hand, my mouth takes hers with the hunger of a starving man. Her tongue dances against mine. Sliding both of my hands up to her face and cradling it between my palms, I pull my mouth away from hers and her eyes move up and search mine.

"You, consume me," I whisper against her mouth. "You are mine and I never want to be without you." I never thought I would ever hear myself say anything like that to anyone but with her, it's a want; a need, a necessity. I see the small curve of her lips as she whispers back " and I don't want to be without you." Picking her up into my arms, I take her upstairs and to my bed.

Chapter thirty-five

C asey

Laying on my side and looking at the magnificent man lying next to me, I let my eyes roam over his perfect body from his muscled biceps and pecks down to his wash board abs. With the sheet pulled up to his waist I can see the dark line of hair running from his belly button and disappearing under the sheet. My gaze wanders up to his beautiful face and tousled black hair, and I watch his stomach rise and fall as he sleeps. I don't think he will ever understand how much he has given me, this man who has protected me from the very first time we set eyes on each other. This same man, whom from that first meeting I saw as an arrogant, egotistical cave man, has become the man that has pushed his way into my heart and soul and somehow has made me fall in love with him and has, unbeknown to him, started to free me from the horrors of my past and brought me back into the world of living. I need to give back to him with all my truths. We've come so far together, and I don't want to keep anything from him at all. I want to lay it all on the line between us and hope that the feelings he declared for me tonight will be enough for him to forgive me, and look past my shame and see the person he has helped to set free.

Rolling over in the bed I moved my hand over the empty cold space next to me. Lifting my head and squinting at the clock it was 9.20 am and I dropped my head back on the pillow with a groan. No wonder the bed was empty, Nate would have gone into work. He is always up at the crack of dawn I just keep using the old excuse of me not being used to the whole different side of the world time zones thing. It did work for a while but I'm pretty sure Nate knows it's a bullshit excuse now, he just lets me get away with it for the moment. Eventually pulling myself from the comfort of the bed, I shower, pull on a sundress and go down to the kitchen and pour myself a glass of water. Seeing a note on the bench, I pick it up to read as I pull myself onto a stool to read the words on the sheet of paper. *Hey Doc, Last night was incredible and I hope it wasn't too much too soon for you. I didn't want to wake you but I will confess I did enjoy watching you sleep for quite some time this morning. I have a heavy day today but come down to my office around 1pm so I can take you out to lunch. Nate.* Dropping the paper on the bench, I chuckle at the sweetness of his note and a plan starts to hatch in my brain about his lunch date.

After being on my knees for around twenty minutes with half of my body inside the bottom cupboards in Nate's kitchen, I finally found what I was looking for a square bread basket big enough to fit in all the other goodies I had found in the kitchen. A small French loaf of bread that I found in the freezer and only had to put into the oven for a few minutes to warm and crisp up. In the refrigerator I found a few different cheeses and olives, a container with chopped up tomatoes, basil and garlic, and some mixed berries, that I put in a sealed container. Pulling a couple of towels from the drawer I lined the basket with one, arranged the food inside, then covered it with the other. Picking up the basket I was just about to head down to Nate's office when my phone started to ring. Holding the basket in one hand and answering the phone with the other, I see Flynn's name appear on the screen. "Hey Flynn how are you?"

"I'm good but you...you sound fantastic babe." He said and I knew from the tone of his voice, he was smiling on the other end of the phone.

"Thanks I feel fantastic."

"It sounds good on you as well. Listen, I just wanted to give you a quick call to say hello and touch base, so I take it everything is good?" he asked.

"Yes, it is, I feel like a new person Flynn," I say, and I hear him sigh down the phone. "I feel like I've been locked in a dark room for the past twelve years and someone just unlocked the door and let it swing wide open."

"I take it the man with the key here is Nate, right?"

With a smile, I give him a breathy answer, "Yes." There's about a twenty second pause on the line when I say, "Flynn I'm going to tell Nate. I want him to know everything, I trust him... I'm in love with him Flynn and ...I think he feels the same way."

"Wow babe, I'm really happy for you...you know that right? I just want you to make sure you know what you're doing, I mean how do you think he'll react to everything ?" he said with concern.

Blowing out the breath I just realized I had been holding in, I said, "I don't know Flynn, I just know it's something I have to do. I have to rip that open door of its hinges and take a chance."

He's quiet for a moment, then I can clearly see the huge grin on his face when he says, " I love you babe, you go for it..You know I will always be here to catch you if you fall."

"I know, and I love you for it".

After I'd ended the call with Flynn, I stepped into the elevator and pressed the button for Nate's office floor. I walked to his door looking around. There was no secretary at the desk, so I knocked on the door and hear Nate's voice telling me to come in. Pushing the door open, I see him sitting behind his huge desk dressed in his usual casual style of jeans and a black silk button down dress shirt. He looks so handsome and sexy leaning back in his chair talking into the phone he has pressed against his ear. I place the basket on his desk and he motions for me to come closer to him. Rounding the desk he turns his chair and pats his lap for me to sit and with a brief look up to his face, I see he's serious, so I sit across his lap and he finishes his call, dropping the phone onto the desk he wraps those thick strong arms around me. Burying his head into my neck and placing a warm kiss against my skin. "So what's in the basket?" he speaks low into my neck.

"I brought you lunch. Think of it as a picnic in your office."

"Mmm, I think I already have something tasty to eat for my lunch right here," he says, kissing the skin just below my ear.

"Now, now Mr. King keep it in your pants until later," I say and swing my legs to stand. I take the food from the basket, spreading it on his desk on a towel in front of him, then I sit back down on his lap taking with me the open container of mixed berries. Pulling out a strawberry, I touch it to his lips and when he opens his mouth I place it on his tongue. I follow that with a dark plump cherry.

"So let me get this straight, I have a sexy woman sitting on my lap hand feeding me berries and you expect me to not get wood, right?"

"Too late for that," I say with a chuckle, moving my ass against the growing bulge under me.

"You're testing me Doc," Nate says in a low growl.

"Always." I give him a wink and break a piece of the French loaf off, heaping it with the tomato and garlic mix, and hand it to him, then make one for myself.

Leaning back in his chair while I packed the now empty containers back into the basket he said, "That was the best lunch I have had for a long time. Thanks baby" "You're welcome." Standing up, he lifts me into his arms and carries me towards the leather couch that sits in his office.

"What are you doing?" I squeal.

"Having dessert." He grins wickedly.

"Umm, we had mixed berries remember?"

"Hmm, now I want your berries." He lays back onto the couch and pulls me to lay on top of him.

"Nate, we're in your office." I whisper.

"I know, don't worry, I plan on having your berry later in bed, I just want to lay here with you for a while ok?." He rubs a hand up and down my back and places a kiss on the top of my head. "Perfectly fine with me".

We lay there for a while just basking in the intimacy of the closeness, with gentle fingers stroking each other. It was a calming end to a nice lunch. The silence was eventually broken by Nate's low voice, "I could get used to this every day you know?"

"Hmm, me too." I breathe into his warm chest.

"So why don't we make this a permanent thing?" he said, bringing my hand up to his mouth and gently kissing my fingers. Lifting my head to look up at him I said "What?....You and me... a permanent relationship? But on the beach you said..."

I started the sentence but he cut me off. "I know, but I also know that I can't let you go, and I'll probably make a shit load off mistakes but I need you, here, with me." I lay my head back down on his chest, taking in the enormity of what he was asking, and the realization that if I wanted it too, then I would have to tell him everything. "Your silence is not reassuring me, Doc."

"Sorry I guess you caught me off guard."

"So what are you thinking ?"

"I'm thinking it might not be as easy as it sounds, you know, applying for an extension on my visa, a green card so I can work."

"That's why I have a great lawyer to take care of things like that and really babe you don't need to work." He starts but I stop him.

"Don't even go there Nate, I will never be a kept woman."

"A kept woman." he laughs, "No I can never imagine that of my tough Aussie girl."

"Nate?"

"Hmmm."

"We do need to talk about a few things... important things."

"Like what baby?" Inhaling a deep breath and letting it out and thinking this is it, it's now or never, but before I could get the first word out Nate's office door flung open with such force it sounded like it had just been ripped from its hinges. The loud bang made us both jump and sit up, with Nate going into instant protection mode pulling me tighter into his chest. "What the fuck," Nate bellowed, then we both looked into the red faced look of horror on Paxton's face.

"Its Lynda, she just rang, she said her water broke," he said, shoving a hand through his already ruffled hair.

Nate moved me to his side and stood up. Walking to his desk and opening a drawer, he pulled out some keys. "Come on, we'll take the Audi its faster." Paxton looked flustered and confused.

"It's ok I can drive" he said to Nate.

"Not in your condition. Come on little brother, let's go get your wife, you're about to become a father." I watched as the blood drained from Paxton's face, he went as white as a ghost and fell down into one of the chairs. Getting up and going to him, I put my hand on the back of his head and guided it down between his knees. "Just keep your head down there for a few minutes and take some nice slow breaths," I told him. After a few minutes his head came back up, now with some color. "Holly shit, what am I doing?" Paxton said in frustration.

"You're just panicking a little it's ok, just calm down," I soothed him.

"Casey, you need to come, I would feel one hundred percent better with a doctor riding with us." Looking up at Nate, he gave me a quick nod of his head.

"Sure, we'll take the SUV instead" he said opening a draw and swapping keys. As we drove towards the beach house Paxton had Lynda on speaker phone and she sounded pretty calm. It was Paxton who was having a hard time keeping his cool and I kept on giving him a reminder rub on his shoulder, and when Lynda said that she wanted to take a shower before we got there, Paxton did lose his shit. "NO, no shower honey, you might slip."

Lynda's voice came through the line calm and together, "Babe I have never slipped in the shower before, I'm pretty sure I can handle it ok?"

"NO it's not ok, hell Lynda this is not a time to think about preening yourself. Please just sit and wait, we'll be there in about ten minutes." Hearing Lynda blow out air in frustration with her husband, I had to grin when she said, "fine I'll wait." "Thank you," he said sounding relieved but I could tell with the tone of Lynda's voice that she was just placating him and she had no intension of turning up at hospital without taking a shower first.

As soon as we pulled up out the front of the beach house Paxton jumped out of the car and ran into the house with Nate. I was close behind them. Paxton looked around for Lynda and called out to her, "Honey." Moving further into the house, we could hear the shower going. "Fuck me," Paxton spat out as he went to the bathroom and opened the door. Nate and I stood back at the end of the hall but it wouldn't matter where we were, we could hear Paxton's mouthful of curses and coo's at his wife as the sound of the shower stopped. "Jesus Babe, do you ever listen to me?"

"Yes honey I do," Lynda said with a slight touch of sarcasm, then "What are you doing Paxton? I can dry myself" then, "Paxton just go grab my things for the hospital and leave me to dress myself." Then, "Paxton get out of the friggin bathroom," then a sound of a door slamming, lots of banging and cursing, then Paxton moving up the hallway with his arms full of pillows and bags. Nate took some of the things in his arms and they headed back out to the car. I went to the bathroom and knocked lightly on the door. "Lynda, it's Casey." Opening the bathroom door she was dressed in a pair of yoga pants and a long sweater, rubbing a hand over her belly.

"Oh shit Casey, he dragged you here as well?" she said exasperated.

"Its fine, he's just a little jumpy."

"Ha, that's an understatement he's acting like a lunatic." She sucked in a hard breath with her last word and gripped her belly.

"How you doing?" I ask.

"Pretty good I think, that was only the third contraction."

"Ok, and when was the last one?"

Her eyes squint as she thinks "Around fifteen, twenty minutes ago."

"Ok, where were you when your waters broke?"

"In the kitchen, I was just washing up a few dishes." I start to walk towards the kitchen and she follows behind me.

"Did you clean it up yet?"

"No." she grimaced.

"Good, I just want to check that it's nice and clear with no signs of blood in it, ok?" She's close behind me when I examine the pool of waters spread over the kitchen floor. "It's fine, come on let's get you to hospital, somewhere more comfortable to give birth."

"Yes, preferably with lots of drugs," she said with a laugh.

Paxton sat in the back seat with Lynda on the way to the hospital, rubbing her belly gently, placing little kisses on her cheek together with sweet words of endearment. It was a wonderful thing to watch and hear, the love of two people about to embark on parenthood, it made my eyes begin to get watery with the sight. Nate turned to look at me, but I turned too fast for him to see anything, and looked out of the window.

By the time we arrived at the hospital Lynda's contractions had become a little stronger and closer in duration. As soon as Nate pulled up and put the SUV in park, Paxton was out and helping Lynda out of the car and guiding her through the entrance doors, while Nate and I grabbed their bag and pillows and followed behind.

Nate and I were directed into a waiting room, while Lynda was sat in a wheelchair and wheeled down a hallway. We sat for about an hour just idly chatting and laughing at Paxton in panic mode. I had just leant my head back to rest it on the back of the wall, when the door opened and Paxton came in. "She's been examined and they said it could be another few hours, so I came to get her things."

Nate stood and placed his hand on Paxton's shoulder. giving it a squeeze. "Are you ok?"

Nodding, he said, "Yeah, I'm better now we're at the hospital I had visions of something happening before we even got her here."

"Do you want us to wait with you?" Nate asked.

"No man, it could be hours, you two go home, get some food and I'll text you with updates."

"Are you sure?"

"Yeah, I'm good, thanks Nate for everything."

"You're welcome, now go back in there and be with your wife, she'll need someone to swear at." Nate grinned and Paxton came and took me in what I can only describe as a bear hug and said, "Thanks Casey, you're a gem."

"My pleasure, glad I could help". We watched Paxton push through the doors to the maternity ward. Nate took hold of my hand as we headed out to the car and back to the Penthouse.

Chapter thirty-six

Nate

Back at the Penthouse we sat on the couch watching a movie while we tucked into a pizza that we had grabbed on the way back. I sat my cell phone on the coffee table and we relaxed and waited. After cleaning up the remains of the pizza, I lay stretched out along the couch with Casey snuggly in front of me. I felt the instant her body relaxed and her breathing fell into a deeper pattern, and I knew she had dozed off. It had been a long and stressful day, but knowing that soon my little brother would become a father, made it all worth it. It's pretty amazing to realize that it has been just me and Paxton for so long, and now there was going to be a new generation to the King family. How much had our lives changed over the past year, first Paxton and Lynda getting married and the pregnancy, and this woman laying snug in my arms that had been almost thrust into my life and she's made such a difference, made me think about a relationship......and forever, this woman just blew me out of the water.

When the phone buzzed with an incoming text, I reached across and grabbed it. It was Paxton. *Lynda is in full labor, baby should be here soon.* Running my fingers across the letters, I asked if he wanted us back in the waiting room and his quick reply of a smiley face told me that he did. Leaning down and brushing small kisses along Casey's jaw line until her eyes flickered open, I said, "We've got to go baby." Rubbing at her eyes and sitting up, she said, "I'll just grab a jacket".

When we were back sitting in the waiting room she leaned her head against my shoulder and once again we waited and waited until we were startled by the doors opening and Paxton walking through. He looked tired and haggard and elated with pride and joy. The beam of his smile was so illuminating, his face told me everything. "It's a beautiful baby girl," he exhaled. Casey wrapped her arms around him.

"Congratulations, that's wonderful, how is Lynda?" she asked him.

"She's a champion, I can't believe she did that, I am so amazed." Taking my brother in a bear hug, I said "I am so proud of you."

"Well come on in and meet the new King in the family".

Following Paxton and taking Casey's hand, we walked down the hall and into the room where Lynda lay cradling a small bundle. Leaning down I placed a kiss on her forehead. "Hey momma, how you doing."

"Tired but fantastic" she beamed.

I looked down at the little pink cherub face amongst the folds of the blanket and looked back to Lynda. "She's beautiful," I said. Casey gave Lynda a kiss on the cheek and looked down at the baby. "Oh Lynda she is so precious." Lynda looked up at Paxton. "Here babe you take her so uncle Nate can have a hold."

"Sure honey" Paxton said, slowly taking the baby and turning to me.

"Paxton I don't think..." I said with trepidation.

"That's right, don't think, just hold." Placing the tiny warm bundle against my chest and moving my hands to where they needed to be, I looked down into her tiny face and just basked in her beauty. Looking up at Paxton now standing next to the hospital bed, holding Lynda's hand, I asked "Have you thought of a name yet?"

"We thought Emily Jean." Paxton said, and a small pang of pain hit my chest.

"After mom?" I breathed out.

"Yeah, what do you think?" Paxton asked me. Looking back down at this beautiful little girl I said, "Hi, Emily Jean, I'm your Uncle Nate." She felt so small in my arms; all I could do was stare at her tiny features.

After a while Paxton said "Ok, Uncle Nate, let Casey have a hold now." Turning towards where Casey was sitting in a chair in the corner, I made my way over to her and placed little Emily in her arms. She stared up at me wide eyed then down at Emily. I watched as her fingers gently brushed against the fine dark hair on Emily's head then along the tight little fist that she had shoved into her mouth. "Look at you," she softly cooed ."You are so beautiful." When Casey's eyes moved up to where mine were watching her, I saw tears brimming in her beautiful blue eyes. I also saw a deep pain and sadness in them. Standing, Casey handed Emily back to Lynda. "I think she may be hungry the way she's attacking that little fist of hers. She is absolutely gorgeous guys."

"Thanks Casey," Lynda said.

Saying our goodbyes and giving them both some privacy so Lynda could feed Emily, I took Casey by the hand and back to the car. She was quiet on the drive back. I glanced quickly at her several times, but I could tell her shutters were back up in full force. Once we were in the elevator I broke the silence. "Are you Ok?" "Yes fine, I'm just so tired." Nodding at her response, although not completely happy with her excuse, I needed to let it go for tonight and give her space and some sleep.

Opening my eyes to what sounded like a wounded animal in pain, for just a second I had to think if I was having a nightmare. Sometimes I have, on occasion had flash back memories from my time in the military but as I turn my head, I see Casey moving her head back and forth on the pillow, her face twisted into a painful grimace and covered in perspiration making her hairline look damp. Her hands fisted into the sheets at her sides. Leaning up on one elbow and running my fingers across her cheek, I speak in a low tone, trying not to wake her up too abruptly. "Casey, it's ok baby, I'm here, you're ok." Her eyes flick open fast as she gasps in a breath. Pulling her into my arms and stroking my hand along her back I soothed into the hair on top of her head, "Shhh, I got you." After several moments, her breathing changed from panting to a steady pattern. Pulling away from me she sat up on the side of the bed.

"Sorry I didn't mean to..." her words trailed off as she rubbed her palms against her eyes.

"No, don't be. Was it a bad dream?" Shaking her head and standing, she said, "Something like that. You go back to sleep. I'm going to go down and get a cool drink." As she walked towards the door, I got up and pulled a pair of sleep pants on that were on the floor next to the bed and followed her. She turned and placed her hand on my chest. "I'm ok, go back to bed"

"Nope." Already knowing me so well, she sighed, turned, and went down to the kitchen. Pulling out two glasses she poured us both a glass of juice.

Watching her sip juice from the glass, I said "Talk to me."

Looking down at the glass in her hand, she said "Just a bad dream."

"Wonder what brought it on?" I said to myself. but she heard me and shrugged her shoulders. Looking up to her, I asked "Was it the baby?" She stared at me momentarily, then shrugged her shoulders again, I knew I had to tread carefully with whatever I said next, but I needed to. "I remember once you said that you couldn't get pregnant, you just never said why." I watched as she bent her head to the side and rubbed at her neck.

"The scars, I told you I had an accident," she said.

"And you were told what? That it's impossible?"

"Not impossible, but improbable.... A million to one chance they said," she said in a low tone.

"I'm sorry Doc, I can see how today would have stirred up some emotions for you."

"Yeah, I guess." Draining the last of her juice she took both empty glasses, rinsed them and put them into the dishwasher, her body language letting me know this was a subject she didn't want to get into and I have learned the hard way to not push too hard. "Coming back to bed?" she said.

Looking at her and grinning, I said, "Hey you never have to ask me that question twice."

"I mean to sleep you pervert, you have to get up for work in a few hours." Pulling her into my arms and placing a soft kiss against her lips and smiling. I said. "I know, doesn't stop me from trying though." Taking her face in my hands, I rubbed both thumbs along her cheeks, tilting her face up so I could look into her eyes. "You know you can talk to me about anything right?" She nodded, and I brushed my lips over hers once more, before we went back upstairs and got into bed.

Within the next few days Paxton had taken Lynda and his beautiful daughter home, and he was taking some time off from work to stay with them both. Casey's low mood had disappeared and we made plans to go down to the beach house over the weekend and spend time with Paxton, Lynda and Emily. When I had first mentioned it, Casey thought that maybe they would like to spend some alone time getting to know their new baby, that was until Paxton rang and insisted that we come and spend the weekend and how they would feel more confident knowing there was a doctor in the house. Casey had laughed, and told him that she was not a pediatrician or an expert on babies, but as far as he was concerned a doctor was a doctor and so when I finished work late Friday afternoon, we packed the SUV and headed down to the beach house.

Chapter thirty-seven

C asey

Friday night Paxton and Nate manned the BBQ, while Lynda and I sat and talked babies, not my most favorite subject but looking at the beaming face of a new mother, I couldn't help but share in her happiness too it was quite infectious. I loved being here at the beach house, it was a whole world away from the bustle of the city. The constant smell of the salty breeze, the sound of the ocean waves crashing over the sand, and the calmness of the house. It was a wonderful place.

After dinner Nate tried his hand at holding Emily again. I couldn't help but smile watching his awkward big hands moving gently around her and the intense, frightened look he had on his face the whole time he held her. He was so focused, I watched as he gently stroked his fingers across her dark fine, wispy hair, how her little hand gripped onto his finger and how he spoke softly to her, telling her how beautiful she was. I almost went into a trance-like state watching and admiring him, and I felt a slight pang in the middle of my chest as I realized how much of a loving father he would make some day and how I may not be able to provide him with that child. Every time I think about the relationship between us it always points to the same conclusion. Logically I don't know if I can give him a fulfilling life with a perfect ending, and I'm not sure if the feelings and chemistry we have for each other will be enough to get us through either.

On feeling the sting of tears starting to well behind my eyes, I excuse myself to the bathroom, where I sit and compose my thoughts and try to deal with the tug of war my head and my heart keep having. Sometimes I just wish I didn't have to think so deep into things and just take life as it comes, warts and all. What I needed was to find the right moment to talk with Nate, tell him all my thoughts and fears about everything, just simply communicate and absorb his strength. Satisfied with that thought and deciding that if I stay in the bathroom any longer it would cause Nate to seek me out, I felt calmer and relaxed enough to go back out.

Seeing that Lynda had taken Emily into the bedroom to nurse her, and with no signs of Nate or Paxton, I headed out to the back porch and stretched out on a sun lounger and let the cool breeze drift over my skin. It was so relaxing and serene that I must have dozed off, because I awoke to the low sound of Nate's voice against my ear. "You look so sexy when you're sleeping."

"Wow I didn't mean to fall asleep," I said with a yawn.

"Come on," he said holding out his hands to me."Let's go to bed." Pulling me up to my feet, he wrapped his arms around my waist, pulling me snuggly into his body. "I intend to do wicked things to you," he growled.

"Really? In your brother's house? What if he hears us?" I whisper to him, and he presses an open mouth kiss against the side of my neck.

"Then I might have to gag you, unless you can achieve a silent orgasm."

"Hmm not sure I can be that silent," I smile up at him.

"Then a gag it is," he chuckles as he pulls me inside of the house, bolting the door behind him.

Waking the next morning snuggled up to Nate's warm body, my face pressed against his chest and my leg over the top of his, I smile to myself as I remember what we did when we got to bed last night.

He didn't use a gag, but he did cover my mouth with his hand at one stage, when he had me losing all of my senses as he drove me to the edge of madness and back repeatedly for at least three hours. I could see through the small gap in the curtains that it was light outside but deciding I would much rather be exactly where I was right at this moment, I snuggled in deeper, closed my eyes and went back to sleep.

It was a perfect weekend of swimming, walking on the beach, and for the first time in my life I actually felt like part of a family. The feelings that were coursing through my body were unexplainable like my body, mind and soul were clean and all the years of scars were healing. I felt elated, euphoric, I felt.....free, and it had been given to me by this perfect man that had somehow taught me to trust and have confidence and power to take control of my thoughts and feelings. I know that I can lean on Nate's big muscular shoulders if I need to. I know this and I feel it, now I just need to convince my brain to have as much confidence in me as my heart does and rid myself of these feelings that chain me to my past. It's time to cut them off and get rid of the weight once and for all.

Leaving the beach house late Sunday afternoon, we drove back to the city and got back to the Penthouse just as it was going dark. Nate dropped the bags in the entrance and headed for his home office, while I scoured the fridge looking for something quick and easy for dinner. Pulling out some left over lasagna, I slid it into the oven and set the timer. Then I headed upstairs to take a long soak in the bath, my muscles were aching from all the weekend swimming and walking. Turning on the water and pulling off my clothes, I leisurely slid into the warm water and reveled in the depth of the tub, leaning my head back and closing my eyes blissfully.

The bathroom was warm, steamy and quiet but I heard him when he entered, and felt him when his naked body slipped in behind mine, adjusting my body so I was cradled in between his legs."Mmm, you feel so good," he groaned into the side of my neck.

"You don't feel too bad yourself," I whispered back to him. Taking the soap in his hands he rubbed it into a lather, then dropped it into the water. His soapy strong hands slowly moved up my arms and to my breasts, taking them in his hands and rubbing in circles covering them with small soapy bubbles, and when his fingers touch my already hard, puckered nipples, I let out a small gasp of pleasure "Your nipples are so sensitive," he almost moans against my cheek, and slowly starts to gently suck and kiss from the back of my ear down my neck.

"And your sensitive part is pressing hard against my back." I moan as he keeps soaping my breasts, then his hands glide down my stomach and disappear under the water to my sex, then to the inside of my thighs. Moving them open and up until they are now draped over his own thighs.

"You feel so fucking good," he breathes as he rubs his fingers over and through the sensitive area between my legs. I close my eyes and lean my head back into him, turning my head so his wandering lips are closer to my own, his tongue skims over my bottom lip before his mouth takes mine in a deep passionate kiss. With tongues dancing and lust heating between us, his hands slip back under the water to my ass and he lifts me slightly up and places himself at my entrance. "Open up for me baby," his voice now sounding low and urgent. I open my legs as wide as possible in the limited space of the tub and feel him as he pushes into me, my inner muscles stretching to accommodate him.

"Oh fuck," I let out as he buries deep inside of me, right down to the base.

"Mmm, that's exactly what I am going to do to you." He rasps. With his hands spread on the inside of my thighs, holding them open, I start to move in circles against him, the sensation of pleasure sparking up my spine. I run one of my hands under the water to where his balls are and I cup them into my palm and give them a gentle squeeze that makes him buck up into me with a moan. Sliding my fingers up, I can feel where we are joined and he is moving in and out. I stroke his shaft as he comes out and moves back inside of me. "Jesus baby, what the fuck are you doing to me." Moving my fingers just that little bit higher to the nub of my sex, I run my fingers back and forth against it, sending more shivers through my body. Nate slips his hands further under my ass until he is lifting me up and down on his hard throbbing shaft, driving himself deeper into my body and I feel my orgasm beginning to rise and my legs start to spasm. "That's it baby, give me everything," he grunts into my ear. Pushing myself harder down onto him as I climb that hill of ecstasy and with the sound of water plashing over the side of the bath and onto the floor and the groans cutting through the steam of the room, I reach the pinnacle that I am reaching for and what I need. Tingles flickering over my wet skin, I tremble as I scream out his name and he follows me with his own primal groan and fills me with his heat.

Both panting and trembling with pleasure after our frenzied water play, he strokes his hands over my arms soothingly as we both come back down to earth. Once the water started losing its warmth we were out and dry and slipping in between the soft sheets of the bed. I was encased in his arms, my cheek against his chest, just where it loves to be, as we both fell into sleep.

Over the next few days it kind of felt like we were getting into a domestic routine. Nate went into work and because I didn't have to be so enclosed in such tight security any longer, I spent a lot of the day exploring the city and taking it all in. And at night, Nate and I would either go out and take in the night life or better still, just stay in, cook a meal together and laze on the couch, which was always followed by love making sessions somewhere in the Penthouse. Paxton came back to work, calling me down to his office one morning so I could go through some papers that he needed me to read through and fill out so he could start the ball rolling on my

H-1B visa so I could hopefully find some employment while I was here. There was also the messiness of applying to the United States Medical Licensing Board if I planned on practicing here as well. I left his office with all the papers promising that I would spend the day going through them and getting them all back to him ASAP. The thought of Nate financially supporting me was not on my agenda, and I felt some relief in knowing that my bank account was still healthy enough for my needs for the foreseeable future.

Looking at the time on my phone it read 9.15pm. Breathing out a sigh, I placed the chicken that I had roasted earlier into the fridge next to the salad and resigned myself to the couch. I sent him a quick text to see if everything was all right, this was late for him, I mean it's not as though he has to drive a long way to get home, right? He usually texts me, even if he's going to be a few minutes late. Minutes pass and still no reply. This is not like him at all. Tapping on his name to call him on my phone, it rings once but goes straight to voice mail. I look for Paxton's name in my phone but just as I am about to press it, the elevator pings and the doors open. Standing, I open my mouth to speak, but stop as I look at Nate's thunderous face. Its full of fury and rage, and his steel eyes pierce into me like knives. Storming over he stands rigid on the other side of the table and throws a large manila folder onto the table, followed by several small memory sticks. I look down at where the scattered papers fan over the table and gasp, placing my hand over my mouth to try and hold it back. "I think we need to talk Casey....or is it Catherine?" he growls. Looking from the papers on the table up to his face, his head tilted to one side, eyebrow raised, all I can do is collapse back into the soft leather of the couch and let the shock waves ripple through my body as I feel all the blood drain from my face.

Chapter thirty-eight

N ate

Earlier......

Looking down at my watch I see that its almost five pm and I start to save the files that I have been working on for most of the day and close down the computer. Paxton had arrived back at work this morning looking like the cat that ate the cream. I was under the impression it was the new mother that glows, but it seems my little brother has caught the new father glow as well and it didn't take him long to get back into the thick of things. In fact, I think it may have taken him a whole fifteen minutes in his office before I had a new contract in front of me to peruse, and one glance at it told me that this was going to be a long day. However I also have no intension of spending any more time behind this desk when I have my beautiful woman waiting for me just a few floors above.

Standing to leave, I'm stopped by a knock at the door. Looking up I see Paxton entering with a large file in his hands. "Paxton?" He stands in front of me and in his eyes I see a flash of apologetic regret. "What is it? Is it Lynda, Emily?" He lowers his eyes to the ground and slowly shakes his head and his behavior is worrying and his silence is angering. "What the fuck is going on?" I almost yell in frustration, and finally he speaks.

"I got those back ground files today."

"Okay..." I let out slowly with curiosity. I'm not entirely sure what the hell he's talking about but I encourage him to keep going.

"Casey's back ground files." He says.

"Okay," I repeat.

"And...Nate I...." he trails off shaking his head again, then he hands me the file he's holding and reaches into his pocket and pulls out what looks like several small memory sticks. "You need to watch these here in the office, in private, ok?"

So many things are running through my mind right now, but the look on Paxton's face is telling me that whatever I am about to see is not good. "I'll be in my office when you need me." He pats me on my shoulder and walks out. Looking down I look at the memory sticks in my hand and take a seat back in front of the computer, flicking it back on and slipping the stick marked with a number one on it into the dock at the side and pressing play.

It looks like a news story. Looking in the bottom corner I see its dated the 9th of September 2004, with the headline story that reads " Kidnap Victim Found After 3 years In Captivity." Then on the screen flashes a picture of a young blonde headed girl, and I pause the video on her. Narrowing my eyes, I zero in on her face...those eyes, and it hits me like a baseball bat. This young girl is Casey, but the name under the photo reads Catherine Taylor. A male newsreaders accented voice comes over a flash of different photos and movie clips of an old house, a car, a middle aged well- dressed couple, photo snaps of a small blonde haired, blue eyed girl on the beach, riding a bike. Smiling, she looks adorably happy. Then a clip of a guy, being led away from the house by a cop, his hands cuffed behind him, his head shaven and looking down at the ground until he reaches the police van then he briefly looks up at the camera with a sickening grin that makes me feel uneasy, before he is pushed inside and the door slams behind him. With my eyes so busy on the pictures that are now inundating my screen, the voice of the newsreader seems to have blurred away into my office and I have to restart the whole thing, this time concentrating on what is being said.

"In breaking news today, teenage kidnap victim Catherine Taylor has been found alive early this morning. Catherine, the only daughter of successful power lawyers Corrine and David Taylor, went missing 3 years ago at the age of 14. Catherine's parents received a ransom note 2 days after the teenager disappeared from her home. Corrine and David Taylor publicly rejected paying any money for the safe return of their daughter, as they feared she was already dead. Police continued their search and investigations, which finally led them to suspect 25 year old Max Sullivan, a meat worker, who one night had bragged to a bunch of friends that he had his own slave at home. The barman, who had overheard the conversation, called police on a gut feeling about the young man, and it paid off, leading police to a small farm house where Sullivan lived alone. When police raided the home, Catherine Taylor was found chained to a mattress in the basement. Catherine Taylor was taken to the local hospital in what police called an appalling, emaciated condition."

Standing up, I headed for my bar and poured myself three fingers of Jack into a tumbler and threw it back, before I poured another one. My stomach was churning and rolling with bile, and I needed something to help me get a grip and enough courage to go back to the computer and continue...

I spent hours looking through the file in front of me and watching countless news clips, photos, statements and files from the trial of Max Sullivan, until I had pieced it all together. Catherine was the only child of older parents who were both lawyers. It seemed that Catherine came along later in life for Corrine and David Taylor and I got the idea she was an unplanned distraction for the power couple. Late one afternoon, 14 year old Catherine went down to the corner store to get some milk, when she was grabbed off the street and bundled into a car by Max Sullivan. Sullivan, who had seen the Taylors one day in the local news being interviewed outside their large and expensive- looking house, noticed that it was close to where he worked at the local abattoir so he decided to start watching the house and he noticed that Catherine was mostly there by herself. The day she had gone to the corner store, he decided that Catherine was going to earn him some serious money.

Grabbing Catherine and shoving her into the back seat of his car, he knocked her out quickly with a cloth saturated with chloroform, threw a blanket over her and drove her out to his farm house, where he had her gagged, hands tied behind her back and chained to the wall by her ankles. He stripped her of all her clothes and there she sat on an old mattress on the floor. He had intended to send the Taylors a ransom note which included the shirt she had been wearing that day, demanding payment for the return of their daughter. Apparently his dumbass plan was to get them to drop off the money somewhere for him to pick it up, and he was just going to dump Catherine off on the side of the road somewhere. However he didn't expect the Taylors to refuse to pay any money for their daughters return.

In court the dirty looking, skinny youth told the judge that he had no idea what to do, so he thought he might as well get something out of the mess he had created, so he raped her repeatedly, beat her, and performed all other forms of depraved sexual fantasies out on this small 14 year old girl, for three fucking years. When the judge asked Sullivan what he intended to do with Catherine, he said that after a while he was getting bored, so he decided to stop feeding her what little amount he was, apparently he wanted to see how long a human could last without any food or water. Like she was some kind of experiment, he wanted to study her as she slowly deteriorated. He wanted to watch her as she slowly died. Picking up a handful of the police evidence photos they showed an emaciated, small, filthy child. Other photos showed different snapshots of bruises, cuts and weeping sores, over almost every inch of her body.

Throwing the pictures onto my desk, I poured myself another drink and knocked it back so fast it hardly had time to touch my tongue. I needed something right now to burn this nauseated feeling that was in my stomach. I needed the world to stop spinning right now and give me time to process this. I slammed my fist down onto the desk.

In all the god forsaken places I had been during my years in the military, and all the shit I had seen, there is nothing that could have ever prepared me for what my eyes had just been subjected to. Sitting back down in front of the computer, I plugged in the last memory stick. This news coverage was dated a year later. Max Sullivan had been sentenced to 20 years imprisonment and once again Catherine Taylor suffered another blow to her life when both of her parents were killed in a head - on car accident while driving home one night. Typing Catherine's name into my computer, I looked for anything recent on her, but there was nothing that I hadn't already seen. She just disappeared off the face of the earth. Did I blame her? Shit no. So now I understand why the secrecy. I'm guessing her friend Flynn had everything sealed and hidden and provided her with a new identity.... a new life.

I pushed at the computer with fury and it slid off the desk and hit the floor with a loud crash. Standing and walking to the large floor to ceiling windows, I leaned my forehead against the cool glass and stared down into the city lights. I have no words, my mind is reeling with images that I cannot comprehend. I can feel my blood pumping through my veins like lava, filled with a violent anger and rage. I keep trying to swallow back the bile that I can taste in my mouth. All I can see is that fucker Max Sullivan's pissy little face, and I want his blood. I want to wrap my hands around his throat and slowly squeeze every bit of life out of him and watch as he slowly dies. The thought of it makes my hands clench into fists so tight I feel like my skin is going to split.

My door opens and Paxton slowly walks in where he finds me now pacing back and forth in front of the windows. Looking up I see the look on his face. He is silently judging where I am right now and, honestly, I have no fucking idea. Paxton shoves his hands into his pockets and hesitantly speaks. "Nate." I hold up a hand to stop him from asking anything else. Continuing to pace, and running both hands through my hair, I hear him let out a large sigh, exasperated. "Nate, we need to talk about this, before you wear a hole in the floor." Stopping and turning to face my brother.

"Did you watch that?" I ask him pointing to everything that was splayed out on my desk. He took a moment before he answered me.

"Yes, I did." Returning to the bar, I grab the bottle of Jack and as I am just about to fill my glass tumbler up again, Paxton places a hand over the glass."That's not going to help Nate."

Looking at him through narrowed eyes, I say, "Oh believe me Paxton it fucking helps."

"How? This is something you need to talk about with Casey. All the alcohol is doing is masquerading everything."

"Good, I want it to, I want it to numb my brain so fucking bad that I can't think any more," I spit out.

"No Nate because when the blur lifts from the booze you're still going to have to face it, that's if you want to," Hearing the low tone in his voice, I lift my head, looking at him sharply.

"What the fuck is that supposed to mean?" I yell into his face, and he takes a step back.

"Calm down, I just mean you do have options here."

"Options? You mean like just going to her and saying something like oh, sorry Casey you're just too fucked up for me to have in my life, so I'll just crap all over you like everyone else has done through your whole life, and send you packing?".

Paxton's silence pisses me off even more and the next minute I have the front of his shirt in both fists, pulling him up so his face is inches from mine. "Is that what you would have done to Lynda if the tables were turned?" I growl, looking into his eyes, and I pin- point the moment he gets how much I feel for this woman. His body now slack, eyes looking down at the floor, he slowly shakes his head.

"No." Releasing my grip on his shirt, and walking over to my chair, I sink into it. "I'm sorry Nate, I adore Casey, you know that. I guess I'm just trying to protect you."

"It's not me that needs protecting Paxton, it's her, and that's what I need to get my head around and it feels like shit."

"Nate, you can't blame yourself for something that happened years before you even knew her."Paxton said.

"Yeah I know that, but just the thought of someone hurting her, makes me want blood Paxton and the thing that hurts the most is she didn't trust me enough to tell me."

"Look I know what you saw on those news stories is gut wrenching, I get that, but does it really change what she means to you?"

"Fuck no, it changes nothing in her, in fact I respect and admire her even more if that's possible, it's just.... We're so connected, not just in here," I point to the left side of my chest then to my temple, "But in here and I'm finding it hard not to be able to take her pain, her anguish, her worries. She consumes me Paxton, all of me, and the way all this information is spinning around in my skull I'm worried that I won't be able to compartmentalize it logically so that those images won't be flashing across my mind every time I look at her or touch her. Do you understand what I'm trying to say here?" Paxton just nods his head at me. "You need to talk to her Nate." Rubbing a hand down my face I relinquish and agree with a nod of my own.

Gathering the file on my desk, I shoved the papers back into it and shoved the memory sticks into my pocket and headed for the elevator, trying to take some deep breaths on the ride up, trying to calm myself before I faced her. That ball of anger was sitting low in my stomach and the burn from it was rapidly rising again. Looking at the lights of the rising floor numbers, I briefly contemplated pressing the emergency stop button and just staying in this small space until I contained my feelings, but it would be fruitless, I needed to see her right now.

When the doors slid open she was sitting with her legs curled under her on the couch, with her phone gripped against her chest. I saw in her face the look of relief as she saw me. She had been worried, and now, standing in front of her and being the irrational fucking mess I had been in my office, burst through as I threw the file onto the coffee table in front of her, followed by the memory sticks from my pocket. Papers and pictures spilled out in front of her and I was struck with a clenching pain deep in my chest as I see the look of shock and pain in her beautiful blue eyes, as she looks down at them.

Chapter thirty-nine

Casey

Waves of shock pulsated through every inch of my body as I looked down at all the papers and photos that now lay fanned out on the table in front of me. Pulling myself closer to the edge of the couch, I reached out my hand hesitantly and slowly moved them around. Seeing all the broken, revolting pieces of my life like this broke something inside of me. Hope, my hope had just fallen onto the table along with all these white pieces of paper. Looking from the table up into Nate's eyes, I saw a fusion of emotions- anger, sadness, betrayal. He sat on the couch opposite me, elbows leaning on his knees as his hands scraped through his messy black hair. He inhaled a deep breath before he said, "Why?" Looking back down at the coffee table, I bit into my bottom lip and slowly shook my head. "Why didn't you tell me?" Looking back up into his face, I opened my mouth to speak but there were no words and I needed to find some. Swallowing hard and looking straight into his eyes, I tell him the truth.

"I was going to, I just needed the right time." I said hesitantly.

"The right time?" I saw the questioning look on his face.

"Yes, I've wanted to tell you so many times I just...couldn't find the words." He let out a slow breath. "I wish it would have come from you Casey, rather than like this," he said motioning to the mess of papers on the table.

"I'm sorry," I whisper and he quickly stands and starts to pace in front of the couch.

"That's the last thing I want you to be Casey. You have nothing to be sorry for."

"But you're angry."

"Yes I'm angry, I'm fucking pissed but not at you, I'm angry with me." He emphasized the last word by smacking his hand hard against his chest.

Looking at him now confused I ask "What? Why would you be angry at yourself? You haven't done anything. This is all on me. I'm the one who carries all this shit around with me. I'm the one who should have been truthful from the beginning and let you see exactly what you were getting into. I tried so hard to keep you locked out, but you kept chipping away until it was too late to turn back for me." Now I am standing up too and facing him head on. "I'm sorry that I didn't talk to you, it was just too hard to go back there." Nate pushed his hands into the pockets of his jeans and looked down at the floor. With his shoulders relaxed he looked a little calmer now.

"I understand that Casey. I guess I thought we had built up this trust between us and it bothers me that I haven't made you feel safe enough to trust me." He looked so desolate and hurt, I wanted, no needed, to touch him, wrap my arms around this strong man and try and make him understand what's going on in my head, but as I take a step towards him he moves over to the large windows that look out into the night sky and stares out of them.

"It's not really something you blurt out Nate," I continue, as I move closer to him just enough for him to hear my words. "I'm not sure what you want me to tell you that you don't already know." I watch as he closes his eyes and shakes his head. "It has nothing to do with not trusting you, because I do, more than anyone, but I'm tired Nate. I'm tired of constantly running away from my past. I'm tired of it owning me. I'm tired of it squeezing me slowly to death.

I want it to stay in the past where it belongs and not define who I am right now. For all those years I was losing that battle, until I met you, now I feel like I'm not running anymore, but walking. When I'm with you I feel free Nate, and you gave me that freedom to live and trust and ...love." At that last word he turns his eyes to mine and I can see the battle in them that he's having with himself. I'm just not sure what type of battle he's having. "Please Nate, talk to me, tell me what you're thinking."

His gaze turns again to the window and I feel deflated. He's silent for what seems like a lifetime, then he says, "I don't know what to say, I just...what I saw..." he pauses again scrubbing both hands through his hair to the back of his neck.

"Just start by telling me what's going through your mind." I tell him.

"Right now? Everything, too much."

"I'm sorry Nate"

"Stop." I flinch a little at the bite in his voice and he sees it and returns his voice to a calmer tone ."Please just stop apologizing. I just need some time to process everything and get my head straight." With that my stomach sinks. I knew all along this would be the reaction and I can't blame him. I understand that he's feeling betrayed right now, I mean, if I found out the person I had been sleeping with for the past few weeks turned out to be as used, dirty and broken as I am, I would want to run in the opposite direction myself.

"I don't know how to help you," I whisper, looking past him through the window.

"The scars.....they were from him?" he doesn't ask me but tells me and I nod.

Picking up my phone and walking to the stairs, I look over my shoulder and say to him, "I'm going to bed. I think it might be better for you to sleep in your own room for a while, just to give us both some space while you process everything." I tried my hardest not to show him the hurt in my voice but I'm pretty sure he heard, but he also didn't argue or protest and just let me walk away.

Stepping into the hot pulsating water of the shower, I let the build-up of hot tears run down my face and mingle with the water from the shower. I sobbed into the hot spray, wishing it could wash everything away, not just my tears but my past as well. I wish I could go back in time and never apply for the job with International Medical Assist in the first place. Sliding down onto the floor of the shower and holding my face in my hands, I continue to sob, a carousal of images turning in my mind; my parents, Max Sullivan, Peterson, the chains, the dirty mattress, Nate; every image stabbing into my chest like a hot knife, and there I stay until my body starts to shrivel from the water and I feel fatigued, drained and totally shattered from crying for so long.

Pulling myself up and turning off the shower, I wrap a towel around my limp body and grab a t-shirt from the drawer on the way to the bed. Drying off quickly and pulling on the shirt, I slide into bed. My eyes are so heavy and raw that I fall easily into sleep. Dreams take over, and my sleep is restless and broken, waking up from many images I would rather not remember. The last picture I see before I wake to the sunlight is the painful look of betrayal on Nate's face. My body still weakened by the over- load of emotions and thoughts, I pull myself out of bed and walk out of the bedroom. Standing at the top of the staircase silently for a few minutes, I listen for any noise coming from downstairs. Satisfied that Nate has left the Penthouse, I walk down stairs and pour myself a glass of juice from the fridge and drink it down in a few gulps. Looking around I can see that Nate is nowhere in the Penthouse, so I am assuming that he has gone into the office and I wonder to myself just how long the painful silence between us will last. "Just give him some time," I mummer out into the empty room.

I spend the day trying to occupy my time, but when it got to around midday I was starting to feel caged, so I dress in a comfy pair of shorts, sneaker's and tank and go down to the street level and just walk, taking in the fresh air and bustle of the city around- me anything to take my mind away from Nate. I walk into his favorite pizza place and grab a water and a slice of cheesy goodness and walk over to the park to eat. Sitting down on the grass I feel the vibration of my phone in my pocket. Pulling it out. I see Nate's name flash on the screen. "Hey." I answer. "Where are you?" The bite of his words makes me pull the phone away from my ear slightly.

"Just having some lunch."

"I said where, not what."

"Just in the park, why?"

"Hmm, let's see" he starts with sarcasm lacing his voice, "You're supposed to let Nick know if you need to go somewhere."

"Not any more I don't, the threat is over, remember?"

"The threat is never over Casey. Trust me, I'm an expert on these things and I'm still responsible for your safety." The harsh tone in his voice made me flinch. So that's what I am now, a responsibility. His voice broke into my thoughts. "Casey," he barked into the phone making me pull the phone away from my ear.

"Look, I know you're angry but you don't have to yell at me like I'm a child."

"Then stop acting like one. I need to know your safe." He growled.

Blowing out an irritated breath, I calmly say, "I can assure you that I am safe. There is no need to worry, so please Nate consider yourself responsibility- free from me." With that I cut off the call and shut off the phone. I enjoyed the rest of the day to myself. It was nice to put some distance between the King building and myself, and I know he needed some space for now, so that's what I intended to give him.

Later that night back at the Penthouse, I picked up my phone and dialed Flynn's number. "Hey, sweet's how ya doing?." He said with a cheerful spark.

With a sigh I say, "Not good, the shit has hit the fan here."

"What?"

"He knows Flynn."

"He knows?" He repeats. "How?"

"Well you know his brother Paxton is a lawyer and he has connections, they somehow got my file and..."

"Fuck babe, I'm so sorry." He said his voice full of regret.

"Don't be he needed to find out at some stage. I just wish I would have talked to him about it sooner, that's all."

"Sooo, how did he take it?"

"Worse than I ever imagined."

"Wow babe, I don't know what to say."

"It's fine Flynn, I guess in a way I expected it to end, I guess it's just following the pattern of my life." I sighed.

"He's ended it?"

"Not with words but it's put a huge wall between us, and I got the old "I need some time to think" sentence."

"Mother fucker. Why the hell would he do that Casey?"

"Calm down Flynn, I understand it's a lot for someone to deal with in one hit."

"That's not the point babe if someone cares for you they don't let something that happened in your past taint the person they have feelings for. You don't just give up, you fucking fight." I could hear Flynn's anger radiating through my phone.

"He cares, I just don't think he knows how to segregate the 30 year old woman from the 14 year old victim that he saw in those news articles. It was hard, he looked....devastated."

"So what are you going to do now?" Flynn asks.

"I think I am going to come home Flynn. I want to take myself out of the equation and let Nate go, I want to make that decision for him and make a clean break."

"I'm so sorry babe."

"Yeah, so am I." I finished the call with a promise that I would let Flynn know when I had my flight booked and I headed upstairs, laying on the bed and looking at the time on my phone. It was after 9pm and once again Nate had not come home and I started to wonder what had he been doing for the past two nights and what strategies was he using to "process" our relationship. Was he at the beach house with Paxton and Lynda? Or was he still here in Portland? Was he drinking at a bar or a club? Or was he staying with a friend? Or was he out there fucking me out of his mind? And with that thought I suddenly felt ill. No, he wouldn't do that, would he? Fuck! I curse, and pick up my IPod, slip the ear buds into my ears and scroll through the play list until I find something soothing but powerful to make my mind stop drifting into thoughts that I don't want right now. Finding the best of the artist Sia, I press play and close my eyes.

Fresh out of the shower the next morning with a throbbing headache, I dress and go down to the kitchen. Laying on the island bench is a small piece of paper. Picking it up and reading the large black letters it read, "Don't ever hang up on me again." I let out a small laugh of relief that at least I know he's been here, then I screw the paper into a ball and throw it towards the garbage with a flippant curse. "Arrogant Prick." I start pulling open some drawers looking for something to help with the throbbing in my head, and that's where I am when I hear the ding of the elevator and the doors sliding open. I still myself and hold my breath until I see Lynda walking out, a huge carry bag in one arm and baby Emily in the other. I slide the drawer closed and make my way over to her. "Lynda?" I ask reaching out to grab the bag from her "What are you doing here?"

"Hey nice to see you as well," she smiles at me.

"No I didn't mean it like that, I just didn't expect...."

"Yep I know, that's why I'm here." We move into the sunken lounge area and she places a sleeping Emily on one of the couches and places a couple of cushions behind the baby's back to keep her from rolling off. Then she stands with her hands on her hips. She looks good dressed in a white loose fitting summer dress and sandals. "You look great," I tell her and she quirks an eyebrow at me .

"Wish I could say the same, you look terrible." She furrows her brows at me.

"Awesome, thanks," I say defeated and flop down onto the other couch.

"So I was thinking you might need some company."

Looking at her wearily, I say, "Paxton told you didn't he?"

Bowing her head down slightly she said, "Yes."

"How much did he tell you?"

"Everything Casey, but I did annoy the shit out of him until he told me what was going on, I mean Paxton might as well have been walking around the house with an animated dark rain cloud hovering over his head, and Nate, well to be honest the last time I saw him looking like that was.... at his parents funeral." I gasp in shock at her words. "He looks like crap and he's acting like an angry bear right now."

"Has he been staying with you and Paxton?"

"Yeah, he came down the other night. Him and Paxton stayed up most of the night drinking on the back porch."

"This is all my fault, I should have..." I start to say but Lynda cuts me off.

"Ahh should have, could have, would have, it would have made no difference, he would have found out anyway. My husband's a great lawyer and he's even better at finding information, that's what King International Security does, and you are the last person who needs to be sorry. Damn, haven't you done enough of that through your life?" I look at her somber face and recognize that she understands a lot more than I thought.

"I know I'm just not sure where we stand right now, he was so angry and disheartened and he's avoiding me like the plague."

"He's not avoiding you, he's avoiding the situation. I'm pretty sure his anger is not at you but for you." I look at her with a questioning lift of my brow and she continues, "Look Nate is an alpha take charge of all situations kind of man, he's always got his finger on the pulse of everything and now he's faced with something that he had no control over and it will be tearing him to pieces inside. Until he works out how to bury the past and deal with it, he will keep his distance to protect you from him."

"That's crazy thinking." I say slightly shocked at her words.

"No, that's Nate's thinking." Walking over to the huge windows where Nate likes to stand and look out over the city, I cross my arms over my chest and gaze out. "I'm not sure I can do this again Lynda" I say, and she quickly makes her way over to me and stands beside me, placing a hand on my shoulder.

"I think you can, you have fought your whole life Casey. I'm pretty sure you have just that little bit more in you, just hang in there babe." I give her a weak smile and a silent thank you, then both our heads are turned towards the couch at the tiny soft gurgling sounds coming from it. "Someone's awake," Lynda sings as she crosses to the couch and picks up the small body incased head to toe in a lilac colored jump suit and places her against her shoulder with a supporting hand on her back. "She needs feeding so I hope you don't mind me flashing a nipple."

"Of course not," I laugh. "Go ahead I'll make us some lunch, you are staying right?"

"I would love to," she says, and as I start getting things out to prepare some sandwiches for us. I look up at Lynda feeding Emily and I feel a wave of joy flush through my body at the friendship and support that this woman has given me.

Chapter forty

Nate

After Casey had gone up to her room I had to hold myself back from running up after her, taking her in my arms and asking her to help me process all the crap that was going through my head, but she was right I needed some space and time away from her because I didn't want to say something in anger that I might regret later. Right now, my mind is stuck in "Pure Anger mode." Grabbing a beer from the fridge, I snap the cap on the top and take a long pull of the chilly liquid taking it into my home office and sitting down at my desk. My phone chirps with a text. Looking down at the screen, it's from Paxton. "Hey bro, do you need anything?" I quickly send him one back. "Would love to come stay at the beach house for a few days," pressing send then another quick chirp. "No problem, I'll be ready to leave in about 20 minutes, Ok?" I sent him a text back "I'll just grab a bag and meet you in the garage." His return text is just a picture of a thumbs up.

I finish off my beer and quietly go upstairs to my room and grab a few toiletries and a change of clothes, then head down to meet Paxton. We drive in silence apart from some low music coming from the radio. I don't feel like talking and my brother knows me well enough to know that, so I lean my head back against the head rest and close my eyes. I am totally drained, physically and mentally, and I try to clear my mind by concentrating on the movement of the car and the low music and it must have worked because the next minute my eyes open as we come to a stop and we are parked outside the beach house.

Grabbing my bag out of the back seat, I walk up the front stairs and wait while Paxton unlocks the door. "Do you want a beer and a chat?" he asks me.

"No man, I'm just going to crash, but thanks." I give my brother a light slap on the shoulder in thanks for his offer and make my way to the spare room. I drop my bag, then myself, onto the bed.

My last thought is of the last time I was in this bed, she was curled up next to me, pressed against my chest. My eyes droop and I am engulfed by exhaustion and sleep.

The next morning as we drive back into the city, I sip on my hot coffee and pop a couple of pain killers into my mouth. My head is feeling like I had been on a heavy nights drink fest and I was now sporting one hell of a hangover. "Are you going to see Casey today and talk to her?" Paxton blurts out.

Looking at him I shrug and let out a breath, "Yeah, maybe."

"Good, get it all out in the open Nate."

"Easier said than done." I say giving him a sideways look.

"Yep, well it needs to be done, clear the air otherwise I can see you turning into a zombie." Giving him a nod, I go back to my coffee and the wonderful world of silence for the rest of the trip.

When I get into my office, it's been cleaned. There's not a sign anywhere of the mess it was in when I left last night, where my world started to crumble, where I felt that constricting pain in my chest when I witnessed what she had been through. Just the thought of it makes me feel sick to my stomach, and there, right there, is my biggest fear. I don't want to feel like this when I look at her and I am so ashamed of myself that I just can't seem to take control of how I feel. I glide through the morning in what seems more like a haze of the normal bustle of a busy day. Instead of going through contracts I'm more interested in searching the web for any more information on Max Sullivan. I feel like I need to know everything about him, I want to ruin him. I want to remove him from her past.

At noon I decide to pull myself away from the torture of Max Sullivan before my anger takes over again and I smash another computer. I head upstairs to the Penthouse- it's time we talked. Walking through the open elevator doors, I take in the silence of the place and see nothing. Taking the stairs two at a time up to her room I find it empty. A quick glance in the closet and I see it's full with her clothes and I instantly feel relief that she hasn't taken off somewhere. After checking the bathrooms and home gym I pull out my phone and press the contact number for her phone, When she answers I can tell she is outside somewhere by the way the wind blows past the mouth piece, distorting her voice. "Where are you?" I bite out. I am so pissed that she has gone out without telling me.

"Out having some lunch," she retorts.

"I said where, not what."

"Just out in the park." Needless to say I sounded like a prick throughout our short conversation which ended with her letting me know that I was no longer responsible for her safety, and hanging up, leaving me with a dial tone in my ear. "Jesus fucking Christ," I curse, as I head back down to my office, clearing my browser of what I had been looking at this morning. I needed to clear my head with some work, right after I send a quick text to Nick telling him that Casey is having lunch in a park somewhere in walking vicinity of the building and that he needed to go track her down and watch her without being seen.

The next day I went up to the Penthouse at the crack of dawn just to grab a change of clothes. It was quiet and I noticed that her bedroom door was closed. I dropped her a note on the kitchen island and went down to my office. The continuing fury and rage that kept building inside my body was making me feel like a ticking time bomb right now, and knowing her stubbornness and smart mouth, we are going to collide in an explosion that wouldn't be contained, so I decided to give us both another day to cool down.

Driving back to the beach house later that evening, I was greeted with a beer and an invitation to come sit out the back. This was a stern order from Lynda. Changing into a pair of sweat pants and t-shirt, I join her out side. She's sitting on the back stairs and I sit my ass down next to her. Flipping the cap off on the beer, I take a mouthful. "I went to your Penthouse today" Lynda says nonchalantly. Her statement causes me to whip my head around to look at her.

"Is she ok?" I ask her.

She lifts an eyebrow at me. "Really Nate? What do you think?" She sound's exasperated with me then says, "She doesn't look like she's eating or sleeping well, she has huge dark bags under her eyes."

"Shit," I say, shaking my head and looking down at the beer in my hand.

"Well what were you expecting Nate, didn't you just do to her what everyone else has done her whole life?" Looking at her I see the boil of irritation in her eyes. "I mean her parents did it to her and now so have you."

"And what exactly do you think I've done?" I ask through gritted teeth.

"Well they left her to go to work, they left her hanging when she was kidnapped then they left her when they both died and now you've done it too."

Standing up fast to face Lynda, fury pumping so fast through my veins I feel it throb in my neck, "I have not left her."

"Well you're here aren't you? Instead of being at the Penthouse with Casey."

"That doesn't mean I have left her." Rubbing a hand through my hair, I grab the back of my neck.

"Then what the fuck are you doing Nate?" Lynda stands up with a defiant hand on her hip, she looks livid. She must be, because I don't think I have ever heard her swear before.

"I'm giving us both some space."

"Fuck space, you should be running to her not away from her, do you care about her?"

"Fuck, of course I do." I spit out.

"Then what is the problem?"

Rubbing a hand over the scruff along my jaw line, I pause for a moment before I say, "Me, I'm the problem".

I see and feel Lynda's eyes on me searching my face for an explanation of my hard admission. "Nate?" Her words are now much softer, and filled with an understanding of the demons I'm fighting with. Starting slow, I began, "I've never had this much inner turmoil before, it's senseless and irrational and it's driving me fucking nuts. My whole life I've had control over everything, my career, my time in the military and the men under me, my company, and my feelings, but with Casey, I have no control over how I feel about her, how I want her, need her in my life, and I have no control over changing her past, and that's ripping me to shreds. I want to protect her, consume her, I want to wrap her in my arms and absorb every bit of pain that she has ever suffered and take it from her, but I can't." Lynda takes a step closer to me and gently runs her hand over my cheek.

"Then that's what you have to tell her, and all that turmoil you're feeling Nate... it's called love." Looking at her soft smile, my eyes searching her moist eyes, I see it. "And love is not controllable it ties you into knots and it makes you crazy to the extent that you think you're going insane, but once you accept what you're feeling and embrace it with every part of you, the feeling is euphoric, inexplicable and all that chaos- and confusion will fade as your love grows stronger and stronger. I understand this is all new to you Nate."

"You make me sound like the innocent virgin king," I grin.

"Well you are where your heart is concerned. Just because you've had a lot of sex doesn't mean that you have experience where matters of the heart are concerned. That was just sex, just something to satisfy the itch in your balls, no feelings or ties to the person, but love, love is a completely different thing Nate, a totally new experience one that takes time to grow. Like a fire, it starts off as a small flame and you stoke it and play around with it making adjustments until you have a roaring strong hot flame. You and Casey started with a flame that was growing until a little water got to it, so now you both need to be tender and understanding with it and coax it back into a fire and keep all that past water away from it." Her theory makes me smile.

"When the hell did you become a love doctor."

Throwing back her head with a laugh, she says, "When I married your brother. You King men are so concentrated on protecting the ones you love, you forget how to step back and think sometimes." I give her a nod in agreement, then pull her into my arms in a warm hug.

"Thank you, " I tell her.

"No need to thank me Nate you deserve all the happiness in the world and so does Casey, so go fight for her."

Laying in bed that night in the spare room, I found myself going over and over what I needed to say to Casey. I need her to understand what my thoughts have been for the past few days, and I need her to know how much I love her and hope that she forgives me for acting like such an asshole. As my eyes get heavy with sleep and with the satisfaction of laying my own demons down to rest, I feel a slight adrenaline surge at the thought of helping Casey slay her demons and putting them to rest for good.

Chapter forty-one

C asey

Slowly opening my eyes, I squint against the sunlight coming through the window and move my head, only to be hit by a throbbing pain. With a groan, I move my hair away from my face and realize that I hadn't closed the blinds last night and now I have the full morning sun boring into my face. Sheepishly I slowly sit up, dropping my legs over the side of the bed, blinking back the sleep and the effects of that weird colored but tasty alcohol I had managed to devour last night while I sat out on the balcony and enjoyed the feeling of the light rain shower. After tossing and turning most of the night with the images of painful dream sequences fading in and out, I eventually got up, went down stairs and rummaged through the bar until I found something slightly palatable. Also in the bar I had found an almost empty packet of Nate's cigarette's and matches so, together with my bottle of booze, I went out onto the balcony, lit up a cigarette and drank the weird colored liquid, slowly, and there I stayed until the bottle was empty and it had been steadily raining for about the last hour.

Looking down at my shirt it was still damp I must have just crawled into bed drunk and wet. Well at least I slept solidly, so that was a plus, but on the negative side I feel like crap and I think someone is in my head wielding a pick axe right now. Getting up and making my way to the bathroom, I pull my shirt and panties off as I go, then I ease into the shower and turn on the water and just stand under the spray, hoping it will somehow drown me. Stepping from the bathroom in what seems like hours later, I feel somewhat more human now I have washed and used most of the toothpaste to get rid of the disgusting taste of an old ashtray out of my mouth. I pull on a fresh pair of panties, a pair of shorts and t-shirt, then pull my wet hair up into a bun. When I open the door to head downstairs, I smell the aroma in the air of freshly brewed coffee and something else.

Slowly walking down the stairs and walking into the kitchen I see a white box sitting in the middle of the table. Lifting the lid, the box is full of several different types of Danish pastries, so fresh my mouth starts to water. Lifting my head I glance around but see no-one sooo... I slip my hand into the box and pull out a flaky square of buttery pastry that has a line of dark chocolate covered in powdered sugar on top of it. Bringing it up to my mouth and taking a bite, I moan at the taste. "Nice to see they taste as good as they smell." A deep voice from behind me makes me jump and swivel so fast I almost drop my piece of pastry heaven. Nate walks into the kitchen and pulls out two mugs from the overhead cupboard and fills them with hot coffee, placing a mug on the kitchen island close to me, then taking a sip from the other mug in his hand. As he leans against the bench I watch as his eyes move over first my body, then my face.

"You look..." he starts and I finish the sentence for him.

"Yes I know, like shit."

"I was going to say tired." He finishes.

Pulling myself up onto a stool, I say, "Yeah well, it was a rough night." Looking up at him he looks at me puzzled. "Let's just say I decided to help myself to something in your bar, thinking it might help me sleep."

"And did it?." He said, quirking a brow.

"Yes, but at the price of a throbbing headache." He moves to a drawer and pulls out some ibuprofen, sliding the box towards me before filling a glass with water and placing it down next to the box.

"Why were you drinking?" he asks softly.

"I told you I couldn't sleep, I thought it might help, I also borrowed one of your cigarettes too...Yuck."

"Sounds like you had yourself a party."

"Yeah, whoopee doo for me hey?" I say making a twirling motion in the air with one finger. When he chuckles at my comment, I look at him. He looks, weary but so fucking good, his black hair mussed and tousled, a dark shadow of hair grazing along his jaw, black t-shirt stretched over his wide muscled chest and thick biceps down to a low slung pair of jeans.

As I finish my pastry in between swallowing the ibuprofen and sipping the coffee he studies my every movement, but he's silent while he drinks from his own mug. Then he says, in a low serious tone. "We need to talk."

Leaning my elbow on the bench with my hand against my cheek, I sigh."We do." He places his mug down on the marble top and pushes his hands into his pockets. "I'm not sure where to start." He looks out across at the windows, then back to me. I close my eyes at his words and softly say, "It's ok Nate, I understand." I swallow back my emotions which have risen into my throat. "I don't need any explanation, it's a hard thing for anyone to deal with, and I understand, I do, but please don't make it any harder than it is," I start to babble. I just want to get this over with quickly, no more waiting, no more uncertainty, no more pain for either of us. "I know how hard it's been for you, but after everything you've given me let me give you something back. Let me spare you the shame and embarrassment of what you saw and now know. I understand that you can't be with someone like me and it's fine. It hurts, but somehow I will learn to live with it. I've had it all my life. I don't know any different than the shame and disgust I feel for myself ." I jump when his hand slams down on the marble bench, making it shake.

"Stop! What the hell are you talking about?" he growls at me, and that sound makes me stop for a moment and take a breath. "I'm apologizing to you," he grits out, pointing a finger at me punctuating his last word.

My jaw drops, shocked "What? What for?"

"For being a total asshole, for walking away from you."

"No, no" I shake my head and he makes his way around the kitchen island until he's standing right in front of me then reaches out, taking both of my elbows in his hands.

"Listen to me, what I did was wrong, I distanced myself from you because I was trying to protect you, I was filled with so much rage and fury and anguish that I wanted to protect you from seeing any of it." Dropping his grip on my elbows he turns and walks towards the wall of windows and stares out.

"I'm sorry." I whisper and he looks at me.

"For what?"

"For making you feel that way. Hurting you is not what I wanted to do, you gave me so much of my life back Nate, you helped me to feel again, you dropped a rope into that deep black hole I was in and helped pull me up out of it.... You gave me freedom and all I gave you in return was secrets and distrust so.... That's why I am going to give you your freedom Nate."

Taking a step towards me, his eyes dark with confusion, he says "What the hell do you mean?"

"The last thing I ever wanted to do was to cause you so much pain and confusion, and that's why I'm going home and letting you go back to your life, the life you lived before I came into it."

"The fuck you are," he yells so loud it makes me cringe, then he takes the few steps to close the gap between us. "I can assure you that you are not going anywhere." His words are deep and slow, like he's making sure I hear him, then he points at the couch and barks out the words. "You will sit and you will listen." Keeping my eyes on his,

I slowly lower myself down onto the couch and after a few minutes of him pacing back and forth he drops down onto the couch across from me, propping his elbows on his knees and bracing his fingers together.

"The anger that I had was not aimed at you, it was aimed at me." I start to interrupt him but he holds up one hand and stops me. Taking a deep breath, then letting it out slowly, he says, "I've always been in control of everything in my life, and I mean everything, and I have seen some horrific things in my life, but when I saw what you had gone through, it made me sick to the bottom of my stomach. Not only for the way you had suffered for so long, but because I had no control over it. Inside it burned me with so much anger and guilt because I pushed you to break and give in to me, then I pushed you more until our passion became rough and wild, and I hate myself for that, and I hate myself for not listening to you. I should have taken things much slower and I'm disappointed with myself because I thought we had built up a trust between us."

"But we have," I blurt out.

"Then why did you feel like you couldn't tell me what was hurting you?" The sadness and pain in his beautiful grey eyes hits me like a sledge hammer right in the middle of my chest.

"It wasn't the lack of trust Nate. At first it was out of habit, a lifestyle that I have been used to for years I was born in shame and it has followed me around all of my life."

"Don't say that," he says, shaking his head.

"But it's the truth, I was born because of a broken condom not out of parental love, and once I arrived they always made it clear to me that I was a dirty mistake that they were ashamed of. I could never do anything right for them, and when I was taken I was more of a shame for them to deal with. Hell, they loved me so much they didn't even pay the ransom money." I feel the sting of tears prick at my eyes. "When I was found and taken back to them, they weren't overjoyed or relieved that I was alive, they treated me like I was a dirty piece of garbage." I looked up into Nate's pained face. "You know what my own mother said to me one night? She said the best thing that could have happened to me was if I had died at the hands of Max Sullivan because I was too broken, beyond repair, and it would have been better for everyone." I see the vein in Nate's neck grow tense and his nostrils flare in anger as he grinds his teeth and curses under his breath .

"Mother fuckers."

"The only person I have ever had in my life that I trust fully is Flynn, until...you. I'm sorry for bringing all this turmoil into your life, you deserve better."

"Don't say that" he yells and stands from the couch moving around the coffee table until he is in front of me. He bends down and pushes my legs open until he is cradled in between them rubbing his hands up my thighs until they stop at my waist. His thumbs gently move to stroke against my sides, looking deeply into my eyes, his own piercing into me with so much emotion in them. "You are the only woman I want, you're the only woman I want to deserve Casey. I am in awe of you baby. I want you in my life. You may have brought turmoil into my life but fuck, I am so glad you did, and I cannot and will not be without you." My eyes search his for some kind of validation and I see so much reverence and adoration in them and it makes my heart swell with so much love for this man. I feel my tears break free and slide down my cheeks as I place my hands on either side of his face, feeling the scruff under my palms and we just lose ourselves in each other's eyes, silently communicating to each other how much we feel, and we stay like that for what feels like hours, until I watch his eyes fill with a strong determination as he says, "I need you in my life, at any cost. I've fought with my own insecurities and I will not let you go." He leans his forehead against mine. "I love you Casey and everything that comes with you, your past, your present and your future. I want all of you, the good, the bad and the broken. I love every inch of you with everything that I am, you just have to let me love you…understand?" When he moves his face away from mine I see the love and conviction in his eyes and I feel it in his touch, and because of the love that he is pouring into my soul, that forked path in my life is clearer than it's ever been before, and I'm taking the path marked future with him. I watch as his eyes study mine as he waits for a response and I give it to him as I move my mouth closer to his lips and whisper, "I love you so much."

He closes the gap between us with such force I'm pushed back into the back of the couch, his mouth taking mine with a needy, greed- filled passion. He snakes a hand around the back of my head deepening the kiss, while his other arm moves around my waist. With hot tongues dancing against each other, accompanied by a deep guttural moan coming from Nate's throat, I melt into his body. Breaking the kiss, he breathes out in a harsh breath "I need you baby, I need to be connected to you," and when I nod he stands and pulls me up with him and almost runs us both up the stairs into his room where he quickly pulls off every stitch of my clothes, followed by his own, and we drop onto the bed, our bodies entwined in each other as our mouths crash together once again. His mouth moves away from my mouth and he starts to nip and bite along my jaw line making his way down my neck and I feel his hot breath and mouth as he sucks against the pulse at my throat. He's ravenous with my body and he soon works his own thick thighs in between my own as he nudges open my legs and I feel his solid length against my sex, sliding against the outside coating himself in my wetness, and when my body starts to grind against him I shiver with anticipation as I breath out one word, "Please," and that's all the invitation he needs to slide inside my body, making me groan in ecstasy with the fullness of him. He waits for just a moment for me to adjust to him and when I run my hands down his muscled back and into the cheeks of his ass I give him a squeeze, urging him to move.

With no hesitation he pulls himself out and then thrusts back in with deep languid strokes that start off slowly until I wrap my legs around his waist and grind my sex harder into him. With a growl he picks up speed and sinks deeper and harder into me, our bodies joined together in a sensual unity of movement and passion, until I am pushed to my limits and let myself crash into an orgasmic wave, moaning into his mouth with pleasure. The sounds coming from my mouth cause him to follow and with a last hard thrust, I feel the heat of his orgasm as it fills me.

Nate stays buried inside my body as he rolls us to our sides and we just look at each other. As our breathing slows, he slides a finger across my forehead and moves my disheveled hair away from my face. "Nate?"

"Hmmm"

"I missed you,"

I watched as his lips curved into a huge smile. "I missed you too, so much" he says, as he slips from the warmth of my body and pulls me into him "If we're starting a new life together we need to promise each other that there will never be anything between us again, no secrets, no lies and definitely no clothes." I laugh as I feel him kiss the top of my head. "I love you so much baby, with all my heart and soul, you are mine and I will never let anyone or anything hurt you."

"I love you too Nate, I love you too".

Epilogue

N

ate

Three months later...

Looking across at Casey as she sits looking out the window at the scenery, I smile, and wait for her reaction as I continue to drive down the secluded road and straight past Paxton and Lynda's beach house. "Hey you, missed the driveway" she says as she turns to look at me.

"I know," I grin at her.

"Ok, so where are we going?"

"There's something I wanted to show you first before we go to the beach house," she grins and looks down directly at the crotch of my jeans.

"I don't think you have anything that I haven't seen already big guy," she laughs.

"Oh the things I can do with that dirty mouth of yours," I say, giving her a wiggle of my eyebrows.

When we come to the end of the road I turn into an open gate way and drive up the winding gravel drive and she scoots forward in her seat, her head darting from the windscreen to the side window. "Where are we?"

"You'll see we're almost there." The drive climbs upwards and over a small hump to reveal a large open space of grass surrounding a white timber house complete with wrap around veranda and an open view of the ocean and beach below. Pulling up out the front and putting the Audi in park, I open my door climbing out and around to Casey's side, and open her door offering her my hand which she takes. "Nate?" she looks at me questioningly and I tug her up the stairs and pull a key from my pocket and slip it into the lock. When the door pushes open we're greeted by the smell of clean fresh paint and the beautiful shine of a polished wood floor that runs through the whole house. "Nate, who lives here?" Ignoring her question and with her hand in mine, I move down the long hallway until it comes out into a huge sun room with a whole wall of glass tri-fold doors. Unlatching one door and sliding it back, we both walk out onto a deck with stairs leading down to the sandy beach.

"What do you think?" I ask her, wrapping my arms around her waist from behind, as she looks out at the ocean.

"It's stunning, but who lives here?" She turns her head to look at me and when I say, "We do," she spins fully in my embrace until she is facing me, her mouth gaping open in shock. "What?"

"I know how much you love the ocean so I brought it for you, for us I mean. I don't know about you, but I am getting a little tired of holding my hand over your mouth to keep you screaming out my name and waking Paxton and Lynda up when I fuck you. You know, this way I figured you can scream all you want and no-one will hear you"

"You are kidding me right?"

"Nope, not kidding."

"Holy shit Nate I...I" she stammers and I place my lips against hers and gently kiss her.

"No buts, this is our home, together, just you and me baby."

"But you work in the city"

"That's ok we'll split our time between the Penthouse and here." Her eyes start to search mine and I can see a small show of insecurity coming through.

"Stop over thinking, I told you you're stuck with me forever- in like never getting rid of me- so this is," I gesture to the house, " our forever, this is our freedom," I say, waving my hand over the ocean in front of us. Looking down at her face as I feel her relax into my arms and leaning her cheek against my chest, I hear her whisper.

"Thank you for being my forever".

After taking a look around the house and Casey excitedly talking about what furniture will go where, with reluctance she finally lets me lock up the house and gets back into the car. As we drive back down the road, I can't help but chuckle at her insistent chatter and excitement over the house. Her smile is spread wide across her beautiful face and her eyes are sparkling with happiness and I feel a slight relief at my decision to purchase the property. Paxton told me about it a few weeks ago and I had tracked down the owner and made them an offer that I knew they couldn't refuse, and now, looking at the joy in my girl's face, it was worth every penny.

After dinner that night Lynda informs Paxton and I that we get to clean up the dishes so the girls can have some down time with a glass of wine out on the deck while Emily is asleep. Paxton bumps my shoulder with his as I place the last dish into the dishwasher and close the door. "She looks like a different woman" he nods to where Casey is sitting next to Lynda on the porch swing idly moving back and forth.

"I know" I smile.

"I'm glad. You two are good together."

"Thanks." I press the button to start the dishwasher, when I hear a familiar tune emanating from the coffee table. Looking over to where Casey's phone is vibrating its way across the wood as it plays, Waltzing Matilda.

"What the hell is that noise?" Paxton asks as I grab the phone and look at the screen to see Flynn's name on it.

"That is Casey's BFF Flynn calling." Opening the screen door and walking over to Casey who stops when she hears the song, and reaches out to take the phone I hold out to her. Pressing the green button to answer and placing the phone to her ear she smiles when she answers.

"Hey, Flynn?" She's quiet while he speaks and I watch as her face changes from the happy glow she normally has to a somber, serious one. She stands and walks closer to me, her eyes darting from mine to the ocean that sits behind me, then she speaks into the phone. "Are you sure?" then, "Ok, I'll get onto it straight away, thanks Flynn. Yes I love you too." Ending the call, she looks straight into my eyes and I see something brewing in them. Placing my hands on her shoulders, I say, "What is it baby, is Flynn alright?"

"He's fine," she says with a small shake of her head and I bend down slightly so I can look straight into her eyes.

"Baby what's wrong?" I watch her swallow and close her eyes as she says.

"I have to go back to Sydney."

"What? What do you mean? Casey look at me what's going on?"

"Max Sullivan has applied for parole and I need to be there to stop him from getting it."

Standing to my full height, I pull her against my chest and rub my hands up and down her back, soothingly, and say, "Then I'm coming with you." She pulls back and looks at me.

"But your business, the company?"

"Paxton can take care of that he's done it many times before. right Paxton?" I look at my brother for confirmation and he gives it to me instantly.

"Absolutely. because there is no way you're going there without him." Paxton points a finger at me while he looks at Casey. I kiss the top of her head and her arms tighten around my waist before looking up at me with uncertainty in her eyes. "Told you before baby, no-one will ever hurt you again, you're stuck with me now." I place a finger under her chin to bring her face up to mine."Ok?" she closes her eyes then gives me a nod, "Now did Flynn tell you when the parole meeting is set for?"

"He said it looks like the 24th of this month."

Doing a quick calculation, I say, "So that'll be the end of next week."

"Nate," she gives me that hesitant look again.

"Everything will be fine, I promise. You just enjoy the rest of your wine and girly talk with Lynda and I'll jump online and book us some tickets for down under."

She sighs and pulls herself up onto her toes to bring her mouth closer to mine. "I love you Nathanial King" she breathes against my mouth before pressing a kiss against it .

"And I love you Casey Tyler," kissing her back I slowly release her and walk back into the house with Paxton trailing behind me as we walk to his home office. Sitting down at the computer, I log into our company flight account "Nate," Paxton says and I look up to see the worried look on his face.

"Don't let that fucker near her,"

"Paxton this is one fight that she will not be taking on alone and I will kill that mother fucker if he even looks at her."

"Just do what you need to do and bring her home, ok?"

"That's exactly what I intend to do brother, and Max Sullivan, you have a whole new other problem heading your way......me".

THE END

Don't miss out!

Visit the website below and you can sign up to receive emails whenever J.Grayland publishes a new book. There's no charge and no obligation.

https://books2read.com/r/B-A-YZUJ-IWYYC

Connecting independent readers to independent writers.